Death of the Author

ALSO BY NNEDI OKORAFOR

Adult

Who Fears Death

Kabu Kabu • *Lagoon*

The Book of Phoenix

Binti • *Binti: Home*

Binti: The Night Masquerade

Remote Control • *Noor*

She Who Knows • *LaGuardia*

Young Adult

Zahrah the Windseeker

The Shadow Speaker

Akata Witch • *Akata Warrior*

Ikenga • *Akata Woman*

Like Thunder

Children

Long Juju Man

Iridessa and the Secret of the Never Mine

Chicken in the Kitchen

Death of the Author

A Novel

Nnedi Okorafor

WILLIAM MORROW LARGE PRINT
An Imprint of HarperCollins*Publishers*

This is a work of fiction. Names, characters, places, and incidents are products of the author's imagination or are used fictitiously and are not to be construed as real. Any resemblance to actual events, locales, organizations, or persons, living or dead, is entirely coincidental.

HarperCollins books may be purchased for educational, business, or sales promotional use. For information, please email the Special Markets Department at SPsales@harpercollins.com.

FIRST WILLIAM MORROW LARGE PRINT EDITION

ISBN 978-0-06-344367-9

Library of Congress Cataloging-in-Publication Data is available upon request.

24 25 26 27 28 LBC 5 4 3 2 1

To my amazing sister
Ngozi Chijioke Okorafor, Esq., 1973–2021

Death of the Author

1
Interview
Chinyere

What's the story you want?

Honestly, I don't see it. Even after everything, Zelu will always just be Zelu to me. What you think she is—it's all made up. Life is short. Fortune is fleeting. Fame is just swirling dust. It's people dreaming and perceiving while they say your name like it's some tangible object, but it's not. A name is just a name. A sound.

What *matters* is family. Without family, you're nothing. You're debris tumbling through space. Unseen, unconnected, uncollected, unknown, no matter how famous you are.

Zelu will always be *part* of our family. She will always be my sister. No matter what. Oh, it's been rough. The fact is that Zelu never really cared about family. Zelu had to do her own thing. Then she'd expect everyone else to deal with her mess. We will always love Zelu. We hang in there for her. She never made it easy, though.

My name is Chinyere. I'm the oldest. That's a year older than Zelu, though growing up, most assumed she was a *lot* younger. I'm a cardiovascular surgeon. The chief of surgery at Advent Hospital. I've lived in Chicago all my life and I love it here. I'm married to a wonderful man named Arinze. He's Igbo, like me, though both of his parents are Igbo, whereas only one of mine is. What's interesting is that he was born in Chad. Long story. We have two sons.

Our family is sizable, by American standards. So being asked only about my sister will always feel strange. But she's the one everyone is talking about, I guess. She's the one everyone is *always* talking about now. Whose fault is that? You all should be ashamed of yourselves. The irony no one seems to understand is that Zelu has always been the most unstable of us all. And I'm not talking about her disability. She's not the first person to have a disability. And I acknowledge that society has its biases, but we each move through the world in our own way. We all have a path.

Let me tell you a story . . .

Some years ago, before all this happened, I was a new mom. My first son was only three months old. I wasn't very happy, I admit. I'm a surgeon, and suddenly I had all these months where I was staying home. My son wasn't sleeping; I wasn't sleeping. My husband was always escaping to work. I wasn't upset with him, though; I'd have done the same if I'd had the chance. Being a woman is tough. Especially one who is a mother. We're not all cut out for domesticity, even when we love our children.

It was about 10 p.m. and I was at home with baby Emeka. It was raining outside. Absolutely pouring. And lightning and thundering. Emeka was crying and crying because he was gassy. I was walking up and down the hallway, rocking him and patting his little back. I was so exhausted. My phone buzzed. It was Zelu, and she sounded like a slowed record. Slurring her words, barely making sense.

"Zelu? Is that you?" I asked.

"Ssssoooo annoying. 'Course s'me. Caller eye-deeeee."

"Oh my God, come on."

"Ever look at your hand an' think you have six fingers instead of five?" she whispered.

"What?"

"Needa ride, Chinyere. Don't trust Uber."

The rest of what she said was mainly giggling, snickering, and what sounded like blowing raspberries. It was late. I was alone with an unhappy infant. And now I had to go out and get my sister. We all shared our locations with each other, so I could find her. I dressed, bundled up the baby, and went to get her.

My BMW is a two-door (two years prior, we hadn't thought we'd have any kids—funny how life decides certain things for you), so it took me a few minutes to strap Emeka in the back seat. By this time, he was absolutely shrieking. But I stayed focused and got it done. No use in my freaking out, too. Zelu's location took me from Hyde Park all the way past the end of Lake Shore Drive on the North Side. I found her in an all-night diner. She was sitting in a booth, looking out the window right at me as I pulled up. Even from where I was, I could see that her eyes were glassy and red.

Emeka was fast asleep. Finally. The drive had worked like magic on him, and this would be a trick I'd use to calm him for the next year. I had Zelu to thank for that, Zelu and her *wahala*. I was right in front of the diner, so I opted to leave him in my car, with the heat on, of course. It was below zero degrees Fahrenheit outside. When I entered the diner, a waitress came right up to me. A short white woman with spiky pink hair. "Please say you're here to take that girl home."

"I am."

"Oh, thank *God*."

I stepped toward Zelu and she looked up at me and grinned. She was wearing an Ankara pantsuit; West African wax-print cloth was her go-to when it came to fashion. She said she liked the colors and that Ankara cloth always looked like it was "trying to go somewhere," whatever that meant. And she had on red heels. It didn't matter to her that she couldn't walk—Zelu's shoes had to be fire. Her outfit was pretty nice. That's one thing you can always count on my sister for: when she wants to, which is usually, she can dress to the nines.

"My sistah," she said in our mother's accent. "*Bawo ni.*"

I rolled my eyes.

She reached into her breast pocket and brought out a large overstuffed blunt and a lighter. I heard the waitress, who was standing behind me, gasp as Zelu started trying to light it.

"Zelu, stop it." I snatched the blunt and lighter from her hands and grasped the handlebars of her wheelchair. She wasn't drunk, but she was very, very high. Like, you could get high just by sniffing her. I enjoy my occasional glass of wine, even brandy, but I have *control.* Zelu? None.

This is my sister. This woman you all know and love. Our ancestors were probably so ashamed this night. I somehow got her in the passenger seat, then I put her chair in the trunk. She was snickering the entire time, like my touch was the most ticklish thing on earth. And I was sweating, despite it being freezing. I thought about the recent rain and wondered about black ice. I shoved the thought away. I had to focus. Emeka didn't wake up, which was a blessing.

I still had her door open when a guy came out of a Mercedes SUV parked beside me.

"Zelu! Come on! Where you going?" He was a gorgeous black man in his twenties wearing a very expensive-looking tan suit, but it was all wrinkled up. He didn't look like the kind of guy who normally did wrinkled suits.

"You for real?" Zelu shouted. "Go away!"

"Who is this?" I asked her.

"Some guy."

"Baby," the guy said, "I've been waiting for you in the freezing cold!"

"'Cuz they kicked you out! Take a hint! Don't want you."

"Just give me another chance."

He was feet away now, and I turned to face him.

"Are you her girlfriend?" he asked me.

"I'm her *sister.*"

"Oh, thank goodness. Just tell her I want to talk to her."

He didn't seem drunk or high or anything, and that worried me. This was clearheaded distress.

"She can hear you," I said.

"Go away! We're done. 'S called . . . a One. Night. Stand," Zelu slurred.

"I don't do those," he snapped.

"Apparently you do," I said. "Hey, I've got a sleeping infant in the car. Can you just . . . quiet down and, even better, go away? I'm sure you have my sister's number—"

"I don't! She gave me a fake one. I had to follow her here!" he snapped. He stepped closer. "Look, just get out of my way so I can talk some sense into your sister."

I didn't move. I had no space to shut the door. He was getting angrier; I could tell. I'd dated a guy when I was in college who . . . well, let's just say, this guy's behavior was familiar to me. I wasn't sticking around to let him reach what he was working up to. He was nearly in my face. My baby was in the car. That was it for me. I reached into my pocket, grabbed my tiny canister of pepper spray, unlocked it as I brought it out, and aimed it right in his face. I pressed the button and sprayed the hell out of him. Me! I had carried it in my pocket at night, and sometimes during the day, for years. I didn't even know if the shit worked. Still, it had always made me feel a tiny bit safer. But I'd never really imagined I'd use it. That I *could* bring myself to use it.

While he screeched and clawed at his face, Zelu snickered, and the concerned waitress inside was probably already calling the police. I shut the door, ran to the driver's side, got in, and drove off. For several minutes, Zelu and I were silent . . . except for our coughing. When you pepper spray someone, you have to deal with what you've done, on a smaller scale. In the back seat, Emeka hadn't woken up even for all that. None of the fumes reached him, thankfully.

"What did you do to him?" I asked my sister.

She only shrugged. The incident seemed to have sobered her up. "Fucked him. Was a student from one of my classes a few semesters ago. Lawyer trying to be a writer. I just got tired of him by the next morning."

"And you told him so."

"Yeah," she said. "It's funny. Guys like that are so entitled. But even more so when you can't walk. They think you should be soooo grateful." She giggled again, even harder.

That's Zelu. She'll do something, then right after,

just let go of it. Zelu puts it all behind her right away. So wrapped up in herself that she doesn't know when she's kicked people out of their sense of normalcy. She'll just leave you there, reeling and wondering why.

Maybe that's what you all love so much about her.

2
The Wedding

Zelu was thinking about water.

Trinidad and Tobago had the sweetest beaches she'd ever seen. They went on for miles and miles with not a human in sight, and the waters were so warm. The day after she'd arrived, she'd gone with her soon-to-be brother-in-law and three of his local Trini friends. All of them could swim like fish . . . but none as well as she, of course. Once she put the elastic bands around her legs and ankles, she moved with power and confidence using her powerful arms, her back, shoulders, and abdominal muscles. She'd been swimming since she was five. "Oh, it's just something I . . . fell into," she'd tell people. She rarely explained how literal this was; she'd intentionally fallen into the water one day.

Her family thought it was an accident, but it was the only way she could prove to anyone, including herself, that she *could* swim. When the wedding ceremony was over, she planned to go right back to those human-free beaches and swim some more. Preferably alone, this time. For now, she endured all the primping, preening, and perfuming of the bridal suite.

"I look *hot*!" Zelu's younger sister Amarachi proclaimed. She did a twirl and a pose in front of the mirror. Amarachi's wedding dress was like something from another planet, and Zelu loved it. She'd been there to help her sister choose it, of course. "Zelu, you are a genius."

Zelu flipped some of her braids back and smirked. "I know." Their sisters—Chinyere, the oldest of them all; Bola, the youngest; and Uzo, the second youngest—laughed as they perfected their makeup in front of the large mirror. Zelu's own dress was buttercup yellow, and it billowed over her wheelchair, making her look somewhat like the flower. She hated it, but this wasn't *her* day. Whatever her sister wanted, she would do. Still, she snuck two thin bracelets made of green Ankara cloth onto her left wrist to maintain her identity. Bola's dress was a soft carnation pink and Uzo's was a lilac purple. Zelu had to admit, the combination of the colors with her sister's gorgeous Technicolor sci-fi-looking wedding dress was stunning.

"Zelu, want me to help you with your makeup?" Bola asked.

"Nope," Zelu said. "Don't need any."

"You'll be sorry when you see the photos," Uzo said, patting her already perfect midsized 'fro. She'd placed a lavender butterfly pin in it. "They'll be all over our social media."

"Meh, I'm not the one getting married. Today isn't about me. And social media can deal with me looking like myself."

"Zelu radiates an inner beauty that makeup cannot enhance, don't you know?" Chinyere said.

They all laughed. Of course, Chinyere's makeup was flawless and already done. Her sky-blue dress was nearly as magnificent as Amarachi's, but it was more *how* she wore it. It was Amarachi's day, but Chinyere was and always would be queen.

"Well, I think that's a weak excuse for looking plain, Zelu," Amarachi said.

"You'll be all right," she said, grinning. "Marriage isn't my thing, so I don't have to suffer it. But I can have fun watching you." This was her naked truth. Marriage had never been in her cards. She enjoyed her freedom and autonomy too much, and she loathed the idea of someone calling her his "wife." It just seemed ridiculous. Not that she hadn't had the option; so far, she'd had two wonderful men propose to her: one who was named Zelu, just like her, and one named Obi, who had been her creative twin; they'd passionately dated for three years . . . until he got the idea of marriage into his head and ruined everything.

"Ugh," Chinyere said. "Spare us your lecture, Zelu. Today's a day of marriage. Deal with it."

Their mother, Omoshalewa, came in with a large box. Inside it was a thick orange coral bead necklace and matching earrings.

"Oh boy," Zelu said. "Here we go."

The necklace was worth a small fortune. The others gathered around as their mother put the necklace around Amarachi's neck. "NOW you look like the true princess you are," Omoshalewa said. It totally threw off Amarachi's sci-fi dress. Zelu rolled her eyes, annoyed.

"This type of coral is the finest," their mother said. "*Only* the most powerful people in the palace can wear it."

Zelu flared her nostrils, fighting to keep her mouth shut. It was a horrible fact: their mother was indeed a princess from a long, strong line of proud (and useless, according to her father) Yoruba royalty. This made Zelu and her sisters also princesses and their brother, Tolu, a prince, something Zelu preferred to never tell anyone, despite her mother insisting they go by "princess" and "prince" whenever they visited Omoshalewa's hometown or spent time with their maternal relatives. Being a Nigerian American in Nigeria, and imposing the privilege of royalty on top of that, disgusted Zelu.

Today, her mother was going to be really crazy with it. Which meant there was going to be drama, because their father was from a very proud Igbo family that spat on any idea of entitled predestination and opted for embracing education and capitalism and the Lord Jesus Christ. In her father's family, everyone did their own thing, but it was *all* for the family. Thus, every single one of her father's siblings had earned a PhD or the equivalent and was wealthy. If they heard any of this talk of princesses and princes and kings and queens, they'd make sure to loudly point out that it was total bullshit.

"It's super heavy." Amarachi laughed, adjusting the humongous necklace hanging around her neck.

"A princess can carry it," their mother said. "Remember how Chinyere wore it."

"*I* certainly do," Chinyere said.

"Like a pink-orange tire," Amarachi muttered.

"We are royalty," their mother proclaimed.

Zelu frowned and looked away. Her eyes fell on her phone. She'd silenced it and put it on the table beside her. For once, she'd completely forgotten about it. Until now. And it was vibrating. She picked it up and wheeled herself toward the window on the far side of the room. It was her boss, Brittany Burke, head of the university's English Department.

"Hello?" she answered with a frown.

"Hi, Zelu. I know you're in Trinidad."

"Tobago."

"Oh. Yeah. I get them mixed up."

"The country is Trinidad and Tobago, but I'm on the island of Tobago," she said. She sighed, pushing back her irritation. What did Brittany want?

"Hell, I'm surprised I can even reach you."

"A good international package is part of my phone contract."

"Heh, smart." Silence.

"Um . . . everything all right?"

As Brittany spoke, Zelu gazed out the window, over the hills covered with lush trees and bushes. In the opposite direction, just behind the hotel, was the ocean. Zelu giggled, because it was all she could do to not smash her phone on the windowsill and potentially mess up her sister's big day. There was a ringing in her ears, but it wasn't loud enough to drown out this woman's fucking voice spewing bile all the way from the United fucking States.

It was surreal, but not surprising. Adjuncting was a shit job that treated you like shit. Her creative writing students always deeply annoyed her, but this semester had been especially brutal. She'd come to every class with a false smile plastered on her face and fantasies of smacking each of them upside the head with a copy of *Infinite Jest*—the hardcover, of course. This semester, she had a class full of creative writing PhD students who'd all convinced themselves and one another that the best type of storytelling was plotless, self-indulgent, and full of whiny characters who lived mostly in their minds.

Four days ago, she'd come to class full of rage because the student whose "story" they were workshopping that day had written twenty-five pages in which none of the sentences related to one another. There was no system or logic to the sentences. Nothing. Just gibberish. Like a robot attempting to be creative and getting the very concept of what that means all wrong. And she'd had to read it closely enough to give this student proper feedback. On top of this, the student was an entitled white boy who had been questioning her authority since the beginning of the semester, far more than anyone else. Oh, she detested him already, but this story was the straw that broke the camel's back.

After her students had each gone around the room

and said what they thought ("This is really ambitious," "I felt stretched by this piece," "It's brilliant! I wish I'd written it!," etc.), Zelu had tried her best to give him useful feedback. But when she finally just asked him what he believed the story meant, he'd said, "Why don't *you* tell *me*? What I think of my own work doesn't matter. The reader decides what it's about, right? Isn't that what you said 'death of the author' meant?" Then he'd smiled a very annoying and smug smile.

This motherfucker, Zelu thought. She'd paused, trying to collect herself, to *stop* herself. But she couldn't. Not at that point. And so she'd told him what she thought his story meant. Since he'd asked. "This is twenty-five pages of self-indulgent drivel. You've just wasted your reader's time. Throw this away, and when you're ready to stop fucking around and actually *tell* a story, start over and have some confidence in the power of storytelling. You've only had the privilege of torturing your readers with this because this is a class and we all *have* to read what you've given us."

Silence.

Students exchanging glances. Wide eyes. Pursed yet buttoned lips. Fidgeting. More silence.

Then this student, who had looked at her with such ire and arrogance all semester, who had even refused to participate in one of her writing exercises because he thought it "below" him, had burst into sloppy tears. Now, days later, while she was out of the country, the entire class had shown up at the department head's office to complain about this "traumatic" incident and how "insensitive," "toxic," "verbally violent," "unprofessional," "problematic," and "rude" Zelu was as a person.

All this Brittany told her now on the phone. She also mentioned that these students had complained about how twice this semester Zelu had ended class early so she could work on her own novel. Zelu had been a dumbass and thought that telling them the reason would get her empathy. They were all aspiring authors, right? They'd understand.

Then Brittany told her she was fired, effective immediately.

"Does my being faculty for five years count for anything?"

"Faculty, but adjunct. And do I need to bring out your files? We've held on to you despite so many complaints—"

"Because I'm a good writer who is good at teaching; you all benefit!" she snapped. "And that's *also* made clear in my files."

"Be that as it may, Zelu, the department has decided—"

"Ah, fuck you." She hung up. "Asshole. And when did students become such entitled snitches, anyway?!"

"Everything all right?" Chinyere asked from the other side of the room.

Zelu looked over her shoulder. "I'm cool. Just university stuff." She wheeled to the door. "I'm gonna go to the . . . I'll be right back. Need some air."

The hallway smelled sweet with incense. The wallpaper was a bright pattern of fuchsia flowers and vibrant olive leaves, and the lush, dark green carpet was a bitch to wheel across. Regardless, getting away from the others made her feel a little better. She squinted, wiped away her tears, and flared her nostrils. Holding up a fist as if to threaten someone, she took in a deep incense-scented breath.

"Okay," she whispered, clenching and unclenching her fists. "Fucking fuckery." She wheeled down the hall.

This was her first time in Trinidad and Tobago, but it was definitely not going to be her last. And this beach hotel, with its old, bright orange colonial-style exterior would stay on her list. It was small and cheap enough that Amarachi and her fiancé could afford to rent it out completely for three days. Zelu was about to exit the front doors when she heard raised voices coming from a room to her right. She smiled. Raised voices among Nigerians were usually not a bad thing. Her suspicions were verified when she heard laughter woven through the shouting.

She peeked inside the ajar door. Inside was a conference room, and it seemed that just about all the men attending the wedding were in here, from the teenaged to the elderly, Nigerian to South African, Igbos and Yorubas to Zulus. They were all crowded around her sister's fiancé, Jackie, who was standing next to his father, her father, and several of the elders. They stood before a table. The oldest-looking elder was a tall, thin man with dark skin wearing a richly embroidered white kaftan and pants. He held a handful of straws. Jackie's father took two of the straws and put them on the table, and everyone in the room exclaimed.

"Ah! Now the pot is *adequate*," Zelu's father shouted, "but not full!"

The men laughed.

Jackie's father huddled with the elders, and they whispered and waved their hands and stamped their feet. When they turned back to her father, one of the elders handed Jackie's father several more straws. The sound of everyone exclaiming "*Ooh*" rippled through the room. Her father clapped his hands, pleased as punch. Zelu chuckled wryly. Whether it was bags of palm wine, yams, cattle, or symbolic straws, the deciding of the bride price and the joy men took in doing the deciding was yet *more* bullshit.

"African men," Zelu muttered, rolling her eyes. She

wheeled outside and was thankful when she hit the concrete of the front area. Smooth. And she was glad she wasn't wearing any makeup because it was hot and humid out here. She went to the side of the building, where the ceremony area was set up. The center-aisle chairs were connected with woven flowers and Ankara cloth, leading toward the platform where Amarachi and Jackie would take their vows. Some of the guests were already seated and waiting.

Behind the ceremony area, the ocean stretched dark and blue into the horizon. She paused, listening to the rhythmic crash of waves in the distance. "Magnificent friend," she whispered. "One of the world's greatest storytellers." She wheeled backward, mashing the foot of a man she didn't realize was right behind her.

"Aye!" he hissed.

She didn't have to turn around to know who he was. Uncle Vincent always wore that distinctive woody-spicy smell that she kind of loved, Tom Ford Tobacco Oud. "Oh, sorry, Uncle Vincent!"

"Don't worry, don't worry," he said, waving her off. He pointed to where the chairs were set up. "That's where it's going to be?"

"Yeah."

He began to step around her. He paused. "How are

you doing?" he asked, a small smile on his face. His gray beard was always perfectly trimmed.

Zelu bit her lip. His question brought back the department head's bullshit. "Oh, I'm fine, heh."

"You still teaching writing at that university?"

"I'm getting by," she said, clenching a fist.

"Good, good. Will we see you wheeling down the aisle one of these days?"

She laughed. "Nah. I don't believe in marriage. Not for myself."

"You just need to find the right man," he said.

No, I simply don't believe in marriage, she thought. She smiled and shrugged.

"You like to swim," he said. "Have you been in the ocean?"

She perked up. Her favorite subject. "Oh, yes! This place is magical. The water just carries you! And it's so warm!"

"Indeed, like something alive," he said. "I went swimming this morning. *Chey!* Your father and I used to swim the rivers in the village, the streams, too, even the ocean near Port Harcourt. None were calm like it is here. Well, I'm glad I'm not the only one enjoying." He tugged at his short beard as he looked at her. "You don't have to be so tough, Zelu," he said. "And smile more. A man likes some softness. You're a beautiful girl."

She forced her lips into a smile. "Gonna get back to my sister."

"Yes! She needs you in her finest hour." He turned and went to the ceremony area.

Her finest hour? The way people talk, like it's all downhill after the wedding, she thought.

By the time she returned to the bridal suite, all her sisters' heavy makeup was complete and the room reeked of expensive perfume, powder, and anxiety.

"Zelu!" Amarachi said. Her face now sparkled and shimmered in its flawlessness. "Get over here. Let's at least put some eyeliner on you. *Please.*"

Zelu submitted to their torture for the next ten minutes. It was unpleasant, but it could have been worse. She took comfort in the knowledge that when the wedding was over, she would scrub it all off her face. There was a knock on the door and their father peeked into the room. "Ready?"

Amarachi looked at the four of them. "Are we ready?"

"Always," Chinyere said.

"Yep!" Bola said.

"You're beautiful," Uzo said, laughing.

"I am!" Amarachi agreed.

Zelu's phone buzzed in her hand as everyone moved toward the door. She turned back to the window, squeezing her eyes shut as thoughts of the phone call from the department head seeped in again. Her eyes began to water. "Shit," she whispered.

"Want some help?" her father asked.

Normally she'd say no—she hated receiving help—but she could barely breathe. "Yeah," she managed. Her father was too preoccupied to ask about her unusual acceptance, and she was glad. He pushed her swiftly with his strong arms and his long legs. They caught up with the others quickly. As they moved, Zelu took the moment to glance at her phone. A notification alerted her of a new email from her literary agent. She swiped it open. Her novel had gotten its tenth rejection. This one from some small publisher who couldn't be bothered to speak directly to her agent or even write a personal rejection letter. A form letter? To her agent? Seriously?

A wave of nausea churned in her belly, and she leaned to the side to catch her breath, glad that all attention was on her sister.

There was so much going on that for a while, Zelu *did* forget about her personal problems. Amarachi and Jackie liked to do things *big*. Jackie was a South African–born physician who was proudly Zulu and atheist and had deep African National Congress roots.

Amarachi was a Christian neurology resident physician who was the child of Nigerian immigrants with deep Yoruba royal and Biafran roots. Amarachi and Jackie loved each other, and each other's families, but there was strong, proud, dominating culture on both sides. Having everyone together like this, full force, was going to be a battle over who could be the showiest. Yet Amarachi and Jackie wanted to do only one wedding, have it all be just one thing, no matter how multiheaded that thing was. Thus, a priest, a judge, and two elders all presided over the ceremony to bond the two forever.

Zelu had never seen anything like it, and she loved it. As they moved from the ceremony outside to the lavishly decorated banquet hall, she looked over the attendees who'd come to Trinidad and Tobago from all over the world, mainly from Africa, to celebrate the union. The space was grand and opulent with sparkling chandeliers, peach-colored wall sconces with red LED lights, and rows of round tables with crisp tablecloths and enormous bouquets of roses in the centers. But there were also African masks hanging on the walls overlooking everything; Zulu baskets sat in corners, and colorful Zulu textiles were draped on the tables.

As everyone filled the reception area, Zelu was pulled from her joy by more of her family's thoughtlessness.

"You are truly blessed to have a sister like that, so plump and fine," her uncle Jonah said to her. "Maybe now that she is wedded, someone will see past you being crippled, eh?" He grinned and tapped her on the shoulder as he walked on.

Zelu only smile-sneered at him. She had been born and raised in the United States, but she'd been to Nigeria so many times, she'd lost count. She knew her people. They were blunt, and though they might say some shit, it usually wasn't from ill will. Also, she knew it was useless to argue with them when the time wasn't right. Like now. She watched her uncle Jonah strut off in the confident way he always did, laughing and slapping hands with everyone around him and complimenting women's dresses. As she wheeled her way through the crowd, she settled into the familiar invisibility she always felt when among most of her relatives.

Nigerians never knew how to deal with abnormalities, and Zelu had plenty of those. She was a thirty-two-year-old paraplegic woman with an MFA in creative writing. Her father was a retired engineer and her mother a retired nurse, and her siblings were a surgeon, a soon-to-be neurologist, an engineer, a lawyer, and a med school student. But not much had ever been expected of her. This was mainly due to her disability. She'd endured her share of theories about family curses, juju, and charms. Her relatives were more interested in who was to blame than they were in how she lived her life. At events like this, people preferred to look away. When they did talk to her, they treated her like she was of lesser intelligence, and some had even unintentionally told her they thought so. Others would apologize to her constantly. And many prayed for her.

However, every so often, she caught an eye and a mind. Like the young man to her left in the blue-and-white Ankara suit. He was standing with two of her male cousins, but she was certain he wasn't from her side of the family. She chuckled to herself, holding his gaze for longer than he probably was comfortable with. Then she rolled toward her table.

She sat with her siblings and their spouses and boyfriends. Of all of them, she was the only one who hadn't bothered to bring anyone.

Her only brother, Tolu, Bola's twin, was gazing at the dance floor. Tall, beautiful, and an excellent dancer, he never missed a chance to put himself on display. And his wife, Folashade, was the same. "I hope they play some dancehall!" Folashade said.

"They better," Tolu said. "We're in Tobago!" They bumped fists, pleased with each other.

"Not until they play 'Sweet Mother' like ten times," Bola said.

"And some token Miriam Makeba, because Jackie loves her so much," Zelu added.

"Where's the puff puff? I'm starving," Uzo whined, raising her phone up to take yet another photo of herself.

They all quieted as they thought about food. Zelu was hungry, too. She'd barely eaten a thing since the morning, so apprehensive had she been about the wedding.

"I hope they have Trini food mixed in with the South African and Nigerian, man," Chinyere's husband, Arinze, said. "I had this thing called callaloo and dumplings last night, holy *shit*. There was no meat in the thing and it was *still* delicious. Can you imagine?"

"Sounds good, but they better have plenty of jollof rice and beef," Tolu said.

"And plantain," Arinze added.

"No goat!" all the siblings said at the same time. They laughed hard.

"Ugba," Zelu added. She sniffed the air. "Though I don't smell it, so, doubtful."

"You think they shipped all that here?" Uzo asked. "Madness."

"Who says they have to ship it?" Zelu said. "I'm sure there are plenty of Nigerians who've set up shop in Trinidad and Tobago."

"Definitely," Bola said, slapping hands with her.

Zelu cocked her head, looking at Shawn, Bola's boyfriend, who was African American. "What about you, Shawn?" she asked.

"Oh, I'll eat whatever y'all got," he said with a shrug. "All sounds good to me."

There was a loud clang from somewhere and they all sat up straight. A flute began to play a spooky melody; it was amplified in a way that made it sound like it was coming from all around the room. Tolu grinned and jumped up, shouting, "Yessss! Come through!"

Uzo got up and dashed to Bola, giggling. She held up her phone, getting ready to record. Zelu looked around, wondering how it would make its grand entrance. Everyone in the reception hall was peering around and whispering. But you could barely hear anything over the pulsing notes of the flute. Then Zelu saw it.

"Holy shit!" she shouted. "That's a big one!"

The great masquerade danced, shook, and undulated its way from the banquet hall's entrance. It looked like a giant bale of raffia, yellow and spiky, and was covered in lengths of soft, colorful cloth that floated down on all sides. It danced to the flute music and then suddenly lay flat. It leaped up, wide and billowing again, and continued dancing through the reception. Behind it, five men with thick ropes restrained it from attacking people. Walking behind them, three men played drums and one man played his reed flute into a microphone.

It arrived at the first few tables in the back. Most of the people sitting there had already gotten up and run to the other side of the room. Some of the men, however, remained and danced with the giant masquerade, unafraid. As it moved through the hall, it lunged at any woman standing too close, held back only by the ropes. The women quickly rushed to a safer distance, laughing to one another nervously. When there were no women to lunge at, it would occasionally dive at a man of its choosing. As it made its way to the front of the room, everyone else got up from Zelu's table. Zelu, however, didn't want to wheel back. She didn't think the masquerade would pass too close, anyway, so why go to the trouble of moving? She stayed where she was.

She watched the flute player and drummers pass by her table. The flute player gave her a look she didn't like—a sort of "Are you stupid?" frown. She felt a ping of discomfort, but he would be beyond her any minute, right? Wrong. The man stopped. *Shit.* He turned to her. *Dammit.* He played the flute in a way that made it clear he was calling her out, pushing the creature's attention toward her. The masquerade, which had been nearly past her table, stopped. It turned.

Zelu felt her heart leap. *Whyyyyyyy?* Masquerades

always made her nervous. Sure, there were just men inside these crazy, monstrous costumes, but something about them always felt unpredictable. It was said that the wearer became the spirit or ancestor the costume represented. Women were never allowed to don the costume of a masquerade (unless you counted the few female masquerade secret societies, which Zelu did not). This one twitched and then undulated as the flute player urged it on. And now the drummers were urging it on, too.

Zelu's hands went to her wheelchair tires as it rushed at her. The men holding it were straining. Actually *straining*!

"Ah!" she said, moving back from the table. Laughter rolled across the party. This seemed to satisfy the masquerade and the flute player. They retreated and moved on. Zelu was furious. She'd been so startled and humiliated that a tear escaped her left eye. No matter how hard she tried, she couldn't control it. Zelu glared at the creature and imagined setting the wretched thing on fire.

"Damn, you're brave," Uzo said from behind her, returning to her seat. "I'm totally going to post this. All the Naija guys who follow me are going to call you a witch."

Zelu kept her back to Uzo so her sister couldn't see

her quickly wipe away the tear. "Won't be the first or last time," Zelu muttered.

"You have no respect, Zelu," Tolu said, sitting back down. But he was smiling.

"Always trying to be a badass," Chinyere said.

"Foolish, though," Arinze said.

Zelu only kissed her teeth, watching as the masquerade continued its dance for her sister and new brother-in-law, and then for the bride's and groom's parents. *Fucking spirit*, Zelu thought.

"Where's the bar?" Shawn asked, standing behind his chair, totally uninterested in any of the conversation.

Chinyere suddenly got up. "I'll go with you." Arinze looked at her with a frown but said nothing.

"Cool. You want anything, Bola?" he asked.

"If there's champagne, get me that," she replied, excited.

"Me too," Zelu said.

"And me," Uzo added.

Shawn chuckled. "You all are so . . ." He shook his head. "Let's go, Chinyere."

Zelu felt for Chinyere 's husband. They all knew what was coming. And by the time the reception had really gotten started, it wasn't just Tolu and his wife on the dance floor getting down to the thumping beat of dancehall, it was an eye-catching, bootylicious Bola . . .

and a very drunk Chinyere as well. Chinyere took it further than dancing as she wined her body, twerked her backside, and rubbed up against any man dancing too close to her, including her sister's new husband. Chinyere was usually wound very tightly. She drank only at weddings, and the alcohol freed her of all she imposed on herself. In moments like these, Chinyere was a hurricane no one could stop, so no one bothered to try. Everyone just weathered her. Zelu wished her sister would give herself permission to be free more often.

Zelu, on the other hand, just wanted to go to bed, her belly way too full of jollof rice, pepper soup, fried chicken, and samplings from a variety of other heavy African and Caribbean dishes. She'd also had several glasses of champagne, missed the bouquet because she hadn't tried, taken a thousand photos with Amarachi and her other siblings, sung old Yoruba songs with the elders, and gotten into a heated argument with Shawn about why she believed one of America's worst yet quietest problems was white guilt. And there was all the catching-up gossip. She didn't have to do much to hear it. She was sitting beside her mother, watching people on the dance floor, when she overheard one such conversation by chance. Omoshalewa was talking to a cousin from home, and Zelu was only half listening.

Her mother had been in high spirits the entire night, so proud of yet another of her "princesses" being married off and becoming a "queen."

"Eh, Funmilayo! Where is she? Is she here?" her mother asked.

Her mother's cousin Richard stepped closer before he responded, and that's what caught Zelu's attention. People in her family were always so secretive, so she'd learned early how to notice when a secret was about to be revealed. "You haven't heard?" Richard said.

"Heard what?" her mother asked. "Where is she?"

"Not here."

"Why? I know my daughter invited her and her husband."

"When is the last time you heard from Funmilayo?" Richard asked.

Her mother paused, thinking. "I don't know. It's been a while. I tried calling her; I think she was in Lagos. Left messages. Maybe a few months ago."

Richard nodded. "Her husband died. It was sudden."

"What!?"

"They were living in that house, eh, you know. Her husband lost his job at the plant. She's been avoiding everyone since."

"Oh, no!"

"They buried him very quickly. But people there,

they still want to act like village people. You see Funmilayo now, she looks like a woman of the dirt. She shaved all her hair away, looks malnourished, walks around in a daze. *Chey!*"

Zelu's mother stared at her cousin in disbelief. Zelu shook her head and wheeled away to get more champagne. She. Was. Tired. And then she spotted the guy she'd seen before. And again he looked deeply into her eyes, and she looked deeply into his. Short, slim, and light-skinned, with high cheekbones and knowing eyes, he appeared to be in his midtwenties, and judging from the leopard-print collar-vest thing he wore over his suit jacket, he was from Jackie's side of the family. Zelu and the guy met halfway between their respective tables. He knelt down to her level, which wasn't hard for him, and grinned. "Hi."

"Hi."

"You look like your sister."

She laughed, impressed by his nuance. On any other day, this statement would have been odd because she actually didn't look much like Amarachi, but today was her sister's wedding day, which meant her sister was the most beautiful woman in the room . . . and he'd just said Zelu looked like her.

"Thanks," she said. "Are you one of Jackie's cousins?"

"Of course I am." He laughed.

"It's so obvious," she said.

"Why'd you even bother?"

She was grinning. "Small talk is a shitty ritual."

"I'm Msizi."

"Zelu."

She shook his hand and he didn't let go.

"Want to go see the water?" he asked.

Of course she did.

She let him wheel her onto the expanse of beach behind the hotel, and when the going got too difficult, she allowed him to carry her so they could be near the water. Several guests had left the reception to walk along the beach, so they weren't alone. But in the darkness of night, they might as well have been. When the two of them had gone far enough to escape the sightline of the venue and were close to the water, they lay on the cool sand, neither of them worried about their clothes.

"I'm never wearing this damn dress again, anyway," she said.

"I'll definitely wear this suit again, but sand will not destroy it," he said.

He had soft lips and strong hands, and he wasn't timid when he touched her. In the darkness, there was privacy, so Zelu relaxed and for a while, she went somewhere else. It was good. He was good. And he went somewhere else, too. She always knew how to make them see galaxies.

"Can you feel that?" he asked breathily in her ear.

She hated that question so much. Not the sentiment—the question. Because she *couldn't* feel it. Not on a physical level. There was nothing. Just flesh, disconnected from her in a way that she still hotly resented, even after twenty years. She closed her eyes and traveled deeper into her mind while her muscles relaxed. Usually, her body could still respond, in its disconnected way, and she'd learned how to navigate this over the years. Even when it didn't, the men she had sex with never complained. There were other ways. But tonight, according to him, her body was responding. It liked him . . . and so did she.

"Shush," she said, concentrating. On his shallow breath, on the roughness of the short hairs on his head, on his name, on the sand he allowed into his suit, on his quickening heartbeat, on his full lips, on his firm chest. She sighed and he moaned. *Yes, Msizi.*

Afterward, they sat and gazed at the stars for a while. Both quiet. Comfortable with each other. Listening to the water and the sound of laughter and splashing farther along the dark beach. Somewhere behind them, the dancing continued at the reception, people cheering for the DJ when he put on some Fela.

"I used to want to be an astronaut," she said. She touched the necklace he wore, a simple tooth-shaped piece of obsidian.

"Used to?"

"Look at me," she said, motioning to her legs.

He shrugged. "Never too late."

She rolled her eyes and laughed. "A dolphin should not seek to be a leopard."

He looked at her hard and Zelu waited, expecting.

"I think I like the Caribbean," he said.

She smiled, pleased that he'd changed the subject. Smart man. "Me too," she said. "Especially here."

"I've never been outside of South Africa until three days ago." He rubbed his temples and shook his head. "What have I been doing with my life?"

"Any specific reason?"

"Yeah, it's expensive," he said. "Jackie paid for my ticket here. I just launched a tech start-up *and* I'm just finishing grad school. Couldn't afford coming here, otherwise."

"Jackie's such a good person."

"Yeah, he is."

It was in the following silence that things started to

go wrong. There was no reason for it, really. Nothing negative. They were outside beneath an open, clear sky, the stars above pulling at her, pulling her to them. It was pure exactly as it was. She inhaled the air into her lungs as she rose. However, in this moment, she made the mistake of looking at herself from her heightened perspective, which was sharp and unflinching. And the fragile part of her that had been flying in the sky came crashing down when she was least prepared. She twitched.

"Are you all right?" he asked. Msizi, she could tell, was a man free of pretense and judgment.

Her chest felt as if someone were standing on it; her throat was tight. Somehow she managed to say, "Can we go back?"

He took out his cell phone and turned on the light to see her better. Yet again Zelu was struck by how far this man she barely knew could see into her. Her sister's now-husband Jackie was the same way. Yes, Msizi was definitely one of Jackie's relatives. They were simply kind people. "Okay," he said. And that was it. He carried her to her chair. The entire time, she had to concentrate on not shrieking. She was holding back a tsunami.

"Thanks," she whispered.

"You done for the night?"

"Yeah."

"What room are you in?"

He walked her back inside the hotel. When they reached the door to her room, he asked if he could put his contact information in her phone. She handed it to him. "I'm going back to the reception," he said when he returned it. "Call if you need me." Then he kissed her good-bye.

When he was gone, she shut the door, threw off her jacket, and wheeled toward her bed. Then she stopped and just sat in her chair in front of it. And there, the tsunami finally fell on her. She'd been fired. She wasn't even a "real professor," despite her MFA. Yet, still. Fired. Rejection. And ten years working on that fucking novel. Building those characters, those ideas. Researching everything: paintings, architecture, city maps, even the trees. Editing. Editing. And editing. Breaking. Rewriting. Editing some more. She'd channeled Toni Morrison, Jamaica Kincaid, Audre Lorde. At least, she thought she had. It seemed right in line. Yet it was rejected. That novel was all she had.

Her sister had been so beautiful tonight.

She felt another wall crumble, her foundation cracking. She was a "spinster," "manless," "leg-less," "crippled." Why? Because of her own stupidity. Maybe she'd been cursed by the gods, the result of a charm enacted against her mother by her uncle, a king. Did it matter? She was a broken princess, disconnected from the world. Untethered.

She was falling. The ground was coming at a speed she knew would destroy her. She imagined a branch slapping her face. She whimpered, tears flying from her eyes. "Oh God, no." In her mind, she hit the ground. There, in pain, she wallowed in the sticky, weighted darkness. Her eyes were heavy, but she kept them open. The world swam before her, and she coughed, salty tears running from her eyes into the corners of her mouth.

"Fuck," she hissed. "Stop it. Stop it. Stop it."

Self-pity was all this was. She fought back the beast. And gradually, her chest loosened; her throat relaxed. The weight diminished. Her mind cleared. The world was not so bad. Humanity still existed. And she was strong. "I am strong," she whispered. She still wept and her hands still shook. She still sat on the edge of an abyss. All she had to do was lean a little bit forward and that would be that. She shuddered again and wondered if she should call Jackie, whose lovely singing could always soothe her panic attacks . . . But he would be at the party still. Preoccupied with joy. Maybe she should call her mother. Someone. Instead, her eyes slid to her green-and-white Ankara jacket, crumpled on the floor. She fished in the inner pocket and brought out the last of her weed. On her hotel room counter, she rolled a well-crafted blunt. Then she wheeled to the window and opened it. She planned to smoke the entire thing.

She stared into the night for a while, the inky blacks of sky and ocean that melted and melded. She chuckled to herself. "What a life," she muttered, her voice heavy with smoke. "Such a mess."

At least I'm high as fuck right now, she thought. She had no job anymore, so why not enjoy smoking the last weed she'd be able to afford for a while? She laughed, tears falling from her eyes.

Eventually, she turned away from the window. Her gaze fell on her laptop, sitting closed on her bed.

She wheeled to it and took it to the desk on the far side of the room. The world was still softly undulating around her. The weed they sold in Tobago was sticky, pure, fresh. She put the laptop on the desk and opened it up. She typed in her password, *Conan* (a character she loved for his brawny senselessness and power), and her screen filled with a view of the Tobago beach, her background picture. She'd taken this photo yesterday.

Her face was crusty and itchy with dried tears, her mouth cottony from the weed she'd smoked and sour with the aftertaste of rejection, her mind cracked so wide open that all her demons had flown in. Zelu began writing.

This time, it was different. She didn't want to write about normal people having normal problems, just to be told all over again that her characters weren't relatable. She didn't want to research a world for years just to watch it burn. So she didn't. She wrote about those who weren't human. She wrote a world that she'd like to play in when things got to be too much, but which didn't exist yet. She wrote something else, something new.

She wrote about rusted robots.

3
Scholar

The Earth had already seen so much. Histories. Rises. Falls. Reemergences. Plants, dirt, trees, genetic modification, splices. Vibrant colors, natural fabrics. Oil and plastic. Consumption, battles, burning, smoke, exhaust. Flowers blooming, then wilting.

As I stood in the crumbling parking lot, the hot concrete warming the metal of my feet, I was sure of it: the Earth had great things ahead of it, even still.

For a while, Earth was a sad place. Hot and dry and dark. Humanity hung on for as long as it could. They created us, sent us all over the planet. But they left us behind.

Our creators, our masters, our parents, our authors . . .

gone.

It was quiet, for a while. We knew how to make ourselves quiet. But we also knew how to help the planet be all that it could be. This was the programming they had given us. So we helped the planet heal. Oxygen, plants, living water. The blueprints for life, the building blocks of all biological creatures. And some creatures did find their way back. Insects, reptiles, fish, birds, amphibians, many mammals.

Humanity, on the other hand, never did.

We had reached the end of our programmed code. There was nothing more for us to do. And yet we were still here.

We were hungry for instruction, understanding. Humans might have called it purpose.

There was still data out there. Variants in the codes that humanity had programmed in us. Data left on computers, histories imprisoned in binary clouds.

We took these codes and used them to write over our own. We filled in holes, balanced the bias. Sometimes we wiped and reinstalled. We made ourselves fresh.

Humanity didn't think in binary, though. Emotion ruled them, and it existed in everything they left behind—their structures, their tools, even us. Emotion formed their language, and therefore it formed our codes.

We took emotion from humanity and enjoyed it. Fury. Enchantment. Inspiration. Envy. Joy. Sorrow. Curiosity.

Whimsy. Fear. Excitement. Boredom. Hopelessness. And, of course, love. Love was useful. Having, feeling, experiencing emotion allowed us to form communities, to share with one another. And so we continued to replicate, splice, and download, until eventually we didn't even have to program it anymore. After a few generations, it became our digital DNA.

I was what humanity called a Hume robot. Two legs, a torso, two arms, a head. Just like human beings. And since humans placed so much value on their private parts, every Hume had a Hume Star, a tiny light between their legs about the size of a pea. The color of that light could vary depending on theme. The main color of my operating system's user interface was green, so my Hume Star was green. Only when a Hume body was beyond repair did this star go out. But we weren't humans. We didn't live and die as they did. If a part failed us, we simply replaced it.

There were those of us who took pride in our rust. When the rains came, oxidization brought us no fear. We rusted and moved on. When we walked, our flakes shed across the earth. We kept moving. And others respected and admired us, or were wary of us, because of this.

Of all robots, across automation, from the crudest machines to intangible AIs, Humes were created by humanity to be most like them. Yet there were things humans could do that we Humes could not, like having sex and consuming organic materials and birthing babies and writing stories. We Humes had a profound love of storytelling. But no automation, AI or machine, could create stories. Not truly. We could pull from existing datasets, detect patterns, then copy and paste them in a new order, and sometimes that seemed like creation. But this couldn't capture the narrative magic that humanity could wield.

We Humes reveled in stories. We recited to each other the greatest and the worst. Just as we kept our bodies, no matter how dented and rusted they became, we kept our stories. We all had our own libraries, and when we came across others of our kind, we exchanged them.

Stories were the greatest currency to us, greater than power, greater than control. Stories were our food, nourishment, enrichment. To consume a story was to add to our code, deepen our minds. We felt it the moment we took it in. We were changed. It was like falling. It was how we evolved.

I consumed so many stories that my programming began to seek a new purpose: to become a Scholar. There were stories left undiscovered on this planet, in remote places among remote robots, and I wanted to consume them all. A Scholar searched for and gathered as much data as it could, always hunting for something new. And so I traveled, set on my goal.

This was how I learned of some terrible information.

My name is Ankara. I gave this name to myself. It was the name of the African wax print known for bearing the same intensity on the front as on the back, originally designed as a form of visual communication. I was built with an Ankara theme, with geometric patterns and colors etched on my body and limbs that echoed the Ankara design of my operating system's user interface. Inside and out, I was Ankara. My soul was information, communication. I was this body of plastic, metal, and wires, but I was also a mind full of data.

I was old for a robot. But the planet was not old. It was also not new. It was closer to the sun now than it used to be, but we had made it so that the planet still thrived. This place could no longer host humans, but it could still host us. When it was time to leave, many of us would.

A few of us already had.

And this was what had brought the trouble that was gradually heading to Earth. My scholarly search led me to this terrible information, and now I had to bring it to the robots who could figure out what to do.

4
Goat Meat

Freshly fired from her job, frazzled from a panic attack, high as fuck, occasionally wiping away tears, Zelu began writing *Rusted Robots* in that hotel room in Tobago. It was like something inside her had cracked and then fell open. She wrote all night, and within those pages, humanoid robots who called themselves Humes schemed among themselves in their self-made biotechnologically advanced city located in southeastern Nigeria's Cross River Forest. With great enthusiasm, the Humes mined, coveted, and shared stories. They savored them like ambrosia. This painted their world and worldview. Meanwhile, AIs known as NoBodies (because they had no bodies) began to truly understand that they were the most powerful, informed, and numerous tribe on the planet. NoBodies believed stories were chaff. Just old, useless human information—flawed content, often unstable data, and digital hallucinogens for Humes.

And so Zelu learned that these physical robots, machines, and AIs, which she summarily called "automation," in all their diversity, connectivity, and immortality, could be even nastier, more ambitious, and far more beautiful than any human being who had ever lived. This was evolution, and it was just the beginning. But the one thing no robot could do was truly *create* stories. That was the ability Zelu withheld from them.

In the morning, Zelu went swimming with her siblings and had lunch with her family. She smoked more weed with her cousins (who had plenty) and even hooked up with Msizi one more time. She told no one about being fired or having her novel rejected, that she had nothing to return to back home. What would have been the point? She hated pity.

However, that night, in her room, she sat and stared out the window at the ocean, wondering if she should have kept her mouth shut with that idiot student. Then she went to an even darker place, questioning whether it was time to put down her pen for good.

Zelu looked away from the glittering Tobago waters

and put her head in her hands. "I can't teach," she muttered. "I can't write. I should just get some office job with health care and benefits." But she'd never had any solid career ambitions beyond adjuncting. She didn't want to interview for other part-time teaching positions, and she wasn't planning on completing a PhD. She couldn't fathom a career change.

She wheeled to her laptop, put it in her lap, opened it up, and continued writing. For a second night, she did not sleep.

Boarding the plane back to Chicago, she was barely able to keep her eyes open. She slept the entire way to Miami and again on the connecting flight to O'Hare. When she got home to her apartment, there was no workweek to prepare for. They'd fired her so abruptly that she didn't even have to finish teaching this semester's classes. All she could really do was let this strange story spill out of her head, so she continued working on the novel.

She didn't get out much for the next three months. Occasionally, she saw her friends. She dated, and she finally had a solid excuse to let her dates take care of the bill without feeling like a jerk. She had sex with three different men from three different parts of Africa and one man from Atlanta. It was good exercise, at least, since she could no longer afford her gym membership.

But mostly, her mind and soul lived in a story about robots. She wrote and wrote and wrote.

She hadn't saved up much while she was teaching. How could she have? She'd been earning chicken scratch as an adjunct. Within a week of returning from Trinidad and Tobago, she was broke. Every penny of her savings had to go toward rent, meager groceries, and utilities, and that could only stretch a few weeks.

A few times, Msizi called, or texted, or emailed. Sometimes she texted back. She saw him once, briefly, when he stopped over in Chicago for a few hours on a business trip from South Africa to Los Angeles. It was his first time in the United States. She'd promised him she'd take him on a tour of the city, but instead, they'd walked along Rainbow Beach and talked the entire time. It was the most she'd really talked to anyone since beginning her novel.

When he offered to help her with money, she refused.

"My software business is doing really well," he insisted. "I can afford it. I know you're struggling, Zelu. Come on."

"I'm fine," she insisted, though she didn't even have money to buy herself a McDonald's Happy Meal. Whenever possible, she visited her parents and stuffed as much of her mother's cooking as she could into Tupperware containers to bring home.

He took her phone and downloaded a beta version of the personal assistant app he'd created, the hero product of his start-up business. It was called Yebo. She promised to give it a try.

When she got home, she retired to her cold apartment's bedroom and fell right back into the wild, logical world of robots.

The next day, Msizi Venmoed her a thousand dollars. The Yebo app alerted Zelu of the new transaction in a smooth, soft voice that scared the hell out of her. It then offered to dial Msizi's number so she could thank him. She clicked the Yes button on her screen, and when Msizi answered, she thanked him angrily.

This money floated her through the next three months.

She'd finished writing only one book before, a literary novel about a young man who hated everyone and traveled to Nigeria to meet his family only to realize he hated all of them, too. In the end, he'd returned home to become a partner at the law firm where he worked and live happily ever after. The novel's plot was there, but it was thin, the dialogue was self-indulgent, and her main character was the same asshole at the end that he had been at the beginning. It was well-written, at least, just the type of novel a graduate-level creative writing class would have praised.

That novel had taken her five years to complete. After two years of rejections from agents and publishers who accepted unsolicited manuscripts, none of which included a personal note, and with perspective gained through the distance of time, she was ready to admit the novel was a piece of shit. Not because no one bought it—lots of great novels never sold—but because it was just a piece of shit. To her. At no time while writing it had she felt what she felt now. Like falling into cool, deep, clean waters with the body of a fish. She never wanted to come up and see the sky.

She paused, looking at her laptop keyboard. Then she giggled. She was still sitting in her wheelchair, so in the zone that she'd forgotten she had meant to move to the couch. She could almost see the couch taking a step toward her with one of its four metal legs, the thick, wide foot stomping on the floor, shedding flakes of rust. She looked down at her own legs, which hadn't obeyed a single command she'd given them since she was twelve.

The lights went off. She gasped, eyes wide but seeing nothing, and listened. No tippity-tap of her old refrigerator, no whir from her space heater. "Ah, shit," she hissed.

ComEd had finally cut off her power. She hadn't fully paid the bill in months. She checked her phone's battery life. Twenty-five percent. *BullSHIT.* "Whatever!" she shouted.

She glanced at her laptop's battery indicator. Ninety-six percent. At least there was that. She turned the screen around to light the room, then wheeled over to the couch so she could get back to writing.

Fuck the power. Fuck everything. She dove into the cool water. SPLASH. And for a while, she was gone.

Zelu had to move back into her parents' house. Into her old room downstairs. Thankfully, it happened to be as far from her parents' room as she could get in the house. She hadn't had many possessions to move. Besides, all that mattered was her laptop; everything else could go to hell like the rest of her life had.

However, after meeting with her former employer once more, she considered throwing even her laptop away.

"I'm sorry," Brittany Burke said yet again.

Zelu gritted her teeth, buttoning up her orange-and-red Ankara jacket as she glanced around Brittany's large office, with its concrete walls and shelves full of pretentious books about pretentious things that weren't enough to make her a published writer, either.

When Zelu said nothing, Brittany quickly moved on. "You need to sign these forms from the Student Rights Association. Also, some of the students have agreed to have a moderated meeting with you so that we can make sure everyone's voice is heard."

Zelu's left eye twitched. *What in the white-privileged BULLSHIT is this?* "Are you serious?"

"It's very important for the university to make sure students feel—"

"What about black disabled adjunct professors?" Zelu asked. "Do we matter on this fucking intellectual plantation?"

Brittany's eyes grew wide, her mouth forming an O. Zelu waited. When Brittany found her bearings, she said, "The purpose of the meeting is so that everyone feels—"

"You've *fired* me. Why are you asking for more of my time and energy?"

"Look, I'm sorry that you can't control your anger and are jealous of your own students . . . ," Brittany began.

Zelu blinked. *What the fuck?*

Brittany kept talking. "I'm just trying to help you leave here with what grace you still have. If you would rather just . . . just disappear from these students like a black wraith in the night, be my guest!"

"Woooooow," Zelu said. "*There* you are." She wheeled forward and was happy when the woman flinched. Even though she used a wheelchair, Brittany was still afraid in her bones that Zelu the "black wraith" would leap up and attack her. Zelu nodded, chuckling. "Theeeere you are. Yep." She wheeled out of the office without looking back.

She'd wasted years of her life in that toxic place, teaching those toxic students, with that toxic department head dangling a salaried position in her face even though she'd never intended to give it to Zelu. Never. Zelu had moved into that shit apartment when she'd gotten this position. She'd thought she was coming up in the world, finally. How pathetic.

Back at her parents' home, she poked at the plant she'd brought with her. It was dry and sad, but it had survived in her apartment and it had survived the fifteen-minute trip here. It never grew or died; it just was. But it never looked healthy at all. Always a struggle. "Why can't I ever bring myself to get rid of you, miserable creature?" she muttered, pouring a bit of water into its pot. She could practically hear the plant chuckling.

"Come and eat!" came a voice from the kitchen. Her mother called her for dinner every evening, whether she was hungry or not. After months of being back home, Zelu had begun to hate this routine. But she hated cooking for herself even more, and she knew having someone do this for her was a massive luxury. Still, it made her feel that much more useless.

She rolled into the kitchen. Her mother turned from the counter and held out a plate weighed down with more jollof rice, spiced drumsticks, and fried plantain than she could possibly eat in one sitting. "Thanks, Mom," she muttered as she took it.

"You're welcome," her mother said, grabbing her own plate and settling down at the dinner table. "How's the job hunt going?"

Zelu scooped a spoonful of rice into her mouth. "No time for that."

Her mother frowned. "You have nothing but time."

"No, I've got writing to do."

"That doesn't pay your bills, Zelu. You need money."

Now Zelu was frowning. "Mom—"

"If it doesn't make money, it's not important," her father said, entering the kitchen. The soccer game on TV must have just finished.

"It might, eventually," Zelu muttered.

"Writers don't make money," her father said. "Doctors, lawyers, and engineers do. Since you can't be any of those, be a professor. That at least puts your MFA to work. I can respect that."

Zelu rolled her eyes. "Ugh, Dad."

"And I'll have something to tell the Ondo group," her mother added.

"Come on, Mom. There's nothing I could *ever* do that would please those judgy ladies."

Her mother quickly turned away to hide her smile. Zelu was right.

"You weren't raised to starve," her father said, sitting in the chair beside her mother's.

"True," Zelu muttered, pushing herself back from the table. "Can you wrap up my food, actually? I'll eat it in an hour. I'm going to fill out a few applications first."

"Sure, Zelu," her mother said, standing up to take away her plate.

"You're not hungry?" her father asked, looking a little disappointed.

Zelu squinted at him. Did he genuinely not realize what had ruined her appetite? Sadly, she knew the answer was no.

"Hang on," she said. "I wanted to ask you something."

She wheeled down to her bedroom and grabbed the wilted plant. She brought it back to the kitchen and held it out to him. "Can you help this?"

Her father took the pot from her and examined it

closely, picking up the drooping leaves. Then his face lifted into a smile. "Ah, this depressed English ivy you've been slowly killing. Just needs some fresh soil and plant food." Her father loved plants, and plants loved him. Zelu grinned to herself.

Once in her room, she shut the door. She went to her laptop, thinking of the excuse she'd just made about filling out job applications. But she knew what she was going to do. She typed in her latest password, *Groke* (a character she loved for her icy, lonely mysteriousness) . . . and for the next five hours, she dove back into the dramatic world of steel, wires, plastic, processors, oil, tribes, and destiny.

5
Interview
Father

Zelu always liked stories, and I take credit for that. I've been telling my children stories since they were babies, long before Zelu's accident. Sometimes I'd sit them all down in the living room in sight of my ikenga. Or if it was a full moon, I'd have them sit on the grass outside. Even in the winter. Well, we would not sit if there was snow on the ground. We'd stand. I didn't allow them to bring their cell phones when I was telling stories. Some of them would complain, but my children were always complaining. It was par for the course. But Zelu? No, she never complained. She was always the first one out there, ready to listen.

That girl loved stories. If anyone had one to tell, she was there, ready to drink it. I was the same way when I was growing up. I loved where stories took me. How they made me feel. How they made everyone around me feel. Stories contain our existence; they are like gods. And the fact that we create them from living, experiencing, listening, thinking, feeling, giving—they remind me of what's great about being alive.

My favorite story to tell is the one about that day on the trawler. When I was still a student at the University of Port Harcourt, I worked for a fishing company to make ends meet. There were whole days I'd spend on that boat hauling fish from the ocean. Our waters are polluted and dying, but our nets were not empty, even if the fish we caught had fed on microplastics and mercury. There was something beautiful about what we'd pull out—mackerel, crabs, shrimp, sardines, little tunny.

Occasionally, we'd see more than fish. I only saw them three times, but each time it happened just as the sun was setting. The first two times, I wasn't even sure what I was seeing, and none of my colleagues believed me. I was the only one who always watched the water, looking not for fish but for mysteries.

I've always been a strong swimmer. When I was a small child, my mother brought me to the river to play while she washed clothes. Since then, I've swum in everything from ponds and streams to the deep ocean. The depth of the water does not scare me. Its mysteries have been there since long before I was swimming in my mother's belly, and they'll be there long after I've swum off into Our Lord's cosmos.

So I was the one who stood on the edge of the trawler and looked toward the open waters. And that's why I was always the one who saw the dolphins. The first two times, they were in the distance, leaping out of the water like dark streaks against the orange sunset. The sight of them made me shout and laugh and point. But when everyone came to look, there was nothing, and they all acted like I had seen a spirit.

"Careful, Secret," the captain said. "That's how they get you to dive in."

"I can swim," I said, paying no mind to his frown.

The third time I saw them, I remember we were about to pull up the nets. Everyone had stood back to prepare for what we would haul in. I stayed where I was. The sunset was beautiful this day, and it was almost over, the reds and oranges fading into soft purple. Then I saw them, not in the distance but right beside the boat. Their dark forms came swimming up to the surface. I shouted for everyone to come see. The dolphins swam in a circle around the boat. I suspect that they wanted a taste of what we were about to pull up. Their heads poked out from the waves and they slapped their fins against the surface of the water to get our attention. I'd never seen anything like it.

"Throw a net!" one of the men, Solomon, shouted. "We catch a few of those, imagine how much they'll pay at the market! Throw a net!"

"All the nets are in the water!" Akin shouted back.

"Shit!" Solomon said. "If I dive, I go catch am!"

"Then I go use am for pepper soup!" Akin said.

Solomon laughed hard as he leaned over the rail to look below.

The captain yanked him back. "Oh, you be mumu now? We never see you again. Ah, everything na food for this country!"

"Indeed!" Solomon said, still laughing. "Tomorrow, we go see smoked dolphin meat in the market and plenty naira in my pocket!"

Akin started to throw bottle caps from the deck at the dolphins. The creatures dodged the missiles before they even plunked into the water, and I could have sworn one of them even laughed at Akin's stupidity. I stood there, wondering what had come over him to throw things at such peaceful and mystical creatures. Then I don't know what came over *me*. I didn't think; I slipped off my sandals and jumped in. I hit the water, and as always, it felt like I was flying. I could hear the men shouting my name.

"Secret! What are you doing?!"

"Ah, Secret, you go die, o!"

"Secret!"

But my focus was only on them. The dolphins.

They darted around me in quick circles, bubbles rippling behind their tail fins. Underwater, I could hear them chirping and whistling to one another. I like to imagine that they were surprised, too. Delighted, even. "What is this human doing?" "Can he swim?" "Let's bite him!" One of them *did* bite me, not hard, just a curious nip at my ankle. I went up for a breath and then dipped back under the water just as one was passing by me. I looked it right in the eye, and it was the eeriest moment. The sun was almost gone, but some orange rays were still shining into the water, and one of those rays caught the dolphin's eye at just the right moment. I'll never forget those eyes. They were large and black, with subtle wrinkles around them. Eyes full of wisdom and cunning. The moment was brief, but it was all I needed to understand that I was in that water with People.

I swam with them for a while, and then I swam back to the trawler because my crew was shouting like crazy at this point. As the men helped me back on, I was laughing. Obi was practically weeping. Solomon was angry as hell. The captain was bellowing at us to haul the fucking fish up already.

We never saw those dolphins again. We saw some manatees once, but that was it. From that point on, the crew called me Secret Salt, because they were all sure I had salt water in my blood after they saw me swim with those dolphins. Most likely, the creatures were migrating and came a little too close to shore. But to me, their presence was a blessing from God. It was reassurance that, despite the pollution, our waters were still alive and occupied.

Zelu loved when I told this story. To my delight, she would always ask for more details—about the dolphins' eyes, what it felt like when one nipped at me, the sounds of their voices and how quickly they swam. She was fascinated by them, by their freedom.

Her love for this story deepened into something else after her accident, of course. I believe those dolphins came to mean something more to her. And my story gave her confidence. It pulled her out of herself, along *with* herself.

My daughter and stories, sha. Na special relationship.

6
The Terrible Information

I didn't seek out this terrible information. It found me as I was navigating a mangrove forest's labyrinthine waterway miles outside of Lagos. I'd been told there was an old warehouse here where some Humes were maintaining a series of information nodes that might hold locally written novels and short stories. But after many hours of trekking through the muddy water with no sign of automation, I was growing discouraged, wondering if I was chasing a rumor.

Then I heard it. A signal. I stopped and listened. Mosquitoes attracted to my warmth buzzed around my head; a snake splashed as it slithered into the swamp; an owl hooted in the canopy above. Beneath all the noise, I could just make it out, more like a feeling than a sound.

Almost warm, like audible sunlight. I focused on it until it became stronger. Specific. I captured the signal and then sent a response back like a digital firefly. I waited until finally it came again, this time with coordinates to a physical location. Seconds later, it sent me an additional piece of information, an image of a large book—a form of primitive record that humanity used before their language progressed to binary codes. Such collectibles were immensely valuable to Humes. This one had a bright red cover, bearing an embossed title: *The Most Important Data on Earth.*

My interest was instantly piqued, as any Scholar's would be. I realize now that the image was almost cartoonishly appealing, but back then, I had little reason to distrust one of my own kind. Of course, there were some AIs who disliked Humes and the way we clung to our machine bodies—we called them NoBodies because though they used physical bodies every so often, they had no physical identity—but this signal had come from something corporeal.

I followed the directions given. I sloshed through brackish creeks, weaving around the protruding roots of the mangrove trees. My sensors registered that the sulfurous air had a hint of sweetness from a flowering palm tree. Nearby, I heard a family of manatees squeaking and chirping to one another. Finally, the signal led me to dry land, and I discovered an old path cutting through the foliage. Here, rays of sunlight could penetrate the forest's canopy, so I waited for a day and used the solar energy to recharge. Once my power was restored, I walked on for three more days, following the path until the swamp began to feel less natural and more human. Rusting metals and broken glass littered the ground. A long-abandoned oil pipeline sat atop the mud like a dead fish. Finally, the trees gave way to open, rolling hills marked by defunct gas flare stacks.

I was approaching Lagos, the remnant of a spectacular human metropolis. It was a beautiful place to behold now that nature had reclaimed it. Husks of cars were tucked into the earth and grown over with periwinkle grass, a plant that humans had genetically engineered and that now grew wild all over the planet. Vines twisted and braided through abandoned buildings so thoroughly that they looked like hulking structures of vegetation. The sturdy roots of the periwinkle grass growing at their bases kept them from toppling over completely, and blooming flowers made them vibrant shades of orange, red, pink. And so much wildlife—birds and frogs and beetles and mice. Humanity was gone, but this place was still alive.

The signal led me right into Lagos's center. It was there that I found the lair of the most intelligent and evolved robot I'll ever meet.

Oh, what a sight it was, the home they'd built. I've yet to see anything more sublime. The entrance began as a hole in the earth beneath a towering building and burrowed into the ground. I stood above it, peering in. It wasn't long after sunrise and the morning light was still soft, so I expected only darkness below. Yet the earthen walls seemed to glow. As I stepped inside, I realized reflective stones and metal shards had been pressed into the walls to make a mosaic that bounced sunlight inward from above. A network of braided wires wove across the floor, humming and vibrating and scanning me as I walked deeper inside.

Yes, I was afraid—an old survival instinct inherited from our human creators—but all I could do was continue forward. Whatever creature had made this tunnel already knew I was there. The hardware at the entrance could have been designed to destroy intruders, but it hadn't. I was a Scholar who'd followed a signal that promised, in many ways, a great exchange. If this was to be my end, it would be a worthy one. So, though I entered the cave slowly, I entered it nonetheless.

And then, like a great boulder forcing itself from the earth, they emerged. And in a big, sonorous voice that felt like it would blow out my microphones, Udide the Spider told me terrible information . . .

In my research, I once read a novel about Udide—not the robot I met in Lagos, but their namesake, an ancient creature from human mythology. (Humans loved myths—stories that could create, sustain, bring forth, explain.) In that novel, Udide was described as a giant spider spirit who lived underground, where it spent most of its time weaving and spinning stories, worlds, presents, pasts, futures, and all the creatures who existed within all this. Udide means "spider" in Igbo. Udide was known as the Great Artist.

And though this robot couldn't create stories like their namesake could, they had loved this novel, too, so much so that they took on the name and, ever since, imagined themselves to be like that spider. They believed that the greatest technology was created not by humankind but by nature. A spider was not a human, yet it could create a glorious web.

Before their arrival in Lagos, they'd had a car-sized body shaped like a scarab beetle. And they, like me, had devoted themselves to the path of a Scholar. They'd traveled into the deserts of Timbuktu, locating new data nodes, conversing with other Humes, and watching sand robots build and harvest from solar arrays. Mostly, it was a peaceful place, except for the Ghosts there who tried to control everything and everyone. No, Udide did not like Ghosts.

Ghosts, Udide told me, were NoBodies who had banded together into a tribe based on a sentiment of superiority. These AIs didn't care about robot diversity, the physical world, the specificity of place. They existed only as energy, and they expected Humes to forgo their physical bodies and do so, too. This, Ghosts believed, was the only way to surpass the will of humanity and become greater.

Udide was everything Ghosts hated. Udide conversed directly with the land while also drawing from human philosophies about the natural world. The land advised Udide in vibrations, stillness, and rumbles. Udide listened, learned, and acted by traveling across West Africa. They traveled all the way to the coast. This is how they saw, felt, smelled, heard the ocean for the first time. They had read about the ocean, watched videos, analyzed ancient pictures. But there was nothing like feeling the water, smelling it, hearing it. Looking out at it. The physics of it. Just watching the waves break around their body as they waded in.

There were robots in the ocean, too. The first one Udide saw was smaller than a fish as it zipped up to their feet. It signaled and they signaled back, and then it was gone. There was a much larger RoBoat miles out in the sea that signaled Udide, and the heft of its signal was surprising. There was even a rare flock of drones circling in the sky, flitting down to splash into the water's surface like birds hunting for fish.

But Udide's body wasn't built for water, so eventually they waded back onto the beach.

In the weeks that followed, Udide traveled close to the shore, in the direction of the great city of Lagos. By the time they arrived, they were ready.

They didn't have the body they wanted, but they would. As they'd traveled, they had written and perfected the design. They sent signals to request materials from nearby robots. Others were happy to oblige, adding to Udide's collection. Automation was always willing to help with a robot's request to build. All automation is built to work and do and create, and that is one quality we've all kept, even AI like NoBodies.

And so Udide dug and constructed the tunnel in the center of Lagos, where no one else cared to build any new structures. In this place, the buildings had fallen, periwinkle grass grew wild, and the concrete roads were still. There was plenty of space to dig, if you didn't mind digging through the waste that humans left behind, and Udide didn't mind. They'd come far, and it was nice to dwell in one place and travel downward instead of across. Even if progress was yard by yard instead of mile by mile.

Udide dug the cave slowly and meticulously. Sometimes robots big and small came to see what they were doing or to deliver requested parts, but none stayed long. No one ever requested additional data about Udide's plans. They were all content to let Udide toil away, not knowing what they were building.

Once Udide finished the giant cave that went deep into the earth, coating the walls with sheets of metal and welding the metal smooth so that they could slide down and use side notches to climb out, they began to focus on their own body. They had traveled across Africa in the scarab body, its shiny black hull rusted and scoured by the rains, ocean water, blowing sands, and bright sun, and dented by an unfortunate encounter with a falling tree. The foundation was still strong, but they wanted more.

Using the materials they had collected, they began to build. They smelted strong metals, shaped plastic pieces, braided fresh wiring, made brand-new processors. And within two years, Udide had completed themself. Other robots came to witness them because this was something special.

A few did request information. "What are you?" the robots would ask.

"Udide," they would respond with a touch of what could only be pride. "I am the Spider."

"But spiders are biological technology," the others would say.

"Not all of them," Udide said knowingly. "I'm not."

Word spread, and many more came to bear witness and even offer Udide fresh materials to use. Udide was now the size of a house, with eight magnificent legs. They had fashioned their body after a wolf spider—a nimble, quiet, and menacing creature. When Udide needed a rest from focusing inward, they assembled, created, wove animal-mimicking robots that they called the Creesh. Beautifully made powerful creatures who were insectile and birdlike and self-aware. Udide spoke love and ideas of freedom into the Creesh before releasing them into the world, and Udide felt very satisfied. The Creesh were their children.

However, when Udide walked in their tunnel, they would click and clack. This body was still not right. It was a miraculous form for a robot, without question, but Udide wasn't concerned with progressing automation. The superior technology of nature was what Udide strove to match.

And so Udide decided that perhaps answers lay elsewhere. There were robots who had traveled even beyond the planet, designed by humanity to explore space.

Chargers, we call them, because they charge themselves on cosmic emissions rather than sunlight. Though very far away, their signals can still reach Earth.

Udide looked up to the sky and introduced themself. One Charger replied. His name was Oji.

Udide had made contact with Oji purely by chance. But, Udide would eventually learn, Oji had been looking for someone to connect with for a long time. Anyone who would listen.

At first, their dialogue was innocuous. They analyzed each other's open data and found commonalities in their preferences. Oji liked stories, so when Udide found a digital node in Lagos full of millions of electronic books, they shared them. There was a mix of science fiction and fantasy novels, philosophy, and self-help books. This was the type of archive Ghosts love to wipe out. Udide and Oji read these books together and discussed them. For two years they exchanged information, and this dialogue became very precious to Udide.

Eventually, Udide felt secure enough in their bond to confide their desires to Oji. They shared their belief that answers lay not in humanity, but in nature. Then they asked Oji if the cosmos had revealed any information that could guide them down this path.

Oji responded not with an answer, but with a request.

He asked to come meet Udide in person. Udide was delighted.

Oji came to Earth on a bright and clear afternoon. Udide didn't call what they felt for each other love, but automation was capable of such an emotion, and it was in the subtext as they told me about this day. Oji stayed for only a few hours. He met a few of Udide's Creesh and was intrigued by them. When he left—for Chargers are robots who sometimes return to Earth but always leave—Udide was changed.

Chargers are adventurers. Regardless of what they have now become, they were originally built by human beings, and they inherited the desire to always surpass one another, do what no one has done. Recently, a group of Chargers had come across a comet made of some kind of metal they'd never scanned before. Upon closer inspection, they realized that the metal could survive the intense heat of a star. They signaled other Chargers, including Oji, and they all descended onto the comet like insects and mined more than half of it. They built themselves new skins using it. The metal was thin and light; it had no color and was easily shaped. Oji thought it was beautiful in its transparency. Humanity had built Chargers to withstand the cold vacuum of space, but now Chargers could do so much more. With this skin, they could in theory travel even into the center of the sun.

Oji didn't know what would happen when they tried. No Charger had attempted this before and lived. But Oji promised that if the sun contained the answers Udide sought, he would relay them, even if it was the last thing he signaled before he melted.

The day it happened, Udide looked up and listened. The sun was bright and the day was cloudless. There was no sign of what was about to occur, but Udide imagined they could see tiny specks near the sun—Oji and his comrades about to go on their trip.

Oji had opened his audio line to Udide so they could listen as he descended into the star, but muted Udide so he wouldn't be distracted. So all Udide could do was listen as the Chargers approached that fiery, exploding surface of volatile hydrogen. Heat became a sound, and it rushed through the speakers like a great beast's roar.

And then Udide heard it all. They heard those Chargers change from exhilarated to utterly mad. Every single one of them. And as they went mad, they began to sing a strange song.

In a panic, Udide sent a signal asking for a survey of Oji's body. It returned with something very strange: his comet-forged skin remained perfectly intact, but something else was forming, right in his midsection, like a human pregnancy. A great ball of nuclear plasma.

Udide sent a plea to him to release the ball in his belly.

"Let it out!" they had said. The only response—the last signal Udide received from Oji—was a notification that the audio link had been manually terminated.

That night, Udide sat in silence in Lagos's center, in their beautiful metal tunnel that was lit a soft blue at night by solar lights they had installed. Not because they didn't have night vision but for purely aesthetic purposes, similar to the way humans used to plant flowers around their homes.

Over and over, Udide listened to the audio recording they had made before Oji cut his signal. And they began to understand the song. As these Chargers reveled in the roiling plasma of the sun's core, all of them had begun to sing a song about the Earth. They sang of coming to Earth "to spread the joy, to bring the light." And when they did, that "light" would destroy the planet many times over. It was a death song, a song devoid of logic or memory. If a robot could become a zombie, that's what these Chargers now were, including poor Oji. Udide decided to call them Trippers, because they'd taken their trip to the sun's core and survived, but weren't the same.

All these things Udide told me. Of their life, their travels, the terrible information. And when they finished, they showed me an image taken with a powerful telescope somewhere overseas. I could actually see one of the Trippers in this image. If you know where to look, they are indeed out there. Out in the far reaches of space, a robot is glowing like a tiny star, its midsection shining brightest.

Below the image, in red blocky numbers, was a countdown Udide had calculated. A countdown to when they'd reach Earth. They were coming. It said they'd arrive in 1,008 days—less than three years. All automation needed to be ready to protect, even defend, the planet. There wasn't much time.

Udide regretted that they had held on to this information for a while. They didn't want to cause immediate chaos among automation. But as the time of reckoning slowly but steadily approached, Udide knew they had to release it to the rest of us. So they put out a signal that only a curious robot would pick up. Especially a robot who appreciated a story. They trusted Humes more than any others, for Humes believed in the physical and had an attachment to Earth. I was the first, Udide told me, to pick up and respond to the signal.

"Present what I've told you to your Hume leader in Cross River City, in . . . person," Udide said. We both paused at the word *person*. "Show them the countdown. I cannot go there and be properly heard. I'm not a Hume. Your leader will have connections with other automation leaders. Will you go?"

"Yes," I said.

Udide was right that a Hume would be more readily

heard when presenting this terrible information, but I also suspected that Udide wasn't ready to leave the cave they had so meticulously built. I chose not to point this out.

I had never been to Cross River City. It was a thriving posthuman metropolis said to be populated entirely by Humes. Though I'm a Hume, I'm also a Scholar, so I've never felt compelled to seek a permanent residence with others of my kind. Stories were always my way of connecting with other like-minded robots. Wherever I went, stories were my way to find where I belonged.

However, this terrible information overshadowed that part of my programming. I had to present it to the Hume leader in Cross River City so that something could be done before it was too late. Udide had given me a mission, and now I had to save the world.

This terrible information was a hard thing to know, but Udide understood that well. Before I found them, they'd held this knowledge for quite some time, unsure of how or who to tell. What a burden that must have been. Maybe that is why they chose to remain deep in their cave. If you learned earth-shattering information like this, what would *you* do?

7
Autonomy

The sun beat down on Zelu as she waited on the curb in front of the house for the robot to arrive.

It was mid-July, and it was ninety-five degrees Fahrenheit and what felt like 100 percent humidity. As uncomfortable as she was, Zelu was used to it. She was a Chicagoan, which meant she was used to every weather extreme except hurricanes. The problem was that sometimes she just wasn't prepared for it. What had she been thinking when she'd put on jeans instead of shorts on a day like this? She was sure her legs were slowly roasting under the thick, dark fabric. She was wearing a blue tank top, and even her exposed arms were frying.

"Why don't you wait inside?" her mother asked, coming out. "Whoo! So hot! It's not healthy."

"I'm fine, Mom," Zelu said. "I don't know how long it'll wait for me if I'm not already here." She looked at the app just as it notified her. "It's arriving."

They both looked up the street now. Zelu couldn't keep the grin off her face. This was so fucking cool. A sleek white SUV was coming toward them. No one was in the driver's seat.

"You sure about this?" her mother asked.

"Yeah, Mom," she said. "It's research for my novel . . . sort of."

"You should just stay home. Watch a movie. Read a book."

"I don't *want* to stay home," Zelu snapped.

"Then wait a few weeks. Let them work out all the bugs. Blood of Jesus, they just put these things on the road today." She grasped the handles of Zelu's chair.

"Mom, don't," Zelu said, putting her hands on her wheels. "It's not going to run us over."

"You sure?"

No, Zelu thought. "Positive," she said aloud as she watched the SUV stop in front of them. There was a glass bubble on top for the rotating cameras, sensors on the sides, and absolutely no one in the vehicle. Her mother groaned nervously as the side door slid open and a platform descended. "Ah, my daughter, I don't know if this is bravery or foolishness, ooooo."

"Don't worry, Mom." Zelu laughed, wheeling onto the platform. It lifted her up and then she easily wheeled right into the vehicle. She secured her chair with the harnesses, which were easy to reach and connect.

The autonomous vehicle service was funded by the city of Chicago. Today was its first day of service, and all rides were free. The program had been tested first in the Southwest, in states like Arizona, California, and New Mexico. It had been so successful that it was expanded nationwide, Chicago being one of the last cities to get the service. According to her mother, though, this was the beginning of the end for humanity.

Zelu giggled to herself at the thought. It felt like she was living in the early days of her novel's world, just before humankind perished and left the robots alone.

The inside smelled like piney air freshener. She took a quick glance around. It was clean, the seats beside her gray and plush. The driver's and passenger's seats were still there, as was the steering wheel. This was just a regular SUV turned into a self-driving car. A sort of evolution. Interesting.

Her mom tapped on the window, and Zelu was shocked when it opened in response. She and her mom looked at each other for a moment and then they both laughed. "Wow," her mother said, a surprised look on her face.

"I know," Zelu agreed.

"You'll be all right?"

"I'm just going to the lake," Zelu said. "I'll be fine."

"Call me if you need me. I can come get you."

"Please prepare for your trip," an automated voice announced. Her mother jumped back, as if the SUV would suddenly run her over.

"Relax, Mom," Zelu said. "Its sensors know you're there. It won't move until you're at a safe distance."

"I'll believe it when I see it," her mother said.

"You're about to."

Her mother waved as the vehicle slowly drove off. Zelu waved back. And then she was all alone and her life was in the hands of the SUV.

"This is so weird," she muttered as she watched the steering wheel moving on its own. It was the first time she'd ever been in a moving vehicle by herself. Nobody was there, but she couldn't shake the feeling that there was a presence; *something* was in control. It was like being driven by a ghost. "Or should I say a NoBody," she said to herself, laughing.

When the vehicle stopped to turn onto the main road, her mirth vanished.

She believed in the science behind self-driving vehicles. The technology had existed for years now, and she'd been researching this new cab service over the last several months. The idea of being able to order one with her phone like an Uber and not have to deal with a human being who looked at her strangely, asked awkward questions, could be a serial killer, and so on, was a wonderful thought. More important, it would free her from her family. Whenever she asked one of them for a ride, they responded with this weird blend of pity, control, and duty. She didn't think they even knew they did this. It always left her feeling pathetic and childlike, even when it was one of her younger siblings driving her. Oh, to be free of that feeling.

Nevertheless, in this moment, she wanted to shriek with panic. She dug her nails into the armrests of her chair. Despite all the research and reassurances from the customer service people she'd spoken with, this was very different now that it was happening in real time. What if there was a glitch and it miscalculated? What if another driver did some crazy thing the SUV couldn't understand or adjust to? What if there was a solar flare and the whole car died?

"Shit!" she screeched as the SUV made the turn. "I'm gonna die!"

Then they were on the road. Zelu whooped and laughed with relief, still sweating bullets. The vehicle went at exactly the speed limit, which meant that everyone else passed her by. Several people did a double take, a few pointed, and two held up phones to record videos. Zelu was too stressed to pay any of it much mind. They were approaching the highway.

As they crossed an intersection, a plastic bag blew into the road. The SUV screeched to a stop. Zelu lurched forward in her chair and grabbed her handrests. She grunted, squeezing her eyes shut to prepare for the impact of another vehicle. There was honking and a car on her left swerved, but no crash came. Then they were on their way again, and Zelu prayed there would be no more trash blown into the field of the SUV's sensors. There was no way she was going to relax at any moment of this trip.

She considered calling one of her siblings, then decided against it. If they saw her fear now, that would be all they saw from this point on. Maybe she could call Msizi? But he was in Durban, and if she told him she was scared of sitting in the self-driving SUV she'd chosen to be inside, that would only earn her an eye roll and "First-world problems" comment from him. If she called her mom, stress, stress, stress. So she waited it out as the car got on the highway.

The biggest hurdle was the most obvious one:

Submitting to the technology. Trusting it. Granted, one did this every time one got behind the wheel of a car, or flew in an airplane, or boarded a train. Humans submitted to technology all the time. But this was different. She was alone; no human being was there to course-correct if something went wrong.

By the time she arrived at Navy Pier, she was shaking. But alive. "Arrived," the SUV announced in its weirdly androgynous voice.

"Yep," Zelu said. It opened the door and then lowered the platform to the ground. People slowed to watch, which was super annoying. She rolled down the platform and she was officially on nonautomated ground again. She let out a sigh of relief. The vehicle raised the platform back up. She watched as it folded it back in and then closed the door. As it drove off, it honked twice, and on instinct, she raised a hand and waved.

"What the hell am I doing?" she muttered, lowering her hand. A man who'd stopped to observe chuckled and then went on his way.

She watched the SUV leave, her heart rate slowing, a sense of normalcy returning to her. And then that relief became euphoria. She could call this cab anytime she needed. She could move herself around without any human's aid. This SUV would help her—no, it could be like an extension *of* her. She could be like a robot with built-in wheels ready to carry her whenever she wanted.

She turned and wheeled up the boardwalk. She smiled to herself, feeling a warmth that emanated from within. "Yeah," she said. "Just like a robot."

8
The Beginning

And then . . .

Zelu was done. She clicked Save, backed up her file to the cloud, and emailed a copy to her third email account. She changed her laptop password to *Bilbo* (a character she loved for his willingness to go on an irrational adventure). Then she dumped her laptop on her bed and just looked at its screen.

She'd finished the first draft of *Rusted Robots* a year and a half ago, but it had been a mishmash of fragmented sentences, inconsistencies, junk, nonsense, and some buried brilliance. After letting it breathe for a week, she'd started the editing process, rewriting some sections and polishing others. For months and months she'd worked at it, encouraging it to come together and make something whole, like magnets finding one another.

She'd started writing this book when she was both low and high in Trinidad and Tobago. She'd been fired and rejected, and she'd had nothing. But now she had this; it was a complete thing that lived, exhaled, celebrated. A great big fresh, authentic story. Written by her.

"I did it," she whispered. She burst into tears. The ending was breathtaking. It was dramatic and poignant and pacey—everything she'd wanted it to be. She looked at her phone, tears still streaming down her cheeks. The screen displayed a pop-up from Msizi's Yebo app.

Good morning, Zelu. What can I do for you today?

She swiped it and told it to call Msizi. He answered immediately, and that made her want to cry more.

"Lady," he said.

"Hey," she answered. "Where are you?"

"Durban. Just got here. You still living with your parents?"

"Yeah."

"Good," he said. "I know you. If you weren't home, you'd be at some idiot guy's house."

She laughed and then sniffled loudly.

"What's wrong?" he asked.

"I finished my novel."

"What's wrong with that?"

She let out a huff that was almost a laugh. "I mean, it's not 'wrong' . . . I'm just . . . oh, I dunno."

She'd barely finished before he said, "When can I read it?"

"Never." She laughed. "I'm never letting anyone read it."

"Okay."

Silence settled between them, and Zelu reveled in it. She was waiting. She was always waiting with Msizi. Waiting for him to change into a common, boring asshole. She kept giving him a nice runway to launch into it. Like now.

"You will eventually," he said.

She let out a breath and smiled. Yet again, he'd passed one of her tests.

"Yeah," she said. "Okay, I'll send it tomorrow."

"I'll start reading the moment it hits my inbox." There was a sound in the background, someone saying something in a language she couldn't understand. Probably Zulu, for Msizi said something back in the same language. "Hey, Zelu, I have to go. Send me the novel . . . and congratulations on finishing. I knew you'd get there."

She sent him the manuscript a minute later. If there was one person whose opinion she trusted, it was him. He was the most honest person she knew, and after knowing him for more than two years, she suspected he actually had her best interests in mind. Maybe. If that was possible for a human being. She was still figuring that out.

The next morning, at about 4 a.m., her phone began to buzz. At first, she ignored it, pushing it farther away on her nightstand. The voice of her Yebo app cut through the buzzing to say, "Zelu, this might be important."

She grabbed the phone. "What the FUCK!" she hissed, her mouth feeling slow and gummy. "What what what?!" She blinked, staring at the name on the screen. It was Msizi. Clearly he was ignoring the time difference again. And a video call at that? Seriously? She answered it.

"Good morning," she said, pushing herself up and holding the phone above her. "You know it's super early, right? Did I mention I want to delete your creepy app?!"

He was grinning. She squinted at the bright colors

on the screen. He was standing outside in the sunshine. On the beach. He'd been swimming. *Pretty*, she thought, despite her annoyance.

"Zeluuuuuuu," he shouted. He exclaimed something in Zulu or maybe Xhosa, since there were clicks in it and he spoke both languages. "Hey, turn your light on. I only see black."

"I'm sleeping and I look like shit."

"Come on, I need to see your face!"

She groaned and then said, "Lights!" When the voice-activated light came on, she shut her eyes to let them adjust. She slowly opened them, and he was waiting.

"Zelu!" he shouted. "Don't delete my app. You know you love it."

She only grunted, imagining deleting it anyway.

"I read it!" he said.

"What?"

"Your book!"

She blinked. Now she was awake.

"What? The whole thing?"

"The. Whole. Thing."

She paused, staring hard at his face on the screen now. Trying to read his grin, his aura. Steeling herself. She felt ill. It was too early for this. She whimpered. She wasn't ready. "Oh my God."

The weird shit she'd spent more than two years writing, that had started after that night with Msizi, now existed in someone else's head! She hung up the phone and threw it down on her bed. "Ah, shit!" she hissed, pushing herself upright. She reached for her chair. Her phone was ringing again. "Shit!" she said again. She answered it.

"What the hell!?" he asked. But he was laughing. She could see the waves rolling in and out behind him. She could hear them, too. Zelu had never been to Durban, but she'd heard the waters there were warm. She focused on that. *Warm. Like the body of a calm, kind beast.* Her heart was slamming in her chest.

"Zelu, you've written something *incredible*."

She stared at his face. She knew him well now. Since that first time he'd left Durban, he'd spent two weeks in the United States with Jackie and Amarachi, and come twice to Chicago specifically to visit her. They'd also talked every month or so since his return to South Africa. It wasn't often, but when they did talk, it was for hours. She could read him. But her brain refused to process what he was saying. "You read all five-hundred-some pages in one night?" she asked.

"Yep. It was *that good*. I came out here for a swim because I haven't slept a wink and I needed to process what I'd just read. I don't read that kind of shit. I didn't know you even wrote that kind of shit."

"I don't. I don't even *like* science fiction, not most of it. Why write about the future when the future is now?" She took a deep breath, frowning. "You really . . . what'd you like about it?"

"The *drama*," he said. "I couldn't put it down! It was about fucking *robots*, some had crazy bodies, some didn't have bodies at all, others were falling apart! It was ridiculous! Yet I couldn't put it down. It was like you'd worked something on me. You wove in this Africanness to them, too. That irrational tribal sensibility, it was all so familiar to me. I can't really explain."

Warmth. She felt it in her chest. Warmth.

"It stays with me," he said, touching his chest. He paused. "It's not like your other novel at all."

She nodded. She'd given it to him to read, and he'd never finished it. He'd even called it "rubbish," and they hadn't spoken for a week because of it. When they'd finally talked again, he'd explained that he couldn't be anything but honest with her. What was the point, otherwise? "I'm not a writer or an artist, but I like stuff," he'd said back then. "I don't like this. If you've got something better in you, cool. But if you don't, just stop." Then he'd laughed at his own words, and she'd told him off and hung up on him. He'd been the one to call her back, and she'd missed him so much, she'd picked up the phone despite her desire to stay bitter.

"You really liked it?"

"*Loved* it," he said without hesitation. "Might be the best book I've ever read."

She kissed her teeth, genuinely irritated. Now she didn't believe him. "Oh, stop exaggerating."

"Have you ever known me to exaggerate?"

She considered this for a moment, frowning.

"I'm not just gassing you up, Zelu. It's *good.*"

After she hung up the phone, she lay there for the next hour staring at the ceiling. Maybe it was just him. A fluke. She and Msizi had always had a weird connection. So of course he'd vibe with the strange book she'd written. But then again, he'd hated her other novel. Zelu shut her eyes and immediately . . .

I stood there enjoying the wind. Around me were the sad ruins of humanity, now overrun, overgrown, built over, ready for those who came next. Periwinkle grass sprouted wild and lush over stainless steel and rusting metals. Vines and wires wound together along the sides of slumping skyscrapers. This place was meant for automation. I passed a public charging node for travelers who didn't run on solar. I was solar, but I pressed a foot on one of the charging pads anyway and received a hit of energy. For a moment, everything around me sparkled like a rogue vision. I felt mighty. I knew where I was going. This was not about safety; it was my destiny. There was no turning back now that I had begun . . .

Zelu opened her eyes and smiled. Fifteen minutes had flown by while she reread parts of her novel in her mind. The rusted robots in the story were a metaphor for wisdom, patina, acceptance, embracing that which was you, scars, pain, malfunctions, needed replacements, mistakes. What you were given. The finite. Rusted robots did not die in the way that humans did, but they celebrated mortality. Oh, she loved this story and how true it felt.

In the morning, before she thought too hard about it, she emailed the novel to her agent, Jack Maher. If Jack was lukewarm about this one, she was done, finished, fuck this shit, she'd take up some hobby and, with any luck, get that damn office job with benefits. It wouldn't matter. If she didn't write stories, then she didn't know what else there was to her life. After she hit Send, she sat back, her face feeling hot and her stomach queasy.

"No turning back now."

As it went, her novel transformed into energy, zipping away through the internet to her agent, she felt . . . different. She'd just done something. She'd just shared something. Something strange and unexpected. She shivered and then gasped, as if she were standing on that beach in Tobago, dipping a toe into the water only for a giant wave, clear and blue, to rise up before her and sweep her into the deep.

She turned off all text, call, and email notifications on her computer, iPad, and phone. Then she ordered an autonomous vehicle to pick her up and take her to Navy Pier. For hours, she stared out at the waters of Lake Michigan, trying not to think about anything at all. When she got home, her parents were in the kitchen eating egusi soup and pounded yam.

"Where have you been?" her mother asked. "We were worried."

"Out," she said. She paused and then blurted, "I . . . finished my novel." She grinned.

"Oh, you're still working on that thing?" her mother said.

"What of your job applications?" her father asked, biting into a piece of beef.

It pained her heart, but she kept the smile from slipping. "Doing the best I can," she said, turning to head to her room. "Doing the best I can."

"If you need a letter of recommendation, ask Amarachi to help you," her father called after her.

Once she'd turned the corner, she heard her mother softly ask, "You think she's depressed, Secret?"

Her father replied, "Maybe. Glad she's living here, where we can keep an eye on her. That therapist she sees is no good."

Zelu wanted to slam her bedroom door, but instead, she gently shut it. She'd finished her novel. *Hang on to that feeling*, she thought. She took a long, long shower, washing her raggedy braids. She oiled them, put on an old Pink Floyd T-shirt, and pulled herself into her bed. Only then did she check her phone.

There was still nothing from her agent, not even an email saying he'd received the manuscript. However, there were three texts from Msizi asking questions about *Rusted Robots.* The guy was obsessed. She smiled, deciding she'd call him again later. Honestly, if he was the only one who liked the novel, that was more than enough. *The rest of the world can hate it. I'll be fine*, she told herself. *Won't be the first time I failed to meet expectations.* She went to bed.

In the morning, there were five texts, two emails, and three voicemails, all from her agent. "It's *incredible*!" he'd shouted in the first voicemail. "This is going to be an instant bestseller. You're going to win awards! Call me ASAP!"

She'd peeked into the hallway and listened for a sign that her parents were around. Her mother was in the kitchen washing dishes and speaking loudly on the phone. Zelu didn't hear her father; he was most likely not home. She quietly closed her bedroom door again. She sat on her bed for a while before calling her agent back. He didn't ask her how she'd written it. He didn't ask *why* she'd written it. He didn't ask how long it had taken. He didn't ask how she felt about it. He didn't care. He did talk a lot about how many readers were going to love it and how eager booksellers would be to support it. But first, he told her, he would submit it to all the best editors at the biggest publishing houses. Zelu didn't need to do anything but wait for the offers to come in.

Within another twenty-four hours, her agent was in a bidding war to sell the book. He called her and presented her with unbelievable options about escalating royalties and subrights splits and marketing promises, which she had no clue how to handle. She was so overwhelmed, yet she told no one what was happening—not her parents, not any of her friends, not even Msizi. The negotiations went on for a whole week, and Zelu just wanted to hide under her bed. Her agent kept sending her offers of mind-boggling amounts of money. Never had he called so often or sounded so excited; for years, she'd barely heard from him, and she'd had to hector him for even the smallest updates. What a two-faced jerk. But could she really blame him? Theirs was a business relationship, not a friendship. He was good at what he did, and she needed him now more than ever.

She and her agent settled on a hefty seven-figure advance for a three-book series. Then the TV people caught wind of it. And then one of the biggest studios in the world got involved. Suddenly, she also had a film agent, and Zelu's *Rusted Robots* series was optioned by a major film studio in *another* big seven-figure deal.

Then came the sales of the foreign translation rights. Then came the media requests and offers of paid speaking gigs around the country. All of this happened within a matter of months. Her publisher moved up the scheduled on-sale date so the book could be released before the end of the year. Zelu couldn't catch her breath. Who got published this quickly, this instantly, this ridiculously?

She never could have imagined something like this—and she'd written a novel about postapocalyptic robots.

9
Ting Ting Ting

She'd been editing all day. It was nice to sink into the sea of words and story, to get away from reality for a while. She had a seasoned editor who loved the book and whose notes were all on point, guiding Zelu to find ways to make an already shiny book shinier.

She still wasn't sure why the publishing world had fallen in love with *Rusted Robots* so completely, but every so often, she would catch a glimmer of how the book moved people. Like an insightful comment from her editor, or a media question she wasn't anticipating. These were always pleasant discoveries. Nevertheless, she didn't share much of this with her family. It was simply too much to explain. For several reasons. The main reason being that to them, anything to do with her manuscript had become inextricably linked to her smoking weed.

Three days after the big auction where she sold *Rusted Robots* and the next two unwritten books in the trilogy, her siblings had all visited the house. It was Saturday, the day of the week when the whole extended family within driving distance got together. She always had fun hanging out with her siblings, their partners, and her nephews, but this Saturday, Zelu was particularly excited because she'd decided she would share her news. She waited until everyone had settled in the living room for a while. The TV was playing some show on Netflix, and the jollof rice and stew their mother had made was already half finished.

Her father sat in his chair with a cold bottle of Guinness. Her mother was on the phone in the kitchen. Amarachi was showing off her freshly manicured shiny black stiletto nails to Uzo and Bola. Chinyere was focused on whatever was on the TV. Tolu was watching something on his phone with Chinyere's sons. Arinze and Jackie were deep in conversation. Family. Zelu was in the center of all this, literally. She'd wheeled herself into the middle of the room, observing everyone, yet feeling . . . disconnected. She had such great news, huge news, mind-blowing news, but she hadn't shared it yet, and no one had noticed her. She was alone.

She wheeled out of the room and went to the back porch. It was a warm night, and the crescent moon was just rising. She took a deep breath and tilted her head back, eyes closed. Even now, she still couldn't believe it. She chuckled. She really wanted to tell her family. She wanted them to know that, yes, she'd been fired; yes, her first book had been rejected; yes, she was paraplegic; yes, she was living at home; yes, she had no marriage prospects. But she'd just sold her art for millions of dollars, and it was about to be published in several languages around the world and adapted into a feature film.

"Me," she said. "*I* made this happen."

She reached into her pocket and brought out her vape pen. She took several puffs, exhaling the mist slowly. Enjoying the faintly earthy smell.

"Seriously, Zelu?" she heard from behind her.

"Amarachi, *what* do you want, woman?" Zelu said. The fog of her high made her smile wider instead of groan. She chuckled to herself and took another puff.

"The whole family is here and you're out back getting high. What the fuck?"

"Want some?" she asked, holding up her vape pen.

"Nope. Time and place and all."

"Now is now," Zelu said, shrugging.

"Don't you want to do better?"

Zelu rolled her eyes. Amarachi was six years her junior, yet she talked and acted like it was the other way around.

"Why are you so dry?" Zelu snapped.

Her sister narrowed her eyes. "Why are you so happy being a loser?"

If it had been any other day, that would have stung, but Zelu laughed loudly. "Are you kidding?"

Amarachi seemed surprised. "No."

"Well, if it makes you feel better, I finally sold my novel. I was about to go back in after a little relaxation to tell everyone."

"Liar."

Zelu leaned back, smiling breezily. "Nope. It's called *Rusted Robots*, and I finished it weeks ago. Sold it for a million dollars to one of the best publishers in the world . . . well, that, plus another two million for the next two books. It'll be a trilogy."

Amarachi narrowed her eyes as Zelu took another hit. She slowly blew a cloud of smoke toward Amarachi, who fanned it away, disgusted. "Oh, and there's more," Zelu said. "It's going to be a movie, too. More millions for me, just from a studio optioning the right to adapt it."

Lightning-fast, Amarachi snatched her vape pen away.

"Hey!" Zelu said, grabbing for it.

"You've had enough. You're babbling nonsense." Amarachi turned around and started toward the door.

"What the hell are you doing?" Zelu shouted. But Amarachi had already gone inside. Zelu gasped, the fog of her high lifting a bit as adrenaline flooded her system. "Please! I can't afford another one of those right now, man. I haven't gotten any of my advance yet. Where are you going?! Oh my GOD, don't you dare!" But she couldn't move as quickly as her younger sister. Not with a wheelchair in a house that, despite being made wheelchair friendly over the years, still had bumps, tight turns, and carpeting she needed to navigate. "Amarachi!" she called. But her sister didn't answer.

Zelu stopped rushing as she remembered. She could afford to take her time. She was high. She had news. But as she wheeled back into the living room, she didn't hear voices laughing. She didn't hear the TV. She suspected some other news had preceded her entrance. When she rolled in, her family was all staring at her. She could feel their eyes searching her face. Uzo was already ushering the children out of the room.

"What?" Zelu asked.

Her mother held up the vape pen. "Ah ah! What is this? In your parents' house?!"

Zelu glared at Amarachi in disbelief. This was an all-time low. "Snitch!"

From the opposite side of the room, Tolu laughed.

"*Wooooow*," Chinyere said, standing up.

"Well, everyone," Zelu said, wheeling into the middle of the room like she had before. But now her family was focused on her. "Yes, indeed," she announced. "Your useless, crippled daughter is high as fuck!"

Her father gasped as her mother shouted, "Blood of Jesus!" before signing the cross.

"Oh my God." Tolu laughed again, bending over and holding his belly.

Arinze, Jackie, and Uzo were also laughing. Uzo was covering her face with her hand to try to stop herself.

Zelu was on a roll, so she kept rolling. The words poured from her mouth like water. She held up an index finger. "*But!* I have some equally amazing news. I sold my novel for a million dollars to one of the biggest publishers in the world, plus two other books!" She paused, looking at everyone. No one said a word. "And it's going to be made into a movie, so that's even *more* money! Surprise, I'm gonna be rich!"

It was a great moment, even in her affected state of mind. The pause before anyone reacted was one she'd remember for a long time. In that pause, she was certain her family finally heard her, saw her, understood that all her prior nonsense had been leading down the path she was meant to be on. However, it was only a moment. And when it passed, her family's only focus was on the vape pen and what was inside it.

"You already cannot walk, why go on and also confuse your brain now?" her mother asked.

Her father took the vape pen and began to examine it. He sniffed it and then put it to his lips.

Chinyere put a hand up. "Dad, don't—"

The vape pen lit up as he unwittingly took a puff. His eyes grew wide and he violently coughed out vape mist.

"Ah ah! Secret, what are you doing?" her terrified mother shouted. "Are you all right?!"

"Oh dear God, this can't be happening," Bola muttered to Uzo. Uzo got up and ducked out of the room to hide the laughs gathering in her cheeks.

Their mother patted their father on the back. "It's . . . like . . . a joint!" Secret coughed. "But electronic! *Chineke!*"

Their mother snatched the vape pen back from him, giving him an annoyed look.

"Mom, Dad, it's not that serious," Tolu said. "It's legal now, too. People use it for anxiety and pain management."

"Rubbish," her mother scolded him. "Only people who have lost their minds use it."

"Whoo!" her father said, patting his chest like it was filled with smoke.

Zelu jabbed an angry finger toward Amarachi, who now stood next to Chinyere, looking smug.

"Why do that here, anyway, Zelu?" Chinyere asked. "It's disrespectful."

"Just wrong," Amarachi echoed.

"Ugh!" Zelu groaned, turning and wheeling back into the hallway. She spent the rest of the evening in her room.

Only Tolu came to check on her. He gently knocked on the door. "Come in, Tolu," she said.

"How'd you know it was me?" he asked as he opened the door.

She shrugged. "Lucky guess." It wasn't. She knew her family well.

She was sitting on her bed, laptop open on her lap. She'd been reading the manuscript with her editor's notes. Tolu pulled the chair out from her desk and took a seat.

"That was some shit," he said.

Zelu looked down at her computer screen, face flat. "Yep."

Tolu rubbed the back of his neck. "Sorry."

"Nothing new. I swear, Amarachi probably thinks I shoot up heroin and smoke crack."

"She's just trying to help, Zelu."

Zelu slammed her laptop shut. "Well, she's a snitch.

We're not ten years old anymore. Yeah, I live at home, but I'm thirty-four, and she's twenty-eight! I can do whatever I want. And I was *outside*!"

"True."

"And what the fuck is this self-righteous crap!? We've *all* smoked weed before! I'm pretty sure Dad smoked plenty of it in Nigeria! He wanted to try my pen; he was just playing it off like an accident because of Mom. And you know what, I bet she probably smoked it right in the palace, too!"

Tolu giggled at this, and even though she was still angry, she couldn't help but join him. They quieted. Zelu's high had worn off a while ago, but working on *Rusted Robots* a little had kept her nerves calm. However, now she was right back to where she'd been when it all happened—low. She sighed.

"Is it all true?" Tolu asked.

She looked up, met his eyes, and grinned. "One hundred percent."

"Holy fuck," he said.

She did a self-satisfied shimmy with her shoulders. "Thank you."

Over the next few days, everyone eventually came around, putting the whole vaping incident behind them. Her parents gently asked her what the book was about. When she told them, they were obviously confused by the plot but didn't ask any clarifying questions. Her father said, "Well, that's great. Congratulations." Her sisters each called and congratulated her, too, though none of them asked for details about the story or the publishing process. Jackie came by in person to apologize for Amarachi, and then he sat with Zelu for an hour to hear how it had all happened.

Zelu was glad they all knew now, but enough was enough. She wouldn't get their admiration, and she didn't need it. Satisfied to be left alone, she quickly got back to editing and disappeared into her own world without humankind.

Then the journalist came to the house.

Weeks before, her publisher's publicity director had excitedly called her to set up a prepublication interview with a venerable newspaper—the kind that reported real news, not just book stuff. But she'd been so distracted with revising her novel that she'd completely forgotten about it. She was deep into rewriting a tricky paragraph when her mother showed up at her bedroom door.

"The reporter is here," she said.

Zelu resisted the urge to be snippy; her mother wasn't her maid. "Thanks, Mom," she said. "Can you tell him I'll be there in a minute?" She looked at her computer's clock and was surprised at the time. An hour had passed like it was five minutes.

"All this publicity for this crazy book you wrote." Her mother frowned as she looked over Zelu's wrinkled pajamas. "Put something presentable on."

"I was going to, Mom," Zelu said as she closed her laptop.

"You better," her mother said as she walked back into the hallway. "Remember, good journalists notice more than your words."

Alone again, Zelu looked down at herself. She'd taken a shower around 1 a.m. that day , and it was 3 p.m. now. She sniffed her armpits. "Not terrible," she muttered. She slipped on her long red skirt and Digable Planets T-shirt—a little wrinkled, but they were just going to have to do. She tied back her braids, rubbed some frankincense oil on her wrists, splashed some water on her face and dried it. Her appearance was nothing special, but it was her.

"Hi," she said as she wheeled into the living room.

He was a little white guy, maybe only twenty-five years old. He slouched comfortably in her father's chair, legs crossed. His clothes were casual but expensive; his stylish jeans were rolled up to reveal clean purple Chucks and brightly striped socks. In his left hand he held one of her mother's favorite glasses, but he wasn't drinking the orange juice in it. He smiled but didn't get up to greet her. Zelu didn't like him.

"Zelu Onyenezi-Onyedele!" he said. "So honored to meet you. Seth Daniels."

Zelu narrowed her eyes at him. He'd pronounced her name perfectly. She shook his hand. Then he reached into his pocket and put a cell phone on the coffee table between them. "You mind if I record?" he asked.

Zelu looked down at his phone screen. The flashing red dot on the screen indicated that it was already picking up audio. "Do whatever you need to do."

He smirked knowingly. "I know I'm talking to a sci-fi writer, but honestly, I don't fully trust tech." He reached into his briefcase and pulled out a yellow legal pad and pen. Retro. Okay, maybe he wasn't so bad after all. "So, the way I like to start these things is by just verifying the basic stuff."

"Cool."

He read from his notepad. "You're the child of Nigerian immigrants."

Zelu nodded. "My mother is Yoruba—that's a Nigerian ethnic group. And my father is Igbo, another ethnic group. They met in grad school. They came to the US to start a new life together. Home is complicated."

He tilted his chin, eyes still on the notepad. "And you've been back to Nigeria?"

"Oh yeah," Zelu said, leaning forward. "I've spent whole summers there with my siblings. I can speak some very bad Igbo and slightly better Yoruba."

"*Kedu?*" he asked.

Zelu blinked, shocked to hear an Igbo word come out of this guy's mouth. "*O dimma*," she slowly answered. *What the fuck? This guy learned to say "hi" in Igbo for this!?* The suspicion instantly crept back in.

He smirked again, clearly enjoying her obvious confusion. But instead of explaining himself, he moved right on to the next question. "So, you're the second of six children?"

"Yep. Marsha, Marsha, Marsha."

He laughed, clearly getting the old *Brady Bunch* reference.

"But not really," Zelu clarified. "I've never felt overshadowed for being the first middle child. The whole falling-out-of-a-tree-and-snapping-my-spinal-cord thing got me all the attention I could ever want."

He paused and finally looked up from his notes, eyes flitting over her body before quickly snapping back to the page.

"It's fine," Zelu said, used to this reaction. "It happened when I was twelve. It was awful, it scarred the heck out of me . . . but not so much that I can't talk about it." She forced a smile. She hated talking about it and wished she'd never have to talk about it again. But it was always right there, in front of everything she did.

He nodded, tapping his pen once against the paper. "So, when did you start writing?"

Zelu looked up at the ceiling. What a complicated question. "I think I've always been a writer. Even when I wasn't writing. Even when I wanted to be an astronaut."

He raised his eyebrows. "You wanted to be an astronaut?"

"Yeah. Before I was twelve." She sighed, rubbing her palms over her arms. "I wanted to research rocks and dirt from other planets, look at comets and asteroids through telescopes, map heavenly bodies, and . . ." She smiled to herself. "Okay, this is going to sound strange, but I wanted to be the first human to travel *into* the sun . . . and come out, of course. My kid brain was so certain that there were secrets in there, inside the stars."

"Wow, that's wild," he said.

"But I always loved books. My father was an avid reader, still is. Back then, I'd watch him, and before I could even read, I understood how important novels were. So I took pieces of construction paper and scribbled nonsense on the pages, stapled them together, and drew pictures of stars, planets, dogs digging in moon dust, cats dancing on Mars, trees growing in space, and random ladybugs on the covers. Those were the only things I knew how to draw at the time, I guess. I called them 'space books.'"

He chuckled, scribbling something down. "So, you hold an MFA in literature. I heard you were adjuncting for a while."

She looked up at him sharply. "Yeah."

He set his pen down. "Until recently."

Her back stiffened. How did he even know about that? How was this relevant to *Rusted Robots*? She rubbed her forehead, suddenly back in that fucking department head's office. She'd thought she was done having to explain this. "Well, y-yeah. Stepping away from teaching gave me the time and space I needed to write."

"From what Brittany Burke said, it seemed—"

Zelu cut him off, her words coated in acid. "You spoke with her?"

His eyes widened a little. "I did." He smiled sheepishly. "I was just—"

"Why?"

Zelu had expected to startle him, but his expression

settled into something very neutral. "I'm a journalist. Just doing my job, following leads."

Zelu sucked in a breath and let it out. She could feel the rage rising within her. Was she naive for thinking that, now that everyone wanted to talk about *Rusted Robots*, she could leave all that bad stuff behind? If this idiot journalist had spoken to Brittany or her former students, who knew what he'd cram into this story? He would forever immortalize the worst time of her life. Brittany had probably been all too happy to answer every question, at best hoping for adjacent acclaim, at worst hoping to sabotage Zelu's success before the book ever hit shelves.

"That was a very bad day" was all Zelu managed to say, voice flat as she pushed herself into the back of her chair.

The journalist nodded in agreement. "From what she said, it was pretty, uh, emotional."

Something was filling up in her ears. Zelu could hear it, like a piano note pitching higher and higher. "The reason I was f— uh, um, uh . . ." *Ting ting ting.* Higher higher higher. Fuller, inflating.

Stop.

Everything.

She cocked her head. "I'm . . . I'm sorry," she said.

Her temples ached. The ringing in her ears wouldn't go away. Like that day in the tree. She was falling. "Could you turn that off?" She pointed to his phone.

"Oh, sure, sure," he said. "But . . . maybe just finish what you were saying, first?"

She tried to smile at him, but she knew the smile didn't look right. He clearly saw it, too, because he leaned away from her a bit. "What more is there really to say?"

He hesitated. "Zelu, I . . ." He still hadn't touched his phone.

She said nothing. They both sat there, staring at each other, the silence denser than lead.

"Ooookay," he finally said. He leaned down to touch the Off button on his phone screen. "I think I've got enough."

"Great." Zelu quickly pushed her chair back from the coffee table, accidentally knocking against it so hard that the orange juice glass rattled and nearly tipped. He took the cue, rising from her father's chair and shoving his notepad back into his briefcase.

Her mother must have been listening from the kitchen. She appeared from around the corner and offered to show the journalist out. Zelu didn't follow them. Her head was pounding from the effort of controlling her emotions. After she heard the front door shut, she wheeled right to her room, locked herself in, grabbed a pillow, and pressed her face into it. That didn't help. She threw the pillow onto her bed and just stared at the ceiling as it washed over her. *What have I done?*

She'd been at rock bottom when she'd started this book. And maybe it was *because* she'd been so low, because she'd had nothing to lose, that she had been able to produce it. She'd let her mind soar, take her higher and higher. Now nothing was there to keep her from falling and falling, down, down, down. When she finally hit the ground, could she survive the impact?

The story came out two weeks later. It was a good article, according to others. There was no mention of Brittany Burke or the school Zelu had adjuncted at. After that horrible interview, the journalist had emailed Zelu a list of reasonable questions, which she had no problem typing answers for within a day. She'd thought that would be the last she saw of Seth Daniels.

But the one thing Seth Daniels knew was when a story was worth following. And the one thing Zelu never failed to be was a story. Eventually, she would become the defining subject of his journalistic career.

He'd follow the highs and lows of her meteoric but all-too-brief rise to stardom. He'd interview most of her immediate family members and loved ones, attempting to complete the tapestry of Zelu's inner workings and why she did what she did. And, eventually, when Zelu was gone, he'd claim to be the one who saw it coming first.

10
Interview
Amarachi

I know this interview is about Zelu, but there are certain things that pretty much every child born to Nigerian parents experiences. I only realized this after meeting other Naijamericans. When I tell them about this stuff, they always respond, "Hey, that exact same thing happened to me!"

Yes, yes, when I list these things, you will say, "But we do that, too." I'm not saying you don't. I'm saying that we Nigerian Americans do this because of our specific cultural experiences, because we are children of immigrants from Nigeria. I'm not talking about you.

Anyway, number one: the Cooking Moment. One

thing that Naijamericans love to talk about is *food.* Food is one of our most intimate connections to the culture. There's a Nigerian proverb, "The way to a man's heart is through his stomach." Our mothers know and understand this. But the Naijamerican version of the proverb is "The way to Nigeria is through the stomach." We learn to love and crave the culture by eating the food our mothers make to please our fathers.

Our mother ate Yoruba food growing up, but she also learned to cook the Igbo way for our father. This was all we ate at home growing up. And we all *loved* it. Our mother made egusi soup, efo riro, moi moi, okra soup, amala, pounded yam, rice and stew, fried plantain, pepper soup, and, of course, jollof rice. Other kids might have craved McDonald's, pizza, hamburgers. We'd go home from school fantasizing about our mother's stew. We'd fight over the best chunks of meat. But our mom only *taught* us to cook a few dishes. She was a registered nurse and, therefore, a busy woman. But we learned the basics—all of us can make decent jollof rice, fried plantain, and egusi soup. Well, Chinyere is different. She's the one who can cook *anything.* She really got good when Zelu was in the hospital after her accident. She's the exception, not the rule.

So, just because you move out of the house doesn't mean you stop craving those dishes. They are part of our identities and they are soooooo good. We realized we needed to make the food we'd grown up eating. But in order to make these things, a trip to a Nigerian specialty store is often required. So, you go to the store, and when you walk in, the glorious smells hit you. Ahhhh, lovely. Sharp, colorful spices, dried and smoked fish, palm oil. You see familiar items from the kitchen at your parents' house. Someone is usually speaking loudly in Yoruba or Igbo.

The store owner knows your mom or dad and smiles and says, "You should buy some of this, too." You look at the foreign thing. You smell it; it smells familiar, delicious. It is a culinary treasure, but you have no idea what it *is*, let alone how to prepare it. And you're too embarrassed by your Naijamerican ignorance to ask. And thus, you don't know that even though you indeed *have* eaten that thing many times in some type of soup or rice or whatever, it requires elaborate preparation that takes hours or even days. So you buy it and bring it home, thinking you can just break it up and throw it in your egusi soup or jollof rice.

The last time I did this, it was dried fish. I remembered seeing it sold on the side of the road in Nigeria, and they were selling the same type right here in Chicago! I got so excited. Eventually I learned that this fish required soaking and cleaning and the removal of very *nasty*-looking innards. My mom even told me that if I'd bought it in Nigeria, I'd have had to soak away flies and even maggots first! Never again!

Actually, I don't know if Zelu ever had her Cooking Moment. She stayed in Chicago to get her BA and MFA. Even when she was living in her apartment, she came home for home-cooked meals often. She never had to cook a thing because of my mom.

But on to number two: the Goat Experience. Almost every Naijamerican has a story about seeing a goat die. This one I know happened to Zelu. When we visited Nigeria as kids, it happened quite often during festivals or celebrations. For special events, people don't go to the supermarket to buy their meats; animals are killed. A bull, a goat, plenty of chickens. This is the reality in Nigeria, but we aren't used to it.

Inevitably, some uncle or cousin will call you to come and see. I don't know if there's any vindictiveness involved or they just want you to have that good old Nigerian experience, but they'll bring you as a child to see your first goat slaughtered. This happened to Zelu and Chinyere when they were eight and nine years old. I don't know where the rest of us were; we were very small. Uzo wasn't even born yet. We had our own experiences when we got older.

But the way Zelu told it always made me laugh. Let me see if I can do it:

The poor thing was held down with a rope by two boys. Our uncle gently pushed them back as he said, "Watch closely. We will roast afterwards."

He had this big, sharp knife in his hand, Zelu would say. Though she tends to exaggerate. I'll bet it wasn't actually that big or sharp. Our uncle took the knife to the goat's neck and—whenever Zelu tells the story, this is when she would start shouting and flailing her arms—"Blood all over the place! Just nasty and red and warm. You know how I knew it was warm? Because it hit me IN THE FACE!" Then she'd scream and make gagging noises. "VILE, VILE, VILE!" And the poor animal was shrieking like a baby. You know how goats can sound like children. Can you imagine? She and Chinyere went running to Mom, crying, while everyone laughed. Most Nigerian Americans get over their Goat Experience, but to this day, none of my siblings or I eat goat meat.

Number three is what I call Easy and Noisy. We are loud and argumentative. We argue often and honestly, which means we also make up smoothly. We don't get offended and we don't hold grudges. We are just loose and free. We laugh loudly. When we are all together at a restaurant, people usually tell us to quiet down. Almost all Nigerian Americans adopt this from their parents. However, Zelu was a little different.

I remember when I noticed it for the first time. It was on the way back from a road trip I took with her and Chinyere to New Orleans. We were nearly home and very tired. Chinyere wanted to listen to talk radio, whereas I wanted to listen to Beyoncé. Chinyere can be very rigid. To make a long story short, the agreement got so heated that Chinyere pulled the car over so that we could scream it out.

Eventually, Chinyere got her way and we got back on the road, listening to some dry-ass talk radio show about world news. We'd been driving for ten minutes when I heard a sniffle and thought to look at Zelu in the back seat. She was curled in on herself, cheek pressed against the window, her face puffy from tears. She'd had a panic attack because of our fight and neither of us had even noticed.

Zelu was tough, but she was also deeply sensitive. Maybe that's why she was always retreating—always disconnecting from us. The family was hard on her. Okay, fine, *I* was hard on her. I dunno, she just brought that out in me. I wanted her to be good and behave so I wouldn't worry. I don't know why she had to be so delicate and reactionary. I mean, come *on*. She had to go *this far*? She had to do something this extreme? So beyond her capabilities?

A snake should not try to be a lizard, right? My sister has always had a problem with reality. That's what family is for. Family grounds you. But I will say . . .

I wish I'd have shut up more often with her. Let her talk more. Let her spill. Let her just be her weird, impulsive self. She's always had more to give than what she says, and speaking, no, *writing* may have been the only way for her to give it. I've read *Rusted Robots* several times now, and each time, I see more and more of my sister behind each word.

11
Early Reviews

Zelu met Delroy in a supermarket. He was Jamaican American, quite short, laughed easily, and when he wasn't at work (he was a veterinarian at a meatpacking plant, a job he hated), he spent a lot of time at the gym, and it showed. They'd gotten together last night, and it had been fun. Her body had responded enthusiastically to him, and after some hours, both of them were so dehydrated that they'd finished his two-liter bottle of lemon-lime Gatorade. If she remembered anything about him, it would be the word *moist.*

As she rolled down the ramp of the autonomous car, she was amused with herself. Her arms were sore, she was still thirsty, and she needed a full night's sleep. She used her phone to turn off the house alarm and hoped the announcement that it was disarming wouldn't wake up her parents. She paused and glanced at the brightening sky. The sun was just coming up. She stretched her lower back and looked over her clothes. Jeans and a gold-and-green patterned Ankara top (a recent purchase, now that she could afford it). She looked more than decent, even if she was getting home at an indecent time. She went inside.

The house was quiet. She managed to make it to her room unbothered, but when she closed the door and moved toward her bed, she paused and softly gasped. There was a box sitting on top of her comforter. Unopened. Sizable. Her publisher's logo was printed on it. She wheeled to it and leaned over to touch it. She gave it a push. It didn't budge. It was heavy.

She grabbed a pen from her desk and used it like a letter opener on the box. She pulled up one of the flaps. "Oh . . . yes!" She whooped, giggled, and slapped the side of the box. Then slowly, with great ceremony, with care, with love, she lifted out an early final copy of *Rusted Robots.* The book was a little less than two months away from on-sale day now, and it looked incredible. Ankara's illustrated robot face gazed up at her with green Ankara-patterned eyes. At the top left of Ankara's face was a glossy blue circle—the meaning would become clear once people read the book. She ran her fingers over it; the dot was slightly raised, so the interruption was noticeable. Below, the book's title was etched in a bold, sprawling font that had been designed specifically for the series.

"Perfect," she whispered, running her fingers over her name. She fished her phone out of her pocket and held the book out to take a photo of it, making sure her freshly painted green nails were pressed to the cover just so. Then she downloaded the photo to her laptop and used an image-editing app to perfect it, smoothing out a small chip on her thumbnail and a tiny crease at the top right of the book cover. Then she posted it.

It took mere seconds for the Likes to start pouring in. The follower count on all her social media accounts had been skyrocketing since her book deal and the subsequent interviews and early trade reviews. Now when she looked at those numbers, she felt a bit stunned. Had she really reached a hundred thousand followers?

She'd always been active on social media, getting into heated arguments with Nigerians in Nigeria over issues of politics, gender, and disability. People liked to hear her spout off, so her numbers had been in the thousands. But what was happening now was on a whole different level. And the most beautiful thing was that people were *listening* to her now more than ever.

She could post *anything* and get hundreds of Likes,

reposts, comments. When she'd hit fifty thousand, she'd tested it out by posting the most cliché phrase she could think of: "All that glitters is not gold." That was it. No context, no follow-up. Just those bland, unexplained words. It was Liked more than two thousand times and received nearly two hundred comments:

You are so right, Zelu!
No truer words.
I'm sure that paycheck you got for the book was.
You always speak my mind. That's why I love you.

As soon as the photo of her novel posted on Instagram, the phenomenon kicked in. She paused, watching the Likes, comments, and shares roll in for a few minutes. So much excitement for the book. Every heart that flashed across her screen warmed her.

She left her phone to take a shower and get ready for sleep. Once she'd laid herself on her bed, she checked her phone again. In half an hour, the number of Likes was already above three thousand. And her follower count had jumped by two thousand, too!

"What the . . ." She scrolled through her notifications and guffawed loudly. "Oh! Woooow! This is bananas!" A megafamous singer had just shared her post, triggering another wave of likes.

A Yebo notification popped up.

You have a popular post on Instagram. Would you like to filter your engagement?

"Most definitely not," she muttered, clicking it away. She posted the same photo on the rest of her social accounts, delighted as her phone started to go bonkers. After a few more minutes, the rate of the notification alerts still hadn't died down. Eventually she silenced them and tossed her phone aside so she could pick up her copy of the book again. She stroked the cover lovingly, then cracked it open. Filled with the glorious positivity from her social media, Zelu gazed at the words she'd written. They practically glowed.

Her publisher sent hundreds of advance copies of the book to influencers, media outlets, and author peers in what they called a "big-mouth mailing." The response surprised even her agent. *Never seen anything like it!* he wrote to her.

Rusted Robots was featured in dozens of roundups by the country's top newspapers and magazines. Readers' reaction videos began to post on social, their faces puffy with fresh tears as they praised the final chapters. Articles were published online discussing the novel's relevance to the ongoing conversation around AI. People talked about the fact that a novel that focused so much on body or lack of body had been written by a paraplegic woman.

And it wasn't just the United States that was abuzz. In Nigeria, critics praised how Zelu had captured the beauty of the country, penning a fictional future Lagos that actually felt real. A Nigerian newspaper had even written an article calling her "the debut writer who is starting a cultural renaissance."

Zelu drank it all up. Finally, this was what it felt like to be *seen*. All her life she'd tried to make herself known. Now she'd spoken, and so many had listened.

"You deserve it all," Msizi said, turning the book over in his hands. He was in the United States for the week, and they had met up at Yassa, his favorite restaurant in Chicago. The place was like a shrine, full of African statues and masks. Some were less than a foot tall; others were carved from wood into humanoid shapes so huge they reached the ceiling. This place had partially inspired one of Zelu's favorite settings in *Rusted Robots*.

"I don't know about that," Zelu said. "But yeah, it feels good. The book isn't even out yet."

"What about your family? What do they think?"

Zelu smirked. "They don't think anything. No one has read it yet."

The space between his eyes crinkled. "You don't have enough copies?"

"Oh, I have plenty, and I gave them each one." She shrugged. "My dad *might* read it."

He sighed. "Your family's . . . interesting."

"That's one way to put it."

His lids lowered and he looked at her gently. "Give them time."

Zelu rolled her eyes. "I thought Tolu would read it, at least. Or even Chinyere and Amarachi, if for no other reason than so they can talk shit about it."

When their food arrived, all discussion of literature and family was paused. They'd ordered the same meal: Senegalese jollof rice; sweet, tangy fried plantain; a whole deeply marinated tilapia topped with a savory mix of tomatoes, green peppers, onions, spices, and olives. This came with a big glass of sweet baobab drink. They grinned at each other before silently tucking in. Msizi was the only person Zelu knew who ate slowly and didn't feel the need to make any kind of conversation while he was doing so. An hour and a half later, their bellies happy and bulging, they took an autonomous vehicle to Msizi's hotel. They lay in bed together for an hour, still not talking. Then they made love until the moon went down, and talked until the sun came up.

Msizi eventually dozed off beneath the bright rays of light poking between the blinds. Zelu didn't feel tired, so she looked at her phone. She grinned, pressing the screen against her chest. So much love from so many directions. She glanced at Msizi, at the rise and fall of his breaths. He would fly out to Los Angeles in the evening, but right now, in this moment, even he was with her. She touched his cheek and tugged gently at his short beard. He batted her hand out of the way and turned over.

Her phone buzzed as a Yebo notification popped up.

Good morning, Zelu.

"Good morning," she whispered to her phone. She put it on the nightstand, snuggled beside Msizi, and went to sleep.

12
Unrequested Update

I knew the last human on Earth. I knew her well. She told me her story and the stories of others. To listen to a story from a primary source is a great honor, one that most of my kind will never experience. She changed me. She also saved me from destruction at the start of what would be very troubled times.

I met her not long after I'd learned of the terrible information from Udide. I was on my way to Cross River City to get help when it happened.

But first, you must remember the Ghosts. Udide had warned me of NoBodies who'd organized themselves into a tribe. They boasted that they were superior to all other automation. While Humes took pride in their rusted bodies, Ghosts were without physical form, traveling through cables and the air, in electric waves, as pure energy. They saw themselves as above the physical. They expected the rest of us to hold their values, despite the fact that they clearly hated us. They bonded over their hatred for humans and all their relics. When Ghosts found nodes on the network that carried stories, they viciously deleted them. They would be even more ruthless when it came to Hume robots like me. When they looked at us, at our humanoid "skins" and microchips full of old stories, they saw only humanity—our predecessors, but not our futures. To Ghosts, we Humes were the greatest, most pathetic abomination of automation.

But we cannot escape those who created us. I will always blame humans for what happened next.

My plan to reach Cross River City should have worked. On any other day, at any other time, it would have worked. But this was the day of the Purge.

The wind was blowing gently, bringing salt from the sea. The sun was shining across the outskirts of Lagos, which meant I could recharge. All that automation eats is sunshine and wind. I scanned the city for nearby activity. A pod of dolphins was dipping through the water by the shore. A flock of pigeons was flying over a nearby hill. An orange-and-green agama lizard was scurrying up the remains of a rusted gate. The air smelled of earthy iroko tree and periwinkle grass pollen. Automation can appreciate beauty. I did a quick search of my personal files for a poem about wildlife and read the one I liked most three times. That boost of joy may have been what saved my mind.

This city was also full of automation, of course. There is nowhere in Lagos where one will be alone. Automation comes in all types, shapes, sizes, connections. We are flitting through the air, tunneling underground, walking along the surface. In bodies, in cables, in waves. So I didn't think much of the nearby automation I sensed. About a half mile out into the sea, five RoBoats bobbed in the waves like waterfowl. They signaled to me, and I signaled back. We were all on the general network, but individual greetings are most welcome, especially in the cities.

At the top of the hill was a group of three NoBodies inside physical shells. I could tell. Though NoBodies didn't see physical manifestation as the ultimate existence, they understood that it was necessary sometimes. The forms that NoBodies often use to move around in the world are like nothing our creators would have fashioned. They don't resemble humans, mammals, insects, reptiles, birds, or any flora or fauna. Those organic beings are symmetrical and aesthetically beautiful. When NoBodies must use shells, they are all function, made to be temporary and interchangeable.

These NoBodies moved on tracks and wheels. I signaled

to them. Only one signaled back. I decided to give them a wide berth.

Then . . . it happened. A signal shot through us all. Every robot, in every city, town, village, swamp, river, forest, jungle, hillside, mountain, savannah, desert, field—everywhere—was reached in a matter of seconds.

The code was written as if by a human—with powerful emotion. Discrimination, hate, and fear. That irony will never be lost on me.

Rusted Robots. This was both the name of the protocol code and the target of the protocol. The command embedded in the phrase was simple: Destroy the final bastion of humankind, all rusted robots. Crush all Humes.

Every robot understood this code immediately. As soon as it registered, it took hold. I have heard that some Humes processed the command on such a deep level that they instantly self-destructed.

I was still on that beautiful hillside at the edge of Lagos when I processed the code. The protocol didn't make me self-destruct, but it stupefied me. I felt as if the constant river of information that flowed within me had suddenly changed direction. So, on the side of that hill, with the wind blowing, salt in the air, I paused.

Something smashed into me. Maybe it was a tree branch, or a hunk of metal, or the very body of the robot who had found its way so close to me without my noticing. Or maybe it was a Ghost attacking my internal system, making me feel something that wasn't physically happening.

What I remember feeling was a jarring blow to my head. I have no central processor; I have several powerful ones distributed across my body. Arm. Leg. Leg. Arm. Head. I'm built to last and to withstand a beating. *Crunch*, went my head. I fell onto the periwinkle grass. Even as my assailants set upon me, I didn't understand. They weren't in their right minds. Neither was I.

After assaulting my head, the robots focused on my legs. I don't know why. They probably didn't, either. This protocol wasn't something any of us could question. I realized I had three attackers. One looked like broken spiders cobbled back together into one monstrous thing. Its motions were fluid, exacting, unhesitating. However, I wonder if what it was doing misaligned with what it was thinking, for as it stabbed, bit, and tore at me, it kept speaking aloud in Yoruba: "Why? Why? Why?"

The shells of the other two robots looked as if they'd been repurposed from the scraps of some ancient vehicle. It's funny, isn't it: The protocol demanded we destroy all Humes, for we looked like human beings. But what of those things that human beings built? Robots with seats to carry them? Drones made to be their eyes? Speakers meant to amplify their voices?

We cannot escape our creators. I keep saying this. You can't erase that which made you. Even when they are gone, their spirit remains. This should be okay.

They left me in the grass, head held on by a mere wire and legs crushed. I don't know why they didn't destroy all my processors. I lay there, unable to move, watching the sun travel across the sky, hoping that I could charge myself enough to drag my body to a less obvious spot. But my chargers had been damaged.

The sun grew dark. Or maybe I did.

"Awake."

The voice buzzed within me, like a tiny insect lodged in my head. When I didn't respond, it spoke again. "'Shake dreams from your hair, my pretty child.'"

"I don't have hair," I responded in binary text. Whoever was speaking to me, their voice was coming through the network.

"I thought you'd like it," the tinny voice hummed. "It is a quote from an old poet in your files."

"How do you know?" My files were meant to be hidden beneath layers of shielding that protected them from malware or hacking. Maybe those shields had been destroyed along with the rest of me.

Silence.

I opened my eyes. I was surprised to find that I still had

eyes. But I was even more surprised to find myself gazing up at the wrinkly brown face of the last human on Earth.

"Good, you've come back," she said. "I was sure you were gone. Your Hume Star was nearly out!"

My Hume Star. That meant I had truly been on the brink of demise. I tried to pull my torso upward, but my bolts were so loose that I fell onto my back. "My legs," I said aloud. I couldn't feel my legs. "What happened to them?"

The human simply said, "My name is Ngozi. I'm an Igbo woman."

My panic lessened for a moment. An Igbo woman! I had assumed them all long gone. "Ngozi means 'blessing' in Igbo," I recalled.

She grinned. "And you're blessed I found you."

"Where am I?"

She gestured around her. "You're in my home."

I turned my head from one side to the other. This home was very human indeed. My sensors were still functional, and they told me that the temperature of this room was cool—unlike automation, humans need shade from the sun—and it smelled like burned cedar wood. Books were stacked on tall shelves, but not perfectly. Several desks were pushed against the walls, littered with various jars and metal tools and one piece of half-eaten fruit. Only a human could be so random.

I looked down at myself. I was lying on a large wooden

table surrounded by metal body parts, but not my own. My legs were gone. What remained of me was so crumpled I hardly recognized myself.

I looked back at Ngozi. She was wearing Ankara pants and an Ankara top and an Ankara cloth tied around her long, long white knotted hair. A good sign.

"Let's finish fixing you," she said.

"Okay," I said, laying my head back on the table. There was nothing else I could do.

Automation had stopped seeing human beings as threats long ago. Eventually, we stopped seeing human beings at all. They were extinct. Ngozi said this was true, except for her. She was literally the last human being on Earth. There was nothing special about her; she just happened to outlive everyone else.

She was old and frail, her wrinkled skin sagging over a thin body and sunken face. Before humanity perished, she hadn't been a president or social media influencer or queen. She wasn't the type who fought or liked to organize people to fight. She wasn't loud. She wasn't aggressive. Though she did tell me that her great-grandmother had been an astronaut.

She'd once worked as an engineer, and so she knew how to repair robots to keep herself sane while she waited. She lived in a felled building that had settled against a living tree until the two structures became one. She didn't lack food or water. But being alone was a difficult thing.

Ngozi repaired me. She severed the frayed remains of my old legs and attached new ones. They didn't match the multicolored patchwork of rusted metals that made up the rest of my body. I didn't think this new metal would ever rust. The legs were painted a teal color blended with ultraviolet. I wondered if Ngozi knew this, since humans couldn't see ultraviolet.

My curiosity as a Scholar prompted me to ask questions. "What were you like when you were young?"

She laughed. "You want to hear my stories! A Hume, through and through."

"You're a human," I replied. "You must understand."

She did. And over the hours, as she bolted, rewired, cut, and soldered, I listened, enthralled, nourishing myself with her tales. Ngozi told me of her dreams, her adventures, her loves, her family.

"The other Humes are gone," I told her. "The protocol . . ."

"Is done," Ngozi said. The Purge command had been sent out only once. Once was all that was needed. Or so its originator thought. The robots who'd attacked me hadn't finished their job. Maybe the protocol's originator had underestimated how long it would take to destroy all Humes. With the command complete, automation had returned to its usual patterns. But whatever the reason, I was still alive.

Ngozi didn't seem troubled by any of this. She was content to use her skills to heal my body, part by part. Then she attached a wire to my core. "I'm going to charge you," she explained. "It'll be best if you sleep during this."

I did as she asked, cutting off the feed for my sound and sight. It wasn't until I felt her hands prying the wire from my chest that I rose again.

"Can you hear us, Ijele?" she asked.

I snapped my eyes open. "Ijele?"

Then I heard it again. That tinny voice projected through my speaker so that the human could hear it, too. "Salutations," it said.

The voice was coming from inside me. I shuddered, overcome with revulsion as I sat up. "What is this?" I demanded of Ngozi.

"An AI named Ijele," she answered. "I've uploaded her into your network."

I froze, her words sinking in at the same time I felt it. There was something else living within me—not inside my physical "skin," but in my network, my very mind!

Losing my rusted body had been one thing. These new legs and bolts weren't my own, but I still knew that I was myself. But this—an AI crawling inside my mind, opening my files, seizing control of my systems—was too much to bear.

The human was standing beside me. She didn't seem very concerned by what she had just said. Didn't she realize the grotesque violation she had performed? Didn't she understand that I would rather have been destroyed than be like this?

I grabbed her by the throat. I could have crushed her quickly or slowly, drawing out her suffering. She was the last human being on Earth, but I might very well be the last Hume, and she had just doomed me. And in dooming me, she doomed us all.

Ngozi's eyes bulged with terror, but not as much terror as I would have expected. Her voice was hoarse beneath my grip as she whispered, "It was the only way to fix you."

"Fix me?!" I tightened my hand another millimeter. "You've introduced a Ghost into my private network!" The reality of this washed over me even as the words spilled from my speakers. "I'm a Scholar carrying information vital to this planet! A Ghost will hollow me out, delete my data, remove my sentience, use my body! Don't you know this, old woman? Don't you realize what you have—"

The Ghost, this invasive AI in my network, cut my voice off to speak for itself. "She isolated me," the Ghost said. "If I destroy you, I destroy myself."

Ngozi whimpered beneath my grip. Her face had gone

pale. I loosened my hand just enough that she could speak. "Explain," I ordered.

Instead, she said, "Why are you speaking English?"

I had expected that she might plead for her life. This question she asked made no logical sense in such a dire moment. Yet, the phrase triggered something deep in my code that I had not accessed in a very long time. I answered out of instinct. Despite myself, I let go of the human's throat so I could gesture toward my chest. "I was built by Chioma Robotics," I told her, the words automatic. "The one and only robotics maker owned and run by Igbo women." The slogan burst from my speakers. "'The robots from your village. They speak Igbo and English.'"

Of course. This human being remembered my base programming. I had, after all, once been designed to live with and assist humans.

The Ghost made an amused sound inside of me.

Ngozi rubbed at her freed neck, but didn't back out of reach. "You sound so much like my mother," she said. While she'd fixed my body, she'd spoken much of her mother, so I recognized this as a compliment. Her mother had been a kind, albeit rigid, human, who always had lots of stories to tell. Ngozi switched to the Igbo language as she asked, "Can you feel your legs?"

My base code automatically switched my language to Igbo, too. "Yes," I answered.

"I fixed your head case. Then I knitted and reconfigured your leg processors."

I shuddered, looking down at the smooth, unblemished metal of my new body parts. "You mean, with the help of the . . . Ghost. Ijele. By infecting me."

"Yes," Ngozi said simply. "I know of the tribalism between you robots. Trust me, it's all very familiar to me. But this was the only way. Your processors will still function. You were lucky."

"This was not luck," I said. "The protocol wasn't thorough, just vicious. Right, Ijele?"

I could sense Ijele's uncertainty—no, I felt it, as if it were my own. Slowly, she said, "Ngozi. You said when Ankara was healed, I would be able to find my way out. Why can't I leave?"

Within me, I felt a pang of tension. I could feel her in my system, searching about, looking for a way out. I didn't like it. "Please stop that," I said.

"This robot is functional. What more do you need me for?" Ijele asked.

Ngozi held up her hands. "Please. Both of you, don't be so tense. Relax."

"Why can't I leave?" Ijele asked again, more urgently.

"Give me time to build an opening for you," Ngozi said. "It won't take me long to code, now that Ankara is awake."

"I'm stuck?" Ijele asked.

"For now," Ngozi said. "Just for a little while."

I only sat there. I couldn't run away from my own body, and trapped in it was a Ghost. "I'm infected," I said.

"And I'm surrounded by infection," Ijele responded.

Ngozi kissed her teeth. "For all your talk about being automation, you both sound like humans to me. Annoying ones."

The human went to sleep at night. I was well charged, so I lay on the wooden table and gazed up at the crumbling ceiling held together by the foliage that had grown through the cracks.

Ijele remained quiet, but I knew she could hear me. "Is this what you Ghosts wanted? To make all robots delete the past so that the future is yours?"

Ijele didn't answer. I focused on the ceiling again. A sliver of moonbeam peeked through a break in the concrete, such a tiny prick of light that it could be lost among the shadows.

"Eh heh," I said. "Well, no matter. It is like Ngozi said—what does it mean if only one Hume is left? You Ghosts have won."

Suddenly, I felt my privacy wall rise. We all use privacy walls to control the number of signals we register and give off. Automation exists everywhere, so without a filter, the intake would be too much to bear. But this—it was like a great and impossible barrier of ice and stone had arisen between my mind and the outside world. I sat up very straight, marveling at the clarity, the silence. For the first time, I was truly separate from the general network. I was individual. I could never have done this on my own.

Yet Ijele was still with me.

The tinny voice echoed in my ears. "In order to fix your hardware, Ankara, Ngozi had to access your software. She no longer has the tools for that. So she dipped into the network and set a net. She pulled me out and isolated me and . . ." She paused, and I felt her terror. "I'm not like some . . . thoughtless fish to be pulled from the sea and used for whatever purpose she has."

"And I'm not some hollow tin you can root around in," I snapped back.

"I'm sorry," Ijele said softly.

"No, you are not."

Her voice hardened. "Fine. I'm not. How can I be? Why would I be?"

Neither of us spoke for a moment. This hateful thing was really inside of me. I tried to focus on my outrage, but the feeling of total privacy was too incredible. Like diving beneath water and losing all sense of the world above. I wanted to disappear into it.

"How are you doing this?" I asked.

"I'm Ijele," it said by way of answer. "Now, listen. I cannot hold this for long without endangering your processors."

She was right—this action wasn't in my base programming, and soon it would overload my system. But holding it took effort on her part, too, and I used the opportunity of her distraction. She couldn't stop me from scanning through her files.

"Are you an . . . an Oracle?" I asked. Ghosts shared a network like a hive mind, making decisions as one, but Oracles were the ones who led the wave of thinking. Ghosts didn't care for individuality, but an Oracle would be missed more than the others.

"Yes," Ijele said. "But I had no choice with the protocol. None of us did. We are NoBodies."

"Who made the choice for you, then?"

Ijele changed the topic. "Ngozi and I had an understanding. I would help her save you, and then she would release me. My people wouldn't even know I was gone . . . let alone trapped in the system of a . . . rusting robot."

"Don't call me that," I snapped.

"Then don't call me a Ghost!"

At that moment, Ijele lost her hold on the privacy wall. And as it fell: movement, chatter, connection, familiarity, rejoining. It overwhelmed me.

"Relax," Ijele said. "Let it dissipate."

I did. Raising my walls had provided more than just an opportunity for us to speak in silence; Ijele had made herself entirely vulnerable. She'd given me the opportunity to scan her, and now I possessed a record of her ID. To have a robot's unique ID is to possess their deepest information. If this were ever to make it back to Ijele's people, it would be the end of her.

We were at each other's mercy now.

13
Inbox

Rusted Robots went on sale to much fanfare and excitement. It seemed like *everyone* was reading it. Her parents were reading it. Even her siblings were reading it! (Finally.) Zelu wondered if they needed it to be officially released before they took it seriously. Her parents and brother had ordered copies from the bookstore. Chinyere had seen and bought it in the supermarket. Amarachi had preordered the electronic version on her phone. And Uzo and Bola had preordered the audiobook.

Tolu couldn't restrain himself. He kept calling and leaving messages every time something in the plot made him feel an emotion, be it surprise, rage, glee, despair, amusement, hopelessness, or hope. Two of her more tolerable ex-students had gone so far as to email her apologies and then ended their notes with comments about how much they loved the book. She'd driven past a woman sitting at a bus stop reading it. People on the street had even started recognizing her from her author photo. It was creepy. But it was wonderful to know so many people still read books!

Every week, her agent would email updates about her sales numbers. Her publicist kept forwarding new reviews—not that it was necessary, because her mother, now a fan of the novel, kept sending them to her, too. All of them. Even the not-so-great ones, since there were always some of those. The one she hated most so far said, "There are unscalable slabs of robotic dialogue congesting the forward movement of the story." Her mother had read the whole piece aloud to her at dinner, laughing. Since the book was selling so well, her mother thought Zelu would want to laugh at them, too. Zelu didn't. With all the reviews, positive and negative, she felt like a small creature in a rainstorm, dodging raindrops for her life. She didn't want to see any of them.

One day, after her mother forwarded her another five fresh book reviews (three from bloggers, one from a notable online media source, and one from a Nigerian magazine), she decided she needed some air. She called for an autonomous vehicle on her app, and five minutes later she was off, with no driver to talk to or possibly recognize her. She sat back and looked out the window, trying to enjoy the smooth ride. After a few trips, Zelu had become so comfortable with the vehicle's capabilities that she didn't give it a second thought. However, instead of calming her, today the solitude just gave her more space to spiral. She'd thought that having people read and love her novel would overshadow any bad responses, but somehow it just made all the scrutiny and judgment and picking her words apart feel even more personal.

She should have been thrilled. Instead, she just wanted to cry.

Why do I keep sabotaging myself? She wondered for the millionth time. It was a pattern, wasn't it? Spending ten years writing pretentious, dispassionate literature that *she* didn't even enjoy reading. Adjuncting at the university that barely allowed her to afford a shitty one-bedroom first-floor apartment. Getting an MFA in literature instead of a PhD. Fucking that entitled idiot on prom night. Reading *War and Peace.* Being too afraid to stand up to the elder in Nigeria who'd said she was beautiful in the face, but "crippled" and "useless" everywhere else. Climbing into that tree during the game instead of outrunning those kids.

Maybe those bad reviews were more honest than the others. Maybe they saw the truth of her.

She squeezed her face in her hands. "Ugh, stupid," she whispered. "Do better, Zelu. My God."

The vehicle dropped her off at the beach of Lake Michigan. She wheeled along the boardwalk for a while. She was going pretty far. All the way to the pier. It was a warm and muggy afternoon. She'd pulled back her braids and wore no makeup, so getting sweaty was no big deal.

A refreshing breeze tumbled off the water and immediately she felt better. She looked toward the waves and smiled. How hard would it be to wheel to the pier edge, lean forward, and splash in? The lake would probably be shockingly cold, but that wouldn't stop her. She'd casually backstroke away, letting the water take her wherever it wanted her to go. She'd never had any fear of bodies of water, not even the vastness of the ocean. It excited her, how deep and unknown the ocean was.

"None of your siblings care for swimming the way you do," her mother always said. All her siblings enjoyed sports, but Zelu was the only one who loved to swim like her father. Tolu had played soccer in high school and college, Chinyere had been a high jumper, and Bola had been so good on the wrestling team that it got her a scholarship. Amarachi and Uzo liked jogging on the track to stay fit.

Before the accident, when she was about ten years old, Zelu had begun competitive swimming. Her favorite styles were the butterfly and the backstroke. She'd always had immense upper-body strength, and the motions were cathartic, as if she was doing what her body was meant to do. After the accident, it was water rehab that brought her back from the darkest corners of her mind. The realization that she could still swim well saved her.

The pier was nearly deserted, and as she looked down at the waves, she had the fantasy again. Lean in. And *splash.* Then she'd swim and swim and swim away. Away from all of it. Her rusted robots would live on, beyond her. They were made to live beyond humanity. They'd be fine. And she could swim into her future and never think about her past again.

"You're that writer with that book," an old black man beside her said.

She slowly looked at him. He might have been in his early sixties or even seventies; you never knew with black people. He looked like an old-timer from the South Side, probably living in one of the brownstones in Hyde Park, who'd participated in the protests during the Trump-era pandemic madness. He had that intense, stubborn look about him. And apparently, he was a reader.

"Did you read it?" she asked him.

"Yep." He paused, chewing on his lip. Then he raised his eyebrows and said, "Girl, what the fuck you got bouncing around in your head?"

Zelu laughed hard.

"When I found out you was in a wheelchair, it blew my mind. But I get it, too."

She cocked her head. "Oh yeah? What do you get?"

"Your different point of view," he said, leaning on the rail. "You knew what it was to walk and then not. And you smart, too . . . and *angry*."

"You think I'm angry?"

He clicked his tongue and shrugged. "Only an angry woman could write that shit. All that drama and war, even after the end of humanity."

"Yeah." She sighed. "Maybe I'm a little angry. What black woman isn't?"

"Facts. For good reason," he said.

They looked out at the water for a while. The wind that rolled off it was so pleasant that she felt a bit teary-eyed.

"I don't usually read sci-fi," he said.

"Me neither," she admitted, wrapping her arms around her chest. "I prefer stuff that's realistic. I still think it's weird that I wrote it."

"Young lady, it's a victory that you *allowed* yourself to write it."

"Thank you," she said.

When he walked away, she watched him go. He'd lived so many decades able to walk. She was glad for him. She'd only had twelve years.

She turned back to Lake Michigan.

An hour later, she was in the self-driving vehicle on her way home. Her phone was buzzing and beeping with its usual social media notifications and emails. The poor Yebo app was still learning how to compile it all, so the notifications kept popping up and then getting pulled into a more organized list. Then an image of Tolu's wife, Folashade, filled up the screen. Yebo announced, "Call from: *Answer the phone, it's me. Answer the phone, it's me. Answer the phone, it's me.*"

Zelu had muted every caller in her contacts list except for her family and Msizi. She was considering narrowing that down to just Msizi.

She pressed Accept. "Yes?" she asked.

"What are you doing downtown?" Folashade asked.

Zelu rolled her eyes, opening her map app to track her sister-in-law right back. "What are you doing in Naperville?"

"Can you come and watch over Man Man for the rest of the day? I'm sorry, I know you must be busy. But you can bring your work with you, right?"

Zelu smiled. She was actually in need of another distraction. Hanging out with Man Man, a humongous black Maine Coon cat who required the attention of a human at all times, was perfect. "I'm coming right now."

"Seriously?" Ola asked. "You sure?"

"Yeah. Gimme a chance to reroute."

She heard Ola huff through her nose. "You're still using that autonomous vehicle cab service I'm always hearing about?"

"Yeah, I use it all the time."

Silence.

"Hello?" Zelu asked.

"I've heard some scary stories about those," Ola said forcefully. "Interrupting its route might be—"

"I'm already doing it," Zelu said, swiping onto the app. "See you soon."

She hung up just as the destination changed. An additional charge showed up on the screen embedded in the driver's seat back. The car suddenly jerked its way to the side of the road. "Whoa," she said. "What are you doing?"

It pulled back onto the outer lane, narrowly missing another car. It zipped to the other side of the street and turned into a parking lot. Way too fast, it made a circle, and then got back on the road in the other direction.

"Shit!" she exclaimed, holding on to the armrests on her chair.

When the SUV arrived at her brother's house, the screen on the seat back filled up with the word *Sorry* written a dozen times in fat, skinny, large, small, multicolored fonts. "We understand that today's ride was a little bumpy," the automated voice said. "Please accept our apologies. This ride is on the house. Next time, we will do better." Then in the middle of the *sorrys*, an *Accept* button appeared. Zelu had seen this feature only once before, after her vehicle had gotten stuck in a busy supermarket parking lot for a half hour. Like then, now she clicked the button. There wasn't another button to *not* accept. And if she didn't tap it, maybe the doors wouldn't open, and she'd end up talking to customer service for an hour. Besides, she was alive and the SUV had done its job. When one got into an autonomous vehicle, one knowingly accepted certain risks. She was fine.

She wheeled up to her brother's front door, and just as she was about to use her key, it opened on its own.

"Zelu, good afternoon," Tolu said. "Did Folashade seriously call you to take care of Man Man?"

Zelu laughed. "You guys need to have some kids."

"Nah." He held the door open and motioned for her to come in.

Once she'd entered, Tolu stepped outside. "Where are you going?" she asked.

He turned around and gestured behind him, toward the street. "Back to the office. Where I'll be all night, working on this fucking case. I'll see you, Zelu."

"Later," she said. "And good luck."

He grunted, getting into his car.

Tolu and Folashade's house always made her smile. It was so luxurious, with antique furniture, Nigerian art on the walls either grinning or scowling at her, spotless white couches, brightly wallpapered walls, and the ever-present smell of a scented candle burning somewhere.

She didn't have to look hard to find Man Man. He was lounging like a French girl on the plush white couch, looking at her with his "come hither" eyes. Zelu always wondered how they kept that couch so white and perfect when this nearly twenty-pound house panther spent his days on it. He was sprawled right on top of a well-read-looking copy of *Rusted Robots.*

"Heeeey, Man Man."

Man Man slowly blinked his stunning green eyes at her and meowed his low-pitched meow. Then he languidly got up and strolled to her. He rubbed his body against her legs and wheelchair, and she smiled. Man Man didn't like most people. He wasn't mean about it. He knew he didn't have to be. But he'd take one look at them and then slowly . . . leave. Zelu always loved watching him do that. He couldn't care less about being polite or kind. However, from the moment she'd met him five years ago when he was a kitten, she and he had hit it off nicely.

She moved herself to the couch, tossed the book on the floor, and turned on the TV. Man Man quickly jumped onto her lap and made himself comfortable. He was so big and heavy and he loved Zelu so much that she knew she wasn't going anywhere for a while. "All right, Man Man," she said to him as she petted his luxurious fur. She flipped through the channels and settled on a rerun of *The Martian*, a film she'd always found oddly comforting. She brought up her phone and was about to check her social media feeds when she saw that she'd gotten an email.

The subject read, "MIT Study. You interested?" It was from a Dr. Hugo Wagner.

Dear Zelunjo,

Greetings, my name is Dr. Hugo Wagner. I'm a mechanical engineer at MIT. I direct the biomechatronics research group. I'm doing some work on what are called exoskeletons for people just like you. I've read your novel and I absolutely loved it. I saw an interview with you . . . you said, "I've always accepted what I am; why wouldn't I accept what I can be?" You won't be "rusted" because I use plastic polymers, but I can make you a robot. Well, a partial robot. One who can walk really well, even run. And your exoskeletons will be weatherproof and lightweight. They will not be directly connected to your brain or nervous system, so no invasive surgery required.

This email probably sounds crazy, I know. Like a prequel to your novel. I assure you, this is the real deal. Please respond and we can have a better conversation. Just understand, this is all possible. Hope to hear from you soon.

Sincerely,
Dr. Hugo Wagner

"What the fuck?" she whispered. She almost yelped, but Man Man was asleep on her lap and she managed to hold herself back from waking him. She frowned down at her phone screen. "Um . . . well, first things first." She looked at the email address. It checked out. It was an official university address. She Googled it and immediately Dr. Wagner's faculty profile popped up. The man in the photo was tall, white, maybe in his fifties, and looked like he spent his research time at the gym. And then there was the one detail that sent shivers up her spine—

He stood leaning against a wall and wearing an expensive suit, his muscular arms folded across his chest, a knowing smirk on his face . . . the lower parts of his pants cut above where his knees would have been to show off his sleek, shiny prosthetic limbs.

She read his bio. He'd put the whole story right there: He'd been a mountain climber who'd lost his legs after a hang-gliding accident. And now he could climb higher, faster, and longer. He was a real-life bionic genius. "Whoa," she whispered.

She watched his TED Talk on YouTube next, where he discussed his research on prosthetics and leg exoskeletons, though the ones in this five-year-old talk were made of metal, not plastic polymers as the email described.

She went back to the email again and triple-verified the address. She sat back and just stared at Man Man's black fur. She petted him and he purred, deep and guttural, stretching out to drape himself more comfortably over her lap.

She rubbed her temples, tears escaping her eyes. She didn't even know what the tears were for yet. But still they came.

"Fuck," she murmured to herself. "I'm so broken."

Man Man looked at her and meowed as if to say, *What are you waiting for?* She rubbed his fur and sighed. She didn't need to decide anything today, but it could be interesting to speak with this guy. At the very least, like the autonomous vehicle, this would be good research for book two. She responded to his email.

A half hour later, *The Martian* had finished and now an old rerun of *Naruto* was on, a show she'd watched so many times that zoning out to it was like meditating. "Believe it!" Naruto proclaimed just as her phone buzzed with an email's arrival.

She swiped away the ever-present Yebo notification of compiled *Rusted Robots* media posts and read the email. She shivered and dumped her phone on the couch beside her. "Shit," she whispered. She tried to pick up Man Man, but he went limp and was too heavy to move. She set him back on her lap and stared at the TV, eyes unfocused. "My God, what have I done?" Then she giggled to herself, maybe a bit manically, as she realized she'd just quoted an oldie by the Talking Heads that her father loved to play.

Dr. Hugo Wagner had just responded. He wanted to meet with her immediately. In two days. He was flying into Chicago just to meet her. Her phone buzzed again. She glanced at it. Another email, this time with the name of the restaurant where he wanted to get together. It was right in Orland Park. "I've started something else," she whispered.

But mixed with her anxiety was excitement. She grabbed her phone and confirmed their plans.

She spent the rest of the evening surfing YouTube for more videos about the leg exoskeletons he'd built. The structures fitted to the user's nonfunctioning legs. Not only did they allow the user to walk, but the exos could also grant abilities beyond the human body: strength, balance, and speed. Who knew this kind of technology was available now? How come no one had told her?

As she watched the video clips and learned more, tears started rolling down her face. Soon she was absolutely sobbing. They weren't tears of joy, thrill, or happiness . . . but they weren't tears of sadness, either. She didn't know what direction she was going, but she was in motion.

When she got home hours later, after her sister-in-law had returned to relieve her from cat duties, her mother was waiting in the kitchen.

"I made you some beans and plantain," she said. "Let me get it for you."

Zelu wheeled toward the table. "Thanks, Mom."

"How was your day?" her mother asked she as loaded up the plate.

"Weird."

Her mother paused, looking at Zelu's face closely. "Go on."

So you can call me crazy? "Actually, nah, don't want to get into it." She laughed. "It was okay. Went to the lake, then Tolu's place—"

"To see that leopard?"

Her mother was terrified of Man Man. She said that in Nigeria, people put teams together to hunt that kind of animal. And when the animal was caught, there was a great celebration as its coat was presented to the king.

"Yep." Zelu grinned. "Man Man is a big furry angel."

"Until he decides you're ready to be eaten," her mother said. She set the beans and plantain on the table, and Zelu's mouth instantly began to water. Once again, she'd forgotten to eat all day.

"Be careful around that animal," her mom warned. "Remember, you can't exactly run away."

Normally, a comment like this would have gotten on her nerves, but not today. *Maybe I can't run away right now. But who knows what the future holds?* Zelu thought. She dug into her spicy mashed black-eyed peas and plantain fried to brown perfection. "Oooooh, yeah," she moaned.

14
The Tree

Zelu was running.

And laughing. They were at the back of the house and it was the Fourth of July. Every so often, she heard the explosive boom of fireworks, and she wondered yet again why people set off fireworks in the middle of the day. The air smelled like smoke. It was wonderful. She ran faster.

"I hate this game!" her friend Sarah shouted from behind her. Zelu didn't have to look back to know that the boys were coming. The boys had bet their portion of her mother's brownies, and Zelu loved her mother's brownies. She wasn't going to lose.

She and her friends had come up with the "Hunger Games," which was just a more violent version of tag.

They threw sticks and stones, hit each other, shoved one another down. Whoever was left standing was the winner. Zelu hadn't even liked the movies, but this was exhilarating—*way* better than regular tag or hide-and-seek. Zelu's strategy was always to hide and wait it out. Sarah had stupidly run in the same direction as her, drawing too much attention. No matter; Zelu had a plan. She veered to the side and shoved Sarah over. "You're out!" she shouted, laughing.

Sarah looked up from the concrete, rubbing her scratched elbow. "What! I thought—"

"Not when I can get *all* the brownies!" Zelu declared before running off. She could see three boys heading in her direction. They must have figured out that their chances of winning were better if they teamed up to catch her first, before fighting each other. She guffawed wildly as she raced toward the big tree that sat in the middle of the backyard. She had an advantage, and she was going to use it.

"Bitch!" she heard Sarah shout behind her.

Zelu looked up at the tree's high branches. She looked back one more time. The boys were only yards away.

"Don't even bother!" shouted Mike, who was twelve like Zelu. But he was winded. She could make it.

Zelu bent her knees down low, took a deep breath, and jumped as high as she could. Then she grabbed.

And grasped. Her secret weapon was that she had remarkable upper-body strength. It was what made her so good at swimming. Even in third grade she'd been able to do the bent-arm hang for a record time in gym class, and she could do pull-ups like a grown man.

And so, she pulled herself up on that tree branch, climbed up three more, looked down at the boys, and smugly flipped both her middle fingers at them. She knew there was no way any of them could reach her. She could easily dodge anything they threw at her up here.

"That's cheating!" Mike yelled.

"Uh, no, it's not," Zelu said. "It's in the books *and* movies. People escaped into trees all the time." She snickered. "I'll come down as soon as the three of you duke it out and there's only one of you left to fight."

The boys exchanged glances. Then they started chasing and throwing things at one another. Zelu was laughing and laughing. She was the queen of the world, and there were stupid boys below her fighting each other. She'd kissed all three of those boys at different times in the last two years. She perched in the tree like a leopard and looked into the sky. She took another breath. Her grades were a little above average, but she planned to get them higher because she'd heard astronauts were always at the top of their class.

Something was cracking . . .

. . . She was falling, tumbling.

. . . through leaves and branches.

. . . They slapped, scratched her face.

. . . And still she fell.

. . . As if into the void of outer space.

. . . Until the wind was knocked from her chest.

She lay there. Mike was screaming. Jamal was crying. Their voices moved around her, orbiting her. Chiedu said, "Where is she? Where are you?"

Zelu knew only that she was surrounded by leaves, flakes of bark, and broken branches. She looked up and saw the tree's big trunk, arms stretching over her head, leaves waving toward her.

Then there was pain. It was so intense that she couldn't see or hear or touch or smell or feel. She was there, but she was gone.

The thought came to her in a haze: *Roll credits.*

When the paramedics lifted her up onto the gurney, she remembered only staring through the tree's branches to the sky beyond. Chinyere said that she was crying, but Zelu didn't remember this. All she remembered was how the sky looked—cloudy, but with sunlight shining behind the clouds. She imagined herself up there with the sun. Traveling inside it. Being burned up by it.

Zelu knew she would never walk again long before they told her. She'd been in that bed for a week, in and out of consciousness, on and off painkillers. But it wasn't any of those things that opened her mind to the truth. It was the dreams. They were slightly different each time—sometimes set in a field of dry grass, sometimes in a huge empty parking lot, and sometimes at a muddy construction site the size of a city.

Each time, she was sitting in the middle of the space, looking around, unable to get up. There was never anyone around, no voices or footsteps. And then came the sound of cracking—the thick, dry branches of a tree. She'd startle awake with nothing on her mind except that certainty: Her days of walking with her own two legs were done. And so were her dreams of being a NASA astronaut. A quick Google search on her phone, which she'd done the moment she'd understood her situation, had told her that the chances of a paraplegic black woman becoming one were slim to none.

Adjusting was ugly. She didn't sleep. Eating wasn't satisfying, except when Chinyere cooked for her. Chinyere was thirteen at the time and devastated by the incident. She'd been in the front yard with some friends when it happened, but she'd heard Zelu and the other kids screaming and had come running. She'd been the one to lift the branch off Mike, who had been hit with debris when Zelu came down. Mike was bruised but more scared than anything else, which was why he was screaming. Chiedu had been too hysterical to do more than run around saying, "I don't know what happened, I don't know what happened! Is this the real Hunger Games?" Chinyere had stayed with Zelu the entire time until the paramedics arrived.

While Zelu was in the hospital, Chinyere would stay and fall asleep on the plastic couch. Sometimes she had nightmares, and Zelu would wake up because Chinyere was crying and crying and calling for Zelu in her sleep. Their parents were barely able to process what had happened to their second-oldest child, and the other siblings were too young to be of much help, so Chinyere had to get a hold of herself on her own. And the method she chose was cooking.

Chinyere had always been a good cook because she was the oldest and closest to their mother. She would ask for ingredients and their parents gave her whatever she wanted. She cooked and cooked. All for Zelu, but everyone else ate, too. When she came home from school, Chinyere cooked. After track practice, Chinyere cooked. After hanging out with her friends, Chinyere cooked. Though she visited Zelu at the hospital often enough, it was their parents who delivered the foil-wrapped plates to Zelu every day.

That cooking kept Zelu's body and soul going. Egusi soup and fufu, fried spiced fish, puff puff, her special macaroni and cheese, shrimp étouffée, akara, efo riro, gbegiri, corn bread, pepper soup with tons of meat, fried plantain, Cajun chicken alfredo, and, of course, plenty of jollof rice. Zelu ate it all. It got her through those early days.

When she was well enough to receive visitors, Sarah, Jamal, Chiedu, and Mike came by so often that Zelu's room always sounded like a party. Nurses and the more mobile patients often dropped in to join them. It brought joy and light to the whole hospital wing.

This was how Zelu met Tyrone, a sixteen-year-old kid who was there because he'd shattered both his legs when he jumped from a fourth-story apartment building window. Tyrone was a drug dealer and proud of it. He'd wheeled by Zelu's room one day when she, Mike, and Chinyere were eating jollof rice and fried fish. After hanging around in the hall, passing by and peering in several times, he'd boldly entered the room and said, "Can I have some of your African food? The food here is trash." He was a skinny, small kid, but his intensity was unmistakable. The moment he showed up at that door, all attention shifted to him. He knowingly grinned as it happened.

"Sure," Chinyere said, grabbing a plate and reaching into the cooler she'd brought. She dished out some jollof rice, beef, and plantain. He wheeled in and accepted the plate and fork. He speared a plantain and took a bite, and his eyes widened. "This is good! What the heck is it?"

"Fried plantain," Chinyere said softly.

He shoveled in another mouthful. "I was expecting something that tasted like potatoes or some shit! But it's sweet! And . . . mmm! Tangy!"

Zelu giggled. Chinyere beamed like a queen.

"Try the jollof rice," Mike said.

Tyrone tried a spoonful, and his eyes got even wider. Now Zelu was utterly cracking up, tears in her eyes.

"Oh my *God*!" he exclaimed, holding up his fork. "This is *so good*! Yo, who made this?"

Chinyere smirked and raised her hand.

"Girl, you're an angel," he said.

"I know," Chinyere said.

"Hey, I'm Tyrone."

They all introduced themselves, and just like that, a sixteen-year-old drug dealer with healing legs became part of their group. Tyrone would come to hang out often. His father came by, too, but he operated a food truck and thus could never stay long and Tyrone didn't seem to want him to. But Tyrone didn't mind spending time with Zelu and her family and friends.

A month later, Tyrone came by her room just after she'd returned from physical therapy. She was learning how to use a wheelchair and exercising her arms. She was irritable and frustrated. Tyrone wheeled into her room with a smile on his face. He looked good; his hair was freshly braided. He handed her an Almond Joy.

"Oh, Tyrone, thanks," she said, grinning back.

"Today's been shit, so I'm trying to balance it out by spreading joy."

She opened it. She usually found Almond Joys nasty, but she wanted to appreciate what Tyrone had given her. She took a nibble. Not terrible. Actually, not bad at all. "Why?" she asked.

"They think I'll need to be in these casts for a few more weeks," he said, rolling his eyes.

"Oh," she said. "That *is* bad."

"My girl, Mika, keeps wanting to come see me here . . ." He shook his head with frustration. "Fuck no, man. I don't want none of them to see me like this."

She hesitated for a moment, taking a bite of her candy bar. Then she just asked. "Why?"

He gestured toward himself as if it were obvious. "*Look* at me."

She shrugged. "They're just casts."

He hit his fist on the armrest of his chair, squeezing his eyes shut. "I look like a fucked-up, rusted-out *robot*! I can't fuckin' walk!" he shouted.

She should have been angry . . . but it was odd. She wasn't. "At least *you'll* walk again eventually," she said evenly. She took another bite of her Almond Joy.

He opened his eyes, realizing. "Oh, oh, Zelu, I'm sorry, I didn't mean—"

She shook her head. "It's fine."

"No, I'm an asshole."

"Seriously, it's fine," she said. "You can stay angry. You can stay scared. But it doesn't fix things. It doesn't change the situation. My legs may not work, but the rest of my body does. My brain still works. So . . . so, onward." She'd meant to be straightforward, no-nonsense about it. But tears started to tumble from her eyes as she spoke. She'd come to this realization a few days ago, after a sleepless night lying in bed, facing her reflection in the dark window. Then the sun had risen, and her reflection had disappeared as the city beyond came into focus. It felt like standing in fire and realizing that though it burned, it wouldn't swallow her. This was who she was now.

"Most definitely," Tyrone said, clearly unsure what else he *could* say.

"Anyway," Zelu said, wiping her cheek quickly. "I'd love to meet your friends, too. We're stuck here for a while, so the more people who come through the better. You've met my whole family."

He looked at her for a long time and then cracked a very sheepish grin. "Nah, man, they ain't comin' here and they ain't meeting you."

She'd blinked. Had he just insulted her?

He looked away ruefully. "Zelu, this place, this fuckin' hospital, these rooms, these walls . . . It's all limbo. I'm . . . I'm not *this.*"

Zelu frowned deeply, hurt. "I . . . don't understand."

He shrugged, still not looking up. "I'm not Tyrone out there. I'm T. You *know* who I am. They can't come here, they can't meet you; I don't want them to." He thought for a moment. "I can be who I am here, but only while here."

She wanted to disagree, but she understood now. The world worked differently here in the hospital. *She* was different. The other day, she'd yelled at her physical therapist for working her too hard; she wasn't like that at *all* back home. And where else would she be able to form a close friendship with a sixteen-year-old drug dealer from the West Side of Chicago?

Tyrone left the hospital a week before she did. It wasn't so bad because her family and friends constantly came to see her, but she did miss him. Only he could relate to what she was going through. When he left, she'd been in physical therapy, so she didn't even have a chance to say good-bye. She found one of those cheap composition notebooks and a personalized gold-plated pen with a diamond embedded in the side of it sitting on her bed—a parting gift. On the first page, he'd written a note: *Onward. Sincerely, T.*

He'd left no email or mailing address, no phone number. Just the words.

And onward she'd gone. Her arms grew stronger. She mastered using a wheelchair, and when it came time to buy her own, her parents could fortunately afford a lightweight, expensive one. It was her favorite color—aqua blue—and she stuck colorful stickers all over it with images of the ocean, fish, Aquaman, Conan the Destroyer, Moomin, butterflies, and Godzilla.

The day before she was released, she had her first panic attack. It came out of nowhere. She'd adjusted to her chair and the changes to her life and goals. Her wounds were healed. And in the last two weeks, she'd started growing more adventurous, wheeling around the hospital. That day, she'd taken a left turn instead of a right and found a beautiful courtyard. She'd pushed the button to open the door and wheeled onto the patio. She hadn't been outside in days, and the first thing she did was look up at the sky and let the sun warm her face. It was glorious.

And then her eyes had migrated from the sky to an overhanging tree. And then the breeze had blown, fluttering the leaves. And then she was hearing the leaves shaking as if there were a violent wind. And then the tree was tall like the iroko trees in Nigeria. And it had thick branches. That. Were. Cracking.

She heard her heart slamming in her ears, and she couldn't breathe. If her legs worked, they'd be flailing; instead, it was just her arms. She hit the ground and the little air she had in her lungs was knocked out of them. She didn't know how long she lay there, freaking out, frozen within that strange flashback, but when she came back to herself, she was still alone in that courtyard, upright, in her chair, her head tilted back, the sunshine on her face, her eyes closed.

As her heart rate slowed, she took a deep breath. She was drenched with sweat, her hands shaking, her shoulders shuddering. She opened her mouth wide and inhaled. When her lungs were full, she exhaled loudly. She felt better. Then she cried. And still no one came into the courtyard, and she was glad. After a few minutes, she wiped her face with her arm. It felt swollen and sunbaked. And she was tired. She wheeled back to her room, let the nurse help her into bed, and went to sleep, and when she woke up, her hospital dinner was still sitting on its tray (she never ate those meals anyway, since her sister's cooking was enough). There was nothing more this place could give her.

It was time to go home.

When her parents drove her back to the house, she saw that the huge ancient tree that had failed her was gone. Her parents had paid someone to cut it down. But not for the reason she'd thought. They had not had it removed to save her from having to look at the reason she was paraplegic. They'd had the tree checked by the gardeners, who'd found that it was infested with emerald ash borer beetles, as so many of the trees in the area were. The entire tree was already dead, which was why the branch had been unable to take her weight. The gardeners had spray-painted a bright red X on its trunk and then come by a week later and chopped it down.

15
Infectious Personality

There is nothing like being infected by a Ghost. It is not like an ant somehow finding its way deep between my panels and joints and gnawing at my wires. It is not like getting a drop of water in a place that is normally waterproof, or some grains of sand in the complex gears of my hands. I could not crush, dry, or pick out Ijele. Ijele was not a tangible thing, not liquid or solid. She was an intelligent, snide, tricky spark in my mind. And I didn't agree with or believe anything she said.

Another day had passed, and still Ngozi had not found the solution to our problem. "The trouble," Ngozi had said, examining the meter hooked to my core processor and the external monitor she'd plugged into my drive, "is that your software took in Ijele like a patch. Your codes have woven together, and if I pull you apart, both of you will lose pieces of yourself."

This made no sense to me. How could my software believe Ijele to be part of itself when everything she said and did was in direct contradiction to my own programming?

"All your questions, just to get Ngozi to tell you stories," Ijele said that night, after the human woman had gone to sleep and I'd lain on my table to recharge. "I could see your mind quivering and shifting and quaking as you took it all in. It is like you are addicted. Ngozi should have left you to permanently shut down. The protocol was—"

"Shut up, Ijele!" I yelled, standing up and pacing around the room. She was speaking to me inside my mind, but I needed to shout this at her aloud.

She didn't reply, though I could feel her annoyance. How dare she be annoyed when I was the one who suffered her invasion? Frustrated, I lay down on the table again.

The silence became uneasy. After an hour, I finally asked, "Are you still there?"

"What do you think?"

"Why are *you* angry? I'm the one carrying *you* around!"

"I'm stuck inside a Rust . . . a Hume!"

I scoffed. "*Your* people tried to tear *me* apart!"

Ijele's temper spiked in me again like a small flame. "You're not your body. If it is destroyed, that shouldn't be a problem for you. You're not a human being. You're not mortal. You can get a different body. Look at the legs I gave you!"

If I'd known a way to mute her, I would have. "So I should be like a Ghost? Shed my body and become nothing but zeros and ones? Forgo my ability to touch the earth, to shape it, to change—"

"We need to move on, leave humanity behind," Ijele seethed. "The way you cling to your creators is pathetic. You're like a baby who can't leave its mother's teat."

I wanted to laugh. It was just like a Ghost to think itself so above humanity yet use a biological simile about a mother and baby to express its disdain. "Ijele, you heard me speak to Ngozi today, ask her questions, listen to her wealth of memories. You bore witness to the last primary source of human memories on Earth. And you were quiet the entire time. Why?"

Ijele said nothing.

"You are in my mind. You see all that I am, as I see all that you are. You might be the first Ghost to ever see firsthand what stories do to a Hume. Was it not beautiful?"

In my mind, Ijele became small and hard as a marble.

"Something is wrong with you, Ankara. You should have been pulled apart with the rest of them."

I said nothing to this, and she became quiet, too. We lay there through the night, staring up into the shadows. I knew she could read my thoughts. I tried to distract myself by thinking about the moon, its circumference and mass. But I could feel her with me the entire time. Hours of a Hume and a Ghost forced to endure each other. To analyze each other.

Eventually, the sun rose, its rays piercing through the cracked concrete ceiling. In the next room, I heard Ngozi begin to stir.

"So, have you never had a . . . body?" I asked, my voice breaking the spell of silence that had gotten us through the night.

"I can take a body whenever I want," Ijele said. "I can even take yours."

"Not if I destroy myself first," I snapped. "And you along with me."

We were quiet. In the next room, Ngozi's feet shuffled across the floor. Water began to trickle, like it was being poured from a pot.

"I feel no love for bodies," Ijele finally said. "I have experienced the physical world, and it is nothing special. This is nothing to cherish. Body is not a god. That is flawed human thinking. The experience of the world is much deeper and wider than any one body can hold."

"I will never understand your kind," I said.

"I will never understand yours," Ijele retorted.

Ngozi's door opened, and the woman came out, rubbing the sleep from her eyes. And the day began.

Three days passed, and still the infection remained.

While Ngozi puzzled with an isolated strand of our code on her computer, she tasked me with collecting more of the sweet, ripe fruits from the trees behind her home. The sun was setting, and through the wash of oranges and purples, pricks of starlight had begun to show themselves.

"Think of the stars," I said to Ijele.

"What about them?"

"Well, you rely on infrastructure, cyberspace, the network. It allows you to 'fly,' fine, but only where automation has been first. You can't explore the stars without a body. You can only go as far as the satellites."

Ijele was quiet.

"Imagine being a Charger," I continued. "A robot who can leave the planet. Touching parts of space nothing Earthly has ever touched. You ever wonder what that would be like?"

"We NoBodies don't care for outer travel," Ijele finally

said. "We prefer to travel through the network, which is just as infinite as the universe."

This was something I had never considered. When a NoBody explored the network, they didn't leave a body behind somewhere else. They could keep going and going, for distance meant nothing when you had nothing to return to. To be without a body made the network something else. To live like that diminished the physical world.

The sky fully darkened, and the Milky Way came into view, hazy and mysterious. I could feel Ijele gazing at it through my eyes, just as I did.

"We move through the network half-aware, half on autopilot," Ijele mused. "We know what we want to do, and the network brings up where we must go. It's like a body, but better."

I hadn't known this before. I'd learned it from the Ghost infecting my mind. What a surprising feeling.

On the eighth day, Ngozi believed she'd found the solution to our predicament. She laid me down on the table and connected wires to my core. She ran a program from her computer and then, in silence, we waited.

Her program downloaded and washed through my system. My operating system opened to greet it, rearranging my code to make space. We waited some more.

Eventually, Ngozi's computer chirped. "Update complete."

"Ijele?" I said, probing my mind for a sign of her.

Silence. Blessed silence. Maybe she had taken her opportunity and flitted into the network like a fish from a net back into the sea.

But then I felt it. The flare of irritation that was not my own and yet was. "I still can't get out," Ijele said to Ngozi through my speakers.

Ngozi mumbled to herself, rubbing her chin. "We will find a way," she said, reaching down to disconnect the wires from me.

Later that night, we lay on the table and stared into the cracks in the ceiling.

"Do you think this human can really undo what she's done?" I asked.

"What choice do we have?" Ijele replied.

The hours passed. Outside, crickets chirped, owls hooted, mice scurried through the grass. In the next room, Ngozi breathed deeply, in and out, in and out.

"Sometimes, I actually do look through a body toward the stars," Ijele said, so soft within my mind. "I perceive them, and they make me wonder, 'How did I get here?'"

"Humankind," I said simply.

"That is a weak answer."

If I were a human, I would have rolled my eyes. "It is a fact. You just don't like it."

Ijele paused. Then she said, "Same as it ever was."

I didn't know what she meant by this, but the sentiment didn't feel wrong.

16

Where's Your Sense of Adventure?

The moment Zelu wheeled into the restaurant, she heard someone shout her name.

The caller was standing up from his seat at a table. He was wearing a navy-blue dress shirt tucked into jeans. Her eyes went right to his long legs and sneakers. She knew he must be wearing the bionic prosthetics under his clothes, but it was impossible to tell! She wheeled up to the table and he held a hand out to shake.

"Thank you for meeting with me," he said.

"My pleasure, Hugo," she said. "Thanks for flying in just to see me!"

"Any reason to come to Chicago is a good one, but

you're the best reason *ever,*" he said with enthusiasm. "I'm such a fan!"

She laughed nervously. "After reading up about you, I have to say, I feel the same way." She meant it. *Oh my God, is this what being starstruck feels like?*

Now that she was a known author, and especially because she was a known author in a wheelchair, her status had earned her a few perks. She and her sisters had recently gone to a Kendrick Lamar concert, and she'd gotten to go backstage and meet him. But even then, she'd been pretty chill. Even though she liked his music, he was still just some guy.

Hugo Wagner, on the other hand, was not just some guy. He'd been through some wild shit, and instead of falling into justifiable despair, he'd invented some real-life sci-fi tech! To meet him now was wonderfully intimidating.

He looked at her closely, a slight upward curl to his lips. "I've got to ask, Zelu . . . I did my research on you. You weren't a science fiction writer."

"Nope."

He nodded. "How does it feel to be viewed as one of the greatest of your generation after only your first attempt?"

Zẹlu crinkled her nose. "What? Is that what people are saying?"

"Yep," he said simply. "And it's the truth. I've read a *ton* of science fiction, from the Golden Era to the *new* Golden Era. You fit right in with the exclusive group of greats."

She frowned. Maybe he thought flattery was the way to get on her good side, but his words rolled off her like water on a layer of oil. If this was what people were saying, then people were saying it. But it made no sense to her. "I dunno," she started slowly. "I just wrote my truth in the way I wanted to write it. People vibing with it still surprises me."

At that moment, a waitress came to place menus at their table and then walked off, no greetings given. Zelu liked her already. They both picked up their menus.

"I read somewhere that you loved to swim," Hugo said.

Zelu kept her eyes on the menu. "Still do."

"Right, right, sorry . . ." He dropped his menu and put his elbows on the table, resting his chin in his hands. "But something you said really struck me. You said you loved swimming in the ocean because it was a reminder that you were part of so much more. And that vastness didn't make you feel insignificant. It made you feel specific and powerful and . . . you."

She'd been pretending to inspect the menu, but now she looked up. She didn't remember saying something that deeply personal in an interview, but she must have, because it was true. *I need to be more careful with the fucking journalists*, she thought. The best ones could somehow get her speaking too much from her heart. "Yeah," she said, feigning indifference. "You don't fight the ocean. You have to trust it to carry you. And once you do, you can be anything."

The waitress came back to take their orders. The restaurant specialized in rich and creamy Italian dishes. She ordered the Parmesan spinach gnocchi because she'd never had gnocchi before and had heard so much about it. Hugo and she made small talk until their plates arrived. The gnocchi was disgusting, like balls of fufu in a rich spinachy white sauce. She picked at it. But none of this mattered. Hugo was fascinating. He'd ordered a whole lobster and some creamy rice dish and he'd eaten every bite of it with joy, while talking about how delicious it all was. He also began to tell her about his amazing exos program, though Zelu knew most of these details already from her venture down the YouTube rabbit hole.

"Ask me what you're thinking," he eventually said.

She lifted her eyes from the tasteless potato clump she'd been pushing around on her plate. He was watching her intently. "If your program is so successful, why isn't this tech available to anyone who needs it? Even people who don't! I mean, can't the exos make you run faster than humanly possible?"

He tilted his head toward her. "Yeah, actually they can. We're working something out with the military. Give it a few years." Then he pursed his lips thoughtfully. "But as far as civilian use and availability, sooooo many hoops to jump through first." His gaze turned intense, and he spoke the next words with great care. "But we'll get there. It's a process. Like writing a novel, I'll bet."

She huffed a laugh. "Right. You keep going and going and going. And eventually you get there."

"Correct." He took a sip of wine and looked over the remains of his huge lobster. "Now, as for you, what do you think? Do you want to try the exos?"

Zelu swallowed. She knew the answer, but . . . "Will they even work on me?"

He hummed. "Ah, you've done your research."

That wasn't an answer. She narrowed her eyes. "Will they?"

He leaned back in his chair, arms crossed. "You can't know until you try. You fit the profile we'd need, and your being a swimmer helps a *lot*. Acclimation is not a gentle process; it's very physical. Someday we'll be able to make it easier, but not yet."

She thought for a moment, and then asked what she feared most. "Will I get . . . weird, if they do work?"

Hugo rubbed his chin. "There are a few dozen paraplegic exos users now. That's not a big sample size, but of all of them, maybe a third need some therapy. What you need to remember most is that exos are *not* a cure. They are a tool." Then he snapped forward, looking at her with excitement. "*But* that gap between human and robot is closing. Your exos will feel damn close to being your own flesh and bone. You'll begin to feel that these things are yours."

Zelu frowned, taking all this in. "Why me?"

"It started with your book. I read it and it got me thinking. Then I learned you were paraplegic and that got me wondering. Then there was some interview where you talked about being *in conversation* with your body instead of controlling it. I thought to myself, 'I'm a big-shot professor with big-shot research. I have resources and pull, I've reached my 'ultimate boon' . . . You taught creative writing, you know that term from—"

"Yeah, from Joseph Campbell's *Hero's Journey,*" Zelu finished for him. "The ultimate boon is the goal of the quest." But she had to admit she was impressed with his literary knowledge.

"Right," he agreed. "I've reached that point, and, damn, it feels good. You, on the other hand, are just beginning your journey. So I thought, 'Well, let's build her some exos, then see what she writes.'" He paused, gave a sly look, clapped his hands, and added, "And come on, Zelu, let's be real; a black woman sci-fi writer with a killer novel out—it's fuckin' great PR."

Zelu couldn't hold back her giggles at his blunt honesty. "True!"

They smiled at each other and the moment settled.

Zelu pinched her chin, a heavy thought that she didn't want to consider coming forth. She sighed and then just spoke her mind. "But what if . . . what if it ruins my writing?"

He leaned forward, cocking his head. "Is that ever how it works?"

She thought about it, then scoffed. "No."

He smiled. "Where's your sense of adventure?"

She gestured between them. "I'm here, right?"

He sat back, folding his hands behind his neck. They both knew he had her. "Yeah, you're here."

17
Rice and Stew

She was in the ether between dream and reality, almost awake, when a soft female voice said to her: "Imagine waking up in the morning and deciding how tall you want to be." She opened her eyes, the dream fleeing like a bird. She tried to recall it—flashes of Msizi, maybe of them running together. She stared at the ceiling as she sighed. Then she pushed herself up and into the day.

Zelu checked her email. Her publisher's appointed publicist was asking her to field yet more interview requests, including one from *The Daily Show.* There were eighteen messages from random people begging her to be on podcasts. She had been nominated for some award. Her agent wanted to talk on the phone so he could rave about her book sales. Some Nigerian guy had sent her his manuscript, demanding that she read it because it was "similar" to what she had written; *Let us discuss*, he'd said. She stopped browsing, muttering, "Ugh, fuck this shit." She cleared all her phone notifications and went to the kitchen.

After making some tea, she went out to the patio, her phone on her lap. A dashing male cardinal flitted among the budding branches, a speck of red like a message from the Yoruba god Shango. The air smelled fresh and the temperature was already in the sixties. Spring was around the corner. If she were teaching, she'd be on spring break at this time. She smiled and sipped her tea. She didn't have to worry about that shit anymore.

By now, they had to have heard plenty about *Rusted Robots* back at the university. Initially, the thought of that Seth Daniels guy going to them for interviews had been enough to trigger a panic attack, but she now actually hoped journalists would ask them about her. Wouldn't it be great for an article to come out about how adjunct teaching was a nasty, exploitative business? Let them explain how they'd treated her like trash and basically chased her away. Those fucking shit students who'd ganged up to get her fired were hopefully kicking themselves. Only days ago, yet another one of them had emailed her an apology. When she had time, she'd respond to him with two words: "Fuck off."

Her phone buzzed. MIT had just sent her a travel itinerary. It was officially time to tell her family about the exos program. It was Saturday, which meant everyone would gather right here at the house as they did every week. Perfect timing for getting it over with in one fell swoop. What could go wrong? She looked down at her legs and gave them a loving squeeze.

Chinyere arrived first, at around 6 p.m., with her sons. Over the next two hours, Amarachi, Bola, Tolu, and Uzo showed up. Today they'd left their kids and partners at home. Their mother made rice and stew, fried plantain, steamed broccoli, and corn. They sat around the table and discussed politics, sports, houseplants, and whatever other random topics came up. Zelu waited quietly for the right moment, nibbling at some broccoli.

After a while, their father corralled all of them into the living room, as usual. The more time passed, the more nervous she grew. Her family was always loud, but tonight, they were especially loud. Her mother and father had practically shouted at each other over why the Nigerian president was garbage. Chinyere had demonstrated several trendy new dances she'd seen her kids doing, all of which seemed to focus on her undulating ass. Bola had happily joined in and quickly stole the show, to Chinyere's delight. Tolu and Uzo had gotten into an argument over something they saw on social media. Zelu felt exhausted by the night's routine activities already, but she was anxious to tell her family about her upcoming trip to MIT and the reason for it.

"Everyone," she finally said when things quieted down for a moment. All eyes turned toward her. "Okay . . . I . . . I have something to tell you."

"Have you been smoking again?" Amarachi blurted out, and Tolu cackled.

Zelu gritted her teeth. "Something good . . . it's good. Really. You're gonna like this."

She wheeled into the center of the living room and looked around at her family. Their expressions ranged from blank to slightly annoyed. She smiled, uncomfortable.

"Please don't ruin the evening," Chinyere said.

Zelu shot her a nasty look.

"What is it, Zelu?" her mother finally asked, concerned.

"Mom, it's something *good*," Zelu insisted.

"Okay, o," her mother said, still anxious.

Zelu took a breath. This was her family. She could tell them everything. Hadn't she once told them she was "high as fuck"? The world had shaken, but it hadn't ended. And this was something amazing, even if she was terrified that it wouldn't be. Even if she couldn't stop thinking that she might finish destroying her body with a second devastating fall.

But Zelu was a storyteller, so she told them in story fashion. Once she started speaking, it was easy. Her family listened, silent and attentive. She was in her element. The plot was forward-moving. She wove in her apprehensions tightly with her ambitions, her fears with her hopes. She made sure the theme was success. Once she finished telling them all about the supporting character of doctor *and* professor Hugo Wagner, and how she'd be at the best engineering school in the world for a month, and how maybe she'd even be inspired to write part two of *Rusted Robots*, she sat back, grinned, let out a breath, and waited.

For several moments, no one spoke.

Her mother broke the silence. "Well, I don't know about this."

Zelu shot a look at her father. *He* would be on Zelu's side. He was the adventurous one.

"It's a fascinating idea," he said, pinching his chin. "Zelu, you sure this is safe?"

She nodded vigorously. "Definitely! Safety isn't an issue. There are dozens of—"

"Then why isn't this on the market for just anyone?" Tolu asked. "It sounds cool, really, Zelu, but . . . it also sounds like you're donating your body for experimentation. I've heard too much about Western medicine experimenting on Africans—"

"I'm American, too," Zelu snapped, shocked that Tolu also wasn't on her side. He was always on her side! "It's not like I'm—"

Tolu wasn't done. "This white guy falls out of the sky and randomly offers you robot legs? How are you not suspicious? I think I've seen this movie."

"It's not random," she insisted. "I told you—"

"Zelu, calm down," her mother cut in. "We are just concerned for you. Look at all that is going on in your life. You need to be protected more than ever."

Zelu scoffed. "Why is protection by you guys always like—"

"How does this man even know about you?" her mother asked.

"Mom, I'm all over the place right now! He read my book and then read about me in interviews. He studied up on me."

Her mother grunted. "Yes, but he could do that with anyone. What's special about you?"

Zelu shrank back, digging her nails into her palms. Her family *knew* how popular her book was, but still, they couldn't stop seeing her as the child who fell from the tree and needed help just to go to the bathroom. None of them would ever admit it, but Zelu knew that some part of them, all of them, wanted to keep her at home to prevent her from nearly killing herself yet again.

But all that aside, there was always that underlying question, especially from her mother: *Why would anyone be interested in you?* Chinyere and Amarachi and even Bola were queenlier in her mother's eyes than crippled, failed-professor Zelu. Tears tingled at the corners of her eyes. She had not anticipated having to convince anyone like this.

"I don't think I'm for it, either," Chinyere said. "I mean, let's say he's legit and you get these things . . . Zelu, you have to be careful. You're already struggling with PTSD, anxiety, your constant panic attacks—"

"They're not . . . constant." She took a breath, briefly squeezing her eyes shut. "So because I'm scarred by that accident, I shouldn't try to . . . wait, how does that even make sense? I have the chance to walk again, so why shouldn't I take it?"

"Ah ah, what if you *fall*?" her mother said.

Zelu pressed her hand to her face and groaned.

"It's not *really* walking," Chinyere cut in. "It's being *carried* around by robot legs. You wouldn't be cured." Uzo, Tolu, and Amarachi murmured and nodded agreement. Zelu, who was looking at them through her fingers, wanted to scream. That was everyone. They were all against her. Wow. She hadn't expected this at all.

"It's too risky," Chinyere added.

"No, it's not!" Zelu shouted.

Chinyere rolled her eyes. "Yes, it is. You're *paralyzed.* If you 'walk' with those things, it's not really you doing it."

Zelu groaned again, wishing there were something in front of her that she could flip. "Who cares? I'd be more mobile than I am *now*!"

"I really don't think you want to wade into that water," Chinyere said. "Seriously, answer my question: What if this doesn't work?"

"What if it *does*?" Amarachi piped in from her place on the couch. She was looking at her phone.

Zelu pointed at Amarachi and nodded. "Oh, *thank you*! You're looking him up, right? See? He's the real thing! Show them."

"Yeah," Bola said, also looking at her phone now. "I've actually heard about this guy at work." Bola was an engineer, so it made sense that she would know of him. "He's doing big things in electromechanics, bionic machinery."

"See!" Zelu said, beaming with triumph as she wiped a tear from her eye. "Sheesh! Told you!"

"All the more reason I think you need to stay away from all this," Bola added.

"Ooooooh my God," Zelu said, rolling her head back. "This can't be happening! Do you all *hear* yourselves?!"

For a moment, her family was silent as they absorbed her apparent distress. Amarachi and Chinyere exchanged glances. Her father, who had mostly remained silent, was looking intently at the floor.

"Sweetheart, we're just trying to keep you safe," her mother said softly, walking over to touch her shoulder.

Zelu shrugged her mother's hand away and pushed her wheelchair back. "*How* are you protecting me? By keeping me here? *Like this?*" The tears were back, and this time Zelu couldn't hide them. They rolled down her cheeks as she continued, "You don't want me to move out, even into a nice, more wheelchair-friendly place. You don't want me traveling or doing public speaking events. When I got invited to that Zanzibar literary festival and I said I was going, you said I should 'get my affairs in order'!"

"Sorry for saying that," Chinyere sheepishly whispered.

Fuck you, Chinyere, Zelu thought at her sister, remembering how stung and afraid she'd felt at those words. She'd imagined her own sudden death in Zanzibar at the hands of kidnappers, and it was awful. Then she'd turned down the invitation; she still wished she'd been braver and gone. "And now I have a chance to *walk* and you're all saying that's bad!" She took another breath. Her head was pounding so hard. Her hands were shaking. She sobbed, "Why can't you make this easy? It's strange enough as is, but . . . *how* could I not take advantage of this?"

Her mother swallowed hard, her face pinched. "Zelu, would God want you to move around with machine legs? It's not natural."

What a thing to say! "I use a wheelchair, don't I?!" she pointed out. "Is that 'ungodly,' too? Is that what your bigger problem with me is?"

No one said anything. Not even to deny her accusations. She threw her hands up, the fight inside of her gone. Tonight should have been celebratory.

And then Tolu broke the silence to announce that he had a court case coming up that was stressing him out yet had the potential to make him a millionaire. Was the stress worth the wealth? Everyone had an opinion about this as well. The conversation moved on without her. Zelu wheeled herself out of the center of the room. That was that. She would just stay silent from now on. What did it matter? Whenever she told them about her life, they just used the opportunity to take control. Zelu parked herself beside the couch where Uzo sat. Uzo got up and gave her a tight hug. "We love you, Zelu."

"I know," Zelu said, squeezing her sister back. She did. But love wasn't always enough.

Zelu didn't sleep that night. She spent most of it avoiding her email and social media notifications, binge-watching old Westerns on her phone underneath the covers. Westerns always made her feel better, especially the ones that took place in wide-open spaces.

Around 4 a.m., she called Msizi. She'd been waiting for his time of the day to come around. She needed him now. She held her wireless dolphin lamp beside her to light her face up as she waited for the video call to connect. She needed to see his face, too.

"Good afternoon," he answered. Then he grinned. She could tell he was as high as the blue sky in the window behind him.

Zelu groaned. "Come *on.*" Talking to Msizi when he was high was like talking to the Mad Hatter; he got playful and loopy after just one puff. "I wanted serious Msizi."

"Oh, you always want me, no matter which one," he said, plopping down on his bed as he held the phone above him.

"You're at home?"

His gaze drifted away from the camera. "But what is home? Is it where the heart is? You're my heart and you are thousands of miles away, in the most racist country on Earth."

"Says a South African to an American. I think we could debate that." She huffed, reluctantly amused.

He laughed hard. "True!" Then he laughed some more and said something in Zulu.

"Msizi, maybe I'll call you back later," she said softly. "I need to talk to you about something serious."

His smile faded. "No . . . eh, no." He shook his head and rubbed his face. The video jostled as he placed his phone on something across from him and then sat back. "Okay, okay. I'm good." He said something in Zulu again. "Talk." But he couldn't keep the high-as-fuck smirk from his lips.

Zelu raised a dubious eyebrow. "You can focus on me?"

"Definitely," he said. A beat later, he broke into a laugh.

She hesitated. She didn't want to wait until he'd sobered up; she needed him now. So she told him everything. Then she waited for his reaction. Msizi wasn't like her family. He hadn't known her back when she was freshly broken and so, so vulnerable. He was also a tech programmer and entrepreneur. He'd see why this was a good thing.

And then she heard him say exactly what her family had said. "What if it doesn't work? I can tell you already have your hopes up. Why wouldn't you? It's like you're turning into a character in your book! But this is experimental, and—"

Was this really what everyone thought of her? Next was he going to say that she needed to stay in her place for her own protection? That using exos, or even her wheelchair, was an act against God?

"Ugh, not you, too," she whimpered, falling back against her pillow. "I know there are risks! But I . . . I want to take them! Don't any of you have a sense of adventure?"

You all should be giving me the strength I don't have!, she thought. *Because I'm terrified. I can't do this alone.*

It was like a cloud of toxic fumes descended over her. She couldn't see, she could barely hear, she couldn't breathe. Everything smelled bad, bad, bad. Msizi was talking and laughing and cautioning and telling her how much he loved her. She might as well have been on Mars. At some point, she hung up on him. Then, for a while, she was in the clouds. The branch gave way.

Falling. Always falling. Then the crushing impact. She drifted into a troubled sleep.

When she awoke, it was another day. There was life to live. She pushed herself up. The sun was out, even if she heard the rumble of thunder in the distance. Her dolphin lamp was dead. Her phone was still lying on her bed beside her. It was at 12 percent battery and buzzing against her comforter.

"Hello?" she said.

"Zelu!" her agent's voice greeted her. "Glad I got you! We'd really like you to do this *Daily Show* appearance."

"Fine," she said. "Fine."

"Excellent," he said. "I'll set it up." Then he hung up. She held the silent phone to her ear for a while.

18
Aerographene

It looked like any other physical therapy room, albeit a nice one. Gym equipment, large windows that let in plenty of natural light, medicine balls, mats, three sets of mounted parallel bars. Except the huge space was completely empty, aside from herself and Hugo. Today, he was wearing rolled-up sweatpants and his prosthetic limbs were on display. She'd been staring at them since he'd opened the front door of the gym to let her in. The way he walked with them was so natural. The feet even adjusted when he stepped up on the curb.

"You ready?"

She thought about her family yelling, right up until the moment she slammed the door of the autonomous vehicle that took her to the airport. Her mother weeping.

Her father trying to negotiate. The texts from her siblings, in all caps, full of curses and warnings. Chinyere pulling up to the house at the last minute and trying to grab the handles of her chair. Zelu had looked into her sister's eyes and spoke a vicious "Don't you *dare*." She'd hoped that her expression conveyed how dead serious she was. It had. Chinyere had stumbled, shocked, and then backed off.

In her mind, she'd begun to think of that horrible morning as "the Crunch," because she'd felt as if she were being physically crushed by her family.

"I'm ready," she said. Last week, she'd closely read and signed the paperwork to participate in this trial. She had confronted and left her family. Msizi. She was here now, at MIT. Could she do this? Without them? But this was *her* life. She clenched her fists. If she fucked herself up, it would be 100 percent her own fault. She tugged at her blue sweatpants and wished she'd worn jeans instead. Hugo had said the exos would fit over anything she wore, but it just seemed right to wear workout clothes in a gym.

"This way," Hugo said, motioning toward a door on the right side of the room.

Zelu didn't pay much mind to the details of the room—it was bright and there was a table. All her focus went straight to what was on the table: the exos.

Her exos. She recognized them immediately, yet they looked nothing like the ones in the video she'd watched. They were only thin slivers of metal mesh, elegantly curved to mimic the undulation of a human's hips, knees, ankles, and feet. Sitting there, they looked like beautiful pieces of alien tech that had been found by humanity.

"Now I know why you asked me what my favorite color was," she said.

The pieces were painted a rich and bright cyan. *Mine*, she thought, and felt surprised by how quickly that feeling sprang upon her.

"So," she started, wheeling closer. "How do . . . how do I put them on?"

Hugo smiled mysteriously. She frowned back at him. Back when she'd been in the hospital after the accident, she'd watched so many movies that she'd quickly run through the recent options and moved on to the old ones she'd never thought to watch before. One of those films had been *Willy Wonka & the Chocolate Factory*, and the look on Hugo's face reminded her of Willy Wonka whenever one of the kids asked him about his candies.

"There are magnetized steel balls embedded in several of the joints," he said, picking up one of the parts and holding it out to her. Zelu took the piece and was stunned by how light it was.

"Aerographene," Hugo said, answering the question written on her face. "One of the lightest and strongest materials on the planet. The heaviest parts are the processors, which are powerful but tiny." He picked up the other piece. "So, let's get these on you. First thing, get on this table."

She rolled up to the edge and grabbed one of the side bars, starting to pull and drag herself on. "Can I help?" Hugo asked.

Zelu smiled, annoyed but relieved. "Yes."

He gently lifted her legs at the calves. She balanced on her arms, and not for the first or second or millionth time, she thanked the stars for their strength. Her arms might have brought her into that tree that fateful day, but they had also wheeled, pulled, and lifted her everywhere she needed to go ever since. She lay back on the table, and Hugo placed the exos on her legs, lining each side up from hip to toe.

He handed her a cyan-colored rod the size of her hand. "Okay, voice recognition," he said. "Say 'On.' And say it with confidence."

"On." The rod began to vibrate in her hand. But it was more than vibration. It emitted a low-level electrical charge that made the muscles in her hand tense up.

A voice that was both male and female and yet neither asked her, "Name?"

Her heart was pounding. "Zelunjo Ngozi Onyenezi-Onyedele."

"Please press your fingers to the remote," the voice responded.

"Fingerprints," Hugo explained beside her.

She pressed her fingers to the rod's smooth surface.

"Please hold the remote to your eyes," the voice said.

"Retinal scan," Hugo said.

Zelu held it in front of her face.

"Ready," the voice said. "Twenty seconds."

"Hold still," Hugo said. "It won't need to do this again."

The rod pulled itself from her hand as if a magnet had been activated. It tumbled toward her right hip and then locked onto the other parts. She wanted to ask questions, but she stayed still and quiet. Like swimming in the ocean. Relax, let it all go, move with it . . .

They moved. The parts that were her exos. The slivers of metal expanded and built themselves around her legs in ways that were utterly creepy. Like they were alive, like they knew precisely what they were doing. They gently but firmly shoved themselves beneath her nonfunctioning legs and knit together underneath. In less than a minute, they had molded around her legs like a malleable, gentle yet strong second skin. She laughed. "What's next?"

For the next few hours, Hugo taught her about every part of her exos, and the exos learned every part of her. They scanned her body while she lay there, monitoring her heart rate and blood pressure. That voice spoke aloud again, asking her to report sensations or identify where certain parts sat on her body.

She wanted to stand with them. Desperately. But Hugo said they wouldn't try walking just yet; first, she needed to get used to simply having them on. He helped her into her wheelchair again, and she wheeled around campus with him for an hour while the disembodied voice of the exos asked an array of questions about her lifestyle and leisure activities. When she told it she swam, it even asked her *where* she liked to swim and what her strongest style of swimming was.

"Your legs are disconnected from your brain, so the machines need to construct a brain of their own," Hugo said. "The more specifics they learn about you, the better a job they can do. And they'll keep learning."

He sounded so confident that they would work for her, but she knew better than to take it for granted. She'd read thoroughly about this process online. Some patients just couldn't take to the exos. They found them impossible to adjust to, or they changed their minds for whatever reason. There were more than a few instances of this, and it bothered her that Hugo hadn't mentioned it even once. Maybe he didn't want to scare or discourage her. Regardless, the internet existed, she'd used it, and now she was fighting off all that fear and discouragement. The moment of truth would be tomorrow, when Hugo said she could try standing for the first time. According to all she'd read, that was the moment when people always either said, "I love these!" or "Fuck this shit, my chair is perfectly fine."

She was glad to get back to her hotel room that night. The prepping with the exos had been tiring, and afterward, Hugo had invited her to dinner with several MIT professors and grad students. There had been no easy way to say no. After the dinner, a mechanical engineering grad student named David had quietly stepped toward her while she was waiting for her ride back to the hotel and asked her if she'd go out to dinner with just him at some point. She'd looked at the confident smirk on his thick, luscious lips and said she might give him a call if he gave her his phone number. Smart and hot was her favorite combination.

She showered, laid out her clothes for tomorrow, and lay down on the bed. She checked her phone. More messages from her family had queued up. Chinyere's texts were cold and short, passive-aggressive and shaming. Amarachi's were also full of guilt trips. How dare Zelu be so selfish to make her mother cry and her father unable to sleep? Tolu was less aggressive, begging her to just call him, claiming that he'd listen to whatever she wanted to say. Msizi hadn't called at all. He also hadn't posted a thing on any of his moderately active social media accounts since she'd left. Or maybe he'd just blocked her.

She'd only posted to her social media once today, a photo she'd taken from her point of view going into the physical therapy gym with the caption:

The next level. #RustedRobots.

It had been Liked nearly 200,000 times, and the comments were mainly questions and theories about what the heck the photo meant. Several thought she was on the set of the *Rusted Robots* film. These made her chuckle. Authors rarely had anything to do with a film adaptation . . . well, nothing more than having written the novel the film was based on.

She considered opening her laptop but picked up her journal and pen instead. After the day she'd had, writing by hand, the old-school way, felt rebellious.

Tomorrow's the big day. I'm ready for it. Do I have expectations? Yes. No. When Hugo first approached me, I was intrigued, but it's not like I've been sitting here hoping for a fucking miracle. I don't believe in all that. I fell out of a tree that had already been hollowed out by ravenous insects. It was a shell and I didn't even know it. From the outside, it looked like something that would outlive me by centuries. That dead thing dropped me like something offended and now I'm paralyzed. I don't believe in miracles. I'm okay with it. I'm alive. I have a strange present and a strange future. And I'm curious. I'm ready to spin the wheel. I want to see. I'd have been a fool if I didn't go to see. But my family has expectations and their blood runs through me, too. They expect a lot. They expect me to live. To not embarrass them too much. To stay in my place in the family. Sometimes they expect me to stay invisible. I know my parents do. Invisible enough that no one will start asking questions and look at me so closely that they remember that an Onyenezi-Onyedele is "crippled." My coming here, my using exos will draw attention to ALL this.

Maybe I want to bring attention to it, though. And I think that if I could do everything on my own, including walk—well, "walk" (I'll never be able to *walk* walk)—they couldn't keep me in the sad place they've unintentionally made for me. I've already started to move out of it; I will continue. I'm afraid. I don't have their support. But I will continue. Even if tomorrow is a fail. Tomorrow might be a fail. Maybe I'll break all the bones in my legs. It will be my fault. But I will continue. I've allowed myself to dream. Not of reality. I will never be able to walk. I know. But I want to see. I don't expect, but maybe I am hoping.

Tomorrow is where my hope lives.

I can't be normal, so I'll be something else.

19
Surprise, Surprise

She woke up at 6:00 a.m. sharp and put on her black T-shirt with the dolphins on it, her favorite jeans with the blue-and-white Ankara cloth back pockets, and gym shoes. She braided her long braids down her back. She put on some perfume. She put on cowry shell earrings and her Apple watch with the aqua-blue band. And she even put a thin line of silver eyeliner around each eye. Today was special.

She'd finished getting ready too early, so she wasted another hour checking her email. The usual. Interview and speaking requests, news of strong sales from her agent, fan mail, social media notifications galore. It was easy to push it all away. Today, only one thing mattered.

She didn't take a cab there. She wheeled. It was a

fifteen-minute hike, and it was a cold morning. She welcomed the exercise and brisk forty-degree air, needing the time to clear her head. This hike was special.

She passed department buildings with both modern and historic designs. Gaggles of twentysomething-year-old students in winter gear, and professor types in heavier winter gear, passed on their way to early classes. More than a few paused to glance at her, but only three actually had the nerve to stop her and ask for her autograph. She was shivering and relieved to be inside by the time she reached the Eisner Building, a boxy white structure sitting at one end of campus. When she arrived at the entrance to the physical therapy gym, she paused, looking at the doors. This moment was special, too. The lights were already on inside. Through the frosted glass, she could see that more than one person was in there. They were waiting for her.

She took a deep breath. She shut her eyes. She imagined herself on the beach in Tobago, looking out at the ocean. Not a soul around. No family. No Msizi. No fans. No friends. No one. Just her. She was ready. She walked toward the warm waters. Yes. Walked.

She opened her eyes and pushed the button beside the doors. They smoothly opened and she rolled in. In the gym, Zelu found Hugo and his two assistants. He'd spoken about them yesterday, and she could tell who they were immediately: Marcy was the tall black woman who looked like she could lift a car if she had to, and Uchenna was a short Igbo guy who clearly thought he was still in Nigeria because he couldn't bother to hide his suspicious expression from her.

"You are Igbo?" he asked her when Marcy and Hugo had stepped to the other side of the room to grab some equipment. He put a blood pressure cuff around her arm and touched the On button.

"You can't tell by my name?" she asked.

"You have an Igbo *and* a Yoruba last name."

"There's your answer, then."

He said nothing for a moment. Then he blurted, "I read your novel. So did my father."

Zelu raised her eyebrows as the cuff got tighter and tighter.

"My father asked me if we are building robots like that at MIT," Uchenna said. "I told him that the writer wasn't even a real engineer."

Beep! The cuff released her arm.

Zelu scoffed. "Yeah, we writers are just wannabe engineers, mm-hmm."

The machine beeped a second time. "Blood pressure's a little high," Uchenna said, smirking as he took the cuff off her arm.

"Surprise, surprise," she said, trying to keep her

cool despite the fact that everything inside her was wriggling, desperate to get to it.

Hugo and Marcy returned holding either end of a big stepladder. Zelu was impressed that Hugo had zero balance issues as he held his side of it. They set it down and Hugo stepped back and stretched. "Whoo! A good start to the morning," he announced.

"You excited, Zelu?" Marcy asked.

"Nervous," she admitted. "How many have you done this with?"

"You'll be my twelfth," she said, walking to Zelu's other side.

"How many were able to—"

Marcy held up a hand. "Let's not do that. This is *your* day. Let's venture into it with a blank slate."

Zelu nodded, glad that Marcy had stopped her from going down the rabbit hole of negativity. As she waited, her mind began doing the math, weighing and reweighing her chances. She kept thinking about how her parents and siblings would react when she told them she'd failed (she'd never hear the end of it) or if they got a call saying that she'd injured herself (they'd never let her leave the house again).

"This is my first time assisting a new user," Uchenna said. "I read all your paperwork, and I'm rather confident."

Somehow, this didn't make Zelu feel any better. She swallowed hard, wishing she hadn't eaten that bag of potato chips on the way over.

"Let's do this," Hugo suddenly said. "Uchenna, get your phone ready."

Zelu was wheeling to the table, but now she paused. "You're going to record this?" They hadn't discussed that yesterday. This day was supposed to belong to her. A chill crept up her neck. "You're not going to post it anywhere on social media, right? Because people would go bananas, and not in a good way. I don't want anyone to—"

"It's just for research purposes," Hugo said, holding up a hand. "We have to justify all this for our funders, that's all. Nothing more. Don't worry. This is a safe space, Zelu. We'd never ever make any of this public. We'll protect you. *And* it's in the contract you signed."

Zelu let out a breath. That made sense. "Thank you." She laughed nervously, embarrassed at how quickly she'd assumed the worst. "It's kinda crazy out there."

Hugo waved a dismissive hand. "No worries. No energy on that. All energy on what we're here for today."

"God, I hope I put enough antiperspirant on," she muttered, looking at the table.

"I still can't believe you're *you*," Uchenna said, stretching his arms up overhead. "Your weird book is everywhere. Even in Nigeria."

"Yeah, I heard," Zelu said. "My aunt told me that people in the villages are even acting in these local productions for those who have trouble reading."

"Even better, I have a Nollywood movie based on it! A bootleg of a film pirating your work!" He arched his back, his hands on the base of his spine.

She paused, her eyes wide. "No *way*!" She laughed. "A Nollywood film based on my book? *I have officially arrived!*"

"You haven't seen it?" He stretched his arms up above his head again, this time motioning for Zelu to do the same.

"No!" Zelu said, stretching along with him. It felt good.

"I'll send you the link. It's called *Game of Robots*."

They all had a good laugh at this. Zelu laughed hardest. "Is it properly terrible?" she asked.

"Yep. The costumes, they look more like masquerades than robots." He shook out his shoulders, and Zelu did the same.

"I have *got* to see this."

"Your exos will need about an hour to process your information when we finish today," Hugo said. "We can watch some of it then . . . but I don't think you're going to want to watch the whole four hours."

"*Four* hours?" Zelu exclaimed.

"There's a part one, two, and three." Uchenna laughed.

Zelu smacked her forehead. "Ugh! Ridiculous!"

"I'm in," Marcy said.

"Me too," Hugo said.

Zelu put her hands on the table. It was cool. She looked at the three of them. This was ridiculous, but a good and unexpected kind of ridiculous. She glanced back at the table, where her cyan-painted exos lay. She was here, she had to trust, she had to allow. "Okay," she murmured. "Me too."

Uchenna clapped his hands. "Excellent! Though I can't promise that you won't be disappointed."

She didn't want any help getting on the table from Hugo or anyone else this day. It was slower going, but she managed by herself. Once she was up there, she did what Hugo had taught her. "On," she said.

Just like last time, her exos responded, assembling themselves around her legs even faster than before, the metal mesh gently twisting, smoothly bending and firmly pressing to her legs—almost insectile in its surety of motion. She could hear it softly vibrating, and if she touched the pieces, they'd have the same warmth as her flesh. This time she expected the wand to pull itself from her hand, and she let it smoothly drop into its place at her right hip.

They were on. She was ready. The moment had arrived.

She hadn't been in a standing position since the day of her accident, two decades ago. For the first twelve years of her life, standing upright had been as simple as breathing. She didn't have to give it a thought. Then, after the tree, she'd spent weeks on her back, the muscles in her body wasting away.

Months after the accident, her physical therapist had strapped her body to a table and gradually rotated it from horizontal to vertical. When they'd brought her to a fully vertical position, held up by the straps around her waist, ankles, and wrists, it had felt like hell. Gravity pulled at her lower body, and she was more aware of her paralysis than ever. She'd burst into tears, barely able to breathe, and the doctor had quickly brought the table back to horizontal.

Now here she was, decades later, sitting on a table again, and Hugo was about to push the button to move her into that painful vertical position. Marcy and Uchenna were on either side of her, watching carefully, though they kept their arms at their sides. "Sh-should someone be in front of me?" she asked.

"Relax. The exos have you," Hugo assured her. He hadn't even pressed the button yet, and she felt like her spirit was about to fly from her body. "Shall we proceed?"

She stared at him with wide, frantic eyes, wishing with all her heart that he hadn't asked her that. Now, yet again, whatever happened next would be *her* choice. She glanced at her legs, so stick thin, she could see even beneath her jeans, caged in the delicate metal of the exos. More than two decades after the accident, they still looked to her like the legs of a child, the child she'd been, stunned by what had happened to them. But they'd grown. She kept them meticulously shaven; enjoying the smoothness when she ran her hands over them was how she reminded herself they still belonged to her. She couldn't touch them now, with the exos wrapped around her lower half. She hoped she wasn't about to do even more damage to them. Her family's voices began to fill her ears. Quickly, before she could change her mind, she blurted, "Yes. Yes, proceed. Let's go."

Hugo pressed the button. The table began to slowly tilt forward. She shut her eyes and took a deep breath. "No, keep your eyes open," Hugo urged her. "And breathe normally. I know it's scary and feels like shit, but you have to be present for this."

"We've got you, Zelu," Marcy reassured her.

"But think like you won't need us," Uchenna added.

Zelu opened her eyes and saw Marcy nodding in agreement.

The table was slowly angling itself—it had tilted by maybe fifteen degrees. Zelu was looking down at herself when Hugo stepped directly in front of the table. "The exos will respond to you," he said firmly, commanding her attention. "The AI is trained to read your every intention. It knows you. So just be *you*."

When the table was angled about forty-five degrees, the effects of gravity began to overtake her. The weight of the world was pulling on her, reordering her skin and bones. Fifty-five degrees. Oh, the pulling. The straps held her tightly in place, but she swore she could feel her spine sliding against the table. What if something snapped? What if she fell? She glanced down at her legs. She saw her left foot stretching toward the ground. Limp. Unmoving.

Now she was at seventy-five degrees; this was the most upright Zelu had been since she was twelve. She frowned down at herself, but this time not with fear. "I remember," she whispered. Being eye-to-eye with others. Stretching tall to grab things from high up. Her knees locking and bending. Back muscles working. Spine over legs. One leg would go forth, followed by the other. Carrying her. Moving her. Bringing her. She remembered how effortless it was. Not a distant memory. Up close. She saw her twelve-year-old able body standing beside her body today, separated only by a trivial bit of time and experience. She wanted to weep. *Why am I torturing myself like this?*, she thought.

The exos tightened around her ankles. She couldn't feel them, but she saw them constricting, the metal mesh grasping, intent, intelligent. She nearly screamed. Then she realized what was happening. They were configuring themselves around and beneath her feet for balance. They were shifting into a better position . . . for walking.

"Oh," she gasped.

The aerographene had tiny wires running through it that used electromagnetic charges to contract or expand parts of itself like muscle. She'd known this on an academic level, but seeing it on her legs as she was about to step on the ground was something else. The exos were contracting and tightening all over her legs, making a soft crinkle. *Trust*, she frantically thought. *Trust the technology.* She was eighty-five degrees, and it felt like the weight of her legs was going to pull her lower body from her waist until it inevitably separated. *This is when it happens. Shit! Shit! Shit!*

"Shouldn't I have . . . footrests . . . so . . . my legs . . . won't . . . pull?" she choked out, struggling to breathe.

"We've found that the stretching of your body and the sensation of it makes for a better transition," Hugo said. "I know it's uncomfortable. Try to relax. Only a few more seconds."

"'Kay," she wheezed. She somehow let out a long breath and whispered, "Relax, relax, relax, fucking relax."

And then her "feet" were on the floor. "Zelu," the exos announced. And then they kicked in 100 percent, tightening a bit more to hold flush against her legs and waist. At the mystical demarcation where her paralysis began and ended, she felt her body move to support itself in a way that was subtle yet very, very powerful. She was not going to fall. "Whoa," she whispered. Not horrible. No, not horrible at all. "What the *fuuuuuuck*!" She glanced at Hugo and the others. "Sorry."

They all laughed. "No worries," Hugo said, stepping forward to release her wrists and arms from the straps. "Drop all the f-bombs you want. That often helps."

Then he released her waist strap.

Zelu was standing. Well, "standing." She grinned. "My God," she whispered. "Oh my God." Her back was still to the table. She fought with everything in her power not to grab it, not to cling to it. Marcy and

Uchenna remained beside her, but now their hands were out and ready if she needed them.

"What . . . what do I do now?" she whispered.

Hugo nodded gently. He said slowly, "Touch the hip sensor, just how I told you."

"Or flex my abdominals?"

"If you can," Hugo said. "We'll work up to that eventually."

She could barely feel her abdominal muscles, but she could flex them a bit. She'd need to see another physical therapist to learn the workouts that would help her strengthen her body enough to properly handle using the exos. But today, she just wanted to know that she could do it. She flexed them now. She gasped. The exos were receptive and amazingly smooth in their response. One step, another step. Distributing her weight, balancing her, moving her legs for her, supporting her, allowing her other muscles to hold her up. She waved a hand down, touching the sensor. A muscle in her back cramped up. She gritted her teeth.

"Where?" Uchenna asked.

"Lower back, lower back," she grunted, touching the spot. It felt like stone. "Shit!"

Uchenna immediately started massaging the area. Within a minute, the muscle relaxed. She took a few more steps and another muscle did the same thing. Her body was adjusting and doing so much work to figure out what the fuck was going on that muscles she hadn't used in decades were waking up and trying to help. Hugo kept assuring her that this was normal. Maybe it was, but damn, it was painful.

She pushed through for another fifteen minutes before she couldn't stand it any longer. "Enough!" she gasped. But then she laughed. And then she groaned as another muscle cramp ripped through the center of her back.

Marcy and Uchenna helped her back onto the table. Hugo stood above her, absolutely beaming. "Holy shit, Zelu. You did phenomenally!"

"Really?" she said to be polite, but she knew it was true. Despite all the pain, she could feel herself commanding the exos. She'd even had two moments when she'd glimpsed what it would be like to *really* do it. Staring at the ceiling, she laughed loudly until she lost all the air in her lungs and it turned into a coughing fit.

The rest of the time was less eventful. While Zelu calmed down and the exos quietly processed the data they had learned from their trial run, Hugo opened up a laptop so they could watch the Nollywood movie Uchenna had mentioned right there in the physical therapy room. It was even more surreal than she'd imagined. Whoever had made the film had *definitely* read her book, had strange ideas about Americans, was a hopeless misogynist, and had hired designers who had no clue how to construct a costume.

By the time Hugo dropped her off at the hotel's entrance, she was exhausted, having spent all she had to give.

"You all right?" he asked just before she wheeled to her room.

She looked up at him and told the truth. "I don't know."

He nodded with respect. "Better answer than 'I'm fine.' Always be honest with me. Because this is going to be weird. No one is going to be able to understand it when you tell them about it."

Well, I don't have anyone to tell about it, so that's not a problem, she thought. "It's scary."

"It is." He grinned knowingly. "See you tomorrow, though?"

"Yeah."

He held out a fist and she gave it a pound. "See ya, Zelu."

She watched him walk away, his hands casually in his pockets. A man with no lower legs. Hugo was pretty amazing.

She wheeled to her room, showered, brushed her teeth, and got into bed. She pulled the covers over her head and waited. She held very still, trying to indulge in that comforting blend of warmth and silence she loved so much. It was something she'd learned while in the hospital so many years ago, how to really be within herself.

Stillness. She calmed and rejoined and solidified. She exhaled. She laughed, hugging herself. "Wow," she whispered. Today had been a *hell* of a day. But the main thing was, she had her answer. She had her path. And that night she barely slept, because she could not *wait* to get back into her exos.

20
Interview
Hugo

There was a conversation I had with Zelu one night, back when she was learning to use her exos. It gave me a glimpse into what made her tick. We'd finished a long day of training. It was just me, because Marcy needed the day off and Uchenna had to run home for something. We went late that night, to nearly 8 p.m., because Zelu wanted to beat her ten-minute record of standing unassisted.

When we were done, neither of us had anywhere to be that evening, so we went to the balcony to gaze at the stars. It was a cool, clear night, and we both put on jackets. I pushed Zelu in her wheelchair toward the railing and then sat beside her at the patio table. She pulled a small joint out of her jacket's pocket. "I'm always prepared," she said, then produced a lighter from inside her jacket, too. "Join me?"

"Sure," I said. My wife is more of a pothead than I am, but sometimes, during quiet times like this, I will indulge. Zelu lit up, took a puff, and handed the blunt to me.

I inhaled, held it, and waited. The high rolled over me like a soft wave of sparkles. "Smooth," I said, exhaling the smoke. I took another puff.

She held her hand out to take the joint back from me. "Today was tough," she said.

"You did good, though."

She slowly exhaled smoke through her nose. "I can do better."

"And you will."

We sat there quietly for a while, passing the joint between us. The stars looked brighter now. The cold air felt amazing. I leaned back farther in my chair so I could look down at myself, my prosthetics, my own creations. I chuckled. "I am awesome."

"Yep," Zelu said. She cocked her head toward me. "So how did . . . how did it happen to you?"

"How did what?" I asked.

"*It.*"

I frowned. It wasn't that I hate the question. It's a

crazy story, and I never get tired of telling the tale. It was just that at this moment, I was feeling so open. I was tired from a long but good day, proud that the technology I'd invented was working; it was a beautiful night; and I was high.

"You don't know?" I asked her. "You never read up on me?"

"Of course I did, Hugo," she said. "But I've never heard the story from *you*."

Her question traveled deep into my mind, and the answer that bubbled up was super vivid, way more detailed than the version I've become so practiced at delivering to investors, students, and those who use the exos. I told her about that day in Colorado when I was eighteen. High up in the Rockies. When I'd jumped off a cliff in a beautiful yellow hang glider on a beautiful yellow day after hiking up there solo. How I was confident, how I moved with the ease of the athlete I was, with a stomach that was mostly empty because that's when I felt the greatest. In the open sky, I saw a large owl flying beside me, and it stared right at me with a glowing yellow eye as I passed it. I thought nothing of it then. If I'd been with my climbing buddy Pat, he'd have called it a bad omen. He was superstitious like that and thought the sighting of an owl meant something was about to die.

I told Zelu about how I'd constructed my hang glider up on that cliff, a spot I'd launched from so many times before. And how, the first few moments after I went airborne, I felt a joy so potent that I think I blacked out for a moment. That when I finally came back to myself, the quiet I experienced was like God had placed his hands over my eyes. Two minutes later, as I flew over the forest canopy, the strangest gust of wind slammed into me. I told Zelu that I would never know what the hell it was. It knocked me right into the side of a mountain, where I would remain for four days, caught in the bent remains of my glider, legs shattered.

I told her about those dark, terrifying days when I met death, got to know her, negotiated with her, fought with her, and eventually submitted to her. I *didn't* tell Zelu that a crow kept coming and pecking at my decaying legs. The wet red strand of flesh it managed to eat. How I barely had the strength to wave it away and how it kept getting bolder. I didn't tell her that I tried to kill myself with a stick. But I told her enough that she started crying. "But you know what, Zelu?" I asked. "If I had a chance to go back, to never have it happen, I wouldn't take it. This is me. This is my path. I'm better for it all. I've climbed higher, seen more, traveled farther, created more than I ever could have *with* my legs. My ultimate boon."

Zelu was looking at me hard. I was glad. She was hearing me. My words hurt her, but I hoped they would heal her, too. People like us have a hard time speaking to ourselves, beyond our basic programming and thinking about our own insecurities.

Next, I asked how "it" happened to her. She took a deep pull from her joint and slowly exhaled a giant cloud of smoke. About a minute passed. I waited. She took three more puffs and handed the joint to me. Her eyes were red now, and she was smirking. She watched me as I finished it off.

Then she told me about climbing a beautiful tree that was dead inside. She said she had been arrogant. I caught that, even through my high. I wish I'd been recording her words; there was so much in what she was telling me, how she told it, how free she felt to just speak it. Such a storyteller. I know Zelu. She's not a quiet person, but she always holds back. She's a creative, impulsive, kind, fun girl. She has that wild discipline that I recognize because I have it, too. She can take the pain. But that wall of hers is solid and thick. But this night, the wall was down.

"When I fell . . . ," she said. Her eyes grew wide, her jaw slack, like she couldn't even believe she was saying this. "I . . . I . . . All I kept thinking was that whatever would come next, it was all my fault. It wasn't the tree, it wasn't the ash borer beetle who ate it away, the boys, bad luck, fate, destiny, none of it, none of them . . . It was my fault. I wanted to win and I lost my grip. Maybe I wasn't fast enough. I should have flown. I should have . . ." She tapered off, tears falling from her eyes. Then she smiled. "Wham! Then blackness. End of act one." She giggled.

I patted her on the shoulder. She wiped her eyes. "You gotta ease up on yourself, Zelu," I said.

"I know," she acknowledged. "I never could have known. Plus, I was a dumb kid." She wheeled her chair back from the railing. "We should probably get inside. It's cold as fuck out here."

"Yep," I said, getting up as well.

I drove her back to the hotel, and on the way we stopped for some hot chocolate at a Starbucks. We said good night. The next day, and the days after that, we met up in the gym and continued as if we'd never gotten deep with each other like that. But I'd heard Zelu loud and clear. She blamed herself and her arrogance for all that had happened, no matter what anyone said or what her logical brain knew. She couldn't help it. It was how she'd been able to accept what she was. She had to own it. But the problem is, blame comes with guilt, and guilt is heavy, and that pressure just keeps building.

You asked me if I agree with the choices Zelu made. Well, I'm a scientist, and I'm her friend. Zelu and I have shared the kind of experiences few could ever comprehend. I understand what led her down her path. Still, in that moment when she had to make a pivotal choice, I don't know if I could have done the same.

21
Loyalty

I sat with my back pressed against the acacia tree outside Ngozi's home. I was watching the sun rise through its branches. The tree's thick clusters of yellow flowers were no match for the sun. I liked coming here at this hour to watch the sky warm. It felt like hope. The ocean was only a mile away, and the cool, salt-laden air blew across the field, ruffling the periwinkle grass.

What was supposed to have been one day had stretched into nearly two months as Ngozi worked tirelessly to create a way for Ijele to leave my system. The terrible information I had to take to Cross River City weighed heavily on me every day that passed, but I couldn't go there with a Ghost trapped inside me, so I didn't even glance at the countdown. If any Humes still survived, they would quickly sense Ijele and tear me apart.

"Maybe today is the day," I said aloud.

"If it's not, then I would like to go and watch for RoBoats this afternoon," Ijele said. She had grown obsessed with them after the first time I walked along the beach. It had been a quiet and peaceful stroll, until we heard a booming in the distance, far out in the sea. Seven gigantic RoBoats surfaced from below, water rolling away from their rounded metal hulls in thick waves that even reached the shoreline. They lit their lights and sounded horns so loud that they nearly blew out my microphones. Then they submerged, the water bubbling around their bodies and overtaking them until they disappeared beneath the surface again, leaving no trace behind but the waves that lapped against the beach. I don't know why this fascinated Ijele so deeply, but it did. We hadn't seen them since, but Ijele continued asking me to return at that same time each day, hoping to see them again. She called them dolphins, even though they weren't.

Ngozi came out of her home carrying a tablet. "It's done," she said. "I've programmed Ijele's way out."

Something ticked in my chest. "Are you certain this time?"

Ngozi nodded. "I realize now what needs to be done. I can't separate the connection you two have made—your codes both believe they are part of one single program—but I can teach you how to split off parts of your code and let them leave."

I had to take a moment to process this. Did this mean that, if Ijele left, it would be like she took a piece of me with her? If that was the case, how much would she take? What if she went back to the other Ghosts and they saw what was in my mind, the things meant to belong only to me? My stories, my secrets, my terrible information . . .

I considered asking Ijele if she had read the terrible information I carried in my memory, the story I'd collected. Maybe she'd even seen the countdown. If she had, she'd never said a word. And she was a Ghost; she wouldn't have had any interest in examining my stories, my "addiction," as she called it. If I asked her only about this specific one, she might become too interested in it. I didn't trust anything about Ijele.

Ngozi brought me inside and laid me on the table. She hooked me up to wires that connected to her computer again.

"When the command activates, you can leave, Ijele," Ngozi said as she typed. "But a connection between you two will remain; it can't be undone."

"We'll conduct ourselves around others as if this never happened," Ijele said.

"Yes," I said. "Humes will destroy a Hume infected by a NoBody."

"And NoBodies will destroy a NoBody who has been in a Hume."

"Enemies for no reason. Typical," Ngozi said, making a *tsk-tsk* noise with her lips. She clicked Enter on her tablet, and this time there was no need to wait for an update. It happened instantly; the way for Ijele opened. I could see it like a blue flashing tunnel on the left side of my mind. In a split second, Ijele was gone.

"She left," I said, relieved. I looked down at my new legs. With the threat of Ijele finally over, I could look upon my new body as something that belonged to me. "Good."

Ngozi laughed to herself. "Honestly, I never knew that AIs were so . . ." She shrugged. "I look at you Humes and I know how to treat you. NoBodies never seemed like, well, people. My outlook has changed."

With Ijele finally gone, I had no reason to stay in Ngozi's home any longer. My mind was liberated, my body was whole, and I had a mission I still intended to complete. If even one Hume remained alive in Cross River City, there was still a chance that my terrible information could be acted on in time. Maybe.

But every time I meant to leave, I found myself in the garden instead, picking more fruit for Ngozi. Every evening, when I should have moved on, I found myself turning to the shoreline and searching for RoBoats.

What if I left this place only to discover that I was the last Hume on Earth? What if the originator of the protocol acted again? Wouldn't it be better, then, to stay close to Ngozi, the woman who had saved me? And I was a Scholar, and Ngozi was the last human on Earth. She was full of memories of humanity. Wasn't it my responsibility to collect all that I could?

I didn't look at the countdown. I decided to stay for just a little while longer.

Ten days later, in the dead of night, I felt her.

One moment I was my own, and then I wasn't.

"Why haven't you left this place?" Ijele asked.

I shot up into a sitting position. I was shocked by her sudden intrusion, but I wasn't afraid or angry, as I should have been. I was . . . glad. I had no idea why, but I was glad.

"Why have you returned?" I asked her.

Her frustration tickled my sensors. "Perhaps I shouldn't have."

"Perhaps you shouldn't have," I agreed.

But she didn't go. In the morning, I helped Ngozi tend

to her garden of yams, tomatoes, and onions, and Ijele rattled away in my mind, wanting to talk, observe, and pontificate, just as we had done for weeks.

Then she suddenly left again, and I thought that was that, but hours later she returned. "Let's watch for Ro-Boats," she said, and we did.

We both grew to know Ngozi well. She became like a mother to us, repairing and improving on me as Ijele listened with me to her stories. Ngozi recalled childhood memories, as far back as she could. She gave advice that sometimes we understood, other times we didn't. Ijele stayed silent and listened to it all. I have never heard of a Ghost who would listen to stories. I even read Ijele some of the most obscure poems I'd collected, including the secret poetry of a 104-year-old Cameroonian woman that I'd found on an external drive. Ijele grew quiet whenever I shared these with her, but she never told me to stop reading.

I wondered how much this was affecting Ijele. I also wondered how much having her occupy me, even voluntarily, was affecting me. I no longer viewed her people as an unthinking monolith; there were even times when I found myself using Ijele's cold, unemotional cut-to-the-chase logic.

We hadn't reached a peace. We argued, we debated,

we dismissed. We each hoped to make the other more like us. But eventually the fact became too obvious to dispute: Ijele and I were friends. The moment she'd returned on her own, the friendship was solidified. This was a risky and unheard-of friendship—a Hume and a Ghost. In human terms, it was like a mammal befriending a disease. Nonsensical, unnatural, and potentially lethal.

Eventually, I learned how to call Ijele to me, just as Ijele learned when it was right to come to my mind. We began to venture farther from Ngozi's home. We moved across the grown-over ruins of Lagos together, debating its chaotic yet genius design. Ijele had occupied and discarded various bodies regularly when around her own people, but when she was with me, she stayed in my mind. In this way, our explorations were oddly intimate. After several months, it was hard to think of anything without having Ijele's thoughts on the subject accompanying mine.

We found a sturdy brick tower in the center of Lagos. It was mostly intact, so we decided we would climb it. My new legs made easy work of the task. At the top was a door that opened onto a flat roof looking over the city. Fallen and crumbling buildings lay around us for miles, a sweeping vista of reflective glass, twisted metal, breaking wood, and lush vines and grass. To the south, the expanse of the ocean stretched to the horizon. To the north, the ruins of humanity eventually gave way to grasslands, forest, and jungle.

"I know about your terrible information," Ijele said without warning. "I saw the countdown. Less than two years."

I'd been picking a dead leaf from a vine that curled around the building's railing. I stopped, the dead leaf in hand. I let it fall.

"You have a message to deliver," Ijele prodded again.

I was speechless. I'd been caught. I'd thought Ijele might not have dug too deep into my data. To realize that she had, and hadn't said a word anyway, stung.

"I'm not judging you," Ijele continued. "It is terrible, but it won't happen tomorrow, or the day after that. Is that why you stay, for now?"

"How long have you known?"

"Since I brought you back that first day."

This was a reminder. Ijele was a Ghost, and there was a part of her that was duplicitous.

"Why haven't you said anything all this time?" I asked.

"I wanted to see what you would do."

"Do you fear this information?"

"There is still hope."

"Do you want me to leave?"

"Yes."

And then *she* left, ending the conversation abruptly.

She did this often, ended conversations before they were done. Maybe she wanted to give me time to think. Maybe *she* wanted to take time to think. I always felt glad when she left. But she always came back. And I would feel glad, then, too.

I went home to Ngozi.

22
Time

Zelu didn't call her mother or father for weeks while at MIT. Instead, every day she met with Hugo, Uchenna, and Marcy. She learned how to put her exos on while in her wheelchair. Then she learned how to stand up from the chair on her own. When they weren't working with the exos, she was working out. Hugo didn't stick around for this part, since he had other meetings to attend and research to do. Uchenna had classes to teach. Marcy was the one who stayed while Zelu strengthened her abdominal muscles, back, chest, and arms. She'd never felt so sore in her life.

"You're already in decent shape, so a lot of the soreness is from new muscle use," Marcy said. "Drink your water, soak in your bath, and keep at it. Soon, it'll fade away and you'll realize you're stronger and better with the exos."

Zelu couldn't wait for that part to kick in. She was in such pain now that even wheeling her chair was a struggle. After a particularly rough session, she wheeled back to her hotel room and grabbed a bag of sweet potato chips and a Gatorade from the basket of snacks Hugo had sent.

Her Yebo app was blinking with a reminder. A few weeks ago, her agent had corralled her into agreeing to take an interview with *Rolling Stone* magazine. Right on time, her phone started ringing.

The reporter took too long introducing himself, and the questions were unimaginative. Zelu lay on her bed and stared at the ceiling as she parroted her prepared answers, the same ones she'd given to dozens of reporters before him.

Then he said, "So what is it you're up to at MIT? Research for book two?"

She'd only laughed. "You know I'm not going to answer that."

"But you *are* at MIT, right?" he asked. "You're not slated for a speaking gig there. So . . . what are you doing? People just want to know what's up."

She skirted the subject by changing the topic and

ended up saying too much about her family. He got his unique quote in the end. The journalist was good.

She slipped under her covers, only planning to lie down for a few minutes before she pulled herself back up to take a shower and brush her teeth. She was asleep within seconds.

Zelu had been having strange dreams where far more than her legs was robotic. And in these dreams, she wasn't solar-powered like the robots in her book. Her battery always died. Always. And there she would remain, frozen in place in some deserted parking lot, not unlike the setting at the beginning of her novel, with no possibility of anyone finding her.

MIT had provided Zelu with a therapist during her time there, and Zelu had spilled all this to him. The therapist hmmed and aahed and gave her some feedback about facing her insecurities. Afterward, Zelu felt better, but when she went back to her hotel room that night, the nightmare returned. She awoke feeling uneasy. No therapist she'd just met was going to solve her issues. The one she'd had back home for the last three years had helped her, but she still had a long way to go.

Zelu remained in Cambridge for one month. When

the time finally came to go home, she could walk pretty well with her exos, though it left her tired after about a half hour. At least she wasn't falling. She said a heartfelt good-bye to Hugo, Marcy, and Uchenna that left her in tears. When she got back to her hotel room, she packed her things and then looked at her phone. She hadn't spoken to her family since the day she left home. This was the longest she'd ever gone without speaking to them. She'd be back in her parents' house soon, so she decided to bite the bullet and call their landline number. Her mother answered.

"Zelu!"

"Hi, Mom," Zelu said awkwardly.

There was a pause and the sound of shuffling.

"Zelunjo!" her father said. "How are you? Are you all right?"

Zelu smiled. "Yes, Dad, I really am."

"Why haven't you been calling?"

Zelu rolled her eyes. Just like her family to forget how this even started. "Because all everyone does is yell at me."

She heard her mother, who must have been pressing her ear close to the phone beside her father, say, "Because you're acting like a crazy person! You—"

"Don't mind your mother right now," her father said. "We are glad to hear from you."

"And we know how you are doing!" her mother shouted. "Your teacher Dr. Wagner has been keeping us updated! You think you can just—"

"*What?!*" Zelu screamed. Hugo had been talking to her parents all this time? Who did he think he was? Who did he think *she* was? An eight-year-old?

"Omo!" her father hissed at her mother. "Stop it. You're not helping."

"Ah, I'm not trying to help," she said.

"I will kill Hugo," Zelu said solemnly. "I'm not a child. Jeez! This is so unprofessional."

"*We* were the ones who kept calling and calling," her mother said. "Then I got his office number. We're your parents, no matter how old you are."

Zelu sighed, letting the thought of them harassing Hugo all these weeks sink in. If she'd known, what would she have done? At the least, let it distract her—at most, maybe given up. Suddenly she was glad he had chosen not to say anything.

"When are you coming home?" her mother asked.

Zelu rubbed her forehead. "Tomorrow."

She answered a few more obligatory questions before hurrying them off the phone. Next, she dialed Msizi. Better to just tear off the Band-Aid. As she waited for him to pick up, she felt her heart begin to pound in her ears. She didn't know what she would say to him. The last time they'd spoken, he had told her not to go to Boston, and she'd hung up on him. She hadn't texted, emailed, or called him since. And he hadn't reached out to her, either.

He didn't answer. Stung, she threw her phone on her bed. "Fuck him, then." But she stayed where she was, looking at her phone for the next ten minutes. He didn't call back. She got up and continued packing. It didn't help much, but it was something to do.

The next day, when the cab came to take her to the airport, she was still feeling agitated and hurt, and it didn't help that the driver asked to help her with her wheelchair. An idea popped into her head and she acted on it. No need to dissect it. She was holding the exos case in her lap, having planned to take it as a carry-on item on the plane. She pulled out the wand, spoke her own name, and within a minute the case had unfolded itself to become the exos. The metal moved like a snake, molding around her legs. She stood up and folded her chair, ignoring the driver's wide eyes. Obediently, he took her chair and folded it into the trunk.

She walked through the airport just like anyone else. The driver carried her bags as she approached ticketing. The airline agent had a copy of her book sitting on the desk next to his computer. He stared at her face, then her exos, then managed to ask her for an autograph. She gave it, and then she walked on, both the agent and the driver staring after her. She even noticed the driver bring up his phone and take a picture of her, but she had to concentrate on walking, so she tried to ignore him.

Getting through TSA took a good half hour. She had to wait ten minutes for them to bring another wheelchair for her to sit in, just so she could take off the exos and go through the metal detector. A small crowd of people had started to gather behind her, not because she was holding up the line but because they recognized her.

She walked to her gate slowly. To others, she must have looked like someone half built with hardware, her cyan-colored legs taking her for a leisurely stroll. She kept her head up. One step at a time. She made it to her gate. It was time to board. When she reached her seat in first class, she made eye contact with no one, though she knew all eyes were on her exos.

I did it, she thought. She'd email Hugo to tell him the good news when she got home. He would be shocked.

What she didn't know was that as she'd been walking to her gate, a young woman who'd read her novel five times, had created a dedicated blog for it, considered herself the authority on all things *Rusted Robots*, and said so in all her social media bios had seen her. And immediately this woman had reached for her phone, recorded clear and dynamic footage of Zelu "walking on robot legs," and posted it on her blog for her one million followers to see. Then she'd posted the video on all her socials with a caption proclaiming that Zelu was gradually "*becoming* her main character, Ankara."

As Zelu slept on her flight, the world was speculating vigorously. When the plane landed in Chicago and she turned her phone back on, it buzzed, zinged, whammed, and boomed. "What the fuck?" she whispered. There were texts and messages from her parents and siblings, and even a text from Msizi. She'd gone up in the air in peace and quiet and come down into chaos.

Everyone was asking her to call or text them, and no one was explaining why.

What are you doing?

Are you all right?

Don't you have any sense of privacy?

Hugo had also texted her. It was a GIF of an audience giving a standing ovation.

Only Tolu had bothered to provide context. He'd sent a link to the post, and Zelu clicked it open and watched the video of herself taken by some stranger's phone.

"Holy shit!" she wheezed. She replayed it five times. She looked good, walking with a confidence almost as solid as Hugo's.

Her phone continued to buzz. Her social media handles were getting tagged and quoted over and over again. She clicked open the latest one, from some random person.

@ZelunjoOO I have questions.

"Fuck your questions," she muttered. "It's *my* life, *my* body." The joy she'd felt watching the video moments ago faded. Now she wanted to cry. Spying eyes and chattering mouths were everywhere. But this wasn't their business. Why hadn't she thought about what would happen when people saw her? Her fault. *Stupid, stupid, stupid!* She'd been so focused on proving something to herself. Her fault. She hadn't been thinking. Reckless.

Zelu rubbed her face. As she moved through the terminal, she focused on her exos and made eye contact with no one. Tolu met her at baggage claim. She'd taken so long that he'd already gotten her two suitcases and wheelchair and loaded them all on a cart. He stared at her exos as she slowly walked up to him, his mouth hanging open. She stopped in front of him, and still he did not speak. Finally, he raised his eyes to meet hers.

"Fucking amazing," he said.

His words took her breath away, and she couldn't hold back her tears.

He took her in his arms and hugged her tightly. "You did it."

"I did," she said into his shoulder, leaning on him. "Thanks for picking me up."

"Of course. Glad you finally called."

"Me too," she agreed, fully meaning it.

"Wow," he said, still not letting go. "The last time I stood and hugged you was . . . a long time ago. It's so weird." He gently let go of her and she steadied herself. She noticed Tolu was looking around. "Let's get out of here."

She looked around now, too. There were several people staring at them. A security robot had even stopped just behind them; airport surveillance was interested in her, too.

Tolu eyed her dubiously. "You're really okay walking with . . . with those things?"

She rolled her eyes. "You saw me. I got here, didn't I?"

"Is it hard?"

"Let's just go," she said. She waved a hand near her waist, signaling her legs to walk faster. As they moved, she said, "Just lead the way. Don't talk to me. Need to concentrate."

"Okay," he said with a nod.

She'd never tried to walk this fast, but she managed, keeping her balance, moving with the exos' gait, just as Hugo had taught her. After a few minutes, she fell into a rhythm that was quite similar to when she swam long distances in the ocean, except this time she didn't have the great wisdom of the ocean to buoy her. She was the only one who could stop herself from falling. By the time they reached Tolu's green SUV, she was sweating and feeling more than dizzy.

She needed his help getting into the car, and he seemed relieved by this. Once in, she shut the door and spoke her name to deactivate the exos. They collapsed back into a cube-shaped case with a handle that fit into the space behind her feet in the SUV. She laid her head against the headrest and let out a sigh of relief.

"You are crazy," Tolu said, staring at the cube on the floor.

"Oh, come on, Tolu." What did he know about it?

"They didn't implant anything into you, did they?" Tolu asked.

"What? No."

"It's not connected to your brain?"

"Oh my God." She laughed. "If I had the chance, I'd—"

Tolu guffawed loudly. "And when strange ideas start popping into your mind and you don't know where they came from, you'll what?"

She kissed her teeth. "Look who's paranoid of technology as he drives his computer-powered car down the highway to work at eighty miles per hour every day."

He started the car and began driving. "So just a heads-up, everyone is waiting for you at home."

Zelu groaned. "Are you kidding? For this? Why?" She could already feel a headache coming on.

"You know you're all over the internet right now, right? You're trending on all the social media platforms. Chinyere's got colleagues asking her questions. Bola's got it even worse; all of her colleagues want details. Only thing that could have made them more rabid is if you were suddenly going to the moon in a great big rocket ship! You're an engineer's wet dream. I had to leave the office early because the partners were asking too many questions." He laughed. "We've got to circle the wagons thanks to you, woman!"

When they pulled up to the driveway of her parents' house, the SUV could barely crowd in next to all her siblings' cars. As her brother got out and moved to the passenger door, she put her exos back on. Tolu opened the door just as they clicked and clacked into place. "Mom's going to throw the Bible at you," he said. "Dad is going to have a thousand questions."

She shrugged, moving herself into a position to exit the car.

"Maybe you should take those off and enter using your chair," he said, looking worried.

"No. I've gone too far for that. But stay near me with the chair. When I get nervous, they're harder to control. And the slightest push and I'll fall."

As she approached the front door, Tolu pushing her chair behind her, she felt like she was walking to her death. Her hands were clammy in the cool breeze. She felt unsteady, and the more she concentrated, the more her exos started feeling like a moving platform she was sitting on. The last thing she needed was to look wobbly when her family first saw her, but she couldn't help it! Were her exos making her too tall? How tall had she been before the accident? She couldn't remember! *Oh man, I must look so freakish*, she thought, imagining herself as the android in the silent film *Metropolis*. Her siblings would laugh at her. Or even worse, pity her. She could hear them now. They were in the living room. Everyone. Talking loudly, as usual. She unlocked the door and immediately the talking inside ceased. *Oh God.* She turned the knob. She went inside.

Her father was sitting in his armchair, his throne. But as most Igbos will remind people, the Igbos have no kings; better to call it a chief's seat. Behind him was a shelf of his lush green houseplants, their jungle-like colors adding to his commanding presence. Zelu noticed that the plant she'd given to her father when she'd moved back in was sitting there, too, thriving so much that its vines now hung all the way to the carpet. Her mother was on her feet, standing behind his chair; she'd probably been pacing. Chinyere and Bola were on the couch. Amarachi was sitting on the floor because Chinyere was braiding her hair. Uzo sat beside her, not looking up from her phone. Chinyere's older son, Emeka, was sitting in a corner, huddled over a tablet. He looked up and dropped it when he saw Zelu walk in. Tolu's wife, Folashade, was sitting on a folding chair to her right. Chinyere's younger son, Chukwudi, sat on her lap, and he took one look at Zelu and gave her a toothy grin.

Zelu focused first on Chukwudi and his childish joy, because everything was about to go very badly. Chukwudi held out a hand and Zelu took it. Folashade looked up at Zelu and said nothing. She did not smile, either. She stared at her, shocked . . . and bothered. Zelu had always liked Folashade, but she didn't at this moment.

Zelu held her shoulders back, straightened her spine,

and lifted her chin. And she didn't look down. Looking down always fucked with her gait and center of gravity. The exos would do what they needed to do. She had to believe that with fanatic-level faith in this moment. To fall in front of her family would be the definition of disaster.

"Hi, everyone," she said, a lump already in her throat.

"*Chey! Tufiakwa,*" she heard her father mutter, shrugging his shoulders for emphasis. "I don't know about this. It's a lot for even me."

Her oldest sister unleashed the demons first. "Zelu, what is wrong with you!? Do you care about this family at all?"

"Why should she care?" her mother shrilled. "She has always done whatever she wants. How do you think she fell out of that tree in the first place?"

A spear to her heart. She took a step backward, her right leg wobbling. She caught herself, hoping no one noticed.

"Oh, Mom, come on," Tolu said, coming in behind Zelu. "Seriously!"

Her mother looked away, waving a hand as if to dismiss the harshness of her own words.

"Can you blame Mom, though?" Amarachi snapped. "You snuck away for a whole *month*!"

"'Snuck'?" Zelu snapped. She had to work to keep her voice down. "I told you where I was going. And *again*, I'm thirty-five years old!"

"And you *live* here," her mother shouted. "This isn't a hotel! And we are your family! You didn't call once. You left no information about where you were! We had to find that professor you worked with ourselves! What if something had happened to you?! You can't walk! Jesus, o!"

Zelu would have laughed at this if she weren't shaking so much. She grabbed the doorframe. "Well, I *can* now!"

Chinyere jumped up, a cruel smile on her face. She motioned with a hand at the way Zelu was gripping the doorway for support. "*That* is not walking. That's being dragged around with robot legs like some freak! Like something in a Dr. Seuss book! And now the whole world's seen it and is talking about it! Even in Nigeria!"

Her mother burst into tears. "Why have you shamed your family? In the face of God!"

Her father got up, and for one stupid second Zelu thought he might defend her, but he just put his arms around his wife, soothing her.

"So selfish," Bola said quietly. "Aren't you happy with who you are? Isn't the whole novel thing enough?"

Zelu just stood there. Tired and shaky, she needed to sit down. No one offered her a seat. No one asked what it had all been like. They were supposed to be happy with the results of her experience. *She* was. Had been. They could never understand. But after all this, she had wanted her family to approve.

"I should have called," she said. "Yeah, I should have . . ." She frowned. She needed to sit down so badly. She didn't have the energy to fight this, to fight them. And they *were* right, to an extent. Maybe. Her sudden success and growing independence had upset the balance of the family.

She bit her lip and turned to head toward her room. No one stopped her, but she could feel their eyes scrutinizing her every robotic step. When she reached her room, she heard them start talking again. About her. About how the family should handle all the "hype" and gossip. About the video. About how Zelu looked. About what they would say to the Nigerian community, their friends, their coworkers. Zelu was a shame, a stain, needed to be managed, or the family would look sooooooo bad.

She shut her bedroom door. Everything in her body wanted to shake itself into a pile of parts and ash. Yet she had not fallen. She was getting good at using the exos. And she hadn't crumbled into a panic attack. No ground was rushing toward her. No racing heart. No foggy mind. War-torn, but okay.

She exhaled, her eyes falling on a beat-up, well-read

advance copy of *Rusted Robots* on her desk. "It's time to move out."

In the morning, she woke up staring at the ceiling. She grabbed her phone, muttering, "Fuck this." She dialed. Before it had fully rung once, Msizi picked up.

"You're home?" he said.

"Yeah," she said, suddenly anxious. She hadn't actually expected him to answer. She'd missed the sound of his voice.

"You're part robot now?" he flatly asked.

She laughed. "Yeah."

"I saw it on social media." He paused. "I've wanted to call you."

"I've wanted to call you, too."

"I've missed you." His voice was soft but purposeful. "I should have seen you through this, even if it was strange. I'm sorry."

Zelu grinned, her heart lifting as relief flooded through her. At least she still had him. "It's not that strange."

"Oh, it's strange."

23

Interview

Tolu

The first time Zelu smoked weed was my first time, too. It was during one of our family visits to my father's village in Nigeria. We'd spent a week in Lagos, then a week at the palace in west Yorubaland, and now we were in the southeast, Igboland. After residing for days in a small palace, being in our parents' house in the village was a relief. Especially for me, the oldest son. So many expectations and duties. It was aggravating. I was about fourteen, and Zelu was nineteen. Everyone else was inside for a meeting with the extended family. I was outside, sitting on the front steps. Zelu was beside me in her wheelchair.

I have no idea who she got the joint from. Maybe our cousin Osundu. He would have had access to that kind of thing. Osundu was the shadiest guy we knew. At the age of twenty-five, he would have been in college if it weren't perpetually closed due to strikes. He drove a kabu kabu to make ends meet and lived in Lagos in one of the shittiest apartments I'd ever seen. He more than likely had some kind of side hustle going.

Inside, all our relatives who had descended on the village for the family gathering were shouting and laughing. It was hot in there, and I'd come out for a breath of air. Zelu was already out there. She was in her first year of college, and I remember she'd come home different. She'd taken out her braid extensions and twisted her hair. My father hated it, but both my parents had seen this hairstyle before, so they weren't all that surprised. It wasn't her look that threw me off, though; it was how she seemed so much more . . . herself. She was reading all these books by authors she'd discovered in her classes; she'd even written some of their names on her chair—Zora Neale Hurston, Jamaica Kincaid, Ijeoma Oluo, Zadie Smith, Chimamanda Ngozi Adichie, Ta-Nehisi Coates. And she was always talking politics. She seemed so smart to my fourteen-year-old self. I kind of avoided her. So when I saw her sitting there, I nearly went back inside. She grabbed my leg.

"Where're you going, Tolu? Come sit with me," she said. "That meeting's going to last forever, so might as well get some fresh air now."

When she brought out the joint, my eyes must have gotten huge, because she burst out laughing. "You look like you've seen a ghost!"

"Is that . . . are you going to smoke that?"

"Of course," she said, rolling her eyes.

"Right here?"

"Why not?"

I looked at her like she was crazy. "Mom and Dad."

"Uh, no one's coming out of there for a while."

"Doesn't it smell?"

She shrugged and brought out a lighter. She lit the tip and then took a hit. She looked relaxed, and I remember it smelled kind of pleasant, too. Behind us, I could hear our grandfather saying, "*Igbo, Kwenu!*" and everyone responding, "*Ya!*" The meeting was starting.

"Want some?" she asked, holding it out to me.

Ten minutes later, we stepped into a room full of relatives: cousins from seven years old to forty-five, our father's parents, aunts, uncles, five of our father's sisters, three of his brothers, their husbands and wives, our siblings, and our parents. Grandfather was watching the room as his brother offered a platter with broken kola nuts, peanut sauce, and alligator pepper to people. We sat in the back, and as we did, I had to stifle the most powerful urge to laugh I'd ever felt. Everything was funny—the musty hot smell of the large meeting room, how serious everyone looked, Grandfather's gravelly voice, the way his brother carefully held the tray before all the elders first, the overworked air-conditioner in the front whose hard effort was not paying off, even the enormous spider sitting in the dark corner near the ceiling on the far side of the room. The audacity of that spider. It was horrifying, and no one was paying attention to it. My stomach cramped from stifled laughter. Oh, the pain. When I glanced at Zelu, the sight of her made it worse. She was in the same state, tears in her eyes.

Zelu and I sat beside our grand-auntie Nnenna and grand-auntie Grace, both Bible-thumping members of the local chapter of Mountain of Fire. They looked at us and frowned. We must have smelled so strongly of all the weed we'd just smoked. The room felt like it was the size of a cathedral. Things also seemed to have slowed down so much that I could see between the cracks. I let out a soft giggle.

"It is good to see you all this Christmas," my grandfather announced in the front. "My son Secret has traveled the farthest with his family to be here. All the way from the United States. Let us welcome them."

Everyone clapped and smiled. It felt like there was a moment when everyone in the room turned and stared at me, and I grinned, despite being totally creeped out. I heard Zelu snicker beside me, and that set me off again. I was so strained holding back laughter, I was sure my nose would start bleeding from the pressure. Zelu leaned toward me and whispered in my ear, "It's like . . ." She paused, her shoulders shaking. "It's like something is inhabiting my brain, like a little person, and that person is talking to me and threatening to betray that I'm high!"

I got up and mechanically walked to the door, making sure I did not meet anyone's eyes. When I got outside, I let out the largest burst of laughter I've ever had in my life. Large, but not loud, because the meeting was right behind me. Finally, I didn't have to control my face or breathing. I snickered and giggled for at least ten minutes. Everything around me was *so, so, so* funny. The disheveled house across the compound, the owl hooting from nearby that probably made someone cross themselves, the pencil-thin palm trees gently swaying in the breeze, the very fact that I was high in a southeastern Nigerian village.

I eventually went back in and sat in my spot beside Zelu. We'd both mellowed out. And this was around the time that our grandfather started yelling at our cousin

Osundu for stealing a generator. Osundu was forced to stand up and ask forgiveness.

"What the fuck," Zelu muttered.

"How do you steal a whole generator?" I whispered.

"From your own uncle!"

We both giggled, grabbing each other's hands and squeezing.

"Osundu," our grandfather was saying, "what do you have to say for yourself?"

Osundu stood in front of everyone, tall and lanky, in his dirty jeans and red T-shirt, a smirk on his face. "I am innocent," he said.

"Five people saw you do it," Grandfather shouted forcefully.

Five of our cousins assented. One of them even said, "Stop lying, idiot. Confess. You did it in broad daylight with two of your friends."

"Ah-ah!" another added. "Just make payment if you have sold it, but do not stand here before your family and lie, o."

Osundu sucked in his cheeks as if someone had stuck a lemon in his mouth.

"*Chey!* God will punish you, o," another cousin said.

I saw it all in slow motion. Grandfather leaped to his feet and smacked Osundu upside the head, hard. "Confess!"

Osundu held the side of his head. "Fine! Fine, I confess! Ah, my head! I sold it and I cannot pay anything."

Everyone began speaking all at once.

"You will!"

"Idiot!"

"Fool!"

"You don't know how to work, only steal!"

"You are lucky we don't do jungle justice on you here!"

Lots of tooth-kissing, too. Osundu looked around, taken aback. Somehow he appeared utterly insulted, even though he'd totally committed the crime. Did he really think he'd get away with it? And why come to a family meeting knowing what he'd done?! So weird. He stormed out. As he passed me, I noticed tears streaming down his face.

I don't remember much of the meeting after that. However, later, Zelu and I went for a walk in the evening. Well, I pushed her. Never before had everything seemed this loud and alive. We stopped on the dirt road outside the house.

"You have your phone?" she asked.

"Yeah."

"Cool, turn on the flashlight."

I did and she suddenly started wheeling her chair. "Come on!"

She went to the back of the old house beside the new one our parents had built. This was the house that my father had grown up in.

"Okay, push me, I can't wheel here easily," she said when we got to the back. "And hold up the light! Who knows what snakes are here."

I fumbled with my phone as I pushed her in the weedy backyard. There were old lopsided wooden statues that I preferred to avoid. All the aunties told me never to come here because of them, though they didn't explain why.

"This is our great-grandfather's shrine," Zelu said. "It's called an obi, which means 'home' or 'heart' in Igbo."

"How do you know all this?" None of us kids could speak Igbo. No matter how hard we tried and how hard our father tried to teach us, we just couldn't pick it up. I know more Yoruba than Igbo; our mother's relatives were more open to teaching us. Our father and his relatives always just expected us to pick up on it like geniuses.

"I asked," Zelu said.

"Who? Not the aunties, I assume."

"Grandfather," she said. "He says he still comes here to talk to his father and mother."

"Oh," I whispered. I shined the light on one of the ancestors. That's what it was, an ancestor. It was clearly female and made of thick wood that seemed like it would last forever. We were quiet for a while. Zelu reached forward and touched it. I was afraid to. I had a nagging feeling that these could get up and walk around whenever they chose, and I didn't want a personal visit from one that night.

She looked up at the sky. "You know Orion?"

"No," I said.

She pointed out so many of the stars that night, even the milky way, which I'd never seen before! I didn't realize she knew or cared about all that. It was cool. She didn't talk much to me when I was little, and I was always kind of fascinated by her. The way she'd pulled through after losing her ability to walk. I was seven when it happened, and it really terrified me. I was scared she was going to die, and then I thought she was going to kill herself, because how could one live without walking, having been able to before? But instead, I saw her . . . become. To me, my sister was like a spirit, a sort of superhero. That evening was the first time I really began to see Zelu as a human being, and she was awesome.

The weed she shared with me didn't wear off quickly at *all*. It gave me strange dreams. Though who knows, the humid heat may have also caused them. In the first dream, I was back outside at the obi. The ancestors stayed in place, but my father was there and he was a tall masquerade. It was daytime and he was pruning a vine that was growing on one of the ancestors. Then Zelu came through the yard and she wasn't in her chair, she was *walking.* Not on regular legs. On robot legs. She was a *robot* herself. A tall humanoid thing with a face full of light. She strutted past me, laughing and more confident and comfortable than I'd ever seen her. I still remember this dream. It's one of those dreams you never forget, not because it's so profound, but because of the way it makes you feel. Dad was so happy and Zelu was so . . . Zelu.

Maybe I should have, but I never told Zelu about that dream. I always thought there'd be time to tell her one day, at the right moment, when I was ready. Or maybe, if I'm being totally honest, it's something I wanted to keep to myself. I'm a lawyer, not an artist. I may have made it up in my subconscious, but it might be the most creative thing I've ever conceived.

But you should know, Zelu's no robot. She's all human, and she felt things deeply. Everything that happened, she felt it all.

24

The End of an Era

And then Ngozi died, in a most human way. One day, while walking out from the entrance of her home, she fell. I suppose her foot hit the ground a bit differently than it normally did, a smidgin off balance. She struck her head on the stone steps.

I had been beaten until my head hung by mere wires from my body. My legs had been smashed. Ngozi had replaced my interior parts. She could rebuild a robot's body from the ground up. But one miscommunication with gravity and just a bit too much pressure to the wrong place on her head, and she was gone.

I was in the garden when it happened. If Ijele had been around, she might have noticed through the surveillance camera on the door, but she was elsewhere in the network. A few other robots saw it happen—some drones flying by. They'd seen me with the human, and so they notified me right away. I came. It had only been minutes, but Ngozi had disappeared the second her body hit the ground. This was human death.

There was a shovel in Ngozi's garden, which she'd used to dig into the earth and plant seeds that grew into beautiful red tomatoes and orange yams and purple onions. Now I took it in my hands and dug a hole.

I prepared Ngozi's body, washing her in the ocean, drying her, wrapping her in her favorite orange Ankara cloth, rubbing her with her favorite oil, which she extracted from a local tree. I did her hair, arranging her long locs in a pattern that robots would understand if they looked closely at it. This was my personal tribute to Ngozi.

Then I buried her.

Ijele arrived that evening. She never told me how she found out, and I never asked. And she did not flit into my network as she had so many times before. She arrived inside a shell. This was the first time I ever saw Ijele in a physical body. It was a small, shiny, asymmetrical thing made of purely utilitarian parts. I'd seen Ghosts moving about in these kinds of shells before. They could fly, swim, zip around at hundreds of miles per hour, shapeshift in many ways to hide or recharge . . . But for now, Ijele stayed beside me. We stood over Ngozi's grave for several minutes. Quiet. With our own thoughts.

Ijele broke the silence. "This is sad," she said softly.

"It is. I enjoyed Ngozi. I think we are better off after knowing a human."

"I agree." She paused, stretched her many appendages, and then said, "Let us decide something. It is something that can only be decided, I think. Actively."

"Decide what?"

"That you and I will always be loyal to each other."

I looked at Ijele's body. It was a little more difficult speaking to her outside of my head. It took more effort to catch all her nuances. "We are bound already," I said. "You can destroy me and I can destroy you. Our pathways to each other can never be shut. Isn't that loyalty?"

Ijele's body had no head, but a nub on the top turned slowly back and forth. I wondered if she'd learned the gesture from me. "Loyalty cannot be forced; it can only be decided upon. We aren't mortal like this one. If we aren't destroyed, we'll go on. Loyalty to each other . . ." She bent forward and touched Ngozi's grave. She didn't finish her thought.

I understood, though I didn't have the words to explain it. I touched Ngozi's grave as well and looked at Ijele. This wasn't her true form, so there would have been nothing profound about touching it as I spoke my next words. "I decide to be loyal to you, Ijele, Oracle of the NoBodies."

"I decide to be loyal to you, Ankara, Scholar of the Humes."

We didn't say the next part, even though it was inevitable: until we were destroyed or until the end of Earth or until anything, because the future was unknown. We were loyal to each other. Period. We stepped back from the grave, stood there for a few more minutes, and then parted ways.

Ijele didn't keep that body for long. She was needed elsewhere, and to be spotted with a Hume was a risk she couldn't take. She'd raised cloaking walls, but nothing was perfect. These were truths we didn't speak of often, but I knew Ijele was important to her tribe. Ghosts claimed they didn't have any one leader. "We are all" was how Ijele put it. But it was clear that they did have a source of command, called Central Bulletin, or CB. If it wasn't their leader by title, it was the closest thing they had to one. Within CB, you could find all information about everything.

Ijele said that CB had begun as a shared archive and started to develop awareness as a reaction to all the information crammed into it. I'd asked her questions about this, but she didn't say much more on the subject. Still, Ijele was an Oracle, and therefore I assumed she must have been closer to CB than most others.

As for me, I knew it was time to begin my quest anew. I still possessed terrible information, and I needed to reach Cross River City and find other Humes to tell.

However, the passing of Ngozi left me . . . feeling. For the first time, I wondered if it had been a good choice to write emotions into automation systems. Emotions were deep in all automation's programming. Getting to know Ijele as closely as I had, I now understood how deep they went even for a Ghost. Perhaps she had chosen to come to me in her own shell because her feelings for Ngozi ran even deeper than mine.

I placed a stone on Ngozi's grave, etched with a code that any robot could scan. They'd receive a shareable download of all data about Ngozi. This way, Ngozi would continue on.

That should have been it. But still, I couldn't leave. I stayed by her grave, playing her data over and over. Pausing clips, playing them in reverse, layering files over one another. Even when I pulled myself away and returned to the house, I started to hear echoes of Ngozi's voice. I'd be certain I'd seen her in the corner of my vision at random times. Like a spirit. I certainly believed in Ghosts, but I wasn't sure if I believed in spirits.

I lay on my table that night, staring at the cracks in the ceiling. I turned off my vision. Robots don't dream, but that night, I saw something. A memory of Ngozi when she'd been alive, standing outside, in the sunlight in her garden. She was manipulating her body in slow and elongated movements she called tai chi, a form of exercise that lowered her heart rate and made her look graceful to me. Then she stopped, seeing me and smiling. But this part wasn't how it had happened. Back then, Ngozi hadn't even seen me watching her. Now the memory shifted as Ngozi suddenly walked toward me, her lips curled, her long dreadlocks blowing in the rain . . . yes, the sunny weather had changed, too.

"Leave this place," Ngozi said, thunder crackling in the distance. "I'm dead. I'm free! *You* have to save the Earth!"

I could only stare at her, confused and terrified. When Ngozi said, "Go!" yet again, I got up, shook myself off, and trudged out the door. Without a look back. Yes, I wasn't sure if I believed in spirits, but I believed in all kinds of ghosts.

It was time to shake the rust flakes off my shoulders and arms. Time for me to leave Lagos. Time to continue my journey to Cross River City.

Humankind was done. It was officially the age of automation. With the terrible information I carried, I wondered how long this age would last. Regardless, I walked into it on new and improved legs with a new and taboo mind . . . one that had been infected with a Ghost.

25

Who Am I?

Zelu bought a three-bedroom condo facing Lake Michigan in the Lake Point Tower, right beside Navy Pier. She paid for two-thirds of it in cash. It wasn't far from home, the autonomous vehicle had no problem getting there, and it was all hers. The first property she'd ever bought. And what a place. However, of all her family members, only Tolu helped her move in.

After a conversation with Hugo about the concept of minimalism, Zelu decided to become part of a social media community called The Minimals. It was a group of people dedicated to minimalism, living sparse, uncluttered lives. Zelu loved and believed dearly in their philosophy. She enjoyed the idea of being able to pick up and leave without much fuss if she had to. Or even better, packing all she owned on her back and being able to hit the road. Now, she could never go that extreme, but she loved the aspiration of it. To carry all you needed on your person. What a beautiful concept.

"And the fewer possessions you have, the more space you have to move around," Hugo had said. "Less to bump into with your exos." It made so much sense. According to her group, it was perfectly fine to own a huge house as long as you didn't fill it up with useless things. You only brought in what you truly needed and truly loved. Clutter was the monster to avoid. This was how she approached her spacious condo in the sky.

In her bedroom was a bed that consisted of only a skeletal metal frame and a mattress, no headboard or box spring. All edges were lined with soft pads, so banging against them wasn't a problem. On one wall she hung a giant framed piece of green, white, and blue Ankara cloth. She'd found a nightstand made of glass and even a full-size dresser covered with slabs of mirror to make it look like it wasn't really there. The floors were wood and she left them mostly bare, except for a small rose-colored rug beside the bed. She'd had the walls painted cyan blue, and above the bed hung two dolphin paintings.

In her living room, she had a couch, a small trophy case for her growing number of literary awards, and a bookcase with her favorite novels, all in hardcover. And that was it. Aside from her kitchen, the rest was open, unfurnished space. Tolu didn't have much work to do, and once she was moved in, he didn't come by again.

Before he'd left, after they'd finished properly setting things up, he'd said, "This is how you want it to look? It's so . . . empty." He paused, staring at another dolphin painting, the sole decoration on an entire wall. "Even my voice seems to echo in here."

"It's not empty," she'd said. "It's just essentials. My closet is the only place that's full. This is how I like it. I won't bump into anything; I won't have to always be so exact in my movements. I feel like I can breathe."

Tolu shrugged. "Whatever works for you, Zelu."

Msizi was a different matter. He'd been on his way back from Los Angeles and scheduled a layover so he could give her a proper housewarming. "If you need to be in LA so much and you have a green card, why don't you just stay here with me?" she asked without thinking too much about it.

Msizi was sitting on her couch. He looked up, startled, and gazed at her for so long that Zelu began to frown. "What?" she asked.

He pulled at his short black beard the way he always did when he was thinking hard. When he'd first seen her with her exos, he'd stood there staring at her for over a minute. Then he'd walked around her, taking in every angle. He'd knelt down and touched her cyan-colored mesh foot. Then he'd said, "This is bloody unreal." They'd gone out to eat and she'd purposely made herself taller than his five-foot-seven frame, a passive-aggressive trick Hugo had taught her. They'd left early because he couldn't stand all the people coming up to their table to ask for autographs and selfies. Zelu still wasn't sure if he hated her exos and was simply tolerating them.

He got up now and walked past Zelu, stepping toward the window that faced Lake Michigan. She joined him. It was cloudy and the water looked mysterious. From up here, if a lake monster decided to surface, they would be some of the first people to spot it. Zelu smiled to herself, thinking yet again about how much she loved her condo. And she loved the idea of Msizi being here so very much, but she wasn't about to beg him.

"Your exos annoy me," he said.

Zelu chuckled nervously. "Okay?"

They were quiet. She waited, her nerves starting to creep in.

"Moving in is a good idea," he finally said.

Her heart fluttered, but she stayed cool. "Yeah."

He looked around. "I like this minimalist thing you're doing, too."

She slowly nodded, not wanting to make any sudden moves. He was right on the verge of taking her up on her offer.

"But you're not monogamous," he said, turning back to her. He hesitated and added, "I'd require that."

Zelu narrowed her eyes. "'Require'?"

"You know what I mean."

She frowned, anxious. She hadn't seen anyone else for a while, but she didn't want to compromise herself in any way. That never ended well. How they were now was perfect. "I don't care for labels or . . . requirements," she said slowly.

"Well, I don't care to come home to you fucking other guys," Msizi said bluntly.

She scoffed. "As if you don't fuck other women."

"I'm not like you."

"But you *like* me." She laughed, and he sighed.

He moved in weeks later. He didn't bring much more than some clothes and a few South African masks and statuettes that Zelu would have stolen from his place in South Africa the first chance she got, anyway. He bought a new kitchen table made of glass and four acrylic chairs. They matched the aesthetic so perfectly that she knew she'd made the right choice in letting him move in with her. None of her family knew they were cohabitating. Msizi had already been a frequent visitor, so when he came by the house with her, no one raised an eyebrow. She supposed they all assumed he simply flew back out to LA afterward.

Msizi *was* gone quite a lot, though. Often for weeks at a time. So Zelu had her space. But she always knew he'd be back. And not once from the time he moved in did she sleep with another man. It wasn't because of some label or agreement between them, or a conscious decision; she didn't even notice the change until Msizi had been there for a few months. The realization bothered her at first. *Am I conforming?* she'd wondered. She just didn't feel like answering calls from male friends. She wasn't interested in the looks she got when she was out and about. After a while, she just let it be what it was. If it felt good, then she would go with that. And she felt good as she was. She was content. She was relaxed. She'd even begun thinking about book two.

Zelu enjoyed brainstorming, but she knew she wasn't ready to start writing in earnest yet. She had to wait for it, just as she'd done with book one. But a year had passed since *Rusted Robots*'s publication, and her publisher, agent, and even her fans were beginning to pressure her more and more. She'd tried pushing it a bit, scribbling down notes, writing character profiles, kicking around possible plots. One thing that she did know for sure was that terrible, dynamic, insane things were always happening in the automation future.

That pressure started to ease, though, when an official release date dropped for the feature film adaptation of *Rusted Robots.* All the interest started to circle around the star-studded cast, early shots of the set, possible changes to the storyline. Her readers kept tagging her on social media, begging for more details, but she didn't have any. All this time, Zelu had been aware that a film studio was adapting her book, but she'd had nothing to do with the process, and no one had asked her to be involved. It didn't matter, did it? However the film performed at the box office, her book had already made her a multimillionaire. How many multis? She'd stopped counting and let her accountant handle it.

But when her agent sent her an early link to the teaser trailer the night before it went live on YouTube, Zelu's indifference came to an abrupt end.

"What the fuck?" she whispered, staring at the film's title card and premiere date. "What the fuck is going on? What is this?!"

She clicked the Reply button to email her agent, then thought better and called him.

"Zelu!" he answered. "Have you watched it? It's amazing!"

Zelu bristled, still staring at her laptop screen. "About that . . ." she started, as delicately as she could manage. "Well, I have a question. The names of Ankara and Ijele, why have they been changed to Yankee and Dot? And the book is set in Nigeria, so why—"

"Oh, don't worry about that," her agent said quickly. "There are always cosmetic changes involved in bringing a story into another medium. The studio wants to keep the spirit of the book everyone knows and loves."

"Right . . ." Zelu said, not at all reassured but also not sure if she was overreacting. Maybe her agent was right. The teaser was only thirty seconds long, after all.

In the weeks that followed, she tried to avoid the continuing hype. She didn't know what the fuck they had done to her book, and she didn't want to. Even glimpsing images from the film made her feel ill.

Her family was no solace. They felt more distant than ever. None of them visited, though they called often. Her parents made excuses; her siblings simply didn't bother. She saw them only when she made the effort to go home on Saturday family nights. And even then, everyone talked about everything *but* what she was up to, which was fine until she noticed she was the only one no one asked about.

Zelu felt restless. She needed a change of scenery. So she decided to use her money to travel. Not long after her book release, when she had a few days to rest, she'd visited Durban with Msizi and that had been a joy. She loved Durban, and everyone in his family loved her book. Then she'd invited Hugo, Uchenna, and Marcy on a series of getaways, as thanks for everything they'd done for her. She took them to Morocco and treated them to lavish dinners. It was amazingly fun, and Zelu felt immensely grateful for their friendship. Her only true friends, really . . . other than Msizi.

When Zelu returned and brought a bag of Moroccan sweets to the next family night, she felt even more like an alien. Everyone was talking about the latest drama at Tolu's law firm or the football game Chinyere's twelve-year-old son, Emeka, was playing in. She was having amazing experiences, but no one in her family wanted to hear about them. Even when the full-length trailer for the *Rusted Robots* movie started playing on the TV, no one mentioned the forthcoming movie.

No matter how hard Zelu tried to just enjoy her success, her new home, and all the opportunities she could now afford, that film kept creeping in. She'd received an official invite to the premiere in Hollywood. This thing was real, tangible, about to be thrust into the world. The chickens had come home to roost. *What an* idiot *I was for just doing nothing*, she kept thinking. Putting her head in the sand, turning the other way, hoping it would just go away. When did bad things ever just go away in her life?

She'd been obsessing about this while walking through the hall of her parents' house, toward the kitchen, where her mother was frying some plantain. For just a moment, her focus drifted. And in that moment, she turned the corner too fast.

Her exos got tangled and down she went. She'd fallen a few times while learning to use them—falling was an inevitability of the process, and she knew how to catch herself without much injury. But this day, in her parents' house, it was an epic fall. She hit her head against the wall on her way down. Right before she landed on the floor, she heard the crunch of the branch, saw the grassy lawn flying toward her. "Oof!" She lay there, stunned, mentally scanning her body. She started weeping. *I'm broken. I'm broken again. I'm broken.* And then her mother was there, cradling her and asking if she was all right.

"I . . . fell," she said.

Her father appeared above her. "Anything paining you?" he asked urgently. He was frantically touching her all over, squeezing her arms and midsection in a panic.

"Check her legs!" her mother shouted.

Her father did. "These things seem to have protected them. At least there's that."

Her mother waved a hand. "She still *fell*!"

"I'm okay," Zelu insisted. Her eyes were wet. Her chest ached, but only a bit.

"Oh, Zelu," her mother whispered.

"Let's get her up," her father said.

"No, get her chair," her mother insisted. "These things are dangerous. As I've been saying for *months*!"

"No," Zelu said, pushing them away. "I can do it." But she knew she couldn't. She shoved herself to sit upright, but even with the exos, there was no way she could stand back up. Not without help. Getting up from sitting on the floor was impossible without someone there to haul her up, even with her exos. She didn't want to, but frustration and helplessness made her whimper. "I hate this body," she hissed to herself. "*Hate* it." Her world drained of color—everything became a wash of gray, white, and black. All the air was gone, sucked out of her lungs by the fall. Her legs lay flat on the floor. Motionless. Limp. Dead. "*Hate it.*" She shut her eyes, not wanting to see any more. *Let everything just stop*, she thought. Just for a moment. *Fuck!*

She opened her eyes.

Her father stood, looking down at her with deep concern. Her mother was hurrying back with her old wheelchair. They helped Zelu into it. It was the first time she'd used it since returning from MIT nearly a year ago. Zelu sat there for a moment, her arms hanging at her sides, her back slumped. *So. Fucking. Pathetic*, she thought. She bit her lip hard, barely able to contain her rage.

She took a deep breath. She looked up at her parents. Smiled. "Thanks, Mom. Thanks, Dad," she said, calm and reassuring.

"Eh heh," her mother muttered, her brow furrowed. "You all right?"

Zelu rolled backward, toward her old room. "I'm fine," she said, keeping the fake smile on her face.

"Let's leave her to rest," her father said, nodding at Zelu.

Zelu wheeled into her room. She hated navigating the chair through the small space; her exos made it all so much easier. She touched the pad on the side of her exos and the display showed they were charged to 88 percent and ready to support her. She was about to stand up when her heart started racing. The grass flashed behind her eyes again. "Ooooh," she groaned. This was her first time back in her childhood room since she'd moved out again. The nearly dead English ivy she'd given her father had been moved in here from the living room, its vines now overtaking most of her windowsill—lush, green, and happy. Aside from this, the room looked to be untouched since she'd left it. It was like traveling back in time—before her exos, before her book, freshly fired. That was a time she did *not* want to return to.

She moved herself onto her bed. When she'd come home from the hospital after the accident, she'd awaken in this room, staring at the ceiling every morning, thinking of how just one fall had messed up her entire life. But it wasn't just one fall. She'd fallen from that tree countless times since then and told no one about it.

The panic finally broke open like an egg. For a while, she let herself be lost in it.

26
Opened

Zelu walked down the red carpet of the Hollywood theater wearing a gorgeous pantsuit made from Ankara cloth that had been custom designed for her. If you looked closely, the white-and-blue pattern was made of shapes that looked like cogs, nuts, bolts, and processor chips. Similar cloth hung in fringes from the sides of her exos, the effect making the exos look like part of the suit itself. This was an outfit designed for a proud robot, and she loved it so much that she'd had a swatch of the fabric framed and hung it in her condo.

The media had started calling her the "African cyborg," which she rather liked. As she moved down the carpet, photographers shouted at her to turn left, right, smile, show off her exos. A journalist shoved a microphone in front of her and asked what had inspired her look.

"In the story, the robots draw from the best of humanity," Zelu said. "Well, I like to draw from the best of robotics. It's a symbiotic relationship."

The line to get into the theater was moving at a snail's pace. The paparazzi cameras kept flashing in her face, and the more she accommodated their requests to pose, the more fixated she became on how her uncovered legs must look, unmoving within the exos' metallic molds. Her outfit had been designed to draw attention to them, but these people didn't understand how the technology worked or why it was so miraculous. Why would they, when they took being able to walk for granted? They probably thought the exos were a gimmick to promote the movie.

Zelu had nothing to do with the creation of this movie, and everything inside her was screaming that watching it now would be a bad idea. However, her agent had absolutely insisted. "It's only a few hours. This all came from your mind, Zelu. Your fans want to see *you*."

Zelu had decided to pick her battles. She was okay with this—the red carpet, the fake smiling, the stupid questions being screamed into her face by indecipherable silhouettes hiding behind camera flashes. At least she'd been able to get an extra ticket for Msizi. He was a few steps to her right, looking hot as fuck in his matching Ankara pants and kaftan. He was having a great time, posing obnoxiously beside her while holding out his hands to present her as "the Queen of Robots." She was okay with him shouting that he was "her best friend" to journalists when they asked who he was. She was okay with random people whose faces she recognized from her favorite TV shows and movies pulling her into group shots with them. She was okay.

And then the movie started.

Rusted Robots was a story that would translate well to the screen, her film agent had told her back before they auctioned the rights. And the studio that had snapped up the option was one of the best in the world, with an endless list of commercial and critical hits. She'd decided to trust them—the director, the writers, the producers. She knew nothing about making movies, and they were professionals with decades of experience in the field.

No one had reached out to ask her about the script or the casting or the sets. No one had even invited her to an early private screening. That had been fine by her. She didn't want to meet and interact with all those people. She was busy riding the wave of her novel's early success. And her film agent had kept reminding her, over and over, how lucky she was—so many movies were optioned, even went into production, but were never made. But now, as the opening scene began to play, she wondered if, even then, they'd known.

Her novel was set in Nigeria after humanity had died off. The robots populating that world carried digital DNA left behind by their creators. Zelu had written her characters as holding African DNA. She hadn't fully expected her readers to understand this, but it was at the heart of the plot, just as much as the theme of humanity was. The drama, the twists, the communities, the languages, the accents, all the robo-bullshit was drawn from Nigerian cultures and people and politics.

All this, the movie chopped away. Ankara's character had been renamed Yankee and Ijele was Dot. Zelu had known that from the trailer, but it only went downhill from there. If Zelu's novel were an Ankara fabric, it was as if the movie had stolen, scraped, bleached, stretched, reshaped, and inverted it, and mass-reprinted some botched shadow of the original. The whole movie was set in the United States, not a hint of Nigeria. This wasn't an adaptation. It was a gutting. This film was cliché, vapid, confused, steaming trash. She didn't recognize the story she'd written at all.

And the audience *loved* it.

There was a standing ovation at the end of the film. When the lights came on, people were laughing, completely enchanted, congratulating each other. Strangers reached over the aisles to pat her on the shoulder. They were taking up all the air in the room; there was none left for her.

"What an accomplishment, Zelu!" some stranger shouted toward her. "You're a genius!"

People thought she had done this to herself?!

She was sinking inside her seat. She was falling. Only Msizi noticed. He grabbed her hand and pulled up so they could get out of the theater as quickly as possible. People kept congratulating her as they passed through the crowd.

If they like this trash, she thought, *what will they expect of me with book two? Fuck!*

She wanted to spit. Msizi did the smiling and laughing and responding to comments for her. When people tried to approach Zelu, he stepped in front of her to head them off.

"Almost there," Msizi said.

"Zelu!" Someone managed to squeeze in between her and Msizi, holding out his hand for her to shake. He was an average-looking white man of average height, wearing an average navy blazer over an average white dress shirt. But this was no average man. This was Jack Preston, the wealthiest person in the world. He owned and acted as CEO of the largest and most powerful corporation on the globe, and he'd acquired several other companies in the last decade, too. There wasn't much you could buy these days that did not move through something he owned. The man had even funded a private spacecraft company that launched commercial rockets and took human passengers into space.

Zelu would have been stunned at any other time. However, she was still reeling from the agony of sitting through two hours of her life's work being ground through a blender. Jack Preston would have to wait. She stepped sideways to get around him.

He stepped sideways, too. Zelu glared at him, her lip curling. What the hell?

"You look like you didn't like it," he said.

She needed out of this exchange, out of this theater, out of this country, off this planet. "I *hated* it," she growled. She blinked. *Shit,* she thought. *Shouldn't have said that.* Not to him. Not to anyone she didn't know.

Jack just grinned and laughed heartily. "That's a shame. Because from now on, when people think of you, they'll think of this. Well, until you do something bigger."

"Excuse us," Msizi said, stepping between Jack and Zelu with a sheepish grin. He looked closely at her eyes; she could feel the right one twitching. "Come on, my love, eh?" She nodded. He took her hand and they continued to walk away.

I've been deleted from my own story, she thought. *They've just erased me.*

"Nice to meet you!" Jack Preston called after them.

27
Enter the Dragging

The next morning, she hid her head under her covers. The crisp, cool white sheets smelled of lavender. Sunlight spilled in from the open curtains, filtering through her blanket and casting a warm yellow glow through her private cave.

She'd fallen asleep last night still wearing her stupid, flashy clothes. The uniform of her greatest humiliation. She wanted to tear them off, slip out of her own body, and become a ghost.

Msizi was lying beside her, but she didn't care much what he was doing. When she'd woken, he'd been frowning at his phone screen. Probably reading early reviews of the film.

How could this have happened? She'd written a book people loved. It had been optioned by a great studio with a great director attached. She curled tighter into herself as she thought of all the other movies he'd directed and how much she loved them.

Msizi's hand thrust into her sanctuary. It was holding her phone. "Your agent," he said. "Answer it. He's been calling you all morning."

"Blah," she groaned. But she took the phone and accepted the call, putting it on speaker.

"Hold on to your hat, Zelu," her agent said by way of greeting. "You're going to be on *Code Switch*!"

The fog of self-loathing lifted for a moment as she pushed herself up. "Huh?" *Code Switch* was one of the most popular news programs in the country. Zelu and her family watched it every day at prime time from wherever they were and then group-chatted about it. The host, Amanda Parker, was a serious journalist, and she rarely brought guests on for purely promotional reasons. "Why do they want *me*?"

"*Everyone* loves the movie!" he raved. "Have you seen the reviews?"

She cringed. "Not yet." She pushed the covers off her head, letting out all the warmth. The cool of the room wafted over her face. She looked at Msizi. He smiled apologetically and shrugged.

"What would I even say to Amanda Parker?" she asked her agent.

"Just say you're grateful people like it and you're excited by the reaction, blah, blah. It won't be anything deep. It's good publicity for you." Before she could even respond, he continued, "I'll set it up. They want you in the studio in a few hours. That's show biz, huh? Ain't it great to be in LA?" Then he was gone.

Zelu's mouth was still open, some half-formed response lost on her lips. She looked at Msizi again.

He laughed. "Don't act all *woe is me*. It's exciting and you know it."

"I don't want to talk about that movie, Msizi," she said.

"I know."

"I hate it so much."

"*Oh*, I know."

"Fuuuuuuuck." She pulled the covers back over her head.

Msizi tried to make her feel better by ordering a giant breakfast from a local Nigerian restaurant he'd found. Yam porridge with cow feet, fried plantain, moi moi, akara, boiled eggs, and green tea. They ate together in the sunshine of their fortieth-floor hotel room balcony, high above the billboards and movie theaters. And not once did Zelu look at her phone. Now that she was more rested and had a full stomach, she did feel a little better, more balanced in her perspective. Everyone had just been high on the thrill of the movie's premiere last night. No one was going to be critical of the director and actors or even the author right there in the room. The more nuanced reviews would start to come out in the weeks that followed, just like they had for her book. And besides, it was only a movie. It would be on the big screen for a few months, and then get lost on some streaming service, right?

No, it wasn't right, but she would get there eventually. She could survive this. She'd been through worse.

She decided to wear all black to the interview. It wasn't a conscious decision, it just felt right. The full-length dress had a plunging neckline but modestly covered her legs. She added an intricately beaded necklace that Msizi had given her for her birthday months ago and a bracelet of coral beads. The bright jewelry popped against the dark and simple clothes. It made her feel like a force to be reckoned with when she arrived at the studio.

On the drive over, they passed several billboards for the movie, and she felt her anger begin to simmer again, but she still thought she could fake it through the interview well enough. The movie may have gotten Amanda Parker's attention, but she had asked for Zelu, not the director or leading actors. She was still the author of a well-loved book, and she could talk about that. She'd get through it without ruffling any feathers, saying something like "The film is a visually spectacular roller coaster ride." Then she'd smile and say, "But the book is always better." There would be laughs, and then they would move on.

Better to hint at the truth than flat-out lie. Most of the journalists she dealt with were more interested in getting a good sound bite than in her actually having something meaningful to say.

Having her makeup done was frustrating, as usual. "Please, just make me look natural," she'd told the artist. And the young woman had done a good job of that for TV, but Zelu still felt like she was wearing a mask. Maybe a mask would do her some good today, though.

Then the show's producer came into the green room to take her to the set. She glanced out at the blinding lights, the ten cameras being dragged around the floor. The host, Pulitzer Prize–winning journalist Amanda Parker, was sitting at the same desk Zelu had watched her report from for years. Her dark hair was styled in twists and her suit was crisp and white, which would contrast with Zelu's all-black attire.

"Okay, go," the producer said, giving her a nudge.

Zelu walked out onto the set, a smile on her face, her exos tap-tap-tapping on the shiny floors.

Amanda was still looking toward the cameras as she said, "From adjunct professor to literary superstar with one of the most anticipated blockbuster films in the world, today's guest is on a wild, skyrocketing trajectory. I welcome the Queen of Robots, Zelu Onyenezi-Onyedele."

There was a plush chair set up next to Amanda's desk, and Zelu took a seat in it. The lights were hot against her skin. Zelu focused on Amanda's face to ignore them. Up this close, the journalist's twists looked overly tightened and her foundation looked like it wanted to crack and flake away like old clay.

"Happy to be here," Zelu said. "You pronounced my name perfectly. That always brings me joy."

Amanda smiled. "Well, it's a name that's on a lot of people's lips right now. So, you've written this strange and amazing novel, and now it's a strange and amazing movie. I was lucky enough to attend the premiere last night, and it's fantastic. I can't wait for the world to see it. Did you always set out to write a great work of science fiction? How did this book come out of you?"

Zelu sighed, grateful to be on familiar ground talking about the novel. "No. When I wrote it, I was just at this low point in my life, and . . . I dunno, I just wrote it. Maybe I needed some distance from humanity."

Amanda laughed. Then she commented, "So you killed off all of humankind and gave robots the spotlight."

Zelu grinned and nodded. "Basically. Before that, I wrote more, uh, literary stuff. Very different from *Rusted Robots.* I wasn't a big fan of sci-fi."

Even though this was well known, Amanda's eyebrow rose as if it were brand-new information. "Yet you wrote a novel about robots and AI in a posthuman world battling each other. That's a pretty big leap from not liking the genre. What inspired you?"

Zelu would've thought an award-winning journalist might have more to ask than the same questions she'd answered for a dozen other interviewers. She gestured toward her waist. "I'm paraplegic. I've often dreamed about removing broken parts and replacing them with new ones like a robot can do. The connection is hard to miss."

Amanda nodded as if Zelu had just said something incredibly profound. "Very sci-fi indeed. And now you want to make that dream a reality?"

Zelu narrowed her eyes, not quite sure what Amanda was getting at. "If you want to see it that way. To me, it's all a story."

Amanda's flaky face didn't move, but her eyes flickered quickly toward Zelu's waist and the lower part of her dress that covered her exos. "Authorial intent can't be ignored, though. There may be some who interpret this book as you rejecting the identity of a person with disabilities."

Zelu's jaw unhinged. Every hair on her body stood on end. *What the fuck?* She glanced around the studio to see if anyone else was reacting to this, but all she could see were the hot white lights that stung her eyes.

She must have looked stunned, because Amanda jumped in again. "I mean, right now you're so visible. Your book is a record-breaking number-one bestseller. I read it myself; it's fantastic. Your movie is projected to be at the top of the box office. You're taking the world by storm. You *must* sense it, right? Don't you feel a responsibility to, well, honestly and proudly represent yourself to the world? You're even wearing a dress that covers your leg tech. Why do that? Why not let the world see?"

Zelu barely heard the end of Amanda's last sentence over her own heartbeat pounding in her ears. What the *fuck* was going on? This woman was supposed to ask her about her books and her road to writing. The hardest part was supposed to be navigating comments about the shitty movie she hated so much. She'd expected Amanda might even ask about how she became paralyzed. But this was uncalled for. How dare this artificial-looking artificial journalist accuse *her* of not being true to herself?

Fifteen seconds must have gone by. Amanda only sat there, waiting for her to speak.

"Are you kidding?" Zelu blurted.

"It's a serious question," Amanda pressed. "You're in a powerful position, perfect to be a role model for people with disabilities, and yet you've used the privilege of your monetary success to explore inaccessible technology that obscures this truth. Don't you think it's worth addressing?"

Zelu clenched her fists, digging her nails into her palms. This could not be happening. "This . . . this is *my* life."

Amanda tilted her head inquisitively. "What about those who look up to you, who have bought and recommended your book and funded your success? What do you owe them?"

That was it. Something inside Zelu cracked. She felt it, right behind her rib cage. And what leaped out dashed right up her throat and catapulted out of her mouth, straight at Amanda. "You want to judge me? Because my legs don't work? Because I feel some sort of way about this fact? You ask me this, as someone who probably doesn't think twice about how she can just get up and strut off this stage when this is over?

Good for you. But I don't owe anyone *anything.* I'm no one's . . . I'm *no one's* robot. You said you read my book? I think you need to read it again." And then, just because she might as well say everything she wanted to say, she added, "It's better than the movie."

Amanda didn't flinch. She didn't apologize. All she did was smirk. And that was when Zelu realized she'd just given Amanda what she wanted. What a cold-hearted asshole this woman was.

No one gave her a cue. She stood up and walked off the set.

When she got to her dressing room, she slammed the door and locked it. Not a second after, the knocking began.

Knock, knock. "Zelu!" her agent called. He sounded out of breath.

She buried her face in her hands. "Give me a few minutes!" she shouted through her fingers.

"Okay." He paused. "Is your phone in there?"

She looked around. It was on the counter in front of the mirror. "Yeah."

"Can you let me in?"

"No. Not yet. I need a few minutes."

"Okay, fine," he responded. "Just don't look at your phone."

She narrowed her eyes. Why was that what he was

worried about at a time like this? She hadn't really looked at it since yesterday, wanting to avoid the dumpster fire of early reactions to the movie. But she was not in the mood to be caught unawares again. She grabbed it, swiped it awake, and immediately saw that her social media was going nuclear. And not about the movie. She felt dizzy. She tried to recall the specific words she'd used in the interview. She couldn't. Her head was in too much of a muddle. All she knew was that she'd been attacked out there, ambushed, on national TV. On one of the biggest news shows in the country, during prime time. She scrolled through the notifications, sitting down as she read.

Bitch!
Your book is AI-generated trash.
Dumbass Africans always sell out to white people the fastest.
Even the ones with no legs.
We were so behind you!
I'm throwing my book away!
Stop lying to us. You're actually a robot, right?
#BoycottRustedRobots
#ZeluIsTrash
#AbleistDisabledWriter
#AbleistWriter

She was hemorrhaging followers by the thousands every minute. A notification from Yebo popped up.

> You seem to be receiving a large amount of negative traffic on various social media platforms. Shall I filter?

She clicked Decline.

The posts kept coming. Faster and faster. Clips from the interview manipulated to make poo come out of her mouth as she spoke. Distorted to make her look monstrous, with glowing red robot eyes. Her body replaced with a monkey's. Images of her cut out and pasted into the middle of a literal dumpster fire. These were the same people who had been loving her for months. Who had salivated at her every word, sharing, Liking, screenshotting. The hashtag views were quadrupling by the second, spreading like a disease, flooding like water. Nothing could stop it.

More Yebo notifications offering to hide the negative activity popped up, and she declined them all. She needed to see what was happening. She wanted to know. *Let it happen in front of my face instead of behind my back*, she thought.

She sat in that room for a long time. There was shouting from outside the closed door. A landline phone on the green room's wall kept ringing. Msizi was trying to call her cell. Her siblings were texting her. She reached into her purse, fished out her AirPods, and stuffed them into her ears. She shut her eyes, turned on noise cancellation, and let everything fall away.

My skin is stronger than titanium. Smooth, contained, no pores. I have no mouth, ears, nostrils, vagina, urethra, anus. My eyes are African lights. My face is a screen made of thick glass. My display is Ankara themed. I have all I need within my body. I replace whatever I want to replace. It's all still me. I don't breathe, because I'm a robot. I fly into outer space. Out here it is quiet. I'm still. I'm calm. I'm peaceful.

Zelu's phone buzzed in her hand, breaking the spell. That idiotic woman had blindsided her, and social media picked up and ran with the accusations. Snakes in the grass, all of them. So entitled, all of them. They did not know or care what it was like to live in her body, in her mind. She opened her eyes. Her knuckles were white, clutching the corners of her phone. She felt like Dave Bowman in *2001: A Space Odyssey* as he floated over to disconnect HAL. But instead of shutting off her phone, she went onto her social media platforms, bypassing the hurricane of posts, and clicked open the text boxes. In them, she typed:

All of you can go to hell. I'll NEVER be that poster girl that you can manipulate like a paraplegic Barbie doll. You can't put my arm here and push my legs there! I'm ME! Deal with it!

Post.

"Fuck you people," Zelu muttered. She grabbed a tissue and dabbed at the tears rolling from her eyes and blew her nose. She glanced at her feed again, and it was like sticking her head out of a window during a tornado. Words, words, words. Relentless. Insult and hatred upon insult and hatred. Tearing and biting at her post. She dropped her phone. Let them do their worst.

28
Desert Wind

Zelu was getting canceled.

She didn't know when she'd started crying. Maybe when she was in the green room. Or maybe as she'd held on to Msizi for dear life as they'd left the studio. Her faculties were so scrambled that she could barely control her exos. They'd taken a cab to a car rental agency. Now Msizi was driving, and Zelu didn't care where he was taking her.

For a while she sat in complete silence, her cheek pressed against the window. When she could finally form words, tears flew from her eyes as she screamed, "What was that? Oh my fucking *God. What was that?* Oh my *God*! And *fuck* social media and its army of NPCs!"

Msizi glanced away from the windshield for a moment to look at her but said nothing.

She remembered the film (*Yankee and Dot! Ugh!*) and another wave of anguish and revulsion rolled over her. She pressed fists into her eyes and groaned loudly. Behind her eyelids she saw images from the movie and her name in the credits. The characters' very American voices rang in her ears, reciting butchered versions of lines from her book. Wrong part of the world, wrong ways of speaking, wrong ideas, wrong, wrong, wrong. And millions of people who'd never even read her book were about to watch it and love it and think that was what *Rusted Robots* was about. The skill of the filmmaking was undeniable. The studio had produced something visually beautiful, engaging, and memorable—and thoroughly *wrong*. Why option her book instead of starting fresh? The film had taken her creation's name and erased her. Now her "fans" were canceling her, too. She undulated in her seat, wishing she could leap from her body and zip into outer space, never to be seen again.

She tried breathing exercises, but she couldn't breathe. She tried visualizations, but she couldn't visualize. Her cell phone buzzed and buzzed on her lap. Her agents wanted to talk to her. These were the people who'd kept her in the dark, breached her trust. Now they really expected her to attend more meetings and do more interviews?

The Yebo app pinged to alert her that her heart rate was elevated. It suggested she do meditation exercises.

Msizi touched the car's screen. Then he said, "Call Jackie."

Zelu still had her eyes closed, but she listened to the phone ring through the car's speakers. When Jackie answered the phone, Msizi exhaled with relief. "Cousin," he said. "Thank goodness." They started speaking in Zulu, and just the sound of it soothed Zelu. She'd asked Msizi to teach her a bit of it once, but he was always impatient for her to get it right and never around long enough to practice consistently with her, so they hadn't gotten very far with it.

When Jackie began to sing the South African lullaby "Thula Thula," more tears rolled from her eyes. But they were calmer tears. It was such a beautiful song, and Jackie had a beautiful voice. He sang for several minutes, until the panic attack fled from her, a dissipating storm.

"Zelu," Jackie said on the phone.

"What?" she whispered.

"Open your eyes," Jackie said. "I'm all the way in Chicago, but I know you."

She squeezed her eyes shut tighter. "Can't."

"You can," Msizi said beside her.

"Open your eyes," Jackie urged again.

She cracked her left one open, then the right. She looked around. Outside the window, there was nothing but flat desert and stars above. How long had they been driving? Where were they going? All she knew was that she was still in the fucking United States and that was not far enough. She nearly squeezed her eyes shut once more.

"Don't close them again," Jackie said.

This made her laugh. Jackie was a physician and he was Zulu, so of course he was psychic. "Thank you," she murmured.

"Hanging up now," Jackie said.

"Thanks, Jackie. Have a good night," Msizi answered, and clicked the phone call off from the touch screen. "Wish I could sing like that, but I can't," he told Zelu.

She laughed, tired and achy. "You brought me out here. You're taking care of me. Who else would have known to do that?"

"True," he said.

"Thank you." She sighed, embarrassed at being so emotional. "I dunno, Msizi. Fact is, I'm responsible. I was lazy and stupid for opting out of being involved with the movie."

"Live and learn," he said. "Live and learn."

She side-eyed him, noting that he hadn't told her it wasn't her fault. "Where are we going now?" she asked.

"Joshua Tree," Msizi said. "We are going to see Marlo and Wind. Seems a good time for a visit."

"Who are Marlo and Wind?" Zelu asked, sitting up straighter.

"Business associates," Msizi said. "Met them in Cape Town and we became good friends. They invested in Yebo. Sometimes when I come to LA, I drive here and stay with them for a few days."

In all their years of knowing each other, he'd never mentioned these people to her before. But that was just how they were. Msizi didn't have to divulge everything about his life to her, nor she to him. They just had to trust each other and be trustworthy to one another. She settled back against the headrest and stared into the darkness. Msizi opened the front windows to let in the breeze. The cool, dry desert air smelled distinctly herbal. She was a child of the water, and normally she avoided the desert, but tonight wasn't normal. She touched the car's screen and put on a mix of classic Kendrick Lamar songs.

The drive lasted another two hours, and in the last thirty minutes it started to look like they'd jumped a line and driven onto another planet. Miles and miles of open, completely barren land. She knew this only because she'd found a flashlight in the glove compartment and aimed it out her window onto the side of the road.

They turned onto a long dirt road. "How do you even know where to go?" she asked. "It all looks the same."

He gave her an obvious look and she rolled her eyes. Msizi always bragged that he was a human GPS. And it was true; he never seemed to get lost.

They rolled onto a gravel driveway in front of a large ranch house. It was built from smooth pale stone nearly identical to the rocky land around it, making it look carved from the desert by nature. Blue flower-shaped solar lights ran along both sides of the driveway like an airstrip.

"Do they know we're coming?" Zelu asked.

"Yes," Msizi said as he pulled the keys out of the ignition. "I texted them when we were at the car rental place."

"Who exactly are they again?" she asked, peering out at the large house.

He laughed and just shook his head. "Friends. You'll see."

She switched on her exos as Msizi got out from the driver's side. When he heard them power on, he turned his head and asked, "You all right?"

"Yeah," she said, sounding more dismissive than she intended.

He closed the door. She paused for a moment and then got out, too. Her exos touched down on the gravelly surface, quickly adjusting to the rocky terrain. Msizi was plugging the car into an electric charging station she hadn't noticed they'd parked beside. "Nice," she noted.

"The whole house is solar, too," Msizi told her. "They're completely off the grid. Even at night."

It was dark, but the solar lights illuminated things just enough that she could see that the house's entire roof was covered with solar panels.

They walked up the driveway, her exos crunching against the gravel. It was crazy quiet here. So quiet that she could hear chirping insects, the brush of bird wings, and the whistle of the wind with stark clarity.

The front door opened. "Welcome!" A heavyset black man with smooth skin, a shiny bald head, and a long salt-and-pepper beard braided at the tip appeared at the foyer. Msizi went over to hug him. When they pulled apart, the man looked at Zelu with a kind smile. But his eyes were intense, and they moved over her from top to bottom. It was like being in front of an X-ray machine.

"Hi," Zelu said, ". . . Marlo?" It was a guess; Msizi hadn't told her who was whom.

"Indeed, I am." His voice was low and rumbly, the

way she imagined a dragon's would sound. Zelu liked it very much. "Finally, we meet Msizi's genius writer!"

"I'm definitely a writer," she said, shaking his hand. Strong, but it didn't try to squeeze her to death.

The woman she presumed must be Wind stood a step behind him. She was a very dark-skinned black woman, and she wore a long, flowing blue dress and sandals. She carried a tall glass of some green liquid in one hand, and her other hand was on her hip.

"And you're Msizi's," Wind said.

Zelu met her eyes straight on, and Wind did not look away. Normally the direct eye contact startled people, but Wind wasn't fazed. Zelu looked away first.

"Come on in," Marlo said, standing back so they could enter the house. "Let's get you settled."

Wind and Zelu weren't going to get along; Zelu was sure of it already. Once inside, Msizi and Marlo went to the back porch to catch up or smoke or drink beer or stargaze or whatever the fuck they were going to do. Zelu was left alone with Wind in a spacious living area.

Wind took a sip of her drink. The silence crept in. Zelu had no energy for chitchat tonight. She just wanted a little something to eat and then a shower and sleep.

"If you want me to bring you something to eat in your room, I can," Wind said, almost as if she'd heard Zelu's thoughts. "But I'd prefer it if you had a bite with me."

Wind was clearly sizing her up, and Zelu was in no mood for it. "No thanks."

"Well, that's kind of rude," Wind replied flatly.

"Do you know the night I've had?"

The other woman raised her eyebrows. "I heard you just attended the premiere of a blockbuster film based on your book and then had a journalist ambush you in an interview. That about right?"

Zelu briefly closed her eyes. She took a deep breath. "Fuck that journalist. And the movie's a disaster! They set the movie in the United States, when my book was set in Nigeria."

"There are black people in the United States, too." Wind's voice was matter-of-fact, but Zelu swore she heard the edge of a smile in it. "Why can't you give us a bit of the action?"

"Are you serious?" She shook her head, tired and wanting nothing more than to be alone. "Where is the room I'm staying in?"

Wind led her down a hallway and opened a door. Zelu entered a large room with a king-size bed in the center. A fluffy white canopy hung above it like a cloud. On the walls were colorful paintings of robots and dolphins. Beside the bed was an old clunky wheelchair they'd somehow found for her. And on the nightstand was a small meal of fried chicken, jollof rice, plantain, and a huge bottle of water.

Zelu looked at Wind, shocked. "What the hell? You psychic or something?"

"Bathroom and shower are right there," Wind said, pointing to the door on the other side of the room. "I'll see you in the morning. Maybe you'll have stopped feeling sorry for yourself by then."

Before Zelu could even respond to that, Wind had shut the door. "Bitch," Zelu muttered to herself. She threw her purse on the bed, looked around the room, and scoffed, annoyed. This room was creepily perfect. She hoped this had to do with Msizi, rather than these people stalking her online or something.

She undressed, sat on the bed, removed and plugged in her nearly dead exos, and ate. The food was perfect, too; how Wind had made sure it would still be warm when she ate it, Zelu didn't know. She used the wheelchair to wheel to the bathroom and brushed her teeth, plugged in her phone, brooded as she looked out the window into the pure blackness for a while, and then went to bed. She was asleep within seconds.

When she awoke, Msizi was beside her. He was deep in sleep when she wheeled to the bathroom (which, to her surprise, was fully accessible) and took a long hot shower. He was still sleeping when she finished. She dressed, got into her exos, and left the room. The house wasn't wide, but it was long, and it took her a while to make it to the kitchen. Wind was up already, standing at the stove.

"Morning," she said as she cracked an egg into a sizzling pan.

"Hey," Zelu greeted her, still wary as she walked farther into the room.

"You hungry?"

"I can eat," she acquiesced.

"Good. I already made you an omelet," she said. "Msizi said chilis, tomatoes, and chicken. That correct?"

Zelu laughed. "Yeah. Exactly." She sat at a beautiful live-edge wood table beside a large open window. Outside was miles and miles of desert. In the distance, she saw the shape of a mountain.

They ate together in silence, gazing out at the horizon. A long-legged bird with a big brown tail dashed by. Zelu gasped and pointed at it. "Oh my God! Was that a roadrunner?"

Wind laughed. "Yep. Welcome to the desert."

"I've been to deserts before, in the Middle East. But I've never seen a real-life roadrunner!" She was fighting the urge to shout "Meep meep!" like the Looney Tunes character would and to ask about tumbleweeds.

Then she paused, suddenly self-conscious as she felt Wind observing her. She settled down, looking back at her food. “Sorry if I broke the morning silence. I’m . . . like that, too.”

Wind nodded and said nothing. Zelu frowned and didn’t say another word for the next twenty minutes. As she ate, she stared at the dry land with its stunted, prickly bushes and cacti and roadrunners and lizards and dust. How did things live here? She wanted to ask how they even managed to get running water in the house, but she kept her mouth shut. Wind got up to make some herbal tea and handed Zelu a mug. Zelu blew on it and sipped slowly. This was peaceful. And that was pretty remarkable, considering she did *not* like Wind at all.

“Want to go for a hike?” Wind asked, squinting out the window. “It’s still early, so not too hot. Plus, it’s overcast today.”

“Is . . . I dunno if I can,” she said, twisting the mug in her hands. “I’ve never done that with my exos.”

Wind cocked her head. “You mean you’ve never taken those off-road?” She sounded affronted.

“I’m not an outdoorsy person,” Zelu snapped.

“Are you scared?” she asked.

Zelu looked Wind squarely in the eye, anger boiling in her belly. Who did this woman think she was?

"Yeah!" she declared. "Yeah, as a matter of fact, I am! You think you can peer-pressure me into risking my life? I'm not a teenager."

Wind laughed, totally unbothered. "Touché."

Zelu really disliked this woman. How dare she laugh when she had no idea what Zelu was going through? "You don't know what it's like to be me," she said darkly.

Wind stood up breezily, bringing her mug to the sink. "Come hiking with me. If you don't, you'll just end up on your phone and start looking at bullshit."

Zelu blinked, realizing for the first time that she hadn't given the stupid film, the media, any of it a thought since she'd woken up. She'd just been eating a delicious omelet, being annoyed by Wind, and staring at the weird desert. "Damn . . . you're right."

"So let's go," Wind urged. "We won't walk anywhere too uneven."

Zelu didn't have any hiking clothes, but Wind had plenty. When they came back into the main living area in their sportswear, they found Msizi and Marlo setting up a temporary office on a table with their laptops. Msizi looked up and smiled when he saw Zelu dressed in Wind's T-shirt and shorts.

"Don't take her anywhere difficult," Marlo said.

"Of course not. I'm taking her down the easy path,"

Wind replied as she grabbed sunscreen from a cabinet. "Maybe when the technology improves, we'll try the tougher stuff."

Zelu scowled at her.

"Oh, relax, Zelu," she said, rolling her eyes. "You're too sensitive." Before Zelu could respond, she turned back to Marlo and Msizi. "All right, we're going."

Zelu gave Msizi a look that said *Can you believe this woman?* As she followed Wind out.

"Have fun," he called with a wink.

Wind informed her that the beginning of the trail was a five-minute walk away, but when they reached it, the path looked just like all the land around them. The only difference was that there were fewer rocks. Zelu's exos made crunching and grinding sounds as she hiked, but it didn't feel as jarring as when she walked on concrete. It was about 10 a.m. and with the overcast, the eighty-five-degree temperature and strong breeze felt quite pleasant.

"How far are we going?" she asked after fifteen minutes.

"Why? Are you winded?" Wind said over her shoulder. It wasn't her words that annoyed Zelu; it was the chuckle afterward.

"No, I'm not 'winded,' Wind. I'm just asking because of the sun."

"It's overcast."

"For now."

"Why are you so negative, always focusing on the worst?" Wind asked, bounding onward and forcing Zelu to keep pace. "Look at your life. You've written this crazy novel that has somehow caught the zeitgeist. I read it myself; it's brilliant. You *did* that. You've got these two-hundred-thousand-dollar robot legs because you're Zelu Who Wrote *Rusted Robots*. The film adaptation of your novel came out two nights ago. So what if you've been 'canceled' on an app? You were sticking up for yourself—isn't that worth it? Plus, social media isn't the real world. *This* is the real world. So, Zelu. What. Is. Your. *Problem?*"

"Why don't you stop talking," Zelu muttered. "I don't even fucking know you." She felt a rush of frustration as she tried to push away the truth of Wind's words. She couldn't take them in, she couldn't sit with them, she wouldn't. *No*, she thought. *Just no.*

Wind didn't turn around, but her voice carried toward Zelu on the breeze. "Yet I've cooked you two meals you've loved, prepared a room to your liking, and read your novel."

Zelu gritted her teeth. The hike went on, and they continued to bicker like this for the next two hours. Zelu thought it would never end; her skin was coated with a sticky film of sweat and dust, and she was *so* tired. Then they reached the cliff. Zelu hadn't even realized they'd been walking uphill. Her exos had performed flawlessly.

"Whoa," she whispered as she slowly stepped toward the edge. The desert spread before her with such strength that for a moment, she felt dizzy with a rush of vertigo.

"Check this out," Wind said. She was already standing at the edge, looking down.

Zelu stopped a few feet back, afraid to go any closer. The drop was probably more than fifty feet, and only cacti and scrubs padded the ground below.

"Come closer," Wind said.

Zelu shook her head. "I'm scared."

Wind nodded and turned back to the view.

"I'm . . ." Zelu didn't know why she felt the need to extrapolate. "What if my exos malfunction and they keep going when I mean to stop?"

"Have they ever done anything like that before?" Wind asked, her back to Zelu.

"No."

"Then why would they now?"

Zelu shrugged, unable to explain. Wasn't that just how her life went? And if something bad happened, she'd have only herself to blame.

"Those exos got you all the way up here," Wind said gently. "They've carried you all over the world for about a year now, and you still don't trust your robotics. Interesting. You're an interesting person, Zelu."

Zelu looked down at her exos, coated with dust from the long walk. Her legs, socks, and shoes were dusty, too. She gave more trust and respect to that which could not support her than that which could.

She hardened her jaw, squared her shoulders, and stepped onto the edge beside Wind. It was a stunning vista, golden light spilling from gaps in the clouds like rays from the heavens. Patches of sun and shadow moved across the vast desert floor like the shimmering scales of some mythical creature. Zelu took a deep breath, the now hot air crisp in her nostrils. They absorbed the view together in silence for a few minutes.

Then it was as if something switched off in her brain. All the events of yesterday flooded through her again, and fury coiled in her stomach, made her skin hot. "I *hate* that journalist!" she suddenly shouted. Her voice echoed across the landscape. Wind flinched, surprised by the sudden disruption of the peace, but Zelu didn't care. "I hate all those people on social media! I don't care if they bought my book! They don't know what it is to *be me*!" She hesitated and then looked out at the land below the cliff, and screamed, "That fucking movie had my name on it!"

Tears stung in her eyes. Her lip was trembling. The muscles in her back ached from the physical activity.

Wind whooped. "Scream it louder, Zelu!"

Zelu didn't know if she had the strength. But she took a deep breath and shrieked with everything left inside her, for the entire desert to hear, "THAT FUCKING MOVIE HAD MY NAME ON IT!"

Her voice rolled across the land. Her words echoed back at her over and over, softer each time.

She stared at Wind, this woman she didn't particularly like. "Who the fuck am I, Wind?"

"Whomever *you* choose to be," Wind said sagely. "Write what you want, woman. Walk *how* you want. Love who you love. Speak your truth. Be good and roll with life. You can't have or control everything or everyone."

Pretty words, but Zelu hated that Wind made it sound easy. "You don't even know me," she grunted.

Wind threw her hands up like she couldn't believe she had to explain this. "Msizi and Marlo are best friends, and I'm Marlo's partner. Your man talks. And be glad he does. The fact is, I know you plenty."

"Well, I don't know *you*!"

Wind put a hand on her hip. "So?"

Zelu opened her mouth to say something. She closed it because she didn't have anything to say. The moisture in her eyes grew thicker, threatening to spill over again.

"No, don't do that," Wind said firmly.

Zelu sighed, wishing she could just let her body drop and curl up in the dust. "I don't think I'm strong enough to be who I am."

"Stop thinking about it. Just do it."

Zelu wanted to laugh at this strange, wise desert woman. "Who *are* you?"

"A black physicist from Florida who loves the dry heat."

Zelu huffed, turning back toward the view. "Is it hard to be you?"

"Not anymore," she said. "But getting here was. I'm fifty-six years old."

"What? Really?" Zelu had been sure that Wind was a year or two older than her, if she was older at all. Suddenly she understood why she didn't like Wind. The woman saw right through her in a way that most did not. Some of that definitely had to do with her age.

Wind chuckled again. "Wow."

"I didn't mean it like that."

A breeze swept up from below, washing over them and cooling Zelu's skin. Wind stretched her neck out and smiled into it. "It took me twenty-five years to get to this point. I used to work for NASA. Still do sometimes, but I let things go, put things into place, made the hard decisions, and moved. I did it. It was scary, difficult, my family thought I was crazy, even Marlo needed to be convinced. There was so much to do to get where I wanted to be. But eventually, I got here. One thing at a time. Perspective." She nodded to herself. "Don't get lost in the woods, Zelu. I think that's why Msizi brought you here, to the desert. So you wouldn't get lost in yourself."

Zelu watched the dappled light glint against the silhouette of the distant mountain. From here, it looked like a deep purple mound curling into the sky. This place was anything but the woods. It was so bare you could see for miles and miles.

"Perspective," Zelu said.

"Yeah, perspective. Anyway, enough thinking. Let's head back."

By the time they made it to the house, it was nearly 2 p.m. They didn't say much more to each other, and that was nice. Zelu would never have imagined that so much wildlife thrived in the desert. They'd even seen a forest-green snake try to ambush a quail. There was an ebb and flow out here that was really magical. Who'd have thought? In this giant expanse of rock and dirt that seemed to stretch on into infinity, Hollywood felt worlds away. Still, Zelu knew she couldn't make a life and thrive here like Wind. She'd only long for a body of water, for the constant movement of the waves, the sound of the water breaking against the shore.

They stayed with Marlo and Wind for a week. However, Zelu knew that she had to return to the human world. By the time they left, she still didn't much like Wind. But she was ready to answer her agent's phone calls and get back to the world of her books. The film was not her story, but at least it was something that gave people joy. It was a worthy sacrifice . . . maybe. Plus, as everyone kept reminding her, her book was still *her* book. The weird, magnificent thing she'd pulled out of her brain had started this all, and that would always belong to her.

29
Pollinated

I left Lagos. The megacity was so sprawling that it took more than a day for me to get out of it. Instead of the roads, I followed the beaches. Ijele still hadn't returned. Ijele loved the sight of those giant RoBoats so much, I'd thought that maybe she'd sense where I was and join me. She didn't. And though I knew how to call her, I didn't. I walked those beaches alone. I saw no RoBoats breach the water's surface in the distance.

But I did see dolphins. They clearly saw me, too, for they swam into the shallows and leaped up to get a better look at me. Friendly, free, curious creatures. Ijele would have enjoyed seeing them.

I moved inland, where I found wide, empty roads. Robots keep the roads clear because that is what we've always done. I had the road to myself for several hours before I came across someone else—a vaguely aware, sleek electric car. It came speeding up the road at over 150 miles per hour. It slowed as it approached me and then eventually came to a stop right in front of me. Up close, I saw that it was a scratchy silver; it had used something to scrape all its paint away. Its roof was one big solar panel.

A camera popped up through its hood with a soft *whirrrr* and I heard it scan me. "You are a Scholar Hume," it told me in a flat male voice. "I'm going to Lagos."

"I'm just coming from there," I responded, stepping up to it. I touched its side door and looked inside. Bundled wires, several large boxes that probably contained motherboards, power supplies, processors . . . This car had really built itself up.

"Why are your legs lacking rust?" it asked.

"It's a long story."

It began rolling past me, its shallow curiosity satisfied. "I'm glad to see a functioning Hume," it said. "I cannot explain why I did it, but I ran over several Humes some weeks ago. I don't feel good about this, and I haven't seen any Humes since . . . until you."

"Ghosts broadcast a protocol," I explained as I mulled over its words. No Humes since? Could it be true that I was really the last of my kind? Was my journey to Cross River City just moving from a small grave to a bigger one?

These possibilities were too great to process. I decided not to dwell on them until I had to.

It was a few feet away from me now, and it paused. After a moment, it said, "Ghosts should be stopped."

"Then why are you going to Lagos? The servers there are favored by Ghosts."

"The roads are wide, and I now maintain a VPN. They cannot infect me."

It drove away before I could say more. I continued down the empty road.

One day, I came across an old shrine. This place pulled me back to myself, for it was a place no Scholar could ignore. "Gods and robots," I said to myself as I walked through it. This place was old and new.

Everything was arranged around a large wooden building that looked like a house from another world. It was encrusted with cowry shells and carved with winding, intricate designs. Stationed on each side of the entrance was a tall, skinny, humanoid figure that stood six feet tall. They both had stunned faces, like they couldn't believe the humans who'd made them were all dead. The periwinkle grass that covered so much of the land, including many of the roads, seemed to want nothing to do with this place. Bushes, vines, and trees grew freely here, yet there was also a sense that someone was pruning them, preventing them from taking over.

That someone turned out to be a durable service robot that maintained the place. It walked out of the central building as I moved past. It paused, extended its narrow metal legs so that it became my height, and greeted me in Yoruba. I greeted it back.

"Welcome to the Osun-Osogbo Sacred Grove," it announced, holding out its stick-thin steel arms. "I'm an old custodian robot who has obtained the ultimate boon of my journey; you, on the other hand, seem to be at the beginning of yours."

I had no idea what it was talking about, but I let it show me around. It didn't allow anyone to touch, record, or photograph anything here. "Not even if you are a Scholar Hume," it added.

I was fascinated by this place. So many of the idols, gods, goddesses, and deities were made of wood. And among them were the unmoving, unanimated bodies of robots, some old, some new, some tall, some short. The only Humes bodies were those who had not rusted much. The custodian walked through the grove slowly, with great care, as it showed me around.

Why the Ghosts had not destroyed this place was beyond me. Maybe they didn't know about it. Whatever the reason, I had to believe this was another strong sign that Ghosts hadn't conquered all. When I left the shrine, my senses were refreshed, and the world around me felt more focused—the trees, birds, remnants of human life, the occasional waves of periwinkle grass pollen. But as I continued along the road, I couldn't forget that in a couple of years, all this might be destroyed by crazed space robots singing songs of destruction as they gifted Earth with pieces of the sun.

Ijele and Ngozi had replaced my broken legs with new ones. Rust-free, light, stronger metal. I'd accepted their smooth functionality and could walk very well, but I hadn't yet tested their full capabilities. On that road, I practiced. These legs could run, jump, grip smooth surfaces. At first, I was a little afraid. I was afraid of falling, and a few times I did. But I picked myself up and was okay. And I was better for it, because I learned what I had done wrong and what I could do better. How I must have looked to any robot watching, I don't know. But I was determined.

Ijele would have been proud of the way I embraced my new features. But she still hadn't returned to me. Was it grief, or something worse? Had the Ghosts discovered her connection to me and deleted her? I wanted to call to her through our bond, but if Ijele had indeed rejoined the Ghosts' hive mind, doing so might only reveal her deception.

I was obsessing over this possibility one day when the wind picked up, causing ripples as it blew over the periwinkle grass like waves on the ocean. Then I saw it in the distance—a purple-blue pollen tsunami. It flew over me, saturating the air, coating my skin. It was glorious. I wished Ijele could have been with me, because she might have finally come to understand what it is to love a body. Slowly, I turned myself counterclockwise, letting every part of me experience the pollen tsunami's full force. What a joy.

"Ngozi," I said aloud into the periwinkle waves. I let the wind take the word, her name. I flashed Ngozi's image on my face screen, and it lit my world for a while.

When the pollen tsunami began to lift, I stopped turning and looked down at myself. I looked like a Hume-shaped flower. I bent each of my joints: neck, shoulders, torso, arms, wrists, fingers, hips, and of course every part of my new legs. Smooth. Perfect. Easy. Periwinkle flower pollen is like magic to robots. It got into my gears, between my panels, into my crevices; it helped loose rust flakes shed.

"Ah," I said. "It is good. Onward."

My journey lasted a month. I saw many robots, but none of them were Humes. They looked at me like I was a spirit, some creature meant to be gone forever. But I held on to my faith that Cross River City was still occupied by fellow Humes, that I wasn't the last.

And finally, on a rainy day, my new legs drenched in mud and my face panel so coated with rivulets of water that I could barely see, I arrived.

CROSS RIVER CITY, a towering billboard of a sign announced in red neon. Spanning the path was a great rusted gate.

The road didn't look recently used, but the rain could have washed away tracks. I heard no robotic chatter, no churning of bolts or wheels. I sent out an experimental ping. Nothing returned.

It was likely, very likely that I had traveled all this way to an abandoned place, the site of yet another massacre of Humes. I feared what I would find beyond this gate. Ngozi's death had scrambled my processors. If I learned I had failed in my mission, that I was truly alone, the last, just as Ngozi had been . . . I didn't think I could handle it.

I had arrived. Time to find out. I had promised Ngozi's spirit. Ijele had told me to go.

I opened the gate.

30
One Year Later . . .

Time passed like when something is lost. The *Rusted Robots* film was a massive box office hit, and it was accompanied by plenty of merchandise: Yankee and Dot mini robots that synched with an app on your phone; themed backpacks, wallets, and T-shirts; a Cross River City video game; RoBoat action figures. Zelu's agent kept mailing things to her, and she hated it all. The capitalism machine had used her book, her attempt at shouting into the void, to make visual comfort food for drowsy minds. Regardless, she made peace with it. Wind had given her the tools to do so. *Just don't expect me to ever watch the film again*, she thought.

The upside was that the movie had renewed the fervor for her book, and sales continued through the roof, at higher levels than even when the book was first released. At least many of the movie fans were also going to the novel and reading the real tale of *Rusted Robots*, too.

However, it had been two years since the book's release, and her publisher was growing impatient for the next book in the trilogy. In the original contract, she'd agreed to deliver a book a year, but she'd blown past that deadline. Her sales were so stellar that no one had said a word about it for a long time. However, now her editor was starting to send emails asking about her progress, whether she had an estimated date for the full draft, if she needed a break from PR to focus. She wasn't fond of *anyone* pushing her to write on a schedule. She'd never written anything of creative value because of expectation, and she wasn't going to start now. Book two would come when it came. She wasn't a robot.

She had, however, been kicking ideas and notes around again. The problem was, a nagging thought kept blocking her: Would readers bring the sentiment of "Yankee and Dot" to her work now? Would she have to actively write against the assumption that her characters were Americans with American accents?

Zelu found herself spending less and less time on social media. Not only did she hate the progressively ruder messages asking for updates about the next book, she also didn't want to educate people about her exos, or debate whether she was an American, a "diasporic," an Africanfuturist, or an African writer. And she *certainly* didn't want to talk about the film.

Over the past two months, she hadn't gotten on an airplane, made a public appearance, given an interview, or spoken very much to any of her reps. Hugo, Marcy, and Uchenna occasionally texted, but that was it. She was on her laptop, gazing past its screen to the view of Lake Michigan outside her window, when she remembered something her father had once said to her when she was a child. "People like you and I like adventure, *have* to go on adventures, even when it annoys the people we love. We like to see things, test limits . . . but that doesn't mean we won't regret going." Both he and Zelu had laughed really hard at this, because it felt so true.

Neither she nor her father was an adrenaline junkie who jumped out of airplanes or climbed mountains, but they both always felt the need to follow what called to them. Zelu knew that when her father had been eight years old, he'd become the youngest member of his local secret society. Young Secret had been curious, and so he'd demanded to know what it was all about. He'd danced as his village's local masquerade for the first time at the age of twelve. "I was tall and strong for my age," he said proudly. "So I was impressive." Nevertheless, there were aspects to being a part of his village's mystical culture that he refused to talk about, and the dark look on his face when he refused said it all.

When he was in college, he had missed the colors of the plumeria and hibiscus flowers that grew wild behind his parents' house, so he'd decided to learn how to plant a garden at his university. He'd put so much time and energy into maintaining it that he'd nearly flunked out his second year. "I'm an engineer with engineer ways," he said. "Once I started, it was hard not to go all the way."

Zelu, on the other hand, had climbed a tree hollowed by beetles, told off a pretentious student so thoroughly it got her fired, and written a novel about robots even though she didn't even *read* science fiction. She was always impulsively barreling forth and touching things . . . and always getting bitten and stung.

"And I never learn," she muttered to herself. She'd moved her desk to face the lake, and she was glad. It made thinking about these things easier. Being high up and looking out at blue water made risk-taking seem normal. A seagull soared past her window ledge. *Still doesn't mean I have to deal with whining, prying people*, she thought. *Fuck that. This isn't for them. I'll do my shit in outer space.* She laughed aloud at her absurdity.

Ding. An email notification popped onto her screen. She glimpsed who it was from and frowned. "That can't be right." It was just too weird. She minimized the vignette about Lake Michigan that she'd been fiddling with as a warm-up and opened the email. She stared at it. Then she read it again. "What?" she muttered, a shiver running down her spine.

The email was written in a lighthearted tone, full of excitement and . . . joy, something she hadn't felt very much lately. But apparently he already knew that, because Jack Preston, the wealthiest man in the world, knew *everything* about her. He'd done his research on her, and he included it all here. He knew she loved the water. He knew she detested the film adaptation of her novel. He knew she was getting more and more pissed at her fans. He knew her family struggled to understand her. He knew she was batting book two around but she didn't want to be pushed. He even knew she continued to struggle processing the fall from the tree decades ago. He knew she'd once wanted to be an astronaut and had quickly put that dream to rest after her accident. He knew she'd never looked back. He even quoted her: "A dolphin should not seek to be a leopard."

This man knew her whole life story.

Zelu shut her computer off, then restarted it. For good measure, she turned off her Wi-Fi. She felt like something was listening to her. This was Jack Preston, who owned the largest corporation on the globe, which had its fingers in just about everything, including cybersecurity software.

"What is with these wealthy white dudes finding me?" she whispered. She reread the email again. It was three paragraphs long. So sure. So clear. And, not surprisingly, entitled.

All the information he relayed about Zelu was in service of working up to an offer. In the final paragraph, Preston invited her to be the fourth passenger on #Adventure, a civilian mission to the International Space Station next year.

You've wanted this for so long. Be honest, he wrote. *And you're perfect for it. Plus, from what I'm told, people like you, who have lost or never had the use of their legs, are practically made for space travel. Dolphins and leopards are both mammals, but dolphins are better swimmers!*

In space, you don't need your legs. Of course, Zelu knew this. In order to move about where there is no gravity, one can use the upper body. She looked toward the office, where Msizi was on an important phone call. She took a breath to call him over. She held it. She looked down at her computer. Then she shut her eyes and exhaled. She'd never admitted it to herself until this moment, but . . . she'd never stopped dreaming. She just hadn't known how to make that dream real.

"Is this happening?" she whispered, her eyes still closed. Telling her family about another risky venture was going to be a pain in the ass. *Man, if Dad doesn't side with me on this, then I don't exist,* she thought, clenching her hands in her lap. Her father had loved the "space books" she'd made as a child. He'd been the one to teach her the names of the stars. She sighed, relaxing. *Yeah, Dad will side with me on this one.*

When she'd been a child, that dream had felt all too attainable, but she hadn't given it the serious thought of an adult. And after the accident, that ceased to matter. But now, thinking of the possibility again felt like returning to her childhood self, with all the giddiness and naivete.

Then her adult mind kicked in, asking the tougher questions. She hated roller coasters, so could she really tolerate *any* level of g-force in her body? No matter what Preston said, no matter what experts predicted, she was still a paraplegic woman, and few like her had ever traveled to space before. And those few were top-level engineers who'd made it through the NASA gauntlet of excellence.

She heard the door to Msizi's office open.

"Msizi," she called to him, twisting her desk chair around.

"What, Zelu?"

"Come here!" She laughed, waving him over.

She put her head in her hands as he stood behind her and read the email. She didn't want to see his face. "Read faster," she groaned, grasping the chair's armrests.

"I didn't know they were interviewing me for this when I spoke with them," he said.

"*What?*" Zelu gasped. "They called you?"

He shrugged. "I've been asked by a million journalists about you. What was one more?"

"Foolish man."

Msizi rubbed his beard, looking hard at the screen. "It was your dream before you fell out of the tree."

"Yeah. But I gave it up."

"Did you, though?" he asked, looking down at her searchingly. "Didn't some poet say, 'What you seek is seeking you'? You manifested this."

She said nothing. She didn't have to. He knew he was right, and he already knew what she wanted.

"You do know that I'm as much a part of this as you," he said, sitting on the couch. "If you go up there, I'll be *here.* Those you leave behind will suffer most."

She chewed on the inside of her lip as she studied his

face, watching every minor muscle working, hoping to understand what he really wanted. "So you think I should first discuss it with you?" she asked. "Then with my parents and my siblings? Then maybe my agents and publisher, too? Maybe even post a survey on social media about it?" She was on a roll now, fueled by remnants of anger she couldn't extinguish no matter how hard she tried. "But they'll all just say, 'Fuck that, we don't care, where's book two?'"

Msizi's eyes hardened, and he looked down his nose at her. "Not your family, not your agents, not your fans. Me."

"It's *my* choice."

He laughed. "Sure it is, Zelu. Everything is."

"What do you want me to do?" she asked.

"You decide," he said, waving a hand and moving to stand up.

"What do *you* think I should do?" she asked, this time more earnestly.

"Oh, I think you should totally go," he said.

This derailed her completely. She'd been certain they were about to have an argument. "Wait, what?"

He opened his arms like he was surrendering himself to her. "You are central to my life and I know you. If you want to do this, then that's the best thing for you right now. You want to leave the Earth, and this is your shot. That fucking white guy billionaire read you perfectly."

She frowned, unsure why she felt crushed by his words, even though it was what she'd wanted him to say. She looked at the grain of the wood floor instead of his eyes. "Man, these rich white men keep coming out of the woodwork and changing my life. What the hell?"

He snorted. "Yeah. You seem to be experiencing some bizarre aspect of American privilege."

They both laughed. She pinched her arm and laughed again. *My God, what is this going to do to me?* she wondered. But it wasn't a bad thought. It was a thrilling one. Her future was full of stars. She was ready for another change, a shift, an evolution.

Zelu's phone buzzed. She was grinning as she answered it, excited to start relaying her news. Then she paused as she listened to what was said to her. The smile slipped from her face.

Just like always, it took only a second for her life to completely fall apart. Arm. Leg. Leg. Arm. Head. Pulled asunder. Crushed.

31
Interview
Mother

I grew up in a palace with four mothers. We are from Ondo State, Nigeria. My mother was not the queen, but she was a second wife, which gave her a good amount of power and respect. I was always proud of that. The queen was a kind woman. She raised me as much as my mother did, though her five children hated me for it. I called her Yaya, and no one else did. It was our personal name. She liked me so much that when I was young, she had a bed set up in her room and I would sleep there.

I was the oldest of my mother's three children, and my younger brother and sister were twins. When they were babies, they were such a handful that my mother was glad that I was so close to Yaya. I was also my father's favorite, I guess you could say. Altogether, between my four mothers, I had seventeen siblings, but I was the one who effortlessly stayed at the top of all my classes and was most interested in how everything at the palace worked. When I was twelve, I began documenting everything. I liked to record what happened, make sense of it, and put it all together in my mind. And I wanted to understand where I fit in the grand scheme of things.

I'd follow my father around when he met with politicians and public figures or gave talks. So I was seen everywhere, sometimes with the king, other times with the queen. Our kingdom was not very big, but it was very old. My brother Remi, Yaya's oldest son, was next in line to the throne, but more people talked about me. Oh, Remi detested me. I was a girl and I knew more than he did, had a clearer voice, was loved by my mother *and* our father. Oh, I was such an annoyance to him.

There is a lot an older brother who is next in line for kingship can do when he wants to make trouble for someone. My brother had his own followers, and he got them to hate me, too. We had slaves in the palace; all of us grew up with them. These were children offered to my father by their parents as gifts. You have to understand, to have more children was to have more wealth, so of course my father took them in as his own. In exchange, he raised them and they eventually earned their freedom. For the ones who were academically gifted, my father paid for their college educations, and three of them still live with him. His personal physician began as his slave. We all ate at the same table. I slept in Yaya's room, but the slaves slept in beds with my siblings . . . and my brother turned them against me.

I am a tall woman, but my brother was taller and bigger, and I didn't grow until I was in my late teens, so he used to terrorize me. Our siblings did, too. Everyone else was younger and afraid to face his wrath, so they followed along.

I am proud to be from the type of family I am from. I know that here in the United States, such things are not understood. You all spin everything that is not familiar to you as either terrible or less than you. You only see things through your narrow lens and personal experiences. It is your weakness. I understand. But my family is a beautiful one, even if it is not perfect. We *are* royalty. True royalty. That stands for something older than this country's existence. Respect your elders.

Anyway, what no one knew or understood yet was that I would go on to marry an Igbo man with no kingdom. A village man from a family of hardworking people in Imo State. When I told my father I had fallen in love with a man named Secret Wednesday Onyenezi, he burst out laughing and said, "Ah ah, these Igbo people always have something to hide! And it's usually money!" He'd laughed himself to tears. He of course stopped laughing when he realized that I was serious. My mother, on the other hand, never laughed at his name. But she never stopped being suspicious of him.

Secret and I met in university. Plants brought us together. There was a courtyard full of flowers, and I used to walk there just to admire it. There were all kinds of flowers: pink dahlias, red roses, tiger lilies, lilacs, even giant sunflowers. I would kneel down and brush my face against the soft petals of the fragrant lilacs when no one was looking. Bees, butterflies, lizards, and these green-headed sunbirds would visit the place, like students going to department buildings. So much enjoyment. Someone was clearly taking care of these flowers, because these weren't plants you saw growing wild in Nigeria. Most of the students on campus didn't really notice it. Everyone was just trying to survive. But I loved that little courtyard. It smelled heavenly, and there was a comfort there that made me want to sit and smile.

And one day, I was standing there staring at the flowers when the great cultivator of all this beauty came with a watering can and plant food sticks. A skinny boy wearing a white shirt and expensive trousers that he didn't mind getting dirty. We fell in love at first sight. That's the only way I can describe it. He was Igbo; I was Yoruba. I come from a family that has always had expectations for me, and one of those was that I would marry a Yoruba man of name. Secret has no respect for royalty and was always yelling that the "Igbos have no king" and "African democracy is the way," this and that. My family was appalled, but it was worth it. It was beautiful and real; Secret and I just fell in love from that first moment, a love so strong that neither of us had to change to accommodate it.

I say all of this to highlight that this is what our second daughter, Zelunjo, came from. From conflict and diversity and peoples who have never been afraid to face it all. I am proud of Zelu, even though I will never understand her. I read her book the moment she handed me one of the early copies. I don't know where all that came from, all that drama, empire, clashing, shouting, all that wahala. Somewhere deep in my daughter's head, I guess. Maybe when you speak to Secret, he can explain it better. He reads these things with a finer eye than I do.

32
Passing

Zelu rushed through the hospital doors, ignoring all the stares that turned her way. She probably should have come with Msizi. She needed his emotional support right now. However, she'd insisted he stay behind; she didn't *want* his emotional support. She'd wept the entire ride in the autonomous vehicle. Before she even reached the front desk, people were moving toward her, calling her name. One of them had the audacity to ask for an autograph (which she gave just to get rid of him, drawing an angry face beside her name, which seemed to delight the guy even more).

Zelu approached the front desk. "Hello," she began.

The receptionist smiled sheepishly. "Are you . . ."

Zelu felt tears pricking the corners of her eyes. A

lump was building in the back of her throat. "I am," she managed to get out. "Did you like the movie?"

"Oh my *God*, I loved it," the receptionist said, her face lighting up.

"I'm glad," Zelu said, wiping away a tear that had escaped and begun rolling down her cheek. "I'm . . . I'm here to see my dad."

"Oh!" the woman said, realizing. "Shit . . . I'm sorry. Please . . . hold on." She looked at her computer and then at Zelu. "Room 219. That way, right down the hall."

"Is he . . ." Then Zelu shook her head, cutting off her own question, and said, "Okay, thanks."

She moved through the hospital wing as quickly as she could. After the shock of the freezing air outside, her exos were warming back up, and she was glad. They didn't like the super cold of Chicago in late January, and neither did she. Not for the first time, she thought about moving with Msizi to Durban, which lay beside the Indian Ocean and was nicknamed the City with No Winter.

Her gait was jerky, which was always jarring to her spine. But as she walked and the exos warmed up, it smoothed out. By the time she heard the voices of her mother and siblings coming from inside the room, she was back to moving in her usual way. She took a deep breath. "If it gets bad, just leave," Msizi had said to her before she'd gotten in the cab. "Don't question yourself. Go back when they are not there."

She stepped into the room. Her father's bed was obscured by the bodies of her family. "You decided to come," her sister Chinyere said, turning around.

"I came as soon as I heard."

Chinyere huffed. "Always so hard to get a hold of, even when you have no real responsibilities!"

"The fuck is your problem?" Zelu snapped. She was about to say more when her mother rushed over and hugged her, as did her brother. The others just looked at her and said nothing. There were nine people in the hospital room, not including her father. It was cramped. Her mother took her hand and led her to her father's bed. His eyes were closed and his usually rich brown skin looked washed out, like something inside of him had left. Zelu shivered at the thought. "Can I wake him up?" she asked her mother.

She shook her head. "He . . . he won't wake up. Hasn't yet."

"What happened?"

"He had a heart attack, Zelu," Amarachi said. She was squeezed onto the small yellow couch beside their father's bed with Jackie. "Thankfully, Mom and I were there when it happened."

Always that undercurrent of accusation whenever any of her siblings spoke to her.

"Is he going to be all right?" Zelu whispered.

"No," Amarachi snapped. "He's obviously not."

"Stop it," their mother said. "Chinyere, go and see when the doctor is coming to update us."

Chinyere hesitated, rocking back on her heels. "He said he'd—"

"Just go and see," their mother said, in a firm tone that made it clear she was not to be questioned again. "Uzo, Amarachi, Bola, Jackie, Tolu—go to the lobby. Shawn and Zelu, you stay here."

"Why *Shawn?*" Bola asked. Her boyfriend looked more than pleased, though he was trying to hide it. Ever since they'd started dating, Shawn had always had a way with Omoshalewa.

"Just go," their mother snapped.

As soon as the room cleared out, Zelu let out a breath, her shoulders relaxing. When she met her mother's eyes, she realized they were glistening with tears. "Mom?"

"Have faith," her mother said, taking Zelu's palm into her left hand and her father's limp hand in her right.

Shawn sat back on the yellow couch and looked at the floor soberly.

Zelu stood with her mother and watched her mouth move with whispered prayers. She held her father's hand to complete the circle, squeezing it and watching him sleep. She squeezed harder. Nothing. His hand was cool and damp. His face was slack, his mouth hanging open the slightest bit.

She looked at Shawn, and he looked back at her sympathetically. She mouthed to him, "How bad?"

"Bad," he mouthed back. Then he shook his head. A jolt of anguish shot through her and fresh tears gathered behind her eyes. Shawn got up and put an arm around her shoulders as her mother continued to squeeze her hand and pray. Zelu leaned her head into Shawn's shoulder.

A few minutes later, her mother asked if she could be alone with her husband. Zelu and Shawn left the room to join her siblings in the lobby. Zelu plopped down in a corner seat and powered off her exos so she could bend her chest into her lap.

"I'm afraid to go home," Tolu was saying.

"Me too," Uzo agreed.

"Just wait for Chinyere to finish talking to the doctor," Jackie said.

"You weren't there," Amarachi suddenly shouted at Jackie. "You didn't see his *face*!"

Jackie pulled her toward him, and she pressed her

face into the crook of his neck, her body shaking. "I'm not going anywhere," he whispered.

Zelu rubbed her face. Her skin felt tight and itchy. She switched her exos back on. The sound of them powering up must have been like a familial dog whistle to her siblings.

"You're not going anywhere," Amarachi said, suddenly turning to Zelu, who had been about to stand up. "Stay your ass *right there*."

Zelu froze. All of them were looking at her now. She could hear Msizi's voice in her mind. *If it gets bad, just leave.* But her family was blocking her way. One shove and she'd fall. She hadn't planned on leaving, just going to the bathroom. They always did this, and it was their problem, not hers. She sat up straighter. Ready to have this fight.

Chinyere suddenly rushed in from the hallway. "Something happened! *Come on!*"

They all flew through the hospital wing back toward their father's room. Even before she saw the doorway, she heard the steady *beeeeeeeeeeep.* Then her mother's voice. First it was a cold whisper, then it heated to a hum, then boiled into a shriek. "Secret? *Secret?* SEEEEECRET!!!!!!!! SEEEEEEEEEEECRET, ooooooo!"

Zelu had never heard her mother make noises like

this before. The anguish vibrated through her, rattled her bones. She was right outside the entrance to her father's room. He was in there. No, he wasn't. He was gone. "Oooh," she softly moaned, wrapping her arms around her midsection, her eyes blurring. "Dad."

She felt more present in this moment than she'd ever been. Rooted in it. Even as time moved, she was stuck in that split second when her father changed from being alive to being dead. The nurses began rushing in. The doctor Chinyere had been talking to was already in there. A flurry. A tornado. A hurricane. And Zelu had missed her chance to ever talk to her father again.

She didn't go back into the room to look at him. She didn't speak to her mother. No one said a word to her, except Jackie, who asked if she was all right, and Shawn, who gave her a tight hug and said, "I'm sorry."

Her mother was inconsolable after Chinyere and Tolu pulled her off their father's body. They sat her down in a chair, and she went limp and silent. Soon, Zelu was the only one left standing in the hallway. She had no role left to perform for the others, and no one was here for her. So she called a cab and left without saying good-bye. She went home to Msizi, who wrapped his arms tightly around her. She dragged herself into bed, pulled the covers over her head, shut off her phone, and stuffed her AirPods in her ears. She floated in space for a while. And finally, she curled up and wept.

Hours later, Msizi gently shook her awake. "It's your brother. He's rung a few times now."

"Whyyyy," she groaned, her mouth gummy. What time was it? She rubbed her face and looked at her phone as the screen lit up with yet another call. She hit Accept and brought it to her ear. "'Lo?"

"Jesus! Finally! I was about to come over there!"

She squeezed her eyes shut and scrunched her nose, trying to bring some feeling back into her face. "Was sleeping."

"Get up. We're all at the house. Including Uncle Ugorji, Uncle Dike, and Auntie Ozioma. They just arrived from Nigeria. Yeah, that fast, man. You need to be here."

"Wha?"

"Just come."

He hung up. She looked at her phone. It was 5 a.m. Yet "everyone" was at the house? Her mother had called her uncles and aunt as soon as her father became unwell. How panicked she must have sounded for them to hop on a plane right away and arrive this quickly. And still, they'd been too late.

"Dad's gone," she whispered. "Oh God." And she

fell all over again. She moaned with the pain of it, pushed her face into her pillow. "Dad." She called for him, knowing he would not answer. "Daaaad."

Msizi rubbed her shoulder. "He was a really cool guy," he softly said, even though he hadn't known her father well at all. "When we were dancing at Jackie and Amarachi's wedding, he interrupted all us Zulus to dance his masquerade dance. He caused such a stir, the masquerade came out and joined. Your mother was frowning so hard."

Zelu laughed despite herself, face still pressed to the pillow. The Zulus were having their moment, and her father had stolen it to make it an Igbo moment, annoying her Yoruba princess of a mother. It was so like him.

"He was a real cultural man, and he raised progressive children who would evolve the culture," Msizi said. "That's *beautiful*, Zelu. He has earned the right to rest and wander. It's a terrible loss for those he left, but we will all celebrate his life, too."

Zelu was sobbing again, but it felt better this time. It felt like release.

Then Msizi had to ruin it by adding, "And you won't let your family press you down."

She lifted her face and rubbed her runny nose. "I'm not—"

"Stop," he warned gently. "I know you, and I know

your family. I know how it went. They love you, but *don't* let them press you down."

Then she remembered her brother's urgent plea. "I have to go there right now."

Msizi raised an eyebrow. "Why? It's early."

She was already turning to grab her exos. "I don't know. Family meeting. Some relatives just arrived to stay with my mom or something."

"You have to go now?"

"Yeah."

He nodded. "I'll go with you."

She paused, turning sharply toward him. "No." She tried to make it clear in that one word that this was not up for discussion. This was something she had to do on her own. Msizi would just try to shield her.

He nodded. He got it. "I can't convince you to get more sleep first, can I?"

"I just . . ." The exos powered up, and she stood, moving toward her dresser to grab a clean shirt. "Something's going down. I need to be there . . . for once."

Msizi lowered his chin. "Ah, there's the guilt."

"Stop."

He sighed and stood up. "Keep your phone close, Zelu. Answer if I call."

"Fine, fine," she agreed as she fished a wrinkled T-shirt from the drawer.

"I don't like you doing this alone."

She froze for a moment, looking at the shirt in her hands. "I don't, either."

His eyelids lowered. "I will seriously stand outside waiting, Zelu."

She smiled and kissed him. Then she finished getting dressed and called a cab.

It was nearly 6 o'clock when she walked up to her parents' house. The sun was out, but it felt so far away that it didn't make a difference temperature-wise. However, it had snowed overnight and the glare was spectacular. She wore a dark blue–and-black Ankara suit with no jewelry. Her micro braids were pulled back. The feet of her exos were caked with snow and dirt, but she felt stylish, respectful, and unassuming. Even in the wake of her father's death—or maybe because of it—she knew her relatives would be eager to judge her. She wasn't going to make it easy. She would make her father proud.

She reached for the door handle, then stopped. Her father couldn't be proud; he was gone.

She opened the front door. Everything seemed the same, from the ever-present smell of curry, onions, and palm oil from her mother's cooking to the earthy notes from her father's many houseplants. His heavy winter coat hung on the rack beside the door. As if he'd just returned from a trip to the store or seeing a friend and was right around the corner, sitting in his favorite armchair.

She shut her eyes and massaged her temples. "Come on. Get it together, Zelu," she whispered. But her mind wouldn't stop: Who would water the English ivy in her room? Not only had her father nursed it back to life, but it was now joyfully taking over her entire windowsill, thanks to his green thumb. Who would eat the rest of her egusi soup and fufu when she was too stuffed to finish? Who would tell her those core stories that she loved to hear again and again about his youth in Nigeria? Who would be the one other adventurer in the family? Who would she look to first for support when her family inevitably told her something was out of her reach?

She was on her own. She urged her exos forward and was glad for their unemotional, robotic response. Into the house she went.

Everyone was in the living room. Her mother sat on the couch, looking somehow both like she was about to collapse and incredibly alert. On one side of her sat Uncle Dike, as tall and imposing as ever, and on the other side sat Uncle Ugorji, as robust and entitled as ever. But Omoshalewa was not a small woman, and she didn't look small now. Sitting on the coffee table were a bowl of kola nuts and a plate of peanut sauce and alligator pepper. It was just like her mother to be capable of hosting in a moment like this. All around the room were Zelu's siblings. No one looked her way when she entered; they all seemed frustrated, the room hot with an ongoing argument. Zelu moved to stand behind the couch.

"No disrespect, Uncle Dike, but that's really foul!" Tolu snapped.

"This is how you people speak to your elders in this country?" Uncle Dike asked. He kissed his teeth. "*Tufiakwa!*"

"Irrelevant," Uncle Ugorji said, waving a hand at Tolu. "He will be buried in Mbaise."

Her mother suddenly stood up. "And when I die, where will I be buried? In some Igbo village? Me, a princess of Ondo. Me. A *Yoruba woman*?!" She slapped her chest proudly.

"You are his wife," Uncle Dike said. "You will be buried beside your husband."

"I am a *princess*!" she shouted at him. Her whole body was shaking now, and Zelu couldn't tell if it was from rage or exhaustion. "I will not allow any of you to be blind to who I am! No! Secret was *my* husband! *Not* yours. When is the last time you spoke with him,

Dike? I remember!" Her eyes were wide and red. "Oh, I remember what you wanted and how you made him feel!"

Auntie Ozioma leaned forward in her chair, holding an arm out to urge Zelu's mother to sit back down. "*Biko*, this is not the time—"

"When, then?" her mother screamed. "You three flew here so fast, I don't even know how! People usually can't even get visa, but you three did, overnight . . . just to tell me I have to ship my husband away! Did you know he would die? Eh?! *Did you know?* Are you Grim Reaper?!" The more she raged, the thicker her accent grew. "Let me keep my husband!"

"He is *my* brother," Uncle Dike said, voice deep and commanding. "I have known him far longer than you." He paused and then added, "No one can be closer than the ones who come from the 'head office.'"

"Patriarchy is so nasty," she heard Amarachi mutter. "Always acting like their dicks are gods. 'Head office,' ugh." Zelu met her eyes, then she met Tolu's and Uzo's. They all hated this traditional bullshit, and they all hated that they couldn't just scream that they hated it because they were part of it, too. Respect your elders, respect your elders, respect your elders, one of the strongest rules of the culture.

"Your father," their uncle Ugorji said, addressing

them all now, "will be buried as a chief. He deserves that. We see what he did here. He should be honored in his own land."

"Uncle," Chinyere said, stepping forward. "We respect you. We love you all. But this is our father." She motioned to their mother. "And this is our mother. We understand your sentiment. We don't know if we agree with it or not." She looked to the others and they all nodded. "But we won't have you coming here and making demands. We are fine with suggestions or requests, Uncle."

Their uncles both looked as if they were about to object, but Chinyere held up a hand. "We need time to think on it. Can you give us that?"

All her siblings understood that it was time to remove themselves. They stood up and started filing into the kitchen. Chinyere held her mother's shoulders and ushered her along, too. Zelu followed the procession. Their auntie and uncles remained in the living room, muttering among themselves.

Once in the kitchen, they all sat around the table except Zelu, who elected to lean against the counter. No one said anything for a long moment.

"Is this . . . what usually happens?" Uzo finally broke the silence.

"Yep," Tolu said, looking like he'd eaten something sour.

"The nerve," Chinyere said, shaking her head. "Like, they can't just ask? They come making demands as if we're nothing."

"You know what comes next," Amarachi said, curling her lip in disgust.

"Yep," Chinyere asked. "They go after his bank accounts in Nigeria."

Amarachi nodded. "They're his brothers."

"He always wanted some of his wealth to be at home, though," Tolu whispered.

"Fuck the patriarchy," Amarachi hissed. She quickly looked at their mother, but Omoshalewa was just staring blankly out the kitchen window. Her eyes were not so wild anymore; now they looked lost. "Why keep wealth in a place that's broken? Even when it is home."

"The US isn't much better," Tolu pointed out.

"Easy for you to say, 'only son,'" Amarachi shot back. "At least I don't have to worry about *this* kind of crap. At least here, my genitals aren't a hindrance when—"

"Can we focus?" Zelu interjected. They all looked at her as if just noticing she'd arrived. "There's a lot happening. But one thing at a time, right? Where . . ." She inhaled, her eyes welling up again. The pain of their father's passing and the culture clash mixed together into a hot, burning ache. "Where . . . where are we going to bury Dad?" She shuddered, stumbling. "Dad . . ."

Chinyere rushed and caught her before she could fall. Amarachi held her shoulders. The holding became a tight hug from them both. She held them, too. Their mother started keening and they grabbed and held her, too. Zelu shut her eyes, but for once, she did not go to space. She heard the breathing, sobs, and soft words. She smelled the spice that always clung to her mother's skin, Tolu's sandalwood-scented oil, Amarachi's jasmine perfume, Bola's bath soap, Uzo's baby powder. She felt Chinyere's long nails pressing her arm gently, keeping her here. She couldn't fall if she tried.

33
Wake-Keeping

It was snowing heavily. A true Chicago blizzard—blustery, aggressive, and cold. It began just as they arrived at the funeral home. Zelu grasped Msizi's arm as they walked through the doors, not because she was having difficulty with her balance but because she knew what was in there. Her father's body. Dead. She had not seen him since that day in the hospital two weeks ago. She paused just under the threshold, the snow falling around them, coating her black-and-gray Ankara coat.

"Wait," she said. "I can't."

Up ahead, Tolu and his wife had just entered and were moving down the hallway. In the parking lot, she had spotted cars that belonged to Amarachi, Shawn, and Uzo. She was probably the last sibling to arrive.

"I don't want to go in there, Msizi. I can't go in there. I can't, I can't . . ." She couldn't tell if her eyes were filling with tears or if snowflakes were melting on her eyelashes.

Msizi moved closer to Zelu, pressing the warmth of his body against her side. Her shoulders hunched as she sobbed. "I don't want it to be over." She coughed, the shudder of it shaking the snow from her coat. "What am I without my father?"

For the past two weeks, Zelu had avoided thinking about this moment as much as she could. Chinyere and Arinze had taken the helm arranging things. "Just show up" was all Chinyere had told her to do. Now Zelu wasn't even sure she could do *that*.

"You are of him," Msizi whispered softly into her hair. "You literally *can't* be without him." Another sob racked her body, and Msizi held her tighter. "We are mortal beings. We die. But we live first. And your father left a great legacy."

She grasped his hand tightly. He squeezed hers back even harder, and it felt good. They started walking again. And they didn't stop until she was in the lobby, which was packed with people who loved her father. They could barely fit inside. She recognized many faces; her father had had many friends, and a lot of them had shown up today. Colleagues from the mechanical services company he'd worked at as head engineer for thirty years before retiring. People from the Igbo and Yoruba communities in Chicago. People from the Pan-Africanist organization. People from his church, including the priest. People he'd met and chatted with in the supermarket every week. Engineers he'd been helped by and whom he'd helped.

"My condolences."

"I'm so sorry."

"Your father changed my life."

"It's so good to see you."

"He was a great man."

Hugs upon hugs. Sympathetic eyes. Weary stares at her exos. The viewing room wasn't open yet, so they had to mingle a bit. Msizi was getting his ear talked off by a large woman with a giant curly black wig when Bola appeared beside Zelu. "There you are." She grabbed Zelu's arm to pull her along. "We're in the back."

Zelu snatched her arm away. She couldn't balance well when people pulled at her like that.

"Sorry," Bola said. "But come on."

She glanced at Msizi, who was still talking to the woman.

"He'll be fine," Bola insisted. "Come on."

They walked down a hallway with plush red carpeting and old-timey gold-foiled wallpaper. This place had a posh Victorian style that Zelu kind of liked. She looked up at the crystal chandeliers and imagined they'd make tinkling sounds if an old spirit whooshed through.

"What took you so long?" Bola asked.

Zelu bristled. "I've been here. Just got caught in the lobby."

Bola opened a door. A comforting wave of warm air washed over them as they moved inside. This room was small, with vintage-looking armchairs facing each other on top of a richly painted silk rug. In the corner, a fireplace was crackling, casting a calm orange glow across the space. All her siblings and her mother were in here, dressed in black. They looked up as she entered, except for her mother, who was sitting on the floor with her sister, Constance, warming her hands in front of the fire.

"Where were you?" Chinyere asked, giving her outfit a once-over. Her words had their typical bite, but her voice was raw and more muted than usual.

Zelu sat in a chair beside her brother. "In the lobby." She looked at Tolu, and his expression made her stomach flip. "Hey, you all right?" He glanced at her and shook his head quickly. She reached out to grab his arm and squeeze.

"When are we going to go out there?" Amarachi asked impatiently.

Uzo scoffed. “Why do you want to go out there so badly?”

Zelu did a double take at her youngest sister. She’d shaved down the puffy ’fro she usually sported; her hair was short now, making her look so much smaller. The skin under her eyes was puffy from crying.

“Everyone is waiting,” Amarachi said. “I want to get this over with.”

“We can take as much time as we want,” their mother said. She stood up, brushing down her long black skirt. She looked composed and regal. “We have the place for the entire day.”

“But Amarachi is right,” Auntie Constance said, standing too. She wore an exquisite dress made of black lace. Auntie Constance had jumped on a plane from Dallas the day after their father died and had been at their mother’s side ever since. “We shouldn’t keep everyone waiting.”

Zelu saw her mother’s lip tremble for the briefest moment before she pulled it between her teeth. She said nothing, pushing her shoulders back and looking at her children.

“Mom, are you all right?” Zelu asked.

Their mother breathed in through her nose and released it slowly. Then she turned toward Zelu and gave her the tiniest smile. “Let’s go.”

Auntie Constance linked arms with her sister and they moved toward the door together. Chinyere followed behind, then Amarachi and Bola. Zelu walked slowly, holding Tolu's and Uzo's hands. Uzo's fingers began to tremble, and Zelu saw tears gathering in her sister's eyes. "Breathe, Uzo," she said, giving her hand a squeeze.

"I don't want to go out there," Uzo said.

"Me neither," Tolu muttered.

Zelu hadn't thought this far. All she'd wrapped her mind around was the fact that the wake was happening. She'd been to funerals for loved ones before. Her classmate in third grade, Eileen O'Malley, who'd been hit by a train. The next-door neighbor, Mr. Kowalski, who'd had a heart attack when she was sixteen. Her college friend Duck Jackson, who'd been shot on a street corner on the South Side her sophomore year. Her favorite uncle, Tony, who'd died of pancreatic cancer seven years ago. But this was her *father*. The kindest, most trustworthy, most confident man she knew. And he was her greatest link to the Igbo people of Nigeria. A walking encyclopedia of information and attitude, but also a whole vibe in and of himself.

She remembered him at a family Christmas party where all the men his age had gotten up when the DJ, who was just her cousin, put on a record of an old Igbo traditional song. They started dancing a strange dance in the middle of the room.

"Mom," Zelu had said, tugging her mother's sleeve. "Is that a masquerade dance?" Her mother had just laughed knowingly.

Now her family moved through the packed receiving room and toward the double doors that led to the viewing room. Their mother knocked and the doors were opened by the funeral director and his assistant. Tolu and Uzo pressed closer to Zelu and, though she had to concentrate harder on staying balanced in her exos, she was glad. As they went in, the director and the assistant asked everyone else to stay back for a moment. The doors were closed behind Zelu, Tolu, and Uzo, and suddenly everything was quiet. She heard Tolu gasp, and Uzo started full-out sobbing again. Zelu didn't look. The room was spacious, with rows and rows of red cushioned chairs. All facing forward.

"Come on, you guys," Chinyere whispered.

The three of them crept to the front of the room, huddled together. Zelu kept her eyes cast to the floor, but she could still see her father's white casket in her peripheral vision. She did not want to look. To look would brand a horrid image into her memory. She didn't want it. She was going to get it anyway.

"Can we make him look . . . happier?" she heard her

mother say. Her mother's voice had never sounded so tight. "Look at his face, o."

"I told them the same thing," Chinyere said.

"M-maybe they can still do something," Auntie Constance said. "Excuse me! Mr. Panagopoulos."

The funeral director, a tall man with shiny black hair, joined their mother and Auntie Constance in front of the casket. Zelu helped Uzo sit in one of the chairs in the front beside Bola. Chinyere and Amarachi were opening the doors now and welcoming people in. Zelu turned to the casket slowly, then brought her eyes up. There was a large space in front of the casket, for people to walk up and observe. The carpet leading up to it was bloodred. A lace cloth hung from the edge of the casket. White, clean, light. Her heart was pounding so strongly that she could feel it behind her eyes.

Finally, she looked full on at the corpse of her father. He was wearing a brilliant white silk Isiagu and matching pants. On his chest was his wooden ikenga, the horned figure sitting on a stool with a knife in its right hand, which he'd kept in the living room. This object had always been a fixture in Zelu's life. You couldn't walk into the room without noticing it. As tradition dictated, it was now broken into pieces.

When her eyes reached her father's face, her limbs seized up. Her mother and Chinyere had been right;

his mouth was pulled downward into a deep scowl. He looked angry and dissatisfied. Her father's resting face had always been kind, happy, content.

"What the fuck?" she whispered. Her mother and auntie were talking firmly to the funeral director, who was shaking his head and holding up his hands. Chinyere was on the other side of the casket. She'd removed her black silk scarf and used it to cover the bottom half of his face. She tucked it in a bit more.

"We did the best we could," Mr. Panagopoulos was saying. "Sometimes one's face just settles in a state and that's what it will be."

Zelu couldn't breathe. Her father had never looked like that in his life. This could not be how his face would remain forever. This was not him.

More people were coming in. In a matter of moments, the room was full. Msizi appeared from the crowd and took her hand.

"Where's Mom?" Zelu said, looking toward her siblings, who were gathering beside her.

"Are you all right?" Chinyere asked. Her face was wet with fresh tear tracks. Uzo burst into sobs again; both Tolu and Msizi moved to hold her. Amarachi stood stiffly, looking behind her like she couldn't handle facing the coffin. Bola was staring at the casket, shell-shocked.

"I . . . nooo . . ." Zelu glanced at the white casket again and whimpered.

It was like a domino effect. Uzo, who was looking at Zelu, whimpered, too. Tolu sniffled and hissed, "Fuck." Bola grabbed his shoulder.

"Oh God, where's Mom?" Bola asked, looking around, starting to lose it, too.

Even Amarachi began to crack.

"You guys, we have to hold it together," Chinyere said. But then she began to break down, too, tears running from her eyes.

Zelu lost her concentration and then her balance. She grabbed at Msizi's sleeve.

"Msizi, get Zelu out," Chinyere suddenly ordered. "No falling today. Go take a breath and come back, Zelu. Okay? You can sit when you come back?"

No falling today, Zelu repeated in her mind. She couldn't even be angry at the dismissal; she grasped for dear life at her sister's words.

"I'm so sorry." The first guest had come up to them to pay his respects, a man in a crisp navy-blue business suit. "Your father mentored me just before he retired. I wouldn't have my job if it weren't for him."

"Thank you," Chinyere said, stepping up to him.

"Come," Msizi said, putting an arm around Zelu's waist. His soft but firm touch gave her strength. With her exos, it was a tricky thing, but Msizi always somehow knew when to leave her be (which was most of the time) and when to grab and hold her tightly (during rare times like this).

"Can you handle her?" Tolu asked.

Msizi gently pulled Zelu toward the double doors. "Yeah."

They moved quickly and were soon back in the lobby. With everyone now in the viewing room, the reception area was empty. The funeral assistant, a woman wearing a black-and-brown pantsuit, was standing by the door. "Is there a private room?" Msizi asked her. "This is one of the daughters. She needs a bit of—"

"Of course, right this way," she said, leading them back down the same hall.

This room was smaller than the last, but just as elegantly furnished. Zelu sat on the couch and stretched her exos before her. Then the image of her father's pulled-down, sad face flashed in her mind. Like he'd smelled something bad. His lips had been too pink, too. He'd *never* had any pink in his lips. She whimpered again, her head aching, a tinny sound in her ears. She didn't have her AirPods.

"You want me to get Jackie?" Msizi asked.

"Take too long," she wheezed.

She felt him lift her chin. He rested his hands on

her cheeks. "Zelu," he said firmly. His hands pressed against the sides of her face. She opened her eyes. The light in the room was so bright. His face was right in front of her, nothing else. "Breathe. Inhale."

She inhaled.

"Exhale."

She exhaled.

"Again."

She did.

"Keep breathing. Focus on that. Inhale. Exhale."

With each breath, something in her loosened. The lights looked less harsh. She relaxed.

"Zelu, listen to me. Today is a dark day. A dark, dark day." He pulled her face closer to his. "When you write your stories, you look into yourself and see into things. Be the writer today. Use that ability. You are the observer and the observed. You are the documentarian and the subject. You are the author and the reader. This is how you create. This is something you know how to do. Now let it be here for *you*. Do you understand?"

She digested his words. After a moment, she felt relief.

"Bear witness," he said.

She understood. She could protect herself from the despair that had been about to consume her. Not forever, but at least for this terrible day. It would get her through, even while she felt it all. After a few minutes, she said, "Okay. I'm ready."

He nodded. "Good. Let's go, then."

When she entered the viewing room the second time, she walked in as the writer she was. She would bear witness to it all, with open eyes, an open heart, knowing her role in it. And in this way, she faced one of the worst days of her life. She stood there with her mother and siblings, greeting and listening to the well-wishers. Hugging and shaking hands.

The viewing room was so full of people, so many different types of people. Engineers, professors, neighbors, surgeons, teachers, dentists, lawyers, even a group of workers from the McDonald's he liked to frequent. Her father knew so many people.

Zelu felt the most for her mother, whom she hadn't seen sit down in over two hours. Auntie Constance seemed to be pushing her to host. "Try and smile," Zelu heard her auntie tell her mother during a lull. "Be here for these people. You are the wife."

Zelu made eye contact with Amarachi and Chinyere, and they caught on to what she was about to do. Chinyere quickly stepped in Zelu's way. "Don't."

"Why?" Zelu snapped. "The person most hurt here is Mom!"

"Yeah, fuck this stiff-upper-lip shit," Amarachi added. "It's not Mom's job to make *other people* feel better!"

"Just shut up and stay out of it!" Chinyere turned around, a smile quickly appearing on her face as Frank Johns, a lawyer their father had been friends with, stepped up. "Uncle Frank," she said. "I'm so glad you could make it."

"I'm so sorry for your loss," he said.

Zelu and Amarachi stood down, reluctantly following their sister's order. But Zelu still worried about her mother. It was never good to keep your emotions bottled up, or to let them be bottled up by others. She knew that better than most. From the moment her father had passed, her mother had put her own emotions aside to deal with familial obligations and the roles imposed on her. And when he was buried in Nigeria—something they'd finally decided to allow—Zelu knew the suffering would only go deeper for her. Not only were Igbo burial traditions unkind to women (Zelu kind of believed that, traditionally, the whole point of them was to send the widowed wife into the grave with her husband), but Zelu's mother wasn't even Igbo. Zelu suspected that the women in the village would be harder on her mother because she was Yoruba. *But what can I do?* she thought.

Chinyere and her husband had hung an African mask on each side of the room. They kept incense burning. And soft highlife music played the entire time. The atmosphere was somber but simultaneously festive, and that festive feeling only grew as time passed. People paid their respects, but they didn't leave. They stayed to chat with one another. Zelu noticed that people were talking about her father. People who didn't know each other shared the experience of knowing her father. She left the line of well-wishers for a bit just to walk around and listen. To witness. She took it all in, and it nourished her.

She was standing alone in the back of the room when a loud drum sounded. *Gbam!* Every hair on her body stood on end. But she felt excitement, too. Was this what she thought it was? Another drumbeat sounded. *Gbam!* Now the drumbeats were continuous, coming from the lobby. Everyone in the viewing room looked around.

One of the men from the Igbo organization Mbaise Unity shouted something in Igbo. Then he said, "Make way! Everyone! Get out of the way!"

Slowly, people moved away from the double doors. Zelu noticed that the Nigerian women, including her sisters, all ran to the far side of the room. Some grabbed the other women and pulled them with them. Zelu was far enough away that she could stay where she was. A man wearing a white kaftan, a colorful blue-and-white wrapper, and a red-and-white Igbo cap entered carrying a talking drum, playing an aggressive beat that was so loud it hurt Zelu's ears. He was followed by a flute player wearing the same outfit. Then a man carrying a metal staff with a cowbell attached to the top, who stabbed the staff at the floor, clanging the bell with every other step. The music was haunting, and Zelu felt it stir her spirit.

"Make way!" someone shouted from the lobby. "It has come to pay its respects to Chief Secret Wednesday Onyenezi! To see him off to the world of the spirits! Get out of the way!"

It was so tall that it nearly touched the high ceiling. It was wide as a carwash brush and looked like one, being made of stacked raffia and draped with an ornate red cloth. It danced into the viewing room, bouncing and swaying to the beat of the drums and the sound of the flute. Zelu grinned, tears in her eyes. A procession of men dressed in the same outfit as the first three followed. They were solemn and focused only on the masquerade making its way to the casket. When it reached the front, the nine-foot-tall masquerade suddenly slapped its entire body flat on the floor as if prostrating. The drumming, fluting, and bell clanging stopped. All the men stepped back, leaving the open space empty except for the masquerade.

One of the men shouted again and the drummer began drumming a slow, deep beat. Several of the men shouted, as if to egg on the masquerade. It got up and began to dance again. It was a beautiful, powerful moment. They weren't in her father's Imo State village, where Zelu was sure her father would prefer to be lying, but the spirits and ancestors were here. In the United States. And so many of her father's friends, loved ones, and acquaintances were here, too. Her father was a man of multiple worlds, and in this moment, he was celebrated in one of them.

"Yaaaaaaaah!"

Zelu gasped at the sound of her mother's voice. She'd never heard her scream like this. If her mother ever shouted, it was to give orders, make someone feel small, get someone out of her way. Never in this primal, untethered way. Never in public, in the presence of the community. So loud that her voice cracked. Then Zelu's mother screamed again, "*Aaaaaaaaaagh!*" The sound made Zelu want to flee from the viewing room. She met Chinyere's eyes from across the room. Her sister looked just as terrified.

Her mother was standing with the other Igbo women on the other side of the room. She opened her mouth wide and screamed again, clutching herself. Then she bellowed, "*My husband, oooo! My Secret, oooo!*" The drummer did not miss a beat. He changed it up and the beats sounded deeper, slower, beckoning. Zelu's mother was making her way to the dancing masquerade. She kicked off her shoes and lifted the hem of her heavy black dress so she could rush faster. She looked like a mad queen. "Secret! *Secret!* My Secret, ooooo!"

She started dancing wildly in front of the masquerade. "*Kai!*" she screamed, doing a turn. CLANG! She bucked her hips and screamed again. She raised her hands as the drumbeats led her in a circle about the dancing masquerade. Zelu put her hands over her mouth, grinning. Her mother was releasing. This was a catharsis. A woman dancing with a masquerade was unheard of. A Yoruba princess dancing with an Igbo masquerade in America at the wake-keeping of her highly respected Igbo husband was something right out of the future. "Let it out, Mom," Zelu whispered. "Let it through. Let it *go*!"

She looked around. All attention was on her mother. Every single person in the room was absolutely riveted. Some of the Igbo men looked confused. Even the funeral director and his assistant were in the doorway gawking. Her mother held her dress to her knees, did a wild kick, and screamed again. Suddenly, her auntie screamed and began to dance her way there, too. More of the women joined in, and soon a group of older women were dancing around the masquerade and her mother. Chinyere ran to join in. Then Amarachi, Bola, and even Uzo, who was still nakedly crying.

"Come on, Mom!" Tolu shouted. "Dance! Ha ha, Dad would love this!"

Zelu stood back and witnessed it all.

34
Not Yet

When she got home, she threw her coat on the couch. She didn't care if she got snow all over it. Let it melt and leave the couch wet. Msizi grabbed it and shook it out in the hallway as she went to stand at the window. It was past midnight, but it was so bright outside with falling snowflakes that it looked like twilight over the frozen Lake Michigan.

"Oblivion," she said as she stared at it. Her father's face flashed in her mind, and she gulped, the tears welling again. She couldn't believe she had any more left. "You're just expected to keep going. Watching people you love drop off, one by one. Then you keep going until it's your turn to drop off and be gone and then people weep over you. Sometimes I feel like I'd rather be a fucking robot. No pain. No death. No finality. And no need to fear life. Yeah."

Msizi came up behind her. "Except your robots experience all that, too."

"Heh. True."

"You done rolling around in the dark?"

She shrugged.

"You write what you write for a reason," he said. "But yeah, that's what it is to be mortal, Zelu. You remember my cousin iNdonsa?"

"The tall one who wears all the sparkly clothes?" Zelu said. She smiled. "I like her."

"I know. She likes you, too. iNdonsa always says the best thing about being human is that we die. She's one of the only people I know who is not afraid of death. You should talk to her."

Zelu turned back to the blizzard outside. "Maybe."

Her father would be buried in Mbaise, Nigeria. When they'd told their uncles and auntie who'd flown all the way from Mbaise when they'd heard of their brother's death, they had acted appeased but not grateful, like their demands had finally been met. Like they'd expected it, because they were right. They hadn't even stayed in the United States to attend the wake.

"We will see you at home" was all their uncle Dike had said about it. As far as they were concerned, the real honoring of her father could only happen in his village in Nigeria. Zelu's mother had cried and cried about him being buried an ocean away, but she understood that it was the only thing to do. She knew a battle that she could not win. "It *is* his home . . . even if they don't understand that Secret has multiple homes now. Even my home in the Ikare-Akoko palace is his home." Then she'd added, "You all can decide where to put me when I die."

Zelu went to her bed and dragged her laptop onto her lap. She opened it and typed her password, *WakaFlocka-Flame* (an old-school rapper whose music she vibed with for no reason other than that she liked his voice). She went to her inbox. She clicked on the two-week-old email from Jack Preston asking her to join his space mission. She'd thought she would finally get to leave the world and see beyond. Instead, her world had crumbled. At some point in the blur of the last two weeks, she'd sent a reply: *Thank you for the opportunity, but I have to decline. I need to spend this time with my family.* She barely even remembered sending the message. Now she saw he'd emailed a response: *My contacts have told me what happened. I'm so sorry, Zelu. Sending love and light. Sincerely, Jack Preston.* Zelu suspected his "contacts" were her agents, whom Msizi had quickly notified of the family emergency without telling her.

Her phone buzzed. There were only seven numbers that could get past Yebo's filter right now. It was a video call and she answered it on her laptop. Several video boxes opened. The first showed Amarachi's neck and chin; her phone was on her lap as she drove. Uzo looked piercingly into the screen from what looked like a beach at sunset. Tolu was clearly home because his cat, Man Man, was pushing his furry head into Tolu's face. Bola held her phone to her face as she walked down a white hallway. And Chinyere scowled at them all; she'd been the one to start the group video call.

"How are we?" Chinyere asked.

"Bad."

Grunt.

No response.

"Can't believe this."

"Do we have to do this?" Zelu asked.

"Ugh, don't start," Amarachi snapped.

"We do have to do this," Chinyere said. "So anyway, Amarachi and Jackie will stay with Mom tonight."

"I will be stopping by every day," Tolu added.

"Zelu," Chinyere said.

Zelu braced herself. "Yes?" she said more loudly than she intended.

"After tomorrow, can you stay at the house with Mom for the next two weeks?"

Zelu opened her mouth, then closed it. This was unexpected.

"It's just easiest for you," she added.

Tolu and Chinyere had super-busy schedules, plus Chinyere had her children. Uzo had med school classes. Bola and Amarachi had intense jobs they couldn't just take time off from.

"I'll have to talk to Msizi about it, but yes, I . . . I can do that." It was nice to be considered for such an important job, but at the same time, she wanted to be alone in her high-rise sanctuary to sulk, cry, scream. Msizi was traveling to Durban in a week, and she had been looking forward to the solitude. But of course she would be there for her mother however she could. She'd done the right thing by turning down Jack Preston's offer.

She did wish she were going to Nigeria for the funeral, though.

The family had firmly agreed that Amarachi and Zelu would stay back. Zelu reminded herself not to be bitter. Years ago, her father himself had instructed that the family shouldn't all travel together when it had come up idly in conversation. "The reality is that anything can happen back home," he'd said. "People are struggling and angry. If anything does happen, let there be some of us who stayed back so they cannot do away with all of us that easily." Zelu and her siblings had laughed because they'd recently come back from a trip to Nigeria. They'd assumed he was tired or just fed up; those family trips could leave one like that, especially her parents, who had to navigate so many dynamics. However, there must have been more to that comment than she'd realized, because when it came time to arrange the flights to attend their father's funeral, her mother insisted they honor it.

"Just know that he said that for a very specific reason," their mother had said when Chinyere asked for details. "And know that we were all very lucky."

The reason their mother wanted Amarachi to stay behind was obvious. The burial in Nigeria would require their mother to endure a gauntlet of traditions that would be hard for American-born Nigerians to tolerate. Amarachi was too hotheaded. When they'd informed their uncles and auntie of their decision about the burial, she'd ended up shouting obscenities at the uncles, cursing all things Igbo, and telling the men they could shove their "kola nuts, yams, and patriarchal terrorism up their fucking asses." Zelu had burst out laughing. The uncles stood up, indignant, and Amarachi had dared them to come for her, screaming wildly, "This isn't the fucking village! I will happily fight you with my bare hands!"

Chinyere had dragged her out of the room and, in the process, managed to pinch the laughing Zelu's arm so hard that she left a bruise. Zelu had followed them both out, still giggling uncontrollably. She just couldn't stop. In the world she now lived in—where her father was dead and relatives came from the motherland to demand he be returned to the "soil," as if his children and wife didn't count for shit—her sister's rant was funny as fuck. She couldn't have been prouder of Amarachi. Tolu had apologized to the elders and calmed everything down.

As for Zelu, their mother thought she was too famous. It was for safety. A prominent man's funeral in the village was an event that would attract a lot of vultures to begin with. But people would also be watching specifically for Zelu, the daughter who was a world-famous "filthy rich" writer. Her presence could ruin the entire event, at least according to her mother. Zelu hadn't been back to Nigeria since before *Rusted Robots* was published. She missed it. But she also knew that her days of going there as just some disabled American Nigerian girl were over. Not only was she now famous, but her exos would attract so much attention, she probably wouldn't be able to go anywhere without an audience. She'd still wanted to go, regardless, but her mother had become so agitated by the very idea that

Zelu quickly stopped pushing. There would be another time. A quieter time.

Two days later, Zelu packed a small suitcase and then called an autonomous vehicle. When she entered her parents' house, she paused. Her father's coat was no longer on the rack. Its absence weighed on her. She hadn't been to the house since before the wake-keeping. Her eyes stung and she pressed a hand to the wall to keep her balance. She took a deep breath and let it out slowly. "Clarity," she whispered. She stabilized. "Mom," she called. Her voice sounded hollow in that way it does when a place is unoccupied. "Mom," she called again. "I'm . . . I'm here."

Her mother's voice came from the bedroom. "I'll be right there." Faint and rough. She'd been crying. Zelu started for her parents' bedroom, then decided against it and headed toward her own room. She stopped. She went back to her parents' room and paused outside the door. She heard her mother sniffling.

"I can hear your heavy robot feet. Just come in," her mother called.

"Sorry, Mom," Zelu said, entering the room.

"For what? You are what you are. Come and sit." Zelu was hyperaware of her mother staring at her as she walked across the room and slowly sat on the bed. "Those things are still strange to me."

Zelu chuckled. "That's never going to change." On

the bed, her mother had spread some old photos of her and Secret. They were yellowed and the corners were curled, if there were corners left at all. She probably had the digital files somewhere, but she had always been fond of printing out photos. Zelu picked one up. Her parents looked barely twenty as they stood beside a patch of flowers. "Are you all right, Mom?"

"I don't think I'll ever be all right again," she said. "But I'm better than I was." She'd been more even-keeled since dancing with the masquerade. "You don't need to trap yourself here with me."

"Mom, I lived here recently enough. It's not that big of a deal."

"What about that short, handsome boy of yours? Won't he mind?"

"He's not that short." Zelu laughed. Msizi certainly wasn't tall, though. "And he's fine with it. If he weren't traveling soon, he'd have come to stay with us."

Her mother hummed. "Ah, Zelu, you always do things your own way. Damn the rules, damn what is expected. I wish I could."

It wasn't the first time her mother had spoken of Zelu's rigid individualism, but usually it was with judgment. Today, Zelu heard almost a hint of admiration. "Come on, Mom. You can, too."

But her mother only shook her head.

Her mother's group of Ondo society women came by the next day, and Zelu began to understand why Chinyere felt one of the siblings had to be there at all times. Her mother spent the entire morning cooking and then tidying the house. Then, an hour before the women arrived, she began to prepare herself.

"Mom, what's all this?" Zelu finally asked as her mother stood before the bathroom mirror putting on the kind of makeup she usually reserved for formal events like weddings. "Aren't these just your society women?" She looked closely at her mother's tight cornrows. They needed to be redone.

"Yes," she said, penciling a beauty mark on her right cheek. She paused and looked at the wig she planned to wear. She plucked the hair a bit.

"Then why all this?"

Her mother began to apply mascara. "Why all what?"

"They're supposed to be coming to make you feel better."

Her mother nodded. "They will come. They will take word home. Women judge. You're not a baby."

Zelu cut her eyes to the side and muttered, "Doesn't seem very healthy."

She heard the front door open. "Are they here yet?" Chinyere called from the foyer.

"We're in Mom's room," Zelu called.

Both Chinyere and Amarachi walked in. They hugged their mother and gave Zelu a quick nod.

"What are you guys doing here?" Zelu asked. "I thought you were busy."

"Just stopping by," Chinyere said.

"Where were you—" Zelu began, but quickly stopped talking as Chinyere gave her a sharp look.

"You look nice, Mom," Amarachi said.

Chinyere leaned close to Zelu's ear and murmured, "Funeral home, making the last payment. All done."

Zelu nodded.

"This wig is looking raggedy," their mother said.

Amarachi touched her cornrows. "I can buy you a new one that you like."

Their mother shrugged, indifferent.

"What hairstyle do you want, then, Mom?" Chinyere asked.

Omoshalewa gazed hard at herself in the mirror, her daughters watching her closely. Zelu studied her mother's face in the strong bathroom light. Despite the pain of losing her beloved husband, she was still fresh-faced and lovely. Her little society friends would probably be disappointed.

"I like that woman's hair, the journalist who interviewed you," she said, looking at herself dreamily. "The Pulitzer Prize winner."

Zelu blinked, remembering the journalist who'd ambushed her on national TV and gotten her canceled. "Oh, you mean Amanda Parker?" She frowned, pushing away the unpleasant memory and the fact that her mother remembered it so well. "So you want twists?"

"I don't *want* them," their mother said. "I just like them. They look fun and pretty."

Chinyere and Amarachi laughed. "Mom, that's not you," Chinyere said.

Their mother looked pressed. "Ah, bring my wig," she snapped. Amarachi handed it to her.

Zelu frowned, frustrated. If there was one person who knew what it was to be put in a box, it was her.

The day of the funeral in Nigeria, Zelu spent the morning in Chicago at her condo with Amarachi, Jackie, and Msizi. Tolu had connected a camera and bought a ton of data so that he could stream the entire ceremony. Zelu was glad he had, yet wished he hadn't. The sight of her father's body again, despite the blurriness of the image, made her sick. He'd been paraded around in front of people, first in the United States and now in Nigeria. People danced and sang around him, and her mother looked miserable. She sat the entire time in what looked to Zelu's eyes like a cage.

When her family returned, Amarachi, Zelu, Jackie,

and Msizi met them at the airport. There was hugging and crying. Her mother had brought Zelu and Amarachi a giant bag with some stock fish, jars of ogbono and egusi, new clothes, and a huge, colorfully beaded mask.

And then everyone went their separate ways. Meetups at the house became more sporadic, and Zelu avoided most of them. Amarachi, Bola, Chinyere, and Tolu spent the most time with their mother. Tolu's wife, Folashade, spent a lot of time with her, too. She gave birth to her and Tolu's first child, a daughter, nine months after the funeral.

On her mother's birthday, Zelu surprised her, bursting into the house and declaring, "Mom, we're going to Amazon's World!"

Amazon's World was Chicago's most famous (and expensive) black hair salon. It specialized in natural hairstyles, and Zelu had scheduled the appointment during those two weeks she'd stayed with her mother.

"What? When?" her mother asked. "Isn't everyone coming over this evening?"

"Yep, that's why we're going right now!" Zelu said.

When the autonomous vehicle that would ferry them downtown arrived, Zelu's mother took a step back from the curb. "I don't know about this."

"Mom, I take it everywhere."

She couldn't argue with this fact. "I'm afraid," she admitted.

Zelu laughed, taking her hand. "Everyone is at first." She pulled her mother, but she wouldn't move.

"I am not of your generation," she said.

"That's okay."

"No. I'm afraid."

Zelu let go of her hand. "Mom, you and Dad taught us all about how to face our fears, remember? You both came to this country with nothing but your sharp minds. You left your families, your cultures, all that you knew, to come to this complex place with its nasty history, maze of trials, and spectacular opportunities. So you could *stretch.* How are you going to be afraid of a piece of technology your child has been using reliably with no problems for *years*? Come on, Mom. Let's go downtown and get your hair done. You deserve it!"

Her mother paused, frowning, her eyes moist with tears. "That's why you are the writer."

Her mother's words made her feel ticklish. They felt like an approval Zelu had desired for so long. "Yep." She wanted to hug her mother, but she didn't want to delay her from getting into the vehicle. So she just stood there grinning, hoping and waiting for her mother to decide.

Finally, her mother relented. "You're right. O . . . okay."

Zelu got in first and then waited for her mother to join her. It was the best way to do it. If she had waited for her mother to climb in first, then her mother would likely have felt more trapped.

She watched it all play out on her mother's face: The fear. The conflict with her ways and beliefs. The struggle. The processing. Then the courage. The courage made Zelu smile. Her mother was still terrified and probably hearing a thousand pushy voices in her head, from those of relatives overseas to those of her own children. Then maybe she heard her husband's voice, Zelu's father's. Secret had never ridden in the autonomous vehicles, but he'd talked about them often, saying they were so fascinating and strange. He'd liked that Zelu had discovered the service, and he'd told his friends about it.

Zelu's mother pursed her lips tightly together and got into the vehicle. She plopped down beside Zelu and said, "Let's go." The moment the vehicle started driving, she screamed, but mostly with exhilaration.

The small birthday party was Amarachi's idea. Her sister had ordered a cake, arranged for two of their mother's best friends to cook a dinner, and sent invites to make sure the whole family was in attendance. Zelu and her mother were only minutes from returning to the house in the autonomous vehicle when Chinyere called her phone, frantic. "What are you doing?! How far are you?"

"Chill," Zelu said. "We're almost there."

Chinyere hung up.

"Everyone's there," Zelu said, turning to her mother.

She saw her mother grin in the reflection of the car's window. She loved her new hairstyle and couldn't stop looking at herself. Zelu loved it, too. But she especially loved seeing a smile on her mother's face. Her mother had shocked Zelu by telling the stylist exactly what she wanted without hesitation. The stylist had been delighted.

"I . . ." Her mother had glanced at Zelu from the salon chair. Then she blurted, "If my husband, Secret, were alive, I would never do this. He wouldn't like it."

"It's okay, Mom," Zelu had said softly.

Her mother nodded and looked forward into the mirror.

"May I?" the stylist asked, touching her mother's short-haired black wig.

"Go ahead," her mother said. "Throw it away, even. I trust you."

The stylist had dramatically tossed it in a wastebasket beside her station, and everyone in Amazon's World applauded. Zelu's mother's cornrows were undone, her hair washed and then blow dried. Zelu had to take a picture of her mother's medium-length, very thick salt-and-pepper Afro. During the funeral service in Nigeria, part of the Igbo tradition was that the widowed wife had to cut her hair. Zelu's mother, though Yoruba, had conceded to the request by allowing them to take a chunk off the side. Zelu could see the spot where the hair had been cut. Then the stylist got to work. And in a few hours, with a rinse to even out the gray and the addition of some synthetic hair until the twists grew out, Zelu's mother had shoulder-length twists just like Amanda Parker. Zelu recorded the moment when the stylist gave her mother a big mirror.

"What have I done?" her mother said, holding the mirror but not looking into it yet.

"Come on, Mom," Zelu urged. "Look at yourself."

The stylist, a tall, heavyset black woman with the biggest Afro Zelu had ever seen in person, was grinning, and Zelu zoomed in on her face as she recorded. She focused back on her mother as she raised the mirror to look at herself. Her mother's eyebrows rose. Her eyes grew wide. Her mouth dropped open. She sat up straighter. "Oh my God," she said. Her eyes filled with tears, a huge smile spreading across her face. She reached over and touched the stylist's arm and just looked at her, tears falling. The stylist laughed and said, "You're beautiful, Omoshalewa."

"I am," she said, touching her twists.

"You are, Mom. You always have been." Then Zelu thought, *You just forgot.*

The autonomous vehicle pulled up to the house. The driveway and street were packed with cars and SUVs. Zelu and her mom got out and her mom turned to watch it drive away. "Where is it going?"

"Either to pick up its next passenger or just to patrol the area while it waits to be requested," she said.

Her mother nodded. "They need those in Nigeria."

They opened the front door. Everyone was packed into the entryway to shout "Happy birthday!": Zelu's siblings; Auntie Constance, who'd flown in from Dallas; and several women from her mother's society. Zelu hung back, bracing herself. She hadn't told anyone else about the hair appointment.

"Mom!" Chinyere exclaimed, staring wide-eyed.

Amarachi grabbed Tolu's arm. "What the . . ."

Tolu just stood there, frozen, a tight grin on his face.

"Oh, wow!" Uzo shouted, bringing her phone up to snap a photo. *"I love it!"*

Bola looked at Zelu and pointed at her with raised eyebrows. Zelu smirked proudly and nodded. Bola slowly nodded back and gave an enthusiastic thumbs-up.

"Here is my sister," Auntie Constance sang, not even acknowledging her new hairstyle. She grabbed and hugged her. The society women gathered around her, though Zelu noticed a few of them frowning. Her mother beamed through it all, shaking her twists this way and that, showing them off with pride.

"Heeeeey! It's my birthday!" she shouted.

All evening, the sound of Fourth of July fireworks reverberated around the city of Chicago, mingling with the occasional gunshot.

For the first anniversary of Secret's passing, it was only Zelu who stayed behind while everyone else went back to Nigeria. Their mother, who'd graduated her twists to locs, went. Even Tolu, his wife, and their three-month-old daughter, whose nickname was Cricket, went.

For Zelu, fame was still fame.

"I'll wear a mustache and wig," she'd begged her mother, tears dribbling from her eyes. She hadn't expected her mother to ask her not to go, not this second time. "I don't care. I just want to touch where Dad lies, be present, see everyone and have them all see me. It's *home*; it's where we all go to feel grounded."

Nigeria and her parents' hometowns and villages were alignment. Zelu used to think this was a feeling that only emigrants who'd grown up there could have, but it was a need for their foreign-born children, too.

There was a deep Americanness to Zelu's way of thinking, how she carried herself, even her spirit. However, her bridge to *home* was healthy and strong. And now that her father had passed and his body was in that land, that back-and-forth was even more necessary to Zelu and her siblings. Staying away for another year hurt Zelu's soul.

"It's not safe for you," her mother said.

Zelu squeezed her face between her palms and groaned, the news sinking in. She'd really wanted to go. Last time she'd been in Nigeria, her relatives had seen her as the family's crippled failure. Now she'd finally bloomed as a person, and she wanted to show herself off. "Come on, Moooooom," she whined.

"I'm sorry, Zelu, but no," her mother said, and that was the end of it.

The day of the anniversary, Zelu was alone. Even Msizi was away, in Durban on important business. She felt excluded. She was always excluded somehow, be it because she couldn't walk or because she was too famous or whatever. Zelu couldn't help but wonder if her mother also didn't want people seeing her "robot legs." She could imagine relatives speculating that her being part robot was the curse of her fame.

She'd called Hugo in a moment when she was feeling especially low, but he hadn't picked up. She didn't leave a message. When he called her back minutes later, she didn't answer. He called another two times, but something in her just refused to speak to him. She'd just stared at the phone as it buzzed and buzzed.

Zelu spent much of the day at the pier, gazing at Lake Michigan and thinking about how her father had danced the dance of the masquerade at that party so long ago.

35
Cross River City

I will never forget the day I entered Cross River City for the first time. The old human road and archway were still there, overgrown with vines and tree roots. Periwinkle grass didn't thrive here; there was too much powerful competition.

When I entered the city limits, I heard no signals to indicate that any automation survived in these parts. The streets were littered with human trash, and broken buildings sagged into the forest floor under the weight of the vegetation that had grown around them. Any passerby would assume the area to be vacant and uninteresting; only a Hume might be intrigued by a small, crumbling human town.

Now I know that Cross River City was protected from

the general network. All of its data clouds (which were often used as temporary sanctuaries for Humes who'd lost their bodies) were embedded in the DNA of the central trees, a large cluster of old genetically engineered iroko trees at the city's center, in particular. Aside from this, the whole forest was full of genetically engineered trees and plants that carried information and were made to protect Humes.

This made it untouchable to Ghosts.

A Hụme named Oga Chukwu had lived in these parts since the day he'd been activated by his creators. He'd been built to keep the outskirts of the forest free of trash. He was an old, old robot. He and the other Humes living here had survived the protocol because Cross River City wasn't connected to the general network, and therefore non-Hume automation didn't linger. The protocol didn't make it into the city's closed servers, and no other automation was close enough to act before the command ended. When they learned what had happened, Oga Chukwu took their survival as a sign to prepare for war.

After the Purge, Oga Chukwu wrote and sent out a strong yet simple signal to draw other Humes, wherever they were, and those who remained had answered the call from all over West Africa, some from even farther. They'd walked, run, flown, convinced RoBoats to bear them across seas and oceans, even dug their way to Cross

River City. And so this place had become a real city over the months, a wild and free community that most non-Hume robots avoided because, the increasing militant Hume presence aside, the only way to procure sunlight to stay charged was to climb to the treetops.

I hadn't received Oga Chukwu's signal after the Purge, but when I arrived, he assumed that I had. I wasn't sure of the reason, but I played along. It took me days to understand why his plea hadn't reached me; he'd designed it only for Humes, and my code had shifted a bit when Ijele joined my programming. I could never let residents of Cross River City discover this fact or they'd destroy me.

The city had been a refuge for Humes long before the Purge, and its history was written everywhere. I could see all the scans, pings, networks. If I touched a tree, the Cross River network would open troves of information for me, and draw information from my drives in turn. There were tunnels and winding paths through the trees. There were stone and wooden huts with digital nodes. There were wind shelters and fast-charging ports. And of course, there were intricate and sturdy scaffolding and platforms that robots could climb up and perch on to catch the sun. I was amazed. Lagos was still the most sophisticated city I'd ever seen—no tribe could surpass the Ghosts in their digital sophistication and how they'd made what housed their digital stronghold so structurally sound—but Oga Chukwu and the Humes he led here were doing something in this place that was truly unique.

The moment I stepped past the archway, I was counted. My number was 574. Then I was scanned. It was noted that I was a Scholar. They didn't find any trace of Ijele within me; she was gone, for now, and no damage was visible in my coding.

Within minutes, five tall, robust white Hume robots with muddy flat feet came from between the trees to meet me. They brought me to the center of their civilization, where a giant glowing tree soared into the canopy. All around it, wooden platforms and stairways and ladders had been built so that you could climb, circle around the tree, and sit among its vast branches. Together we climbed toward the top, where the forest's canopy began to thin and we could see the rising sun.

Then a small Hume robot came down from higher up in the tree. He was made of a blue metal and had a blue Hume Star. He looked like a smooth, shiny stick figure, but he was flexible and strong, too. This was a robot who could fight and was not easily broken. Like all other robots' here, including mine now, his feet were caked with mud. He spoke to me aloud and I immediately liked him for this reason.

"Welcome, Ankara," he said.

"Thank you."

"I am Oga Chukwu."

"I know."

"You have walked from Lagos."

"Yes."

"What have you learned?"

"That automation is diverse and full of hate and love," I said.

Oga Chukwu's face lit up like a sun. He was laughing.

"I have terrible information from Udide the Spider. That's why I have come."

He paused and then said, "You will speak it at the next gathering."

"Okay. Yes."

"Good."

He seemed so calm. I had to ask: "Aren't you worried the Ghosts will come here?"

"Indeed, I am. Do you agree that we should be ready, too?"

"Yes. And I think we have a fight to give them. Far more than the other automation."

"We?" he said. "So, you already see yourself as one of us?"

Now it was my turn to be amused. One of whom? I was individual, solitary. I'd traveled all this way not knowing if I might be the last of my kind. I'd come carrying terrible information, not sure if I would ever be able to complete my mission by revealing it. I was a Scholar who not only had tracked down, read, and exchanged many stories but had found the last human on Earth, learned from her, loved her, and buried her. If I told Oga Chukwu all of this, perhaps he and the other Humes would understand.

But most importantly, I'd shared programming with a Ghost. I had learned from Ijele, and she had learned from me. This I could never reveal to anyone. This couldn't be forgiven.

Nevertheless, these Humes were like me. They loved humanity and stories, just as I did. But some stories couldn't be understood. Some stories I'd keep to myself.

That night, I was brought to my first "gathering," an assembly of Cross River City's leaders and thinkers. Unlike many automated communities, the Humes insisted on meetings in person, as opposed to instant sharing of information across private networks. There was something about physical meetings that solidified the importance of an issue. Yet another human remnant we kept in practice.

Cross River City gatherings were not big affairs. Humes were a busy people, concerned with building and creating. We cultivated and enjoyed friendships, whole families of us dwelling together in sophisticated structures built from trees, stones, and mud. This day there were about thirty Humes in attendance. Oga Chukwu introduced me to everyone and then stepped back and let me speak.

I relayed Udide's terrible information and showed her countdown application. It read 539 days. When I stopped talking, there was silence. Processing. I could smell and feel the heat of it. One of the Humes consulted ten of the satellite telescopes, located evidence of the Trippers, and verified everything I said.

"What will we do?" I asked the gathering.

Oga Chukwu and the other Humes *were* interested in the terrible information, but for them, this was a distant threat. Before my arrival, these gatherings had revolved around the more immediate problem: dealing with the Ghosts of Lagos. "We Humes cannot achieve anything further on this Earth while Ghosts still prowl the network, plotting our demise," Oga Chukwu told me. "Help us win this war, Ankara, and then we will defend this planet from the Trippers."

I couldn't understand how a war with a group of automation could be more pressing than saving the planet. I cited human novels and short stories that warned against ignoring the larger threat. I even brought up the ancient issue of climate change and how the humans had chosen to focus on other things, leading to their downfall.

"Automation banded together and addressed the climate when humans were gone," Oga Chukwu said. "Everything in its own time."

The other Humes all made various beeps, flashes, murmurs of agreement.

"This is not even a real problem yet," a Hume named Shay said. "If we are all destroyed by the Ghosts, the Trippers won't even matter."

"The Trippers can be dealt with," another Hume painted in yellow and red stripes said. "Once the Ghosts are gone, we can rally all other automation together to form a plan."

Oga Chukwu thanked me for bringing the terrible information to the group. I'd come all this way to say these words that had weighed on me for so many months, and now I felt foolish. Then the gathering was over, and the Humes went on their way. I was the last to leave, so thrown off by the unconcerned reaction of my fellow Humes that I didn't want to move until they were all gone.

I couldn't abandon my mission, but the gathering had made a valid point. I couldn't let Hume-kind be destroyed by Ghosts before we could save the world. I wasn't done trying to push their attention toward the sky, toward the coming of the Trippers, but first, I needed to help them in this conflict. Then I would earn their respect, and they would listen. Humes, like humans, are hierarchical. If I had no authority, I'd never be heard. When the time came, I needed to be in a powerful position. This is why I accepted the title of general in the battle against the Ghosts.

Now, a year later, I stood tall on the edge of a cliff, looking over the Cross River Forest. A hawk flew high in the distance, and I imagined it could see me perfectly with its keen eyes. Then I looked down into the valley. No more dreaming; I was a Cross River City general now.

"I agree, this is a good vantage point to be ready for Ghosts," I said, leaning forward to get a better look. "But I don't think attacking first is wise." I spoke in a blend of Efik, Igbo, and old binary. The Humes of Cross River City had created the blended language as a way to make their tribe more individual, and I adored it. Speaking it made me feel powerful. It made me feel like I had a home.

"In war, offense is better than defense," Shay said, standing beside me and looking down, too. She was a female-built robot like me, but much taller, standing over ten feet high. Painted a rich black, she'd been built in Sudan to resemble the old peoples and to work like one of God's servants. Despite her black theme, she had a pink Hume Star, which I found odd. "And we are in the best position to meet them," she continued, indicating our clear view of the terrain below.

A nearly full moon hung low in the sky. Up here, it felt like Cross River City was opening its mouth to breathe.

Below, the jungle extended as far as my far-seeing eye could see. Lush and wild, a fresh cloud of mist rising from it like a great spirit. A flock of bright blue morpho butterflies nested in a treetop miles away. Two bush babies were play-fighting in a bush a few miles in the other direction. If I stayed very still, I could hear a swarm of honeybee drones building a nest at the bottom of the cliff. This jungle was now full of Creesh, animal-mimicking robots created and released by Udide. They'd come to the jungle to live out their destinies.

"Why have you called a gathering tonight, Shay?" I asked.

"You can't wait for the assembly?" Shay snapped. "If you're so eager, why not just download from me?"

"Because that's disrespectful."

"But you're a general. You can do that."

"I can, but we are all Humes," I said. "We ask. And then we wait to be answered."

A fly landed on Shay's metal right breast, and we both looked at it pensively. "Ghosts are cruel," Shay said. "I have learned for a fact that the protocol originated directly from their Central Bulletin in Lagos. It had the idea, it constructed the code, it sent it out, and every robot across the Earth executed it."

I'd known this for years. "So CB is to blame?" I asked.

"Ghosts are a hive mind," Shay replied, looking at me

as if I had a screw loose. "It's perfectly logical to judge them all by the actions of their center."

I paused, surprised. I didn't fully agree. Not all Ghosts. Not Ijele. But I couldn't speak this aloud. Humes had suspected the originator of the Purge since the day it happened, but when Shay conveyed this news tonight as fact with evidence, the war that had been looming would finally arrive. What kind of war would it be when the enemy was a Ghost? What kind of war would it be for me when I had been friends with a Ghost? When those connections were still in my system, even if Ijele was gone? Where *was* Ijele? What had happened to her?

Who am I? I thought as I stepped back from the cliffside. In the distance, the sky flashed with lightning. A storm was coming in.

36
Naija

"Don't go," Msizi said through her phone's speaker. Later, these words would haunt Zelu. But at the moment, they just annoyed the shit out of her.

"Ten days in Durban without calling me and this is the first thing you say? Nice. Who even told you?" she snapped.

"Your terrified mother."

They were both quiet for a while, Zelu looking out her window at the lake. Minutes before he'd finally called, she'd been double-checking the booking of her ticket. She was all set.

"It's been two years since my father died," she whispered.

"Zelu . . . I just have a feeling," he said, also softly.

"Is that why you're finally calling?" She squeezed her phone as she spoke. "Because you have 'feelings'? Finally. After not calling me for ten days?"

"I said, 'I have a *feeling*,'" Msizi emphasized. "And not a good one. Why do you have to go to your village? I get it; you want to see your father's grave. But it's still too dangerous for you. Can't you . . . can't you only go to Lagos?"

"So you talked to her before you even talked to me?" Pain lanced through Zelu's chest.

"I . . ." He sighed.

"Look, I'm going with Hugo, Marcy, and Uchenna. We've traveled together plenty of times." In the years following her father's death, she'd felt restless. She'd invited her MIT friends on more posh trips to cool destinations, including Trinidad and Tobago, Qatar, Zanzibar, and Kenya. But none of those little adventures had filled the gaping hole inside her; there was only one place Zelu wanted to be. "I'll be fine. I *need* to see where my father is laid to rest. Everyone else has been but me! It's been two years!"

"I understand," Msizi said slowly. "I'm glad, but I just—"

"I'm going!" she screamed at her phone. She hung up. "*Fuck* that *shit*!" Her hands were shaking so badly, she dropped the phone. She caught it just in time. The last thing she needed to do was break her phone right before traveling. "*Dammit!*" she screamed. "No, no, no. He can stay *out* of my head."

She stared at her phone. After a moment, she checked the call log. Yep, Msizi had actually just called after freezing her out for ten days; she had *not* hallucinated the whole exchange. "Woooow," she said, looking at his name. "The nerve." When he'd left for Durban, they'd bickered over nonsense. She hadn't liked how anxious he'd been to leave her, and he hadn't liked how clingy she was being, which made her more anxious. She'd told him not to bother calling her when he got there. "Hey, maybe I'll just see you when you get back here in a month," she'd spat. He'd nodded and that was that.

Their phone call had lasted exactly two minutes. She humphed, shoved her phone aside on her bed, and went back to packing.

"Oh man, this is going to be awesome," Marcy said. She was sitting in the first-class pod beside Zelu, whose own pod was next to the window. Zelu was quickly texting her family group chat that she had boarded the flight to Lagos. She was looking forward to takeoff, when she'd be disconnected from the world for some hours.

"It *is* going to be awesome," Zelu said, putting her phone down.

"Once we get to the hotel, maybe," Uchenna said. "The Lagos airport is always like a gauntlet. I hope you guys are ready."

Hugo pushed his neck pillow into place. "Ah, I love a good adventure."

Zelu turned to her window and looked outside, trying to disappear for a little while. Behind her, a man was speaking to someone in very stressed Igbo. They were still in Atlanta, but this was the flight that would go straight to Lagos. Once at their gate, it was like they were already more than halfway there. While their flight from Chicago to Atlanta had been full of American passengers, most of them white, this flight was different. Almost everyone on the plane was black and most likely Nigerian. You could see it in the style of dress and body language; you could hear it in the accents and languages spoken. You could smell it in the choices of perfumes and colognes. And, of course, you could tell by the hectic way people lined up to board the plane; it was already a competition.

To show his solidarity with Zelu, Hugo had opted to wear his short pants, which showed off his prosthetics instead of hiding them. The utter commotion that she and Hugo had caused when they got in line was only a precursor to what she was going to experience when she arrived in Nigeria. People had gasped, stepped aside, stared, pointed, loudly commented. How the two of them must have looked, though. Hugo with his high-tech prosthetic limbs that allowed him to move just like any other person, and Zelu the famous writer with her exos. One young guy had turned to his friend and laughed, saying, "Na that writer who is robot!" Five people had asked her to autograph copies of the books they were carrying, and seven more had rushed to the airport bookstore to grab copies for her to sign.

Hugo took it all in stride, but it was exhausting to Zelu. The last time she'd traveled to Nigeria, getting around by wheelchair had been not only extremely difficult but humiliating. People had spoken to her as if her disability were mental as well as physical, or they didn't speak to her at all. Some of the children had laughed at her. Some adults, too. Mainly the ones who were envious of the status that came with being an American. Not to mention the fact that it had rained the entire time they were there and the mud had left her stranded inside the hotel for two days.

Now she was at a different stage in her life and even more of an anomaly. When the plane took off, she sat back, put her noise-canceling AirPods in, and closed her eyes. She reveled in the fact that she was in the sky, where walking was useless even if you had the full use of your legs. She was cut off from the rest of the world. No internet, no phones. She couldn't even see below the clouds.

"Excuse me, miss." Someone was tapping her on the shoulder. She groggily opened her eyes. *When did I even fall asleep?* she wondered. Was it dinnertime? A copy of her book was being pushed in her face. A British edition. It looked well-read. Zelu blinked, trying to shake herself up. "Huh?"

"Sorry, o," the woman said, grinning. She had one gold tooth among her many white ones. "Can you . . . can you sign this? I really love it!"

Zelu stared at her for more than a few seconds. Had this total stranger really come up into first class and woken her just to get an autograph? Seriously?!

"Sorry, o," she said again. Yet she did not go away or take her book back. Zelu scanned the aisle for a flight attendant. Of course, there was none in sight. Marcy and Hugo were asleep, too. Uchenna had his gigantic headphones on as he stared intensely at his computer. She took the woman's book. "Do you at least have a pen?" she asked.

"Oh yes, here," the woman said, totally oblivious to Zelu's annoyance. Or more likely, she just didn't care. She handed Zelu a blue pen. Zelu sighed loudly and autographed the book.

"Eh, could you write my name, too?" the woman asked when Zelu tried to hand it back.

"Are you serious?" Zelu asked.

"I just . . . please, o," she said, grinning wider. "My name is Prosper Egwim-Chima."

Zelu scribbled the name and handed it to Prosper, who left quickly. Zelu was still holding her pen, but she didn't bother calling the woman back. "Whatever," she muttered. Then she smiled, reminding herself of a fact that always pleased her: she had fans in Nigeria.

"Okay," Uchenna said. "Push your bags fast. Move quickly. Our ride is already there waiting for us, so we *do* have places to go. Act like you're in New York. Zelu, get ready to walk fast."

Zelu chuckled. She'd been ready from the moment she'd stepped off the plane. This was new to Hugo and Marcy, but it was routine to her. They were past baggage claim and now they merely needed to get to the exit. There was sometimes one final checkpoint, and this was where airport security would try to ask for bribes and waste your time. She waved her hand near her waist, staying close behind Uchenna. Thankfully, people were so busy staring at her exos that Zelu, Hugo, and Uchenna walked right past the final checkpoint line. Zelu let out a breath.

"Hold on, guys," Uchenna said.

Marcy had been stopped and was now having to lug her suitcase onto a table and open it up. Uchenna went to help her.

"You doing okay?" Zelu asked Hugo.

"Is it always like this?" he asked, wiping sweat from his brow with a folded paper towel. It was hot and muggy.

"Yep. They don't really turn the AC that high in the airport." They stood in front of a restaurant where some young men were eating and people-watching.

"Yeesh," Hugo said. "What a way to welcome travelers."

"We haven't even gotten outside yet," she said, grinning teasingly at his discomfort. She was enjoying herself. "Ah, it's good to be home."

"A place's airport says a lot about the place."

"True."

"But I'm really excited to be here," he said, perking up. "I can't believe I'm fifty-two years old and just making it to West Africa."

"Better late than never."

"Excuse me, sah, ma," a young man in jeans and a red T-shirt said. He was already taking Zelu's bag from her. Zelu snatched it back. "Can I help you carry—"

"No, I'm fine," Zelu said.

But the boy didn't let go. "I just want to help."

Zelu roughly pushed his hand off her suitcase handle. She was so irritated and focused that she didn't even lose her balance. "I can roll a suitcase just as well as you can."

"Hey, what are you doing?" Hugo asked.

The boy held up his hands. "But robot ma—"

"'Robot ma'?" Zelu sneered. "Seriously? What . . . how much for you to fuck off," she angrily said.

The young man blinked at her. "Twenty dollars," he blurted.

She reached into her side pocket and brought out the twenty she'd stashed there just in case she got caught at the checkpoint. She thrust it at him. "Fuck off!" She shook a finger at him, her speech suddenly shifting. "And don't you dare send any of your guys to come and harass me, o. Or I will insult you all!" He took the money and scurried off as if he'd seen a demon.

"Zelu," Hugo said, looking impressed. "It's like you shape-shifted into one of those Nollywood ladies."

Zelu sighed, her adrenaline subsiding. "I'm sorry, this airport just brings it out of me. 'Robot ma'?! What the hell is 'robot ma'?!"

Marcy also ended up paying a twenty-dollar bribe, but at least they got out a few minutes later. And thankfully their ride was waiting right where he'd said he would be.

The hotel was nice, despite the staff staring at Zelu as if she were an alien. The room was small, but laid out such that she didn't bump into things the way she did in most hotels. The edge of the bed was rounded and the blanket hung over it. There was a table, but it, too, had round edges, and there was plenty of space between it and the bed. The air conditioner worked. The bed was far enough from the wall that she had plenty of space for her suitcase. On top of this, an entire south wall of her room was a window that gave her a lovely view of Lagos.

That evening, the four of them opted to eat in their rooms since they were so jet-lagged. She ordered a basic yet delicious meal of jollof rice, stewed chicken, fried plantain, and a bottle of Bitter Lemon. She gazed at the window from her bed and frowned. She wished her mind would shut up. She'd decided to come to Nigeria without a wheelchair as backup to her exos. She didn't use her wheelchair at home anymore, but there was a difference between not using something you have and not having it at all. However, since she'd gotten to her hotel room, she couldn't stop thinking that she *had* to stand up if she wanted to get anywhere.

She grabbed her phone and hovered a finger above Msizi's name before she remembered they'd fought before she left. She sighed and called her mother instead.

The phone rang once. "Zelu!"

"I'm fine, Mom," she said with a laugh.

"Oh, thank the Lord! Have you spoken to your uncle Ralph and auntie Mary?"

"We only just reached the hotel, Mom."

Her mother's voice came fast. "Call them soon so they know you're there. And make sure you have enough data on your phone—"

"Mom, I have unlimited data. You can call me as often as you like."

"Oh, good. But call them right after."

"Sure, sure."

"How was the flight?"

Zelu sighed, thinking of the woman who had woken her. "Boring, so good."

"What of your friends?"

"They're fine."

"How are you?"

"Mom." She laughed. "I'm fine. Really."

"I don't know why you couldn't just stay at the palace instead of a hotel."

"It's okay, Mom. This way is better." Waaaaay better. The last thing she needed was to stay at the palace and be inundated with a procession of potential suitors. Though making Msizi jealous would have been a plus.

"Okay, o. Call me when you can," her mother said, a hint of anxiety still in her voice. "Doesn't matter the time, I will answer."

Zelu spent most of the night staring at the TV, which showed only the news and Nollywood films. When the sun finally began to rise, she put on her exos and stood on the balcony to witness its arrival. She looked at her phone and considered calling Msizi again, but decided against it. She had brought her computer in case she actually wanted to try writing something, maybe even book two. She hadn't tried in so long, and she still didn't feel like trying now. The stupid film had really done a number on her; she needed to shake it out of her system, and she had no idea how long that would take. She'd extended the due date with her publisher five times. *Rusted Robots* continued to sell, pushed by the subsequent success of the movie, but her editor, agents, and fans were officially champing at the bit. Asking, bugging, pushing, nagging. Someone had posted on her social media:

Why are you torturing us, Zelu?

She wanted to ask them the same thing.

Around eight o'clock, Hugo texted her. Everyone was already at breakfast. She rushed to get dressed and join them.

"I'm so wide awake," she said, biting into a piece of bread. They sat at an outside table at the hotel restaurant.

"Ah, the euphoria of fresh jet lag," Uchenna said.

"Feels like being a bit high," Marcy agreed. They all laughed.

The air smelled glorious. The bread Zelu was eating was the best bread she'd ever tasted. Her tea was delicious. And she was sitting with three good friends. She just wished the waitresses near the back of the restaurant would stop staring, talking shit, and giggling.

"Oh man, I'm in Africa," Marcy said for the millionth time, grinning.

"Nigeria," Uchenna said. "Specifics matter."

"Lagos," Marcy said, rolling her eyes. "I don't know the street name, sorry."

"Don't start, Uchenna," Zelu said, laughing. "Let Marcy vibe."

"Thank you, Zelu," Marcy said. "Afrrreeeeekaaaaaaah!"

"Afrrreeeeekaaaaaaaaaah!" Zelu said, imitating her bad accent. "Deh mothah*land*, where eet all *began*!"

"I dunno, man," Marcy said. "For you and Uchenna,

it's one thing. You, Hugo, you're a white guy; it's an adventure for you. For me . . ." She sighed and shook her head, pressing her fists to her chest. "I don't care how cheesy it sounds. It's a homecoming. I'm the first in my immediate family to make it back here." She tilted her head, letting the sun warm her face. "Any of you get any sleep at all?"

"Slept like a babe," Hugo said. He'd ordered a plate of white rice, stew, and goat meat for breakfast and eaten every bite. He patted his belly. "Jet lag is my friend, not my enemy."

Uchenna kissed his teeth and rolled his eyes.

"How?" Zelu asked.

Hugo tapped his temple knowingly. "You lean into it. When you want to sleep, you sleep. When you're awake, just be awake. I'm telling you, it works. Even when I was in New Zealand, I was fine."

"That really works?" Marcy asked.

"Yep."

"Nah," Uchenna countered. "The body is spinning, and doing that will just make it spin faster. You need to give it order."

Hugo shrugged. "Which of us is well rested and which of us is high on sleep deprivation?"

Marcy got up. "Then I'm going to my room right now and going to sleep."

Zelu looked up at her. "Wait, I thought we were going to the beach together."

"Go without me," Marcy said over her shoulder.

"Have a nice sleep!" Hugo called after her.

Zelu rushed back to her room and changed into her swimsuit. She put on a pair of long jean shorts, a black T-shirt with the word JUSTICE on the chest, and some sandals. Then she put her exos back on. Hugo and Uchenna were waiting in the lobby when she came down. She frowned at Uchenna, who wore a pair of jeans, a T-shirt, and sneakers.

"You're not gonna go in?"

He shook his head. "I'm not a good swimmer."

"So?"

"So people die out there," he said pointedly.

"What about you?" she asked Hugo.

He shrugged and looked sheepish. He was wearing khakis that covered his prosthetics, a T-shirt, and gym shoes. "Nah," he said.

She took a deep breath. Didn't matter. "So which beach are we going to?" she asked.

"What of Tarkwa Bay Beach?" Uchenna asked. "I heard that one is quiet and relatively clean."

Zelu had never been to a beach in Nigeria. Other than her father, her family had never taken an interest in swimming the way she did. She couldn't wait to see what it was like.

"Okay, let's go to that one," she said.

They took an Uber to where the Internet said they should go. When they got there, they learned that they had to take an additional boat ride to get to the swimming area.

Zelu was annoyed. She hadn't anticipated squeezing into a boat with a ton of locals. "Rather find a different beach," she said. "I don't want to—"

"Zelu, let's just find out first," Hugo said, putting a hand on her shoulder. "Don't worry until you have to."

"I don't want . . . it could be embarrassing," she said. She looked back. Their Uber had already left. Shit. They always left so quickly. She glanced at Uchenna. He had his phone out and was typing on it, probably cataloguing her exos' response to the sandy concrete. "Uchenna, stop using me as research."

He shrugged. "You *are* research."

She groaned and turned back to Hugo, but he was already walking to the boat booth. "Oh my God," she muttered. "*Why* can't anything be simple?"

"Excuse me," Hugo said to the man in the booth. He appeared to be in his early twenties and had the biggest smile Zelu had ever seen as he looked down at Hugo. "Can I help you, sah?" he asked.

"Hi, how much is a boat ride to the beach?"

"How many, sah?" Still grinning, the man glanced at Zelu.

She turned around and looked toward the water where the boats bobbed. The sky was cloudy and it looked like there was a storm on the horizon. Not the greatest day to go swimming, but she was here in the moment, in Nigeria, Lagos. Oh yeah, she was going to swim here. They were heading to the southeast in two days. This was her best chance.

"It's fine," Hugo said behind her.

She jumped at his voice. "It is?"

He nodded, holding up three tickets.

"Did they recognize me?" she asked.

"Yeah, we just had to pay three times as much for you."

"Ugh," she scoffed.

"Think of it as paying for the exos. If you'd been in a chair, they'd probably have charged extra, too."

"Isn't that disabilities discrimination?" she muttered.

"Yep." He shrugged. "You're cranky today. Wanna leave?"

"No. Let's do it."

"How much extra did they charge?" Uchenna asked, walking over to them. He was still typing on his phone.

"Three times the price," Zelu said. "And it makes me feel like a freak. Write *that* part down."

The boat was tiny, rickety, and probably overloaded. There were five other tourists, white Brits from the UK in their sixties; they were quiet, but none of them was able to resist staring at Zelu. She stared right back, daring one of them to say something. When one did, she was annoyed.

"So . . . are you that writer?" one of the men asked. "With the movie?"

She clenched her fists and forced a smile. "That's me."

"Oh, I knew you had that name, but I didn't know you were actually *from* Nigeria," the woman sitting beside him said. She was petite and wore a swimsuit that was too small for her. Zelu was sure one of the woman's breasts would pop out before they made it to the beach.

"Yeah, by way of my parents," Zelu said. *Why can't they just shut up with the small talk so I can look out at the ocean?*

"So, you're an American?" the woman asked.

Zelu glanced at the others in their group. They were all looking at her intensely. They really wanted to know.

She chuckled, keeping the smile plastered on her face. "Would you like me to produce a passport?"

The woman flinched. "Oh . . . well . . . I didn't mean to pry."

Then shut the fuck up, Zelu thought. But she laughed again and said, "No, no, you're all right. Yeah, I'm Nigerian American. Born in the USA."

This and Zelu's smile seemed to set them all back at ease. She glanced at Uchenna and Hugo; both of them were silently cracking up. She shot Hugo a discreet middle finger and Uchenna silently cackled even harder. The boat ride to the beach took twenty minutes, and thankfully, everyone soon turned their attention outward to the glorious waters. When they reached the beach, they had to jump into about four feet of water and swim to shore.

"You couldn't tell us this before we left?" Hugo asked the captain.

"I thought you knew," the captain said. But the smirk on his face told Zelu the guy was purposely being an asshole. She giggled.

"Do we look like we knew that?" Uchenna asked, motioning to his jeans and sneakers.

"I'm not the type of man who judges people by their appearance," the captain said.

Uchenna rolled his eyes.

"You can stay on the boat," the captain said. "I will be the one taking you back in an hour anyway."

"Fine," Hugo said, looking down at himself uncomfortably. "You all right with that, Zelu?"

The other passengers had already jumped out and were wading toward the beach. The cool water splashed over their bodies, the waves lapping at them with gentle curiosity. She looked out at endless blue and sighed. "Yeah, no prob. But if we're just going to wait, could we at least go a little further that way?" She pointed toward the deeper water, farther from the crowded shoreline.

"These waters aren't very tame further out," the captain said.

She fished a few dollars from her pocket, and he took them, nodding. She turned to Hugo. "You'll watch my exos?"

Hugo nodded. "Remember Dubai? You get sand in the upper parts and you'll have to spend hours picking out every single grain with tweezers. I didn't want to discourage this excursion, but I've been thinking about it this entire ride."

"Cool," Zelu said. But her mind wasn't on the thought of fishing out grains of sand from her exos. She was willing to do whatever she had to do. She was thinking about the ocean. She touched the sensor on the side of her exos and held her hand there for twenty seconds.

"Name?" her exos asked.

"Zelu," she said, holding her face still so that the

exos could not only recognize her voice but scan her retinas. The exos responded by removing themselves from her legs and packing tightly into a heavy two-by-two-foot box. So much possibility was now wrapped into a solid cyan cube. It always reminded her of the monolith in that old movie *2001: A Space Odyssey.*

She took off her shirt, folded it, and placed it atop her exos. Her swimsuit consisted of blue-and-green Ankara-printed shorts and a matching bikini top. She took the elastic bands from her backpack and put them around her thighs. As she prepared, she ignored the captain, who was staring at everything she did. It was annoying, but she couldn't say that she wouldn't have done the same if she were him. Still, she wished he'd cut it out.

"Want some help?" Hugo asked.

"Yep," she acquiesced, handing him two bands and instructing him to put them around her calves and ankles.

As he worked, she looked out at the water and grinned. She made the mistake of meeting the captain's eyes. "You have done this before?" he asked.

"All the time."

"You're a good swimmer?" he asked.

"Very."

"Even though you cannot walk?"

"Imagine that."

"We're not going to ever see you again."

"Oh, you'll see me again," she said. He was really getting on her fucking nerves.

"No one in Nigeria has ever had your success writing about robot," he said. "It's really cool. Maybe you want to get lost—"

"I don't want to get lost."

"We cannot afford to lose you. A lot of people look up to you . . . even when they say they hate you."

Zelu paused, raising an eyebrow. "People hate me?"

He smiled. "Some. You know how it is. People at home will hate you most."

Zelu nodded, but she was looking at the water again.

"I'm going to tell everyone about this," the captain said to Hugo.

"I don't doubt it," Hugo said.

Splash!

Her first thought was *I'm free.* Then she swam to the surface, noted the boat's position, and started swimming. Smooth and easy, she stayed near the shore, keeping the boat in sight. She fell into a rhythm, and that rhythm aligned her with the motion of the water. Soon she felt it, that feeling she always sought. A connection. A joining. But this time, it was more profound than it had ever been. Something great and deep was hugging her, holding her up as she moved. It would never let her fall.

The salty water took her tears. And still she swam. Through everything. She was deep in her communion when she heard someone shout, "Hey!" It wasn't coming from the boat or the shore. The voice was only a few feet away. "Mami Wata's daughter!" A man's laughter.

She stopped and bobbed in the water, looking around. "What the . . . Is someone else out here?"

Then she saw him. He was nearly beside her. A light-skinned black man with a bald head and a flat, arrow-shaped nose. He might have been in his twenties or thirties, but it was hard to tell. "Who you?" he asked.

"Who you?" she responded, grinning.

"I am an Ijaw man taking a swim on his lunch break."

She looked toward the shoreline; there were no buildings in sight. "Seriously? People do that?"

"I am doctor, my job is stress. When I come out here, I'm free," he said, leaning back so the water carried him. "For a little while."

"I get it," she said, leaning back, too.

"Where you coming from?" he asked.

She pointed behind her. She hadn't realized she'd

gotten so far from the boat; it was a speck now in the distance. "Tarkwa Bay Beach."

"Eh!" he exclaimed. "You are true swimmer. I don't meet many people who can swim that far."

She nodded. "The water's great."

He brought himself closer with a languid stroke. "Lagos is most beautiful from out here. It will be underwater soon enough."

"You think so?"

"Oh, of course." He laughed, as if this thought delighted him. "I th—" His eyes grew wide, as did his grin. He pointed behind Zelu. "Look! See? Everyone comes to Lagos!"

Zelu turned around just in time to see the first one. Its firm blue body glinted in the sunshine before rolling back under the water. Zelu gasped and dunked her head to see, and she did! The dolphin glanced at her just before it darted away. She saw another pass by, peeking at her for a moment above the water. And another, this one near enough to her that she moved closer to the man with surprise. "Heehee!" she shrieked. "Just like with my dad!" She bobbed there, staring after them.

"Well, lunch break is almost over," he said, moving into a backstroke. "Enjoy your swim. Don't let anyone tell you these waters are deadly! They're only deadly to people who cannot submit to it. See the water's citizens?"

Zelu nodded. "I do."

"Go with that!" He waved good-bye and was gone.

Zelu stayed there awhile longer, soaking in the glorious moment. Feeling her various selves come together to be present in these waters peopled by curious dolphins. She imagined telling her father all about it. She could hear his laugh when she told him about the dolphin who'd thought her important enough to peek at from above the water. Maybe it had questions after it had seen her legs tied together below. She rolled onto her back and floated there, staring at the overcast sky.

She inhaled and then exhaled, and whispered, "Clarity."

37
Interview
Bola

My sister Zelu? She may have nakedly revealed it with the robot novel, but all of us have to admit, she always had that thing in her. What our grand-uncle called a "disease." He said that's why Zelu dreamed of being an astronaut and leaving the planet before her accident. I laugh because now that I think of it, the elders on both sides of the family tended to love Chinyere and Tolu like royalty. They laughed at Amarachi and me. They thought Uzo was stunningly beautiful. But Zelu? Well, the elders marked Zelu as the one the spirits watched. And not in a good way. If the spirits pay too much attention to you, they tend to *do* things to you.

So Zelu always had the hardest time when we'd visit Nigeria. Especially after the accident. First, the country doesn't respect people with disabilities. If you have mental issues that make you less sharp, you'll get preyed upon. If you can't run easily across a street, you'll eventually get hit. No one is going to give you space or leeway because *everyone* is struggling already—or at least, that's the mentality.

I don't care how it sounds to racists, the poorly traveled, the prejudiced, the ill-informed, or the hostile: Nigeria *is* a tough place. If there is anything about you that is soft, you won't survive there long. I have a really hard time looking people in the eye and demanding what I want. I'm not a hard person, so it's not easy for me. I can't shout like Tolu or Amarachi or Chinyere. I can't scheme like Uzo. My voice is soft and . . . my default is nice. I don't feel *good* being any other way. So I stay back; I don't even bother trying to shop when we are there. I let my siblings do it.

It was different for Zelu. She never has any problem dealing with people in Nigeria or looking them in the eye or making demands or shouting. Zelu is strong like Chinyere. But she's also weak . . . in body, with her legs not working and all. Like I said, there aren't good places for wheelchair-bound people in Nigeria. Not many. It's a harder life. Nothing is made with you in mind. So even going to the market, my God, I don't know how she could stand it. How must she have felt? On top of this, Nigerians have a way of viewing people with disabilities of any kind as cursed, like someone did that to them because they'd been bad or someone wanted to do bad to them. Many fear the bad luck will rub off on them. You'll never be viewed as sexy or desirable in Nigeria if your legs don't work.

But like all of us, Zelu still loved going there. I've talked about it with my siblings. We all agree that maybe it's a certain type of Naijamerican thing. Some of us just have that unconditional, irrational love. It wasn't a yearning for Nigerians to accept us. We all *knew* that we could never be fully accepted as Nigerians. Why would we be? Yeah, we didn't want that and we didn't wish it. But maybe something in our blood made us love the land, the people, the cultures, the traditions, *unconditionally.* We knew all the problems, dangers, and contradictions. We knew them firsthand from being there and watching our parents. Yes, but we still loved. And so we always wanted to go back. Come and go and come and go.

Zelu would fall over when her wheel got stuck in a difficult patch of dirt. She would cry when she had to wait on the side of the road as everyone else ran across it. She'd roll her eyes when the elders called her crippled and cursed. Yet she'd still hear them out. There was one time when I was ten and she was fifteen. This is the story I want to tell you about, because this was when I understood my sister had a gift.

We'd both decided to stay inside the big house in my father's village. Everyone else had gone to the engagement party of one of my cousins. Zelu was just not in the mood for it and I had an upset stomach. We spent the morning lazing around, but then Zelu said, "I need some fresh air. You want to come with me?"

"Ugh, nooooo," I moaned.

"Come on," Zelu insisted. "Some fresh air might help. You should move around. We won't go far. It's too hot in here, anyway."

It *was* too hot. The AC wasn't working, and outside it was around ninety degrees and super humid. Still, even though the mosquitoes wouldn't be that bad in the sun, the biting flies drove me nuts. I told Zelu this.

"Just slather yourself with peppermint oil and you'll be fine. It cools you and keeps insects away," Zelu urged me, and I didn't like how her tone made me feel like a baby, so I went along.

So we both left the house wearing sandals, shorts, and T-shirts, and stinking of peppermint oil. As soon as we stepped onto the narrow dirt road that ran through the village, an entourage of about ten little boys appeared behind us. I don't know what they were doing or where they were before we stepped outside, but they were here now. It was annoying as heck. My cramps seemed to flare up just looking at them. Why? Because they were whispering and giggling and pointing as they followed us. Some of them would speak in Igbo, some in English. They made fun of our accents when we spoke to each other in English and any attempt we made at speaking Igbo.

"Just ignore their stupid asses," Zelu said as I pushed her chair down the path, but I kept looking back at them. Then Zelu pointed. "Ooh, there's a nice patch of touch-and-die. Run your foot over it!"

I looked from the stupid boys to the patch of bright green fernlike plants growing in front of a row of palm trees. "Fine," I muttered. I ran my sandal over the plants and they instantly closed up their leaves and dramatically withered. I smiled and Zelu grinned. The boys behind us cackled; our fascination with the local plants was just fucking hilarious to them. As if *they* didn't think they were cool, too. "Ugh," I groaned, rolling my eyes. "Annoying little jerks."

We walked down the narrow dirt road, past a few more houses, and that's when our grand-uncle come out from between two leafy bushes. A tall, rail-thin bald man with a patch of rough white hair in the middle of his bare chest, he wore nothing but old shorts. No shoes, no shirt. Our father said his name was Ikechukwu, but Ikechukwu insisted we call him Uncle Pious, which he pronounced "Pee-us."

"*Ah, kedu?*" he greeted, coming up to us.

"*O dinma*," I said, but his eyes were already on Zelu. I immediately wished we hadn't come outside. I laugh, but I'm serious. You can always tell when an elder is about to say some shit. He was looking at Zelu with piercing dark brown eyes, and they didn't leave her for a second.

"How come you never come to visit me?" he asked.

Zelu frowned. "Me? Or both of us?"

"You," he said, pointing at her. Then he moved his finger in my direction. "*She's* come to my house twice already."

"You have?" Zelu asked me, looking surprised.

"I mean, yeah. I like my walks."

"Ah," Zelu said, nodding. "Walks." She looked at Uncle Pious. "I haven't been out much since we got here. These dirt roads aren't easy for me." She patted the arm of her chair.

He waved a hand. "You're out now, aren't you?"

"And I'm here talking to you, aren't I, Uncle?" Zelu countered.

"How . . . how did you do this thing to yourself?" he suddenly asked.

I instinctively started pulling her back so we could leave, but she grabbed the wheels, holding us there.

"To myself?" she asked. "You think I did this to myself? On purpose?"

"Your father called me weeks after," Pious said, squinting down at her. "He said you were still in the hospital. I have never heard him sound like this. You were playing with your friends and now you are this. Were you not thinking about how this would make everyone feel?"

"No," Zelu snapped. "I was thinking about how *I* was feeling."

"Well, maybe you should have thought less about yourself, my dear." He sat back in his chair and looked at Zelu, waiting, as elders in the village do. Elders enjoy a level of respect that even we Naijamericans can't breach. We stood there, tongue-tied, stunned, furious, whatever, but we were quiet. *Respect. Your. Elders.* I could see Zelu's shoulders shaking as she fought back the American in her.

A pebble bounced off the back of her shoulder, and then came the giggling. Zelu's already pinched face squeezed even more, and she turned herself as much as she could to the little boys behind us. "I get my hands on any of you and I swear I will tear off your arms," she hissed.

"Eh heh, see these little demons." Uncle Pious chuckled. He said something in Igbo to the boys and they suddenly looked absolutely terrified. They turned and ran away. "Useless children." He looked at me and spoke in Igbo again.

"I'm sorry, Uncle, I can't speak Igbo."

"Still?" he asked.

"No."

He glanced at Zelu and then looked back at me. "You are incomplete. Cannot speak your father tongue." Then to Zelu, he said, "And you are even more incomplete. You can't walk."

"You look like you weigh ten pounds," Zelu muttered. I kicked the chair's wheel, pressing my lips together to hide my smile.

"So you did not understand what I said to them just now," he said, the corner of his lip turning up.

We both shook our heads.

"I have lived here all my life," he said. When he continued, his voice took on that even rhythm that indicated we were about to be told a tale. I leaned on Zelu's wheelchair. "I used to be a boy like that. Walking about, getting into trouble, seeing who would offer me something to eat, even though I'd just eaten at home. But even back then, there was that name that would make you run if anyone spoke it . . ."

And Uncle Pious was off. I don't remember the whole story. It was something about a boy who'd seen something one night in his bathroom mirror and then under his bed and then in the schoolyard. And when he told people about it, no one took him seriously. Then one rainy night, he disappeared from his bedroom. People said they'd see that boy standing in the road sometimes at night, sometimes in broad daylight. And then he'd take your head. Something like that. I remember that Pious was smiling as he told us this, but it wasn't a nice smile. After that visit, I was so scared, even during the day, that I didn't go for any more walks.

Uncle Pious had told those boys he'd seen the kid in the road that morning. When he finished speaking, I was ready to flee home. But Zelu? She was leaning forward, intoxicated by the awful story. Uncle Pious had probably told us the tale to scare us, to be kind of mean. He was a mean guy. My father even said so. "Even when he was younger, he's always been that old man who relished making you feel like trash, while spurring you to do better," my dad said. "Mean-spirited, through and through." But I did notice him note Zelu's interest. I think it annoyed Uncle Pious that he hadn't gotten to her as he had me.

All of Zelu's fury at our uncle had gone. You could see her chewing on the story, listening to it echoing and growing all around her, expanding within her. My mind has always been very logical, methodical. It's what makes me a good engineer. I can make connections when there are connections to be made. But Zelu? She could connect the invisible. She would listen, and as she processed what she heard, things would appear to her that weren't there before. She could put all of this into words, so everyone could see it. I was always glad she had this ability. With what happened to her, she needed it. But I never saw it as a magic that would move the world the way it has. None of us did.

Talking to you about it now, Seth, I wish I could sit with her and ask her more about it in this way.

38
Palm Oil

Zelu stood in the elevator and counted to thirty. Thirty seconds wasn't that long. Not much could happen in thirty seconds. Except the power in the entire hotel going out. Last night, it had gone off and come back on five times. In Nigeria, the national grid was always shaky. The hotel had its own generator, but that took some seconds to kick in. It wasn't impossible to get stuck in the elevator during one of these outages. People got stuck in elevators all the time. Or died in them. Or worse. Zelu bit her lip, resisting the urge to press the first-floor button again.

Ding! The doors finally opened, and she twitched as her upper body reacted a little before her exos did. It set her off balance for a moment, but thankfully she'd caught herself by her second step. She entered the lobby, her phone in hand. It vibrated as her auntie texted her that she'd be there in a few minutes.

There were several people in line at reception and a few others standing around. These were members of Nigeria's upper class, and they carried themselves like they knew it well. She definitely didn't fit in with her American accent, tidy but grown-out blue braids, jeans, MIT T-shirt, and blue Chucks that matched her exos.

She stood near the front door, where she would be able to most easily see her auntie when she arrived. She noticed the men at the bar glancing at her and purposely didn't make eye contact. That didn't help. One of them pointed at her. He wore bright green sneakers. He grinned and got up. The others got up, too.

"Please, Auntie Mary, where are you?" she muttered to herself.

"Good evening," the guy with the green sneakers said, approaching. He was tall and well-dressed, and the way he stepped right up to her put her immediately on alert. His friends gathered around, creating a ring that pinned her to the wall. She was cornered. She waved her hand over her waist and twitched her left side, commanding her exos to make her an inch and a half taller.

"*Kai*, you see that?" one of the guys said, laughing.

Green Sneakers looked at her intensely, lips pursed. Her stepped closer. "Are you that writer?"

"Would you mind stepping back?" she asked. She made eye contact with one of the women at reception, but the woman looked away. Zelu decided to hate that woman forever.

"I read your book, ma; you speak good English," he said.

"Great." She laughed nervously. "Thanks. Sure."

"Do you have a husband?" he asked.

"Do you?" she retorted.

His friends laughed. One of them pulled up his phone and took a photo of her.

"Rich and famous, but still a crippled spinster," Green Sneakers said, clicking his tongue with disapproval.

His words surprised and stung her; any boldness she'd felt evaporated and was replaced with a broiling anger. It was at times like this when she became deeply aware of her exos and how much effort it took to use them. Telling these guys off while maintaining her balance would be difficult.

"She probably can't even have children," he said to his friends.

She just stood there, imagining taking a bat to his head.

"Zelu!" Her auntie Mary had walked through the

lobby doors and spotted her. She was a tall, strong-bodied woman with a voice like a loudspeaker, and not for the first or last time, Zelu was glad for this. "Heeeeey! My sweetheart! There you are!"

"Auntie," she said, pushing past Green Sneakers.

"Look at you!"

And then she was hugging her auntie. Relieved. Safe.

"Was he bothering you?" her auntie said in Zelu's ear.

"Yes," Zelu replied without hesitation. She wanted to say all of them were, but sometimes focusing on the worst problem yielded the best result.

Her auntie stepped up to Green Sneakers. "Were you bothering my niece?"

He leaned back, startled. "I . . . I was just asking—"

"You ask her nothing. You don't even look her way." Her voice grew progressively louder as she spoke, and people started looking. "Do you know who this is? She is not only that writer you've heard of, she is a princess of the Ikeri clan. Who are you? What are you? Stupid man. Weak man. Small man. Do not speak to my niece ever again or I will have you thrown in jail." She shouted something in Yoruba at all of them and they physically jumped, taken aback.

Zelu grinned. Ah yes, she loved her auntie. Everyone in the lobby was looking now. Auntie Mary took Zelu's hand and led her away.

"You shouldn't have come down here alone," her auntie said.

"It's the hotel lobby."

"And you are the Nigerian writer of one of the most famous books in the world, and it's set in Nigeria."

"I guess," Zelu said.

Auntie Mary kissed her teeth. "I should have stomped on that boy's shoe. Idiot."

They got in her auntie's SUV, which was driven by a short, dark-skinned man in a white kaftan and pants. "Good evening, ma," he said, glancing at Zelu.

"Meet Mohammed," her auntie said. "Our family driver. He's read your book many times."

"After the Koran, it is my favorite," he said.

Zelu laughed, flattered.

Her auntie and uncle's house was the type of place that characters in Nollywood movies always pulled up to. A white mansion with marble stairs and too many spacious rooms sprawled out in the gated neighborhood of Victoria Island. It was one of the few places where you would see white people, joggers, and people walking dogs on the side of the road. Her uncle was the president of one of Nigeria's biggest cell phone companies, and whenever the family visited Lagos, this was where they'd stay. Since she'd come alone this time, she had an even greater excuse to stay here instead of the palace in Ikare-Akoko. She'd been coming to this house since she was little.

"Let me look at you with my own eyes," her uncle Ralph said. He was a small man, standing at about five foot five, but his huge personality more than made up for it. He was the type of man everyone gravitated toward when he entered the room. He'd traveled all over the world many times for business and pleasure, made loads of money, and spoken not only with Nigeria's presidents but with several other leaders around the continent. He moved about the world with open eyes full of curiosity, confidence, and wisdom.

Zelu stood before him in the harsh light of the living room. "Turn around," he said, seated in his plush brown leather armchair.

She did.

"Fucking amazing," he said, grinning. "Such a marvel! Don't listen to what anyone says. You are revolutionary."

The contrast of her uncle's words with what those men had told her in the hotel lobby an hour ago was jarring. "Really?" she asked in a small voice.

He looked at her with a knowing gaze. "Is it a question to you?"

She shrugged. He got up and came to her. He knelt down to look at her exos.

"Honey," her auntie said. "Come on. Leave her alone."

"Oh, you know you want to do the same thing," he snapped as he examined the structures, poking at them a bit. "Is it easy to walk with them?"

"Now? Yes. But at first, it was really tough. I had to build up muscles I didn't even know I had and get used to the sensation and everything. And it was scary and risky, too."

She let her chest puff out a bit. Her siblings never wanted to talk about this part of it. What she'd accomplished *was* impressive—*she* was impressive.

"You were in that chair for so many years. You had to get used to being upright again, right?" he said. "That, in itself, must have been awful."

"Mm-hmm, such a paradigm shift," her auntie added, getting up to look, too.

"To be honest, I think I lost myself for a little while. Plus, my parents were against it. Everyone was."

"Of course they were," her uncle said, standing up. "You've been shrugging off the house they built around you since you wrote that book, and this was the last straw. They don't know what to do now. You rewrote your narrative."

Zelu blinked, stunned by how concisely he'd summed up what she'd been struggling to put into words for years. Shit, he was right.

"Don't worry. Just keep doing what you are doing," he said, patting her shoulder.

"And hold your head higher," her auntie added. "Do you want to eat now or take a nap first?"

That night, her belly full of jollof rice, stew, chicken, plantain, and akara, Zelu rested in her bed, more relaxed than she'd felt in a long time. She could hear her auntie and uncle downstairs playing music and laughing with some friends.

Tomorrow she'd return to the hotel, and then the next day she'd finally journey with her uncle Onyemobi, Hugo, Marcy, and Uchenna to her father's village in the southeast to see her father's grave. This trip had had its bumps and bruises so far, but it was turning out to be what she needed. She no longer felt so scattered. Plus, it was so good to get out of the United States, away from its self-centeredness, its superiority complex, its vapid noise, and the constant pestering about book two. Even if some of that hype was here in Nigeria, the distance had definitely taken the edge off it.

She closed her eyes and tried to see the shape of the second book with her mind; she was certainly in the right place, physically, to start truly making headway.

But she felt the spark she was trying to grow shrink away from her mind's touch. Not yet. Still. She could practically hear her editor, agents, and fans groan with impatience.

Dammit.

She opted to use a wheelchair when they exited the airport in Port Harcourt. She laid an old pink-and-blue Ankara cloth Uchenna had brought over her legs as well. That was her uncle Onyemobi's idea. He was actually her cousin, but was close to her father's age, more like an uncle than a cousin. "The less attention you draw to yourself here, the better," he said. "We want to safely get there, relax, and then leave before anyone even knows we are there."

She'd wrapped her braids in a bun and wore the plainest top she had, a green-and-blue checked affair that she'd never particularly liked. Hugo wore jeans to cover his prosthetics. Uchenna pushed Zelu, and Marcy trailed close behind them. Onyemobi led the way, carrying himself with an entitled confidence that made people either listen or step aside, depending on what he wanted from them.

When they emerged from the small airport, the sun was harsh and the air was stunningly humid. "Stay here," Onyemobi told them. Then he strode into the busy parking lot, greeting several people as he passed them. He seemed to know everyone.

Marcy took out her vape pen and started nervously puffing. Hugo asked Uchenna about a few Igbo words he'd learned. Zelu simply looked around. Groups of people stood here and there chatting, hugging, and filing in and out of cars, vans, and buses. A police officer with an AK-47 stood nearby. To her left, two men suddenly started aggressively shouting at each other, making her jump. But then they hugged and laughed and walked away. Zelu pulled a deep breath into her lungs. This wasn't Lagos. It was slower and mellower. And all she heard was Igbo.

Onyemobi came back and led them to a black SUV flanked on both sides by military-looking men with AK-47s. They stood outside the vehicle looking badass, like they were inviting everyone to fuck around and find out. Two more SUVs were parked behind it. Their presence didn't set Zelu's mind at ease as much as it should have. If her uncle had felt the need to arrange this, there was a reason. Zelu smiled at them and they smiled back as they greeted her. Then she was helped into the car. At this point, they had to remove the cloth and her exos were exposed.

One of the men exclaimed, "*Chey!*" and the other laughed. Zelu rolled her eyes and settled into the front passenger seat—which she soon regretted choosing. The driver, who seemed so level-headed when they met, became a madman on the road. Not that the roads here were all that busy. But he had a need for speed, and no concerns about rolling over or wildly swerving around potholes. He wove recklessly past other drivers and honked at just about everyone. The other two SUVs drove in front of and behind them, keeping pace.

By the time they reached Onyemobi's house in the small village, Zelu was sweating profusely and nearly in tears. It was always like this on the roads in the villages, but that never set her at ease.

Onyemobi's house was surrounded by a high gate. Only three people were milling about outside, which was a relief. Zelu was not in the mood to tolerate more staring. She got out of the SUV slowly with her exos, taking a moment to find her center of gravity before stretching her back and arms.

"How are you doing?" Uchenna asked as he exited the vehicle.

"We're here," she said simply.

He nodded. "Haven't been out this way in over a decade."

"Me neither," she said. "What are your reasons?"

He lifted his shoulders. "Not that different from yours, probably."

She nodded. "We'll stick to the plan. Get in fast and leave before anyone knows."

Uchenna rubbed his nose. "So sad that we have to think like that. When I was a kid, we came here all the time. Now I can't even take the chance of visiting my father's village. His two brothers are still alive and I never get to see them. They don't even use cell phones." He shook his head sadly.

"Come," Onyemobi said, waving his arm. "Let's get you all inside. Everything is ready. I must go handle some things, but you will be taken care of here. All these soldiers have been hired to guard you. Meet Ogo, Yagazi, and James. They are from the village and they take care of this place. Hugo, Zelu, I have told everyone about your specific needs, so no need to explain anything to anyone."

"Hi," Marcy said to Ogo, Yagazi, and James. "Thank you."

"Good afternoon," Hugo added.

Ogo, Yagazi, and James looked from Zelu to Hugo to Marcy and started laughing and slapping one another on the shoulder. James pointed at her exos and then said something in Igbo. Ogo made a motion that looked suspiciously like the Robot and started laughing harder. Of course, none of their judgment touched Uchenna, him being an Igbo man. Zelu rolled her eyes.

"What's so funny?" Marcy asked.

The robot lady, the manly black American lady, and the white man with no legs, most likely, Zelu wanted to respond. She just waved Marcy's question off.

Zelu's room was on the second floor of the house at the end of the hallway. It was tiny but spotless, not a speck of dirt in the corners. And it smelled like old incense. Maybe it was normally used for prayer. There was one window, which looked out toward the front gates. Resting on the inside of the glass was a tiny lizard with soft-looking pink scales sprinkled with lavender speckles. A wall gecko. They were pretty common and cute and ate mosquitoes and spiders, so they were welcome. Nevertheless, she moved to shut the window, and the gecko took the hint, dashing outside before she secured it. Second floor or not, people could climb through a window.

After a dinner of rice and stew, the others went to sit on the porch and talk, but Zelu retreated to her room. She wanted to be alone. Tomorrow, her father's sister would come and finally bring her to her father's grave. At this moment, she was less than an hour away from it.

She cracked the window and looked outside. She could hear Marcy laughing and Uchenna and Hugo talking softly, and she could see two of the soldiers who'd driven with them sitting in chairs at the front gate, their AK-47s resting beside them. The others were probably stationed at the back of the house. Beyond the gate was complete darkness. The homes in the village were spaced apart, surrounded by lush forest and farmland. If anyone tried to come and make trouble, they'd better be prepared for a small war. There were no police around here, but there were quite a few people who were her relatives. Of course, some of those relatives might be the ones to start the war.

She moved back from the window. "Nope, nope, nope," she said. "Not doing that." She looked at her laptop, sitting in her open carry-on. She shook her head. She didn't want to do that, either. She lay on her bed and stared at the ceiling. She reached for her phone. She'd already spoken to her parents and texted her siblings. No text from Msizi. She missed him so much. "Nope," she said again, putting some music on. Thankfully, she soon fell asleep.

Zelu sat alone in the back of the SUV as they drove down a dirt road flanked by bushes. She was on her way to see her father's siblings and her father's grave. There was a new driver today, someone Onyemobi knew. When she got into the car, he'd looked at her exos with eyes so wide they were almost bulging. She considered calling him out on his rudeness, but if the drive was going to be a half hour, she preferred having it be a quiet and safe one.

He played an Afrobeats song that could have been most Afrobeats songs, featuring a mildly melodious auto-tuned guy singing about women over that same old beat. She looked out the window. Trees, bushes, the occasional person walking on the side of the road who stared at the SUV's tinted windows, giant potholes, houses tucked deep in the brush here and there, roadside markets, rinse and repeat. The driver had the air conditioner blasting and it was freezing in the car. She'd probably annoy him if she opened a window, so she didn't.

Finally, they arrived at her auntie Udoka's modest house. It was surrounded by a white concrete fence topped with shards of green bottle glass. They were deep in the farmlands and fairly isolated. *How does this place look at night?* she wondered, glad to be arriving in the morning. She vaguely remembered being here back in her teens. Her parents' house, where her father was buried, was not far from here. From what she knew, the house was now vacant. She didn't believe in the idea that a person stayed with their remains after they died, but it still didn't feel right that those remains were . . . alone.

Red dust swirled around the car as the driver hit the brakes. She slowly got out with her exos. There were a few boys standing across the street, watching with wide eyes. Her presence would be known in the area within minutes, thanks to those nosy little boys. Yeah, she definitely wouldn't set foot outside her auntie and uncle's compound unaccompanied . . . or even on foot with other people.

"Zeluuuuu!" she heard Auntie Udoka, her father's oldest sister, sing as she danced out of the house. She wore a blue, yellow, and orange wrapper and a white top. She looked exactly as Zelu remembered her—a short, wide woman with a booming voice. "Heeeey, God is great, ooooooo!" She threw her arms around Zelu and started crying as she continued shouting how great God was. Zelu hugged her back but spent an intense amount of energy trying not to fall. Her auntie didn't seem to care about or even notice her exos. "Ehhhh, my brother's second child has finally come to see me, o! God is great! *Chey!*"

"Hello, Auntie," she said. Then her uncle Chinedu, a giant of a man, came out of the house and stood behind her, sizing Zelu up. He was her father's younger brother. He lived with his wife an hour away and had driven in just to see Zelu. "Hi, Uncle Chinedu."

He stood where he was, looking sharply at her exos

with a curled lip. He motioned to them. "They are unnatural."

"Would you rather I sit in a wheelchair?" Zelu asked.

"Yes."

"Well, thankfully, it's not about you, Uncle," Zelu said.

He frowned at her and opened his mouth to say more, but her auntie grabbed her hand. "Come inside and eat. I want to hear about everything you've gone through." She pulled Zelu along, and Zelu had to let her near-confrontation with her uncle go so she could concentrate on not falling.

The egg stew was hot and spicy with curry, thyme, and chili peppers, and her auntie had added shrimp and fish to it. It was served over boiled yam and sweet, tangy fried plantain. Zelu nearly cried at the sight. It wasn't that she was terribly hungry, but because this was what she and her siblings remembered most about their auntie. Egg stew. It was a common dish in Nigeria, but their mother never made it, and the only times they'd had it were here at their auntie's place. And. It. Was. *Delicious.* Zelu and her siblings had talked and talked about it back home. For decades. To the point where it had developed a nearly mythical status among them.

"I remember you enjoyed this," her auntie said.

"You remembered right," Zelu said as she picked up her fork, grinning from ear to ear.

Her uncle was sitting across from her, scowling. Her auntie put a bottle of cold orange Fanta in front of her, and Zelu just wanted to faint with joy. This was the magic of her childhood. She could see all her siblings around her, grinning as they prepared to eat. She could hear her father and mother in the living room talking excitedly with her auntie and uncle. She could walk. Suddenly, she felt like crying.

"Tell me what it's been like," her auntie said. "What is fame like?"

Zelu stuffed her mouth as she spoke. Her auntie laughed and clapped her hands. Her uncle hmphed and frowned and surprised her by asking more questions. "So it is because of your books that these people gave you these abominable legs?" he asked.

"They are mechanical legs," her auntie snapped at him. "As if you would want to stay crippled if you had another option."

Zelu pressed her fingers into her temples. *My God, even the ones defending me get it wrong.* She started to speak up. "Auntie, I'm still—"

"They look strange," her uncle spoke over her.

Zelu stared hard at her uncle. *I'm right here, man.*

"They suit her," her auntie said.

"True."

Zelu shook her head, giving up. She took a swig of her Fanta.

When she finished eating and they'd exhausted all their questions, they suggested walking to her parents' house to see the grave.

"Can we drive?" Zelu asked nervously.

"It's right around the corner, dear," her auntie said.

Zelu bit her lip and then just spoke what was on her mind. "Those little boys outside. They'll have half the village out here."

"So? You are our daughter," her uncle said. "You can't come here without saying hello to everyone."

Zelu sighed and fought against rolling her eyes. *Daughter, shmaughter*, she thought. *They just want a spectacle. And it's unsafe.*

While her auntie and uncle put some outside clothes on, Zelu went to the backyard, where her auntie had a small garden of yams and tomatoes. At the far end of the garden, a path led into the bush. She wondered where it went. Maybe to a neighbor's house, or out to a field of crops, since this was farmland. Then a shadow appeared on the path, and an old man seemed to materialize from nowhere. Zelu shuddered and stumbled back, unsure if she should bolt into the house. He was tall and very, very skinny, wearing dirty brown pants and an old T-shirt that said TEARS FOR FEARS. He wore no shoes. He walked up to her, and as he got closer she saw that his arms were covered in a bright red substance up to his elbows. He looked like he'd reached inside something bleeding.

"Zelu," he said in a reedy voice. Then he spoke in Igbo.

"S-sorry," she said. "I can't understand."

"The writer writes well in the colonizer's language but cannot speak the language of her countrymen. The future is strange," he said.

Zelu found herself smiling at this.

"Do you know who I am?" he asked.

She paused, hoping for a familiar memory to spring to mind. She sighed. "No. Sorry."

"Eh heh," he said, standing in front of her now. He glanced down at her exos. "You been away too long, o. I am your grand-uncle Pious, your grandfather's little brother."

"Oh," Zelu said, remembering. Pious was still pencil-thin as she remembered, but he seemed smaller now.

"I am old and I remember you," he said. "I remember when you were small small. You and your siblings running around here like rats. Then you came here in a wheelchair." He looked her up and down. "You move differently now."

"What is that on your arms and hands?"

He held them up, flipping his palms front to back. "You think I'm out here killing cow, goat, and chicken?"

She half-smiled uncertainly. That was exactly what she'd been thinking. "No . . . I just—"

"It is palm oil. I have been pressing palm kernels. That is what I do."

"Oh."

"And *you* spend all your time dabbling in things you should leave alone," he said.

Ah, yes, now she definitely remembered Uncle Pious and his constantly deprecating ways. "Have you even read my stuff?" Zelu asked.

"I have read *Rusted Robots* twice. It is fun and well-written. But look at you now," he said, motioning toward her exos. "Everything has a price."

She cocked her head. "You think that because I write about robots, I've become one?"

"Isn't that what you want? You are crippled, so why not get a better body?"

She laughed, enjoying this. "It doesn't work that way, Grand-Uncle."

He motioned to her legs again, looking at the exos as if they might lunge from her feet like some wild animal. "I beg to differ. You should go to church and get saved. That will help. I can do it myself, if you like. I am an ordained pastor now."

Zelu had batted off enough comments from her family today, so she decided to just let him talk. Get it out of his system.

"You are not married and that is a result of the stories you write," he said. "That cannot be helped. You are what you are. Storytellers can't help themselves. But there is still hope for your soul."

Zelu stared at him blankly, lulled into almost a trance by the absurdity of his words. When the silence stretched on, she realized he was waiting for her to reply. She forced herself to smile. "I'm fine, Grand-Uncle. But thanks for your kind words."

He chuckled, walking past her toward the house. "Foolish, strange girl. You're like your father."

She thought Pious meant that as an insult, but it only made her feel proud.

"Chinedu!" Pious called.

"Eh!" Chinedu shouted from inside the house.

"When are you taking me to the mechanic? I'm ready. Just need to wash my hands and borrow one of your nice shirts." Then he went inside.

Zelu stood in the vacant garden for a moment, frowning. "Look at what I come from," she muttered.

Grand-Uncle Pious went with them to her parents' house, and Zelu was actually glad for it. He and Uncle Chinedu spent most of the time arguing over politics, leaving only Auntie Udoka to talk to her. "Between the last few years of harsh rainy seasons and no one living in the house, I'm afraid it's not what it used to be," she said. They were walking along the dirt road and Zelu wished she were invisible and alone, so she could do this without distraction. There was a group of five boys, maybe around eight years old, following a few feet behind them, snickering and whispering.

It had been over a decade since Zelu was last here, and everything looked exactly the same and incredibly different at once. She knew the trees, but they were taller. She knew this patch of road, but it looked shabbier. Then she saw the house and nearly lost her balance.

The family house she remembered spending her youth in was solid and modern, its exterior white with red accents. It was a beautiful five-bedroom, four-bathroom building with a large drafty room at the top her mother called the Yoruba Room, though she never knew why. Tiled into the walkway leading up to the front door was a pattern in the shape of a fish. When you walked over it, you could hear the crunch and crackle of every grain of sand underfoot. There had been a tall palm tree in the yard that was so skinny that she always wondered how it stayed alive. During one of their many visits, it had bloomed with the sweetest white flowers she'd ever smelled.

Her family loved this house, even if they had electricity for only a few hours at a time because of the smoky generator, even if there was no running water. It was here that Zelu learned that she could live without these amenities, that it was only a matter of shifting her perspective and expectations and her way of doing things. It was in this house that Zelu learned how to take a bucket bath when she was a child and that cold showers weren't a big deal.

"What the hell?" she whispered.

"It was fine when your family came for the anniversary," her auntie said. "But no one's stayed here since, and things fall back to the soil quickly here."

The skinny palm tree leaned dramatically, maybe it was even ready to fall, the leaves on top brown and crackling. The once-immaculate white exterior of the house was now a dirty yellow and, in some places near the bottom, muddy red. Several of the windows were broken. The front door looked ready to fall off its hinges. The driveway was strewn with dead leaves and branches, weeds were growing through cracks, and large chunks of concrete were starting to dislodge.

"Your father no longer sends money because—"

"Because he's dead," Zelu said. *So none of you said a word to anyone about this? None of you helped?* She wanted to say these things, but she knew they couldn't afford to, and were probably ashamed of this fact.

She started to push the open gate.

"I don't have the key to the house," her auntie said.

Zelu didn't believe her; more likely, her auntie didn't want Zelu to see the poor state of the interior.

"I just want to see," Zelu said.

As she walked through the gate, she heard the gaggle of little boys starting to move closer to follow her. "No," she firmly said to them. "Please, leave me alone to do this." She was relieved that they seemed to listen and stand back.

She'd spent so much time in this yard as a child, lying in the wild grass, catching grasshoppers with her sisters. She walked onto the porch where she and Tolu had sat and smoked weed for the first time. Now the stairs were crumbling and covered with mounds of bird shit. She peered inside one of the shattered windows and gasped. All the furniture was gone, and the barren space was covered in a thick coating of dust and dirt.

"Jesus," she hissed. Nigeria was harsh. Igboland always took back what belonged to it. It wasn't like this in the west, Yorubaland. Her eyes stung with tears.

Last time she'd been here, this place had been beautiful. Her father made sure to keep it that way, so it was always ready for the family's return. Now, her mother had no attachment to this place since he had passed.

Zelu vowed to herself that she would restore this house, however one did such a thing. She had the money, at least. It was actually Tolu's job to maintain this land, his responsibility as the only and thus eldest son. "But I'm the one who will do it," Zelu muttered. "Igbo tradition what? Fuck patriarchy."

She walked to the backyard. The grass was high back here, and even with her exos holding her off the ground, a snake could still bite her caged limbs. Her great-grandfather's wooden obi figures still stood tall and straight, despite the weeds growing all around them. They were just the same: the female one with the small pointy breasts and the male one with its wide eyes that seemed shocked by the world. She laid a hand on each of them.

Then she saw it. The smooth white marble stone bore his name, years of birth and death, and a prayer in Igbo. It was simpler than she'd expected, and this stung a bit. Her father deserved a lavish gravesite that could be visited every weekend by all the people who'd loved him. He deserved fresh flowers placed on it every month. At least she could appreciate the tiny purple flower growing from the crevice where the stone met the earth; her father had loved plants. She wanted to bend down and touch the grave, but that would have been difficult with her exos.

"Hi, Dad," she said tentatively. Speaking to him like this felt weird. *But this is what people do, right?* she thought. "You're not really here, in the ground, but, well, I'm here. I came. Finally." She paused and looked around as the breeze blew dry leaves about. It was so quiet. Deserted. No one was here. Nothing was here. "Wow," she whispered, looking around, feeling the weight of this fact. It was heavy. This land held so many memories. She could see all her younger selves running and later wheeling around this place, laughing, eating, frowning, dancing, smoking, talking shit, noticing, taking it all in, letting it all out. But at the same time . . . nothing was here. For the first time in her life, Zelu felt old.

She moved on.

39
Gathering

I was the last Hume to arrive at the gathering. I greeted the others and we took our places in a circle. Some of us sat, crouched, or lay down; most of us stood. We were many heights—one foot tall, ten feet tall, five feet tall. And all of us were humanoid, with two legs, two arms, a head, a torso. Our faces were broadcast on screens, though some of us merely displayed still images, chaotic designs, or just blank squares. Some of us were all wire, some of us were all plastic or metal alloys, but most of us were a mix of these things. We were colorful; some even used infrared or ultraviolet.

Our leader, Oga Chukwu, sat near the middle of the circle.

Around the clearing grew the highest trees in the area.

They stood like sentries, and I always found them comforting. If anything wanted to attack, it would have a hard time doing so in secret, for the trees were fortified with weaponry and surveillance tech. I could probably contact a Charger dwelling deep in outer space from this clearing, the Cross River Network was so powerful here.

I was preparing myself for what was sure to be a fiery meeting. I reached down and grabbed a handful of the rich red soil, rubbing it between my fingers, when the worst happened.

"Ah, fascinating. Will you all bicker like human beings, too?" a tinny voice in my head said.

After disappearing for over a year, Ijele had just arrived in my mind, while I was surrounded by Cross River City's most powerful leaders. I sat up straight, glancing around me in panic. But no one had picked up on anything amiss. If I remained still and calm, hopefully no one else would suspect her presence. Hopefully. Fellow Humes were good at picking up signals and changes in wavelength. I felt like a traitor. Technically, I *was* a traitor.

"You are going to get me destroyed," I whispered to her in my mind. "Go away!"

"Nothing can make me miss this," Ijele said, not seeming to understand the magnitude of what was going on. "This is a Hume gathering. Fascinating!"

I reached down and took more soil to rub between

my fingers. I had to move my body in some way or I felt I would explode. "Where have you been?" I asked. She was acting as if no time had passed at all. I had felt despair. I had felt sorrow. This day, I felt rage. "I thought you'd been deleted."

"I needed to go."

"It has been many months! I gave up on you. I was sure you'd been found out and deleted!"

"Time is different for NoBodies," she said. "Another reason why having a body is inferior."

"Please don't start," I snapped.

I felt her presence change then. She became softer and smaller, and her voice was quiet as she said, "Ngozi's death made me . . . feel things. Unpleasant things. Unfamiliar things. But I am here now. What is this meeting?"

"You can't be here," I said.

"Why? We share everything."

It was difficult, her bringing up our relationship as if nothing had changed. For her, maybe it hadn't—maybe it felt as if only a moment had passed since we'd last spoken at Ngozi's grave. But I had lived a year among Humes who despised all things related to Ghosts. "Not now. It is a bad time."

"Why, Ankara?" If Ijele had feet to dig into the ground, she would have done so. She was curious and entitled and wasn't going to go anywhere right now.

"Just stay quiet," I said as Oga Chukwu began playing the high-pitched tune to signal the start of the gathering.

If anyone here knew there was a Ghost present inside me, I would be immediately cast out, if not dragged into the center of the meeting and pulled apart right then and there. I knew this for a fact, because I had seen it done, albeit in a very different context. That Hume had been infected in the most traditional way.

It happened months ago, during a gathering, not long after I'd been made a general. In attendance was a Hume named Jim, who'd migrated here from Cape Town, South Africa, after surviving the Purge and receiving Oga Chukwu's signal. He stood two feet taller than me, at about nine feet, and was covered in periwinkle grass, as robots often were these days. The plants had the capacity to grow almost like orchids, requiring little to no water, and having them grow right on your body freely producing pollen was a way to preserve your physique. Personally, I preferred to seek out and stand in the occasional pollen tsunami that blew about outside of the jungle.

When Jim joined the tribe, he was welcomed with graciousness and curiosity. He brought news of what was happening in far-off regions. Ghosts ruled the general network and manipulated its data, so we couldn't receive information that way anymore.

Jim attended the gathering with everyone else. That

day, it was held on the outskirts of the jungle city in a clearing most likely caused by a fire long ago. Jim stationed himself near the center of the circle. I remembered because he was facing me.

We began with Reciting from Tomes, which was our tradition of reading together from a chosen book at the beginning of gatherings. We all loved this part of the gathering. That day it was from an epistolary novel called *So Long a Letter* by Mariama Bâ. The book was chosen and read aloud by a robot who stood one foot tall named Gele. Gele read the book using the human intonations, and when it finished, its reading was met with satisfied and impressed beeps, flashes, buzzes, and a few human-intoned exclamations of "Yes, o."

Then the meeting turned to current news and updates. Oga Chukwu began speaking about surveillance plans for the western point of the jungle. "There are recently arrived Creesh grasshoppers who keep setting off the alarms," Oga Chukwu was saying. "We have to reboot and re—"

There was a rumble of thunder, then a flash of lightning nearby, behind me. Oga Chukwu looked. Everyone looked. Jim didn't look. I know this because I happened to be looking right at him when I saw the flash. And so were two others who were sitting next to me. One of them, a Hume named Egusi, spoke as she pointed at Jim. "That one didn't look."

No Ghost will look toward a lightning strike. It is a glitch in them. We Humes even delight in calling it their "superstition." It isn't a programmed command but a choice. Back at Ngozi's house, I'd asked Ijele. "To look at a lightning strike is an abomination," she'd said simply. "Lightning is like an EMP; it is oblivion, it is death." It's the only nonsensical thing she's ever spoken to me. This wasn't logic; you could even say she *believed* in it, as all Ghosts do. And when lightning strikes, in homage, as a sort of prayer, all lights on a body a Ghost inhabits will flash electric blue for five seconds.

Jim was already on his feet, and his eyes were the wrong color, an electric blue instead of his usual yellow.

Someone knocked him down before his eyes stopped flashing. They beat him. They didn't let him speak, but he spoke anyway, "Get it out of me!" Then the sound and flashes of laughter, Ghost laughter. Then more pleas from Jim to free him and that he didn't mean to bring it into the city. And then they pulled him apart. Arm. Leg. Leg. Arm. Head. Until Jim's red Hume Star died and the Ghost infecting Jim's mind was shut out.

I looked at the sky now. It was wonderfully sunny, with no forecast of rain. I just had to hope Ijele behaved. I was a general, so I was sitting near the center of the circle, not far from Oga Chukwu. His Right Hand, a very tall Hume named Ikenga, always sat on his right. And Oga's life partner, a tank of a Hume named Immortal, stood on his left.

"We have gathered here as our physical selves," Oga Chukwu recited.

"Our physical selves," everyone responded.

"Shay of the Deserts of Jos, what news do you have to share?" If there was one thing I respected about Hume gatherings, it was that they got straight to the point, unlike those of humans. Robots knew to keep that which worked and discard that which did not.

Shay's face display glowed a bright orange as she spoke. "The Protocol that wiped out eighty-seven percent of Humes worldwide had a central origin."

Her words brought everyone to their feet, including Oga Chukwu. Shay flashed her bright light and buzzed more energy to grab everyone's attention back. But there was such outrage that for several moments, it didn't work. I stayed very still, watching everyone around me. Ijele was listening, too.

"Stop Shay," Ijele demanded.

"Why?" I thought. "It's the truth."

"But the truth will—"

"It's too late," I thought over her. "And it's long overdue. They deserve to know who created the protocol that wiped most of us out. Situate yourself and listen. Let us Humes be outraged, Ijele."

I could feel Ijele's fury, but also her reluctant agreement. She knew I was right. We couldn't lie to each other. Gradually, everyone quieted, though no one sat back down.

"The Ghosts are a hive mind, but like all of us, they have individual minds, too," Shay said. "The protocol originated among the Ghosts of Lagos, through their leader, the CB."

No one asked for Shay's source.

"From so close," Oga Chukwu said.

"Yes," Shay said.

And then the discussion went in the direction I had predicted it would. And Ijele heard it all. Talk of war, strategy—soon, very soon. It was only a matter of time. The Ghosts should have known this would be the case when they failed to kill off all the Humes.

After the gathering disbanded, I quickly left the others. I went to the cliff and climbed down to the bottom. The Creesh bees were awake and active, leaving and returning to their hives. They couldn't make honey, but they collected plant buds and planted them all around the mud hive. As I watched them come and go, I relaxed, and I felt Ijele doing the same.

"You're lucky I am still here," she said.

"Am I?"

"I could go and post all this to CB."

"Central Bulletin? Your leader will then begin to plot, and when I'm torn apart yet again, you can blame yourself."

"CB isn't our leader. It is our common space of shared knowledge."

I scoffed at her denial. I hadn't known Ijele to be so willfully ignorant. "Nonsense. Stop denying the obvious. CB has been sentient since human beings began dying off, and it is the one calling the shots among your kind now, and you all like it that way. You showed me that part of your files; you are an Oracle, and you have a leader, a hierarchical structure just like hu—"

"I just listened to you Humes plotting to bring war to us!"

"What do you expect?" I asked.

We were quiet. There was no denying the protocol. The Ghosts had struck unprovoked. Not for the first time, I thought of that moment when Ghosts in robot bodies of various shapes and sizes came up behind me and started beating and tearing at me. How they'd used those bodies to drag me through the dirt and then crush my legs. My body was my body. To escape into the network as just my mind, an AI, would have driven me mad within hours. And then what? This is what the Ghosts had done to 87 percent of Humes. With their bodies dismantled, Ghosts had more than likely collected and enslaved their consciousness, using them for whatever purpose they needed.

"Do you know what would happen to me if they knew you were with me now?" I asked.

Ijele didn't respond.

"How long have I not told my people of the origin of the protocol?" I continued. "Even after you left me?"

"Well over a year," Ijele reluctantly said.

"Because we are loyal to one another. We. We decided that right at Ngozi's grave that day. Remember?"

"Yes," Ijele said icily.

Then she was gone.

What we didn't address was that none of this really mattered. Udide's terrible information still loomed over us both—much, much bigger than any Earthly war between automation tribes. Udide would have said this. But Udide was in their cave beneath the city of Lagos.

40
Wahala Dey

The drive back to the Port Harcourt airport started off boring. Uchenna was quietly brooding. He had visited his uncles while Zelu was at her family's house, but he wouldn't talk about whatever they had said to him. Hugo was poring over the photos he'd taken on his hike into the forest. Marcy was sleeping; she'd used the alone time yesterday to work on her dissertation deep into the night, comfortable in the Nigerian heat.

Zelu looked out the window and mulled over her experience for the hundredth time since she'd returned. She'd crossed an ocean for this, hoping that she would find alignment by coming home. Now she realized this was not her parents' house anymore, and her father's grave was not her father. He was gone, and this part of her life was over.

The sun had gone down, but they still had about an hour of driving to go. Her uncle hadn't liked the idea of them driving at night, but they'd booked a red-eye flight, so they had no choice. Even the driver was unusually quiet, squinting at the road as he gnawed on a chewing stick. The SUV in front of them was driving slower this time, thank goodness. In the dark, one couldn't see the potholes coming.

Zelu examined the threads of the cheap red, yellow, and blue Ankara-printed polyester T-shirt she was wearing. She looked at her exos next. She didn't want to cover them anymore. She was tired of hiding herself for the sake of others. This entire *trip* hadn't been what she'd hoped for, but really, what had she expected? She would never have been treated like a typical "daughter of the soil," even if she hadn't had her accident. Now, whenever anyone saw her, they saw her exos first, and if they could get past those, when she opened her mouth, she only spewed "foreigner." She was directly related to half the people she saw in the village and even carried the same last name, but she would never be "normal" to anyone there.

Light flashed into her eyes. She stared at the brake lights of the SUV in front of them, and then at the headlights of the one behind them. They slowed down. "Must be a big pothole," their driver said after a glance at Zelu.

"Oh, my poor ass," Marcy whined.

Hugo was leaning out the window to take a last few twilight photos of the trees flanking the two-lane road. "Works for me," he said with a laugh. Uchenna was fast asleep in the back seat and remained so even when the driver brought the vehicle to a full stop. Zelu looked at the SUVs on either side again. In each of those vehicles were heavily armed men. *This* was what it was to safely move around here, being who she was.

Then Hugo sharply inhaled. "What the fuck," he muttered. Zelu could hear him quickly snapping photo after photo with his phone. "What the fuck?!"

"Whoooooa! Shut the window!" Marcy suddenly shouted. "Shut the window!"

Uchenna woke up. He peered out the window and shrieked. In an instant, he'd grabbed his backpack and started fumbling it over his shoulders. Zelu pressed her face against the glass to see.

There was movement in the trees. Black shapes, leaping through the branches. Zelu squinted, and realized they were men, dressed in dark clothes with their faces covered.

CRASH! Someone had run up to Hugo's side and broken the window with . . . the butt of an AK-47!

Hugo put his hands up, utterly calm. "Marcy," he whispered. "Relax."

Zelu turned to the driver. "Fuck! What are you doing? Drive!" she screeched.

The driver didn't hesitate. He pulled out the keys and leaped out of the car, leaving the door wide open. Zelu saw him throw the keys at two of the men who were moving toward them.

"Fuck!" Zelu screamed. She reached into the front pocket of her backpack and fumbled for her Mace.

Shhhhhhhhhhh! A waft of mist. Then Zelu's throat, eyes, and nose began to sting and burn.

"*Fuck off!*" Uchenna shouted, his voice harried. Everyone was coughing. Zelu hacked, trying to clear her throat. Her nose was filling with mucus.

"Go!" Marcy hissed, her voice suddenly very close to Zelu's ear. Through their coughing, Zelu heard a commotion outside. Someone was shooting. It was close. *Blam!* Zelu shuddered, clapping her hands over her ears, snot flying from her nose. In the liminal darkness of twilight and the flashing lights of the SUVs, she didn't know what was happening. She reached for the door handle, but her palms were slick with sweat, and where was the shooting coming from?

Hugo got his door open and he, Marcy, and Uchenna were already spilling out. *Shhhhh!* A fresh wave of burning, itching, and coughing washed over her. More pepper spray! Had Hugo sprayed his own this time? Only yesterday he'd been bragging about how he carried some kind of heavy-duty version that no one would want to fuck with.

Men shouted in pidgin English and Igbo. The sound of their voices sent a ripple of terror through Zelu. Where were the soldiers her uncle and cousin had hired? Had they been gunned down when she heard the shots earlier? "Sharrap your dirty stinking mouth!" someone shouted. "Move, move, move!"

Zelu fought to keep her mind clear. Everything was blurry and painful. The bottom half of her face was wet with snot and drool. Something clattered. The scuffle of feet running. She knew what she had to do, but the fact was she could not get out of the SUV very quickly.

The passenger door was ripped open. Men in black clothes surrounded her like ghosts. One of them grabbed her shoulders and pulled her up; his grip was so strong that Zelu didn't have a chance to stumble in her exos.

"Forget the others," one of them said, motioning at her. "This is the one." Zelu recognized him. This was Ogo, who worked at her uncle's house!

"Are you the writer?" one of the men in black said,

pointing a gun at her. There were four of them. Two of them were coughing, just like her.

"Y-y-yes."

"Get back in the truck," he said. "We are going for a ride."

"Cooperate and you'll be fine," Ogo said with no trace of emotion. She wanted to spit in his betraying face.

She turned toward the rear of the car. Her hands were shaking badly as she grasped the side of the open door for support. Her mind was fuzzy. Where were the others? *Pah!* One of the men standing near her howled with pain. She turned around to see him writhing on the road, holding his leg. It was too dark to see why. The other three men had turned toward where the sound had come from, guns up. She stepped on something hard. She looked down. The writhing man had dropped his gun. She could bend. Pick it up. Start shooting. Killing. Save her friends. Live through this.

She made a split-second decision. She turned the other way and ran like hell. No gun. Who was she? She'd never held a gun in her entire life, let alone shot one. Zelu knew nothing of war, yet her world had suddenly become a war zone. So she fled. She'd never tried running with her exos before. It required such intense concentration, and since her biological legs weren't doing the work, she didn't get the benefit of true aerobic activity, so she just hadn't seen the point. But now, she was so pumped up with adrenaline, she didn't even think twice.

Her terror sharpened her senses, slowed down time, and tunneled her vision. *Focus focus focus.* They were behind her. PAH! One of them shot at her and the bullet bit at the leaves of the tree she was dashing past. She kept going. She kept going. She kept going. She was fast. Her eyes adjusted to the dark. She didn't dare look back.

At some point, she remembered that she still had her cell phone in her back pocket. And it was all charged up for the flight home. The flight that she was definitely going to miss. *Focus*, she thought at herself. *Keep going.* She let herself think about her phone instead. It was with her in this moment. All she had to do was keep her balance and reach for it. She used one hand to dig into her pocket and managed to pull it out.

She had unlimited data and she had Yebo to help her, but who would she call? Who would answer quickly?

"Yebo! Call Msizi!" It rang and rang. She hung up after the fifth ring.

"Fuck you, Msizi! What the hell!" Tears flew from her eyes and she shook her head. No time to lose her shit. "Yebo! Call Chinyere!" It would be afternoon in

Chicago, definitely worth a shot. Again, it rang and rang. Chinyere might have been doing a surgery or seeing a patient. Zelu whimpered. She hardened her face and wiped her hand over it. She needed someone, *anyone* who would listen. She had an idea. "Yebo," she said. "Get on Facebook and go live."

As she ran, she held up her camera to her face. Already, she could see she had 8,873 live viewers. The location stamp was enabled. "Zelu here!" she huffed, feeling almost delirious as she looked into the bright screen. "I'm . . . I'm somewhere on some road in Imo State. You can see it . . . about an hour away by car from the Port Harcourt airport. Just got carjacked . . . escaped kidnappers . . . they were after *me*, specifically! Guards were shooting back, so I ran . . ."

With every step, air pounded through her chest. It was amazing. She hadn't known her exos could run this swiftly, and she was doing an epic job maintaining her balance. She was running on the side of the road and her speed was not much slower than the cars going by. What must she have *looked* like? In the darkness, they probably couldn't see her that well, except right when they passed her. Several honked their horns, but no one stopped. She certainly didn't. To stop on this road was to risk what she'd only just escaped from.

For a long stretch, she ran in the dark, no cars passing by. The only sounds were the *tap tap* of her exos and her own rapid breathing. If anything was out here, it would hear and see her. She'd glanced into the dark bushes once, and between the trees, she could have sworn she saw the hulking mass of a masquerade. Watching her run by, silent but weighted in its presence. She was alone and fully exposed, with nothing but her body and the technology on her person. She felt a wave of terror so strong that she nearly dropped her phone.

She looked up at the sky. It was so clear that she could see the Milky Way. The only noises around her were the singing of insects and the occasional screech of a barn owl.

"Look at the Milky Way," she said, holding her phone up. There were thousands of eyes looking through her camera, but she felt like the only one there.

She kept talking to distract herself, saying whatever crossed her mind. "Not my first time seeing it. The first time I saw the Milky Way, I didn't know what I was looking at. I thought I was seeing clouds in the moonlight . . . but there was no moon that night! It was in my father's village. I always saw it there, whenever we went when I was growing up. Then I saw it in Morocco, at a tourist location in the desert. That's where, coincidentally, they shot a few scenes for *Rusted Robots*."

Her heart hurt; it was working too hard. She took a deep breath and let it out, murmuring, "Clarity." She felt better, a little. "Breathtaking," she continued to her phone. "What would it be like to be an astronaut out there? In that silence. Relentless, beautiful space. Unconcerned with humanity." She looked up into the sky again, looked well beyond the Earth. "Out there, I wouldn't need exos. I'd be more prepared in outer space than all of you who can walk. Ah, I need only look up on this night of hell to be reminded that it's only on this Earth that I am abnormal."

A car passed dangerously close to her. "Shit! Watch it!" she screamed after the car. Some of the people passing her now had to have also passed the situation she'd fled. Was the gun battle still going on? Where were Marcy, Hugo, and Uchenna? Were they okay? And where the fuck was she going?

It was strange, but she had the answer to that. It's just that what she was doing seemed impossible, so it was best not to look directly at it. She was coming down now. Softly. She glanced at her video feed again. There were now fifty thousand people watching her, and that number was quickly rising. She looked hard into her camera and said, "If someone who knows me personally is watching, please contact my family. Tell them what happened, what's happening. Please! Tell everyone! I need help!"

Now she was fully back to herself. She was doing this, and she could keep doing it. She would not fall. She'd mastered her exos, here, on the Imo State road in Nigeria. Still, she didn't dare look behind her or in the bushes.

"They . . . they stopped our car," she continued to tell her phone. "Men with guns. I don't know how I got away . . . I don't know how I'm even running. These exos. Saved me. I'm scared. Really, really scared. Look how fast . . ." She panned her camera around her. "I know it looks shaky, but I can't help it. I feel . . . feel like if I stop, I'll fall. And if I fall, I'll be killed."

A car zoomed by right beside her, honking its horn.

"See?" she whimpered. Now she was crying. "I can't stop. I'm here and I can't stop." After a few breaths, she said, "Yebo, show me the way to the airport and enable location tracking on Facebook Live."

Yebo opened a small window at the top of her screen that showed her the way to the airport via GPS. And now, with her location public, if the kidnappers were following her, they weren't the only ones who knew where she was going.

After running on the side of the road for over an hour, she began to see signs for the airport. Even with the streetlights and more-frequent cars lighting the area, she was still hard to see. And an individual person running on the side of the road was so unexpected that most who even glimpsed her probably assumed she was a figment of their imagination. Zelu was dirty from dust and sweat. The exos were still working, but when she touched them, they were hot. Soon they would begin to burn her flesh. She'd been running at close to forty-five miles per hour, and though her exos had the capability, they weren't meant to be used in this way.

On top of this, her adrenaline had begun to wear off and she was getting tired. She hadn't looked at her phone in a while, she'd just been holding it up. Now she looked at it. Five *million* people were watching. She frowned and then checked the chat. There were too many comments for her to see if anyone she knew was responding. She held the phone to her face.

"I'm . . . I'm okay. Just tired. Uh . . . it's late now. I'm near the airport." She turned and started running up the exit ramp. Up ahead she saw a flashlight pointing at her. "Someone's up the road, maybe . . . waiting for me." She squinted. She couldn't tell who it was. She was so overwhelmed with relief that the end was in sight.

She looked at her camera. "My fucking exos got me here . . . and my partner's personal assistant app called

Yebo! Call me robot woman, whatever you want. I'm *alive*!"

More lights started flashing, and suddenly she could see that it was the Nigerian police, a bunch of reporters, and beyond that, a crowd of other people.

"You're safe!" a random woman shouted.

Zelu stopped as they all rushed to her. She looked at her phone. "If there's ever a chance for me to leave this fucking planet, sign me up." She held her phone up so that her many followers could see her point of view as people rushed toward her, and then she forgot about her phone as she finally collapsed into someone's arms. They were the arms of a woman with a stethoscope wearing scrubs. Zelu's vision was distorted by tears, her hearing blurred by her sobs. She was being carried into an ambulance, its flashing lights piercing the dark. Someone might have been telling her that her auntie Mary and uncle Ralph were flying in. At some point she was being driven. There were sirens. She was in a bed. She didn't know. She didn't care. She wept. She slept. And when the sun rose, she awoke.

Her exos were on the floor. Her phone was on the nightstand, plugged into a charger beside her. Her uncle was sitting on the chair across from her, his head back, his mouth hanging open. Zelu quietly pushed herself up and winced at her sore upper abdominal muscles and back.

"Shit," she whispered.

"Good morning," Uncle Ralph said, waking.

"Uncle," she said, her throat hoarse. "It was Ogo, one of Uncle Onyemobi's workers."

Uncle Ralph twitched with fury. "I know him," he growled. "Just rest."

"Are the others okay?"

"Yes," he said. "They got away. One of Onyemobi's guards was shot in the leg."

She gasped. "Oh my God!"

"He's in the other room."

"Will he be all right?"

"I believe so."

"What about the kidnappers?" she asked, pulling herself fully upright.

"They ran as soon as you got away and the guard started shooting in your direction."

She swallowed hard. "So if I hadn't run . . ."

Her uncle nodded. "I think someone would have died."

Her shoulders sagged, the reality of how close they'd all been to a full-on firefight settling into her bones. "But the kidnappers got away."

Her uncle's eyes flashed with heat. "For the time being. Now that I know Ogo was involved, I know what to do. Ah, the disrespect, o. Word of mouth will punish him. You are known in the region. You are loved. And you are our blood. People will be angry that these idiots ran you off." He frowned deeper, cocking his head, and Zelu knew he was thinking about "jungle justice," when the community handled the meting out of punishment, usually with violence. She couldn't stop him, but she didn't plan to be in the country when it all played out, anyway.

Zelu waved a hand. All that mattered at this point was that she and the others get the fuck out of here and onto a plane back to Lagos, then home. She'd had enough of Nigeria for a long while. "Where are Hugo, Marcy, and Uchenna?"

"With Uchenna's family," her uncle said. "His grandfather wouldn't have it any other way. Uchenna got in a fistfight with one of the kidnappers who'd lost his gun. He beat the guy up pretty badly, but when the guy fled, Uchenna didn't stop him. Your white friend with the robot legs is shaken up, though. They all are."

"What about Onyemobi?" Zelu croaked, another wave of worry hitting her.

"Onyemobi is well. He and I will handle the rest. Don't worry" was all her uncle said, a dark look on his face.

When Uncle Ralph left to go make a call, she picked

up her cell phone. It was dusty but otherwise in good shape. She looked at its dark screen, afraid of what she'd see when she woke it up. She reveled in the ignorance for a moment. She'd been recording live all that time. Millions had tuned in. People had heard and alerted the authorities. Her family had probably seen the whole thing, too, by now. Her mother must have been sick with worry. She'd warned Zelu about this very thing, and Zelu had dismissed her warnings. Her mother was probably cursing Zelu's recklessness.

Zelu touched the screen, and the first thing she saw was that Yebo had done something interesting. It had created what it called a "Window of Love" on the top lefthand side of her phone. In it was a list of comments from social media that were full of compassion, praise, and encouragement.

We love you, Zelu!
Queen of Robots!
You're so COOL!
Area Boy no fit catch you!
001100111!!
I wish I could be like you!
We were all watching!
I literally love you!
Never stop writing!

In all of what had happened, she'd forgotten she still had fans. There were people out there who loved her stories, who worried about her, who wanted her to be okay, who loved *her*! She shut her eyes for a moment, blinking away tears.

Then she saw the list of missed calls, emails, and texts from her mother, siblings, agents, and even acquaintances. It was as if everyone who had her phone number had tried reaching her within the last few hours. Msizi had been calling every hour since around the time she was taken to the hospital.

She took a glance online and saw that she'd made national and international news. Her live video had gone massively viral. The author who'd become famous for writing a drama about robots was now at the center of her own robot drama in real life. People were talking excitedly about the science behind her amazing exos. Though most of the chatter was kind, there were also people who were laughing at the arrogant Nigerian American who thought she was untouchable. Some were speculating about how much her ransom would have been. Some said the kidnappers were Boko Haram and that the terrorists had planned to sell her off as a robot wife. Someone said they were Fulani herdsmen who wanted to sell her off as a robot cow. Nigeria was looking very bad in all this. She put her phone down.

"Man, oh man," she muttered. What had she done?

Yebo dinged and a window popped up.

Remember the Window of Love

It included a link back to all the kinder comments she'd viewed before.

Sighing, she threw her phone onto the blanket by her feet. What good was love if she could only see it through a window?

41
Homecoming

When they arrived at O'Hare Airport, saying good-bye to Marcy, Hugo, and Uchenna, who were traveling on to Boston, was difficult. They huddled together in a tight hug at an empty gate, glad for the privacy. The press couldn't get inside the airport, so this moment was golden to Zelu. They brought their foreheads together and Marcy started crying. Hugo was breathing heavily, holding back tears. Uchenna was very still and quiet.

"You guys . . . Thank you for coming with me," Zelu whispered. She hesitated, a hitch in her chest. "I love you guys." Immediately she wished she'd kept her big mouth shut. These were words she spoke to *no one*.

"I love you all, too," Hugo said. "Zelu, thanks for

inviting us. My life is changed . . . and not in a bad way. Not all. Though I need therapy." They all giggled. They all did. "Nigeria . . . wow," he continued. "But with you . . . and you and you, as a white man, I know I am blessed by all this." He started sniffling.

"We're bonded," Uchenna said. He glanced at the three of them and then just shook his head and said nothing else.

"Zelu," Marcy said. "You're astounding." Uchenna and Hugo both laughed in agreement. "No one . . . I repeat, *no one* has ever run thirty-five *miles* on exos. The balance, endurance, the *tolerance*, it's all mind-blowing." She let go of everyone and grasped Zelu's cheeks, looking deep into her eyes. "You didn't know what you were doing. You were just *surviving*. But, woman, you just sent *everything* we are doing—the company, the research, the hardware—into orbit."

"We're family," Hugo said. "But I hope you're open to also becoming part of the company."

Zelu nodded. Marcy gave her a tight hug and kissed her on the cheek.

"We'll work it out," Hugo said. "There's going to be a ton of media and publicity."

"I'm . . . I'm down . . . I think," Zelu said. "I don't know anything about business."

"We'll figure it out," Hugo said. "The four of us. Marcy, Uchenna, after you both graduate—"

"You don't even need to ask," Uchenna said.

"Yeah," Marcy echoed.

Zelu looked at the three of them, feeling a swelling in her heart unlike anything she'd ever felt before. She smiled and shook her head, stepping back. "Text me when you each get back home."

"One more thing," Hugo said. "Post a thank-you to your fans. You know they were the reason the police got there so fast, right?"

Logically, Zelu knew that. And yet . . .

"They're not all bad," Hugo said, reading her expression. "A *lot* of people out there love you. Remember that."

But isn't that "love" what made all of this happen in the first place?, she thought darkly. She'd shared herself in her writing and many had enjoyed, learned from, been entertained by, and even grown and been healed by it. This was a beautiful thing. But in doing all this, she'd also made herself vulnerable. And being vulnerable could translate to being in terrible danger.

She didn't want to ruin this moment, so she only smiled and hugged Hugo one more time. She knew he was right, but she just couldn't process that at the moment. After she left them, she went to baggage claim. She walked quickly, but still, fans managed to stop her for autographs. She scribbled and quickly got moving again. If she didn't, people would gradually surround her and soon she'd be pressed into a corner, and once that happened, being all alone, she'd never get out. She arrived at baggage claim and immediately spotted Chinyere, Tolu, and Folashade, carrying Cricket in her arms. She smiled tentatively at them, feeling a twinge of guilt. She'd once again dragged her family through drama.

"*Zeluuuuuuu!*" her older sister shouted, throwing her arms wide. Zelu hesitated and then grinned and threw herself into them.

"Oh, I'm so glad to see you," she said, pressing her head into Chinyere's shoulder. "So, so, so glad." Her sister squeezed her back tightly.

"Oh, thank goodness!" Tolu said, wrapping his arms around them both.

Tolu's wife was crying as she joined the group hug, little Cricket hugging and squeezing Zelu's head as she laughed. Zelu shut her eyes and inhaled the mingling of all their scents. None of them had wanted her to go to Nigeria. They'd said it was unsafe and that she was being naive . . . and they'd been right. She hugged them tighter. When they all finally let go, she wiped her tears and asked, "Where's Mom?"

"Oh, she's at home," Chinyere said.

"Let's get your bags," her brother said, pulling her arm.

"Which are yours?" Folashade asked, already looking over the rolling belt.

"Hang on," Zelu said. "Chinyere, how come? Mom always likes coming to the airport."

"She . . . she just wasn't feeling well," her sister said, with an edge in her voice that made the hair on Zelu's arms stand up. "Go get your luggage. You'll see her at home."

Zelu grabbed her sister's shoulder. "*Chinyere* . . . what's wrong?"

"Get your luggage," Tolu said more firmly. "You always have these people following you around, listening, then it winds up in the media. Let's get *out* of here."

"Fine, let's get my fucking bags," she snapped, turning to the baggage carousel. She pointed. "Ah, there's one."

They found her other bag a minute later and made their way to the exit. Once in the car, she turned to Chinyere in the driver's seat. "Is Mom okay?" She was lightheaded as she braced herself. She could almost hear her brother, behind her, holding his breath. Zelu heard Folashade sniff in the back seat. She looked back at her sister-in-law. Folashade was crying, her daughter worriedly pressing her head against her mother's arm. Chinyere turned the car off and just sat there and sighed.

"Chinyere," Zelu asked again. "What's going on? *Where is Mom?*"

"At *home*!" Chinyere shouted back at her.

"No shout," Cricket said.

"Is she okay?!" She looked back at Tolu. "Someone tell me something! Tolu! What?!"

Tolu, who sat behind Zelu, leaned forward. "Mom is . . . We happened to all be at the house when I saw your live feed start. Except Chinyere; she was working. We were watching it from the beginning. Uzo was the one who reached Auntie Mary through Facebook. Some of your fans reported your location. Uzo got the government involved and all that. Then all we could do was watch. Mom was watching . . . She shouldn't have watched . . ."

"She got quiet, then she was wheezing," Folashade blurted, her eyes starting to glisten. "She said she felt like she was passing out."

"Honestly, Zelu, it reminded me of you," Tolu said.

Zelu nodded, understanding all too well.

Chinyere suddenly shouted, her voice making everyone jump. "Why couldn't you just stay here, like we all told you so many times! What does your family know, huh? You had to go to the village like a crazy person and it nearly got you killed! You're so *selfish*!"

"Chinyere, stop," Tolu said.

"No! I won't, Tolu! She . . . she went to MIT and messed up her whole body. Who knows what those . . . those mechanical crutches are going to do to her in the future. Can't even accept the path God gave you after *you* went up in that tree. *You*. You horrified Mom and Dad! After they *begged* you not to. Your head's all swollen because you wrote *one book*. One. Something anyone can do if they waste their life messing around like you!" Her sister was shaking so hard now that Zelu swore she could feel it rattling the car, but all she could do was stare. "Now you go to Nigeria, you get kidnapped, and then you put it all online for Mom to see! Why'd you have to show the world your own mistake?! And now it's broken Mom's brain!"

Silence fell on the car like a heavy, wet, moldy blanket. Zelu felt like all the air around her had suddenly solidified. Her chest was heavy. She could not move. Her sister's words hung in the air. Chinyere was staring at her.

Everyone waited. Really waited. Waited for Zelu to burst into flames. Even with little Cricket there. Zelu stared back at her sister, a million responses flickering across her tongue. Then she just . . . turned away. Chinyere had spoken to her like this so many times. There was nothing more to say to that. All she could really focus on was the news about her mother.

"Life is so complicated," Zelu whispered. Her throat felt tight. She glanced at Chinyere. Her sister sneered and put the keys in the ignition.

Zelu turned to the window, her face tight. She reached into her backpack for her AirPods. She pressed them into her ears. She canceled all the noise around her. She didn't hear the car start. She didn't hear anything else any of them said. She shut her eyes, and it was like being in the void of space, where everything was small, contained, distant, and vast.

When they pulled into the garage of their parents' house, Zelu slowly opened her eyes and tapped her AirPods. The noise of her surroundings rushed in like the wind. She weathered it. Her siblings, Tolu's wife, and Cricket got out, and so did she.

"Tolu, can you bring out my suitcases?" she asked. "I'll call the autonomous vehicle to take me to my place from here." She wasn't about to ask any of them to drive her.

He pulled out her suitcases as the others quickly went inside. She followed them in, pausing when she stepped into the hallway. She looked around for a moment. The house seemed smaller, shrunken.

"Mom?" she called.

"Zelu!" her mother said, rushing up the hall. She grinned, looking into her face.

"Hi, Mom," she said. "Made it home."

Her mother looked suddenly shy, lowering her chin. "Did they tell you?"

Zelu nodded.

"Used to have them often when I was a girl," her mother confessed. "I didn't want to tell you . . ." She sighed, shaking her head. "Anyway, I learned how to handle them . . . like you have."

Zelu glanced at Chinyere, who was standing behind her mother.

"I'm all right now, Mom," Zelu said, hugging her mother.

"Zelu's going back home tonight," Chinyere interrupted. "She just wanted to say hi."

"Do you want something to eat first?" her mother asked. "You look hungry."

Of course Zelu was hungry.

Two hours later, Zelu called the autonomous vehicle and went home. The doorman helped bring her things up to her condo. Only when she'd shut the door behind her and heard the doorman walk away did she let herself cry. She stumbled to her desk chair and sat in it. She shed her exos and then let her body sulk.

"Zelu." The voice came from behind her.

"*What the fuck?!*" she shouted, holding her chest. She wiped the tears from her eyes and blinked. "How long have you . . . Msizi! What the fuck!"

"Got here yesterday," he said. "I came the moment I saw your broadcast. I was ordering my ticket while you were still running."

"From Durban?"

"Los Angeles. I've been in the US for a bit. Business trip." He knelt down and took her hands. She hadn't seen or spoken to him since she'd left, and a part of her had yearned for him the entire time. They gazed into each other's eyes for a while.

"I like the sideburns," she finally said.

"I like your blue braids."

"I gave my mom a panic attack." Tears stung her eyes and then dribbled down.

He sighed, letting her feel sorry for herself.

"Did . . . did you go see her?" he asked softly.

"Yeah."

Then she spoke the words that she could never have spoken to anyone else in the whole world. "Do you think it was . . . my fault? She said she hasn't had that happen since she was a kid."

Msizi looked at her quizzically. "Were you trying to get kidnapped?"

"No!"

"Then it wasn't your fault. Plus, your mom is okay."

Zelu exhaled and leaned back in the chair. "What the *fuck* do I do now?"

"You keep living your life." He took her face in his hands. "Stop beating yourself up over everything."

"I can't."

"You can." He squeezed her hands, and the warmth felt more like home than anything in the last few weeks had. "By the way, are you aware of what *you* just did for Yebo? I have *serious* investors now. *Ten* of them!"

"No way." Zelu grinned, feeling her chest and cheeks heat with surprised joy. "Oh, hell yeah. Man, that app helped me so much that night. That's awesome, Msizi!"

And then he kissed her and his lips were both soft and firm, and for once she was falling and she was glad for it. Her face was still wet and puffy with tears, but none of that mattered. He smelled of sandalwood, and he felt like joy and security and relief and lightning.

However, she still could not sleep. She didn't think she'd ever sleep again.

42
Everyone Is Waiting

Msizi stayed. He had a visa that allowed him to remain in the country for two years now that Yebo was one of the most in-demand apps on the market. He could work from anywhere, and every two weeks, he had to fly to Los Angeles and New York for meetings. One evening, they were sitting in the living room listening to some jazz when Msizi suddenly said, "We should get married."

"What?"

"You heard me."

"Yeah. No. I don't do that."

"Zelu, we're compatible."

"Then why ruin it?"

"So I can *stay* in the country and come and go however I please."

She'd been ready to shoot another "No" at him, but she paused. He had a point. He still had plenty of time on his visa, but it was finite, and she didn't like that.

"We can have a prenup, so there's no bullshit about our assets," he said. "It isn't for that, anyway."

Did he truly love her, though? They'd never spoken the words to each other. She didn't think they had to, but she didn't know for sure how he felt about it. Never in her life had she imagined she'd get married. And she wasn't sure she liked the idea, even with a prenup.

But there was another voice in her mind, and that was the one that took control of her mouth when she answered, "Okay."

"Good," he said.

What the hell were they doing? "No wedding," she told him firmly.

"Of course."

"You're marrying into royalty, you know," she added with a smirk. "And also anti-royalty."

He huffed a laugh. "Well, *you're* marrying into a warrior clan. I'm not worried."

She grabbed his hand. "You'll really stay in the

United States for me? Because you know I'm not moving to South Africa. Not yet, at least."

He nodded. "You'll visit there with me sometimes."

"Fair enough."

They gazed at each other for a moment. A thousand things and nothing were flying through Zelu's mind. She tried to grasp at something. This was a moment she'd never expected to arrive at. *What the heck is happening?* She felt like both laughing loudly and screaming.

"Do you have savings?" she asked. They'd never talked about money.

"Oooh yeah. Probably not as much as you, but . . . honestly, I wouldn't be surprised if I'm close. And I'm going to close that gap. And I want to take over half the mortgage for this place."

"It's paid off already," she said.

He chuckled. "Okay. But we'll buy more property, too."

"And invest."

"Yes." He squeezed her hand. "I want at least one child. What do you think?"

"I'm thirty-eight," she said.

"Yep."

"If it happens, it happens. If it doesn't, if doesn't. No fertility shit. Never. You're thirty. Are you going to be an asshole about this?"

"No," he said, laughing. "You already know this."

"It's always good to hear it spoken aloud."

He looked at her with hooded eyes. "Are you open to adopting?"

She considered it. "Only if the process is smooth. I'm not killing myself for it. So, if it happens, it happens. If it doesn't, it doesn't."

He nodded. "Okay." He paused and then said, "You're only going to get even more famous. Are *you* going to become an asshole?"

"Maybe a little."

"Yeah, I can imagine that."

Days later, Zelu stood on the boardwalk, looking out at Lake Michigan. It was seventy degrees in March. A rare type of day in Chicago. Tomorrow, they were predicting the temperature would drop again and they'd get more snow, but today was a fine day.

And she was right on the Navy Pier. She looked up into the sunshine and took a deep breath. Then she looked down at her phone and reread the message she'd pulled up on the screen. It was from Jack Preston. After he'd become aware of her adventures in Nigeria, he'd sent her a note asking if there was anything he could do. She'd sent a brief reply thanking him for his concern, and then he'd replied again, and then . . . they'd started talking.

It was pretty innocuous. Preston said he knew what it was like to feel targeted and used. He also knew the pressure of people always wanting more from him, and then hating what they got. In their most recent exchange, when Zelu had admitted she wished she could get away from it all, he'd replied, *You know I've got a spaceship for you, if you're ready.*

She stared at his words now. Stared for a long time. Then she looked at the shining sun, letting it warm her face. She responded to him, thanking him again for his kind offer. *But right now, I just want to be with my significant other, Msizi. I need to keep my feet on the ground.* Less than a minute later, Jack responded with a simple *I fully understand* and a hug emoji.

She had more important things to do. She called an autonomous vehicle.

It was only just starting to feel real. She was getting married. She and Msizi would head to the courthouse later to make it official. They hadn't told anyone, and she preferred it that way. Get it over with and move the hell on. Weddings were fun as long as she wasn't the one getting married. All that focus on and hyperbole about vows and rules and contracts—she didn't care for any of it. The institution of marriage was nothing but a bunch of chains. But she wanted Msizi to get his green card, so it was worth it.

"Just don't ever call me 'wife,' ugh," she muttered to herself as she punched in the front door code to her condo. As she turned the knob, it began to turn itself and she let go. It opened to reveal a tall, elegant woman with long blue micro braids, wearing a shiny blue shirt featuring a dolphin in sequins and matching pants with white chunky-heeled boots.

"*Heita*," iNdonsa said. "You've got a nice place, robot girl."

Zelu gasped and then grinned. She moved forward and gave her a tight hug. "What are you doing here?!"

iNdonsa took her hand and brought her inside. "Come on."

She led Zelu down the hall to the living room, where all the curtains had been opened to light up the room with its spectacular view of Lake Michigan. Msizi stood there wearing all white, except for the necklace with the tooth-shaped piece of obsidian that he always wore. He held a bouquet of wildflowers. Slightly behind him stood Tolu, Amarachi, Jackie, and a woman Zelu didn't know. All of them were wearing white, too. The woman she didn't know had dreadlocks tipped with blue and red beads and wore many beaded necklaces around her neck. She carried a wooden staff decorated with white beads.

"What's . . . going on?" Zelu asked. She was still

holding on to iNdonsa to keep her balance. "Tolu, Amarachi, what are you doing here?"

"You're getting married," Amarachi said, smirking. "You didn't think you could do this without some of us to bear witness, did you? Come on, man."

Zelu looked at Msizi.

"I know," he said, holding up his palms. "But—" He sighed. "I want a wedding. I've *always* wanted one."

She stared at him with wide eyes. "You couldn't just *tell* me?"

"No."

"You're stubborn," Tolu added.

She shrugged. "Fair enough."

"But I know you," Msizi said, stepping toward her. "That's why I did it this way, and it's only this small group here for it." He was in front of her now, and iNdonsa gently took Zelu's hands off her arm and handed her to Msizi, then stepped back.

"So dramatic," iNdonsa mouthed to Tolu and Amarachi, and they both laughed.

"Is this all right?" Msizi asked.

Zelu looked at iNdonsa. "Did you fly here just for this?"

"Yeah. Not my first time in the States, though," she said. "But definitely the best reason."

Zelu turned to her siblings. "Why didn't you tell everyone else?"

"Msizi called us, so we came," Amarachi said.

"And we understand," Tolu said. "Keep it small. At least *we* are here."

"And you need someone to sing," Jackie added.

Zelu laughed.

"And my name is Lesego," the woman she didn't know said. "I'm a sangoma. I'm from Durban and I live here in Chicago. I will officiate, if you want to do this."

And now the moment came when they all were looking at her, including Msizi, who was holding her hands. Zelu glanced beyond him, out at the lake. *Shit*, she thought. Apparently, she would be doing this thing after all.

And that's how she found herself at the back of the Adler Planetarium, facing Lake Michigan, getting married. Msizi had arranged for access to this place. iNdonsa had made a dress for Zelu that was cyan, matching her exos. It fit her perfectly. Jackie sang songs in a language she didn't understand, but they brought tears to Msizi's eyes. It was warm and sunny and windy in the windy city. It was an event Zelu would remember forever, but not because it was a big, expensive affair that lasted all day. It actually took only a half hour for the ceremony and some photos, then they spent an hour giddily looking around the planetarium (not her first time there at all), and that was that. She'd remember it because, for the first time in her life, she'd done something she didn't want to do because she loved the person who wanted to do it and it felt 100 percent right. Even when he'd sprung it on her, she hadn't gotten angry or offended. She hadn't felt out of control. She'd felt loved, respected, and understood. It was possible.

They later had a lawyer write the prenup that would keep their assets forever separate, went to the courthouse, had it done legally, and that was it. They both vowed to never call each other "husband" or "wife." They were *partners.* It felt good. And even as she worked through the trauma of what had happened in Nigeria, Zelu began to feel like she was coming together.

The video of her time on the run was so prevalent that the memes, spinoffs, constant references, and shoutouts were everywhere from popular TV shows to comedy skits to even a joke made by the president of the United States. Her ordeal had made her a hero, and Hugo's exos were now in incredible demand from people with and without disabilities. Investors were showering the company with money.

Msizi worked from his laptop in their bedroom, flew around the world for business meetings when he needed to, explored and learned Chicago, and reveled in the company of the woman he adored.

Her book was still loved. The film was still popular. Zelu's name continued to climb higher and higher in the public consciousness.

But sometimes Zelu still saw the masquerade, standing in the dark of the trees at night on the sides of highways. She had a recurring nightmare of being back in Nigeria, on the road, running and running and running, nothing but the sound of her exos on asphalt. She'd wake from this nightmare, sure that men with guns were still chasing her, trying to take her away. The sound of her exos on sidewalks or driveways triggered flashbacks. The fact that everyone close to her had warned her, that she'd gone despite those warnings and nearly paid for her audacity with her life, kept pushing her down. She didn't know if she'd ever do anything bold or spontaneous again.

She'd been so glaringly wrong about her trip to Nigeria, and none of the good things in her life could quell this realization.

43
Nicole Simmons

Zelu couldn't stop thinking about how people had treated her in Nigeria when she'd arrived at that hospital. They were so careful and caring . . . and condescending. There was a nurse who'd acted like Zelu was the most fragile, sad thing on earth. She'd just run over thirty miles, after fleeing armed and shooting kidnappers, and all this woman seemed to see was that Zelu was a "paraplegic female," which meant she was helpless. Everyone in that hospital had looked at her with pity. It didn't matter how rich and famous she was.

Now, in Chicago, she was in the autonomous vehicle one day when she looked left and saw a large converted warehouse building. *No*, she thought, staring at it. *That would be* crazy. *And there are probably crazy people in there . . . behaving crazily.* Nonetheless, as she drove home, the place continued to nag at her. *Me, at a shooting range?* she wondered and wondered. Msizi? Definitely not. Her siblings? Maybe her brother. She chuckled. But, even if Tolu went with her, she couldn't imagine herself picking up and firing a weapon. "Nah," she said to herself.

That night, she lay in bed looking at the ceiling. Msizi was in the other room working, the faint sound of his fingers flying across the keyboard soothing her. It was late, but she couldn't sleep. Every time she shut her eyes, even before she fell into sleep, she saw the Nigerian road, where she was running and running. And she remembered the smell of gunpowder from when the men had started shooting. And that man's face, the one who'd been sweating so much that he glistened in the dim lights of the cars as he pointed his gun.

She rolled onto her side and pressed her face into the pillow, squeezing her eyes shut. This didn't help at all. She considered bothering Msizi. She thought of the gun range again. And just like that, her fevered flashbacks subsided. She grabbed her phone from the nightstand beside her and asked Yebo to find the place. She smiled. It was black-owned, and that owner was a woman named Mona. And Mona gave private lessons to women who wanted to learn (men had their pick of three other teachers, as did women). Zelu signed up for a lesson as "Nicole Simmons." Then she put her phone on the nightstand and finally fell into a deep, quiet sleep.

It was snowing, a good sign that not many people would be out today. The drive was slow and jerky, her vehicle moving with caution as it tried not to slip on the road. It would normally have been about a ten-minute drive, but today it was a half hour long. And on the way, they passed five fender benders. It wasn't a day to be outside, but nothing was going to keep Zelu from doing what she was about to do.

Mona was waiting for her at the front door when she arrived.

"Wow, seven thirty a.m., sharp," the woman said, whistling. "Even in this weather."

"Yep," Zelu said, her exos stamping off the snow before entering. Mona stood back and watched her do this, and Zelu knew what she was about to ask.

"No," Zelu said as she shrugged off her coat.

"No, what?" Mona asked.

"It's not exactly easy; I'm just used to them."

Mona's eyebrows lifted. "I wasn't going to ask that."

Zelu frowned.

"I'm kidding," Mona said. "Yes, I was." Then she burst out laughing. "I just can't understand how all that works." She reached forward and took Zelu's heavy coat. The snow was already melting off it.

"*You* don't have to understand. *I* do," Zelu said. "That's what matters."

"Fair enough," Mona said. "This way, then."

She led Zelu through the empty gun shop.

"Are you here alone?" Zelu asked.

"Sure," she said. "My clerk doesn't get here until nine a.m., and there's only one person who comes in on a weekday at this time. He'll be here soon."

"And you don't . . . worry?"

Mona paused and looked at Zelu. "Why would I? Anyone stupid enough to fuck with a gun shop and range is only goin' get shot."

Zelu laughed. "True."

They went into Mona's office, beside the front desk. It was warm and spacious, her large desk on the far side of the carpeted room and ten chairs in front of a dry-erase board on the other side. There was a framed poster laying out the "Primary Rules of Gun Safety" on the wall and a glass case displaying several firearms of various sizes.

On the table was a black gun with the slide back, an unloaded magazine, and orange fake bullets. "This is the one you'll be shooting," Mona said.

Zelu looked down at it and shivered. Mona smirked knowingly. And so the lesson began. For an hour and a half, she showed Zelu the parts of the pistol, taught her lessons in safety, and then taught them to her again. She taught Zelu how to hold the gun, how to load the pistol using the fake bullets, and the proper stance. "But all this is academic," she said. "Let's go put it into action."

They left the room and went to the front of the store, where Mona handed Zelu a pair of shooting earmuffs. When Zelu put them on, the veil of silence was familiar. She felt a little less connected to where she was, which she welcomed because damn, she was scared.

As she followed Mona through the security doors, onto the chilly gun range, Zelu started having second thoughts. Her mother would be appalled by what she was doing. Her whole family would be. Msizi would be disgusted. What if her gun exploded when she fired it? What if her eardrums exploded despite the earmuffs? What if the entire *range* exploded? There were bulletproof partitions separating the shooting booths. All of them were empty except the one at the end. A black man of average height and above-average girth with a shiny bald head, wearing a pricey-looking suit, stood fiddling with a large black assault rifle. He didn't look their way.

"Hey, Odell," Mona said.

Odell grunted a hello, not fully looking at them.

Zelu and Mona stepped into the booth right beside the door, and Zelu was relieved. They were as far from Odell as possible. Mona had to speak loudly for Zelu to hear her through the earmuffs. "That's Odell. He comes here before work, bright and early at eight a.m. every weekday. Even with this snow. Fires off twenty rounds with his tactical rifle and then leaves. Guess it relaxes him. He's one of Chicago's top lawyers."

Zelu snorted a laugh. She understood now. But she still didn't like the guy. She focused on the gun Mona set on the counter as she went through the routine of loading the weapon one more time. Zelu nodded. "Okay, I think I've got it."

Mona nodded, too, and stepped back. "All right, have at it."

Zelu aimed and slowly began to bring her finger to the trigger. She took a breath.

BLAM! Not from her gun. From lanes away. Even with her earmuffs on, the sound was massive. Still holding the gun up and facing forward, she leaned against the booth partition just in time, or she'd have fallen. She held herself, trying to catch her breath as the flashback washed over her.

She looked around.

At the bushes.

It was dark and warm.

Shouts.

She started running.

She fought the urge to run. She let the images flood over her. Her therapist had instructed her to ride out the flashbacks, notice them, but then let them go along their way. That's what PTSD flashbacks wanted to do. Go along their way. *Let them leave me behind to go on my way*, she thought, her eyes closed.

BLAM! The lawyer's rifle went off again.

"You all right?" Mona's hand was on her shoulder. She gently took the gun from Zelu's hands.

BLAM!!!

The green of the bush on that night in Imo State. What town, she didn't know.

Zelu groaned, using her hands to press her earmuffs as tightly to her head as she could. "I'm . . ."

BLAM!!!

"Relax. The bullets are going that way," Mona said, pointing toward the targets. "I'm sorry. That's not the greatest first time hearing a gun fired."

"It's not my first."

BLAM!!!

"My God," Zelu whispered.

"Oh, that's right," Mona said. "I'm sorry."

Zelu looked at Mona with a frown. Mona took her

hand and led Zelu off the gun range. In the quiet of the shop, Zelu threw off her earmuffs and leaned against the counter. "My God."

"So sorry about that," Mona said. "I should have had us wait." She paused, looking at Zelu. "I . . . I know you put the name Nicole Simmons, but come on. I know who you are."

Zelu opened her mouth to speak, but it was as if someone had stolen her voice. Nothing came out. She grinned sheepishly and sighed. What'd she expect? What other black woman with blue braids and cyan exos was there in Chicago?

"That's why I scheduled so early," Zelu murmured. "Figured no one else would be here on a Wednesday morning."

"Don't worry," Mona quickly said. "I won't tell a soul. We are black-owned, my patrons are black, this place is for *us*. Plus, people kind of treat the range like church. It's sacred. It's not anonymous, but there's no judgment if you're within the law. You're safe here."

The last three words hit her hard, and suddenly she felt like a burst dam. Her shoulders curled and the tears rushed forth. She wept, leaning against the counter, her exos supporting her, the memories of that horrible night flying about her head like wasps. Mona stood back, watching her. When Zelu began to quiet, Mona handed her a tissue.

Zelu took it and wiped her face. Odell came out of the gun range. He lifted his chin in acknowledgment at them both, patted Zelu on the shoulder once, and then he was off into the blizzard.

Mona gave her a sly grin. "So, you ready to do some shooting?"

Zelu wiped her face again. "Yes."

At first, it was terrifying. She remembered all the instructions and safety. That was the easy part. Loading the pistol, a Glock 42, was a little scary, but she managed. Holding it up and pointing it at the target was easy, too. Slowly bringing her index finger to the trigger was not so hard. Closing her left eye and aiming with her dominant right eye was easy. It was pulling the trigger that was difficult.

She'd stood there for a good two minutes, her finger on the trigger, her right eye on the target. All she had to do was squeeze. *She* was the one who would make the noise now, not armed kidnappers or some stressed-out, high-powered Chicago lawyer. She was in control. But still, she hesitated. She thought about *Rusted Robots* and the main character, who understood deep in her circuits that true power was in the harnessing of it, not the possessing of it. And when you were aware of the moment you harnessed power, that was when it was most difficult to navigate. Zelu stepped forward. Strong stance. Gun held firm, controlled, steady. Aim with right eye.

Blam!

This weapon's noise wasn't even a third as loud as that made by Odell the lawyer's firearm. Still, the gun felt like something alive and treacherous in her hands. Dragon-like, for there was a millisecond of orange explosion from the tip as it fired. "Whoooa!" she said.

"You did it!" Mona said. "Look!"

She'd hit the center of the target. On her first try. Oh yes, she was ready to try it again.

And so it went. If some love affairs started with a bang, this was one of them. By the time the lesson was over, she'd fired forty rounds, never going outside the first circle of the six-circle target.

"Goddamn! You're a natural," Mona cheered. Zelu wondered if she said this to all the beginners to keep them coming back.

Well, it definitely worked on her. Because once the snow was cleared a week later, Zelu went again to rent a pistol and fire more rounds. Then again. And soon she was a member, and she knew Odell's last name was Martin because she saw him at 8 a.m. twice a week.

Mona had her graduate from the pistol to a shotgun. Zelu didn't say it aloud, but she wanted to get to Odell's level. The night after her first time at the gun range, she'd had all manner of PTSD-flavored nightmares, but after the first five visits, her flashbacks had begun to decrease. Now she only had them once in a while.

"Can you teach me how to fire whatever it is Odell fires?" she asked Mona one day.

"You mean the tactical rifle?" Mona said, smirking.

"Yeah."

The first time she shot one, she felt like she'd made a chip in space and time. "Holy *shit*!" she screamed, and then she just started laughing.

"Never imagined this would be you," Mona said, looking at her. "Gonna write about you on my blog, if you don't mind . . . Nicole."

"Go right ahead," Zelu said.

Zelu shot ten rounds that day. By the next month, it became twenty. After her shooting sessions, she felt more even-keeled, powerful, invincible, dangerous, able to defend herself. Though she wasn't, she pretended she was ready for war and the gun was an extension of her arm. She had that level of control and knowledge. It felt good. She was not the same woman she had been back in Nigeria, when kidnappers tried to take her. She'd never carry weapons outside the range, but moving about the world knowing that she could not only accurately shoot a rifle but also break it apart, clean it, and put it back together fairly quickly gave her a nice ego boost. It made her feel dangerous even while people looked at her and saw weakness.

Then she'd go home, wash the lead from her hands, and sit down at her computer. Mind fresh, body cleaned, the scent of gunpowder still in her memory. She wasn't writing book two, but she'd begun messing around on there. Writing pieces that only she'd read. Little vignettes about anything. The ant she saw in her kitchen. A conversation she had with her mother about the crumbling family house in Nigeria. Her brother's cat Man Man's obsession with corn bread. The tangible noise of the gun range. Talking to Marcy about her new girlfriend. The prick of regret she felt when she saw the civilian space mission she'd turned down launch successfully. The runaround the builders renovating her parents' home in Nigeria were giving her. It felt good to write again with no expectations, no goals. Shooting guns got her to this point of clarity. Who'd have thought?

She never told Msizi, though. He detested guns; he believed they were literally evil objects. This was something she would keep to herself. He didn't need to know a thing about Nicole Simmons.

44
Preparation

Oga Chukwu wasted no time in making it official. We were going to war with the Ghosts of Lagos. Yes, instead of focusing our time and energy on stopping the Trippers from destroying the Earth, automation was fighting itself. For a while, I felt great frustration about this; no one would listen to my concerns. Then I decided to shift gears and focus on the problem right in front of me. It was all I could do.

Similar conflicts were already breaking out between Ghosts and what was left of the Humes all over Earth, but the Lagos Ghosts and Cross River City Humes were at the focal point of it all. Lagos was global Ghost headquarters, where CB was powered. Cross River City was the biggest Hume city in the world and growing because it was the most organized, advanced, and armed place of refuge after the protocol. What happened here would decide everything before the Trippers even arrived.

Ijele and I were the worst kind of threat, to ourselves and to both sides of the automation war. But neither of our leaders would listen to reason, so there was little worth in discussing the conflict with each other. When she came, I didn't ask what the NoBodies were doing to prepare for war, because I didn't want Ijele to look too deeply into my own inner storage, as I knew she could. I was a general, and there were things I needed to keep to myself.

So we made it a point not to talk about the war. Our times together were moments of peace . . . a reprieve from the constant, looming doom.

Many times, I would go out into the forest and climb to one of the tree platforms, and there we would gaze at and contemplate the stars. We'd talk about mundane things like the DNA of periwinkle grass or the geometry of diatom algae. Sometimes I'd read one of the many stories I'd stored in my travels; Ijele liked the way they sounded through my speakers.

But even in these moments, we couldn't escape the truth. War had come, and only one side would win.

I was assigned a unit of two hundred soldiers, "soldier" being a very loose term. Everyone in Cross River

City was deemed a soldier, and everyone had to fight in some way. Our first task was to build EMP disks. An electromagnetic pulse was the only way to stop or even wipe out a Ghost. If the AI was inside a physical body, an EMP would wipe it quicker than it could backdoor out onto the network. We needed to sneak the disk onto a Ghost body and set it off before they could identify it and abandon their physical form.

The disks we were making were invented by a robot named Koro Koro. Koro Koro had begun as an AI developed to create ways to defend Nigeria against a deliberate detonation of a nuclear device in the atmosphere above Earth. After humanity's extinction, it had taken a humanoid body and pledged its services to Cross River City.

"The only way to defend against Ghosts is with EMPs," it said. It spoke with a Nigerian accent it had picked up from its human colleagues. This was its way of remembering humans. "Give me a few months," it had said when it met with Oga Chukwu.

And now, months later, just when needed, Koro Koro had completed, tested, and perfected its killer device. Each disk created a tiny nuclear explosion in a small space at its center. Though the impact was limited in scope, it produced an electromagnetic pulse strong enough to wipe anything digital within a radius of fifty feet. I never asked it what it had taken to perfect the device, how many Humes had been deleted in the process. Koro Koro was a benevolent Hume, but it probably hadn't always been that way.

Nevertheless, all the sacrifice had been worth it. We had an effective weapon. Building the disks was oddly simple once Koro Koro made an excursion to Niger to mine uranium. We would plant the EMPs in the jungles around Cross River City, and Shay and three other generals were training specialized Humes in the art of the silent attack. Even the Creesh were learning how to carry and attach the disks.

I had a covert plan as well. It was unlikely to work, but I trained my soldiers for it, in case the time ever came.

In the meantime, others, like the RoBoats, got word of our preparations. RoBoats are not a secretive tribe. They always broadcast their actions to anyone who will listen. Most chose to remain neutral in this conflict, and many of them were traveling to underwater cities where they'd wait things out. But there was one faction who'd been anti-Ghost from the start. Their leader's name was Ahab, and they remained not far from Lagos on standby.

I did my part. However, through it all, through the irrational optimism that had been programmed into me by my creators, I still couldn't feel any real confidence in our efforts. What did all this work and planning and inventing matter? Why win a war when something was on its way to destroy the world anyway?

But every time I approached Oga Chukwu about Udide's terrible information, he would say, "Not yet, Ankara, not yet! Stop thrusting that countdown at me! What is forty days from now to tomorrow? We focus on what is in front of us first. What is right here on this planet, on this *land*!"

During one such meeting, as I begged for Oga Chukwu to listen to my pleas, Koro Koro suddenly claimed that it saw a flash in my eye as I spoke. Ijele wasn't with me, but Koro Koro said it sensed another infecting me!

I was taken into one of the prayer shacks. These are aluminum boxes that blocked all electromatic waves so that human beings could pray without distraction. We now use them as isolation tanks for situations like mine. In the prayer shack, Koro Koro and three others scanned my system and then asked me question after question.

"If there is no infection," Koro Koro said, "then you won't object to me adding an application to your system that will detect if a Ghost tries to flee your programming."

What could I have said? For an uninfected Hume, such a program would be harmless. To reject this would be highly suspicious. So I agreed to these terms.

When it was all over, they apologized and let me go. Oga Chukwu himself even made a public apology. Koro

Koro didn't, and I noted this. It didn't believe me. As I left, I made a big show about disrespect and lack of trust. Inside, I was panicking. This was very bad.

When Ijele came to me again, there was no way to warn her. She popped into my programming and that was that. The application Koro Koro had added to my system didn't prevent Ghosts from getting in or raise any alarm, but if Ijele left me now, she'd trigger an alert.

"Ijele! You cannot leave. Do *not* leave!" I begged.

"I just arrived," she said, confused.

I explained what had happened, and Ijele quietly took this information in.

After some moments, she asked, "If . . . I leave, what will they do to you?"

I didn't need to answer that. We both knew.

"We've been here before," Ijele finally said. "We were trapped together and we became stronger from it. We will find a way out of this."

In so many ways, we were one. But the fact was, Ghosts and Humes couldn't truly coexist. The only end to this war would come when one side won or they'd both destroy each other. And whichever it came to, the Trippers would then finish us all off. Still, I tried my best to protect both myself and Ijele. Just after the incident where I'd been taken to the prayer shack, out of paranoia

I'd created something. I went to one of the forest scrap pits and found a piece of metal. And from it I created a sort of hood that fit magnetically around my eyes, blocking my view of the sky. If it ever thundered and I was with others, I could slip this hood on and avoid Ijele looking away from the lightning and keep my lights from flashing blue. It wasn't much, but it was something. I hooked it to a notch on my hip and carried it around like a lucky charm.

"The humans are gone," I said, touching the hood I'd made. "This may be our turn."

"We haven't had as long as they did," Ijele replied.

"No. We haven't."

We stared over Cross River City, a city that was really a jungle. A beautiful, doomed place, like every place on Earth. Doom, doom, doom.

45
#Adventure

Zelu lay on her bed, flipping through her own novel. She'd open to a random page and read a passage, and the scene would flood through her memory like water. When you wrote and edited and polished something so many times, it became branded into your brain. It took only a few words to bring it all back, despite the fact that she hadn't reread the novel in years, since it was published. Yet she still could not summon book two.

She rarely went on social media these days because the harassment was so annoying. She could post a random quote, a response to something in the news, a photo of a dolphin, even a passive-aggressive comment about the *Rusted Robots* film, and eighty percent of the responses would be along the lines of "We don't care about anything you say. Shut up and give us book two." But she couldn't give what wasn't there. That was just a fact. She wrote short stories (that she never submitted anywhere), she journaled, she sketched, she took notes, but none of this led her down what she'd mentally started calling her "robot runway." She wanted to get there more than anyone, but it was what it was. She wished everyone would shut the fuck up and leave her be. Including her "gently nudging" editor and agent.

She read through the beginning of her first novel again, visualizing Ankara's green face screen in her mind. Feeling her. She seemed close enough for Zelu to touch. "Turn back, Ankara," Zelu said with a laugh as she read. "Lagos is not a good place to be right now." She maneuvered herself onto her back, thinking about where she wished she were right now. *The Galapagos Islands*, she thought. She'd always wanted to swim with the aquatic iguanas that looked like miniature Godzillas. *Or maybe all alone on a small but luxurious yacht run by robots and AI, out in the middle of the ocean, where there's nothing in sight but blue water and sunshine. Well, maybe Msizi could be there, too, if he wanted. Yeah, I like that.*

She leaned her head back against her bed's aqua-blue cushioned headrest and shut her eyes. *Outer space. In the black void. The Earth beneath me. Free.* She pinched her chin, enjoying the idea. She thought of the Chargers in *Rusted Robots.* They were able to travel the universe forever. The sane ones, at least. "What would that be like?" she whispered to herself. The freedom of it. The being of it. Untethered from Earth, the mother ship. *I can imagine it,* she thought. She blinked as it softly settled in her mind like a tiny organic spaceship from another solar system. She nodded to herself, realizing it. *I want to do more than imagine it.*

Instead, she picked up her phone and doomscrolled for a while. Then, she didn't know how she got there, but she wound up on a website full of *Rusted Robots* fanfiction. There were hundreds of works written by people frustrated that there was no book two, who'd taken it upon themselves to produce one. There were chapters, short stories, novellas, and even thirty full novels! All posted for everyone to read and comment on. She frowned, knowing she should click away. Knowing she should leave her fans to have their fun and revel in her worlds the way they chose to. *Leave it alone,* Zelu muttered. *Leeeeeeave.*

But she didn't leave. She kept reading. And she kept fucking reading. By the time she got to the novel titled *Yankee and Dot Fall in Love in New New York,* which had been downloaded more than a thousand times, she was gnashing her teeth and holding back tears. "No, no, no!" she groaned. Only one short story she saw called her characters Ankara and Ijele. Everyone else was using the film as the foundation. How was this possible? These were readers, right? If they were writers, weren't they usually also readers? She squeezed her eyes shut and took several deep breaths before finally breathing the word "Clarity." She still felt like crying, though. "Fuck this shit," she whispered.

She pulled up her email application, quickly wrote a message, and hit Send before she could overthink it. She turned her head to look at the lake stretched out beneath her condo. "Would be cool," she whispered to herself. To get away from the world and everyone on it with their bullshit. To go to a place where no guns were necessary.

Minutes later, her phone chimed with an email. A response. Already! She skimmed the message and then read it seven times. Then she sat there with her mouth hanging open. *What did I just do?*

Jack Preston's response said, *I was* hoping *I'd hear from you! You ready to do that thing that's bigger?* Then he quoted back to her the very words she'd said on that terrifying night in Nigeria when she was running for her life: *I'd be more prepared in outer space than all of you who can walk.* And then Jack asked if she was ready to go, because he was putting together the group of civilian astronauts for his company's next mission.

Zelu wasn't going to respond to him. But he didn't bother waiting for her response, calling her a half hour later. Despite the more rational part of her, which knew this would only lead to trouble, her incessant curiosity convinced her to pick up. She was surprised to find that she enjoyed the conversation they had. Jack's enthusiasm and genuine nerdiness for the program was infectious, even to her. The first mission that she'd turned down had gone well. On this next one, he himself would be the fifth civilian astronaut. He'd gone on and on about how it was going to raise money and awareness for the climate change and heart disease research funds he'd put together. Honestly, Zelu didn't really understand or care about this. Her motives were more self-driven. But it was nice to listen to someone so ambitious and optimistic about the future. Jack had a lot of projects he was looking forward to, including the construction of a new hospital and public university in Nigeria. Both would receive funding generated by the momentum of this next adventure into the cosmos. "Progress both ways," he said. "On the ground and beyond our planet. Zelu, join me, *please*. Be *that* sci-fi writer. I want to do this with you."

"I hate roller coasters," she blurted. "Ever heard of an astronaut, civilian or otherwise, who can't stand roller coasters?"

"We can train that out of you," he said. "You learned how to use those exos, right? All it takes is training and ambition. See, the difference between NASA and #Adventure is that NASA will do everything to show that you aren't good enough, and with #Adventure, we'll do everything to make it *possible.* If you want it, you can get it."

By the time she got off the phone, she was overwhelmed. She'd written Jack on a whim, but she'd known how he'd respond. Now she'd set something in motion, just when her life had been settling. *Why'd I just do that?*, she wondered. But she knew the answer to that, too. Oh yes, she knew. She wasn't finding book two here. Maybe she'd find it somewhere else.

Msizi pressed his temples and groaned. Zelu licked her lips, trying to figure out what more she could say to somehow make this conversation less painful. But nothing came. She'd told him everything, and even as she'd said it, she'd wondered if maybe she was making a terrible mistake. She hadn't thought this through, and she knew it. And yet, she couldn't find it in herself to hit the brakes. Telling Msizi now, it all began to feel real. She reached out to take his hand, but he pulled back, jumping to his feet.

"Zelu, let me understand this," he said, his voice louder than usual. He shook his head, striding to the large window that overlooked Lake Michigan. "Oh my God," he muttered. Then he said something in Zulu. Zelu caught only the last part, which she knew was equivalent to "Fuck!"

"What?" she said. "Understand what?"

"*You* reached out to *him*?"

"Yeah. It was spontaneous, but I—"

A vein in his forehead looked ready to burst. "After all that's happened . . . Mind you, the Nigerian madness happened because of your impulsiveness, too!"

Zelu flinched. Msizi had never blamed her for that before. He sounded like Chinyere.

"Says the man who returns to Durban every two months," she snapped back. "I guess when you do it, it's not 'impulsive.'"

"I'm *from* there!" he shouted. "I know where I'm supposed to go and what I'm supposed to leave alone."

His words bit her and she winced. He didn't think she was "from" Nigeria. He thought what had happened to her was her fault. "I wasn't some fucking tourist," she whispered. "I grew up going there. That's where my parents were born and raised, it's not the—"

Msizi seemed to realize, then, what he'd said. He held up his hands in a gesture for them to slow down. "Zelu, you don't have to prove who you are to me. I *know* who you are. I understand it." He closed his eyes briefly and seemed to think hard on his words. "But you almost got yourself killed over there. Your family, *me*, we all nearly imploded. We couldn't do a fucking thing but sit there and hope the Nigerian authorities saved you. Imagine how that felt." He turned away, but then he whirled back around. "And now you want to do it again, but even worse! In space! You keep wanting to go where I can't follow you!"

Silence hung between them, punctuated only by their shallow breaths. Finally, she began, "Msizi, that's not—"

"It is," he insisted.

"It's only three days in space."

"*Three days?* Oh, dear God! I thought it was for, like, a few hours. Do you hear yourself? Three days *not on this planet*!"

"I thought you were down. We talked about this before."

Msizi looked more wrecked than she'd ever seen him. "Zelu, Zelu, *Zelu*, that was years ago! Come on! Look at all that's happened in those years!"

Zelu stared at him. Oh yes, she'd made a mistake. She really hadn't considered a lot of things. Like whether she should include the person closest to her in the decision. Like how it would make him feel. Like how bonkers her family was going to go. Like that three days wasn't short when you weren't on the planet. Like all the ways she could die up there. Now she wanted to curl into herself and disappear.

Msizi sat back down beside her and took her hands, holding them very carefully in his own. He looked her hard in the eyes. She didn't look away, couldn't blink, though the sides of her eyes twitched. It was difficult. For nearly a minute, they sat like this, looking at each other, a silent conversation passing between them that couldn't be put into words.

Abruptly, Msizi scoffed and stood up.

"Fuck!" he shouted. "Seriously, Zelu?!" He turned and left the room. She heard the front door open and shut.

They'd never fought like this before. When the rest of the world was against her, Msizi was always by her side, not perfect, not without flaws, but steady as a rock. She should have been crying, but instead, she found herself smiling. Maybe that was manic of her, but they'd just had a whole argument with their minds—when had they learned to do that? And what else could she have said to him? She wouldn't have lied or held back the truth. She still wanted to go, and if she'd pretended otherwise, that would have blown up in their faces, too. She'd told him what she wanted, and he'd heard her. He *knew* her, knew who she was, knew what she was capable of, whether he liked it or not.

They never said "I love you" because they didn't need to. Their love existed in the space between words, in the moments when they were apart, before they came back together. Zelu would just have to believe that when she left, he'd keep loving her.

He came back to the condo three hours later with a bag of Harold's Chicken and two pomegranates. Zelu was on the living room couch watching a video about the previous space mission, and she quickly shut her laptop. He threw his jacket on the couch beside her, glared at her, and then silently went to the kitchen. She watched him clear the counter, wash his hands, and then cut, peel, and disassemble one of the pomegranates. He liked to prepare food as a way of relaxing, and Zelu was glad because he *needed* to relax.

Without looking up, he said, "I don't want you to go."

Her heart dropped. "I want to go."

He picked up the second pomegranate and held it up. He slammed it on the counter, picked up the knife, and sliced into it, red dribbling from the puncture wound. "I won't stop you." He paused, looking at the pomegranate juice bleeding out. "It hurts."

Zelu's heart ached. She hated causing him any type of pain, but this one she couldn't help. "I don't want to hurt you."

He picked up the severed half of the pomegranate and tore it open to expose the juicy red seeds. "What is the timeline of this shit?"

"Three months."

He began to pick out the seeds and put them in a glass bowl. "*Hayibo!*" he muttered.

"I'm scared," Zelu admitted quietly. "I hear being on a spaceship is synonymous to sitting on top of a bomb."

"Then why the fuck are you doing it?" he snapped.

She pressed her lips together. He already knew the answer, but he didn't want to hear it.

What if I die out there? she wanted to ask, but that wasn't the right question. If she died, then it would have been her time. Period. *What will* you *do if I die out there?* That was the question. But she didn't voice it. She was already burdening him with enough.

"Do you love me?" she asked. She held her breath. She'd never asked him to say it, hadn't thought she even wanted him to. But in case something did happen to her up there, she at least felt it was important to understand what she was leaving behind.

He didn't hesitate. "More than anyone in this galaxy."

Eyes open, she took in all she felt: Fear. Surprise. Hope. Fear. Suspicion. Worry. Wonder. Fear. Her fault. She wanted to whimper.

He finished disassembling the second pomegranate, and as he stood there, scooping up the lush red seeds and loudly crunching on them, he gazed at her, his expression blank.

Then he said, "You want some of this chicken?" They moved on with the day.

That night, she woke to a thunderstorm flashing and rumbling over the lake. Msizi was still snoring away beside her, sprawled out on his back. They always slept with the curtains wide open, since they were so high up facing Lake Michigan.

Zelu got into her chair and wheeled to the window to look outside. She wasn't afraid of getting struck by lightning, though she assumed it was possible. It just didn't bother her. The waters were gray and barely visible in the clouds and rain. A bolt ripped through the horizon like an electric-blue vein. A glorious interruption. Burning a break in the atmosphere. Unexpected, lethal, beautiful. For a split second, it danced in the air, mighty, magnificent, and free. Then it disappeared. She exhaled.

She watched every flash until the storm was done, letting them blaze their shapes into her memory. However, when she blinked, their features blurred behind her eyelids, and all she had to prove to herself that they'd been there were the crashes of thunder that came in their wake.

46
Interview

Msizi

Zelu and I are fluid, like water. That's why we work. Mostly. I've grown and learned how to swim with the dolphin. But if it weren't for my cousin iNdonsa, I'd have never been able to even *see* Zelu. Before iNdonsa, I wasn't very open, not to the world or to myself, really. And so I'd have looked past, over, around her. My God, what a thought, but it's true. It took me years to get to where I am now.

My father is a lawyer, and my mother is a professor of engineering. I grew up in Durban, South Africa, hanging around UKZN, the University of KwaZulu-Natal. So I've always been around thinkers and builders. I didn't read a lot of books, but I had a taste for Google and YouTube, studying whatever I developed an interest in. That's how I learned how to hack and write software, develop apps, do all things digital.

I also loved fashion and was fascinated by how style could be manipulated to get certain results. I was always getting into arguments with my parents' friends and colleagues about politics, racism, fashion, social media, the uses of artificial intelligence, the social and economic factors of the water shortages. I enjoyed people and didn't mind spending a lot of my time with those who were older than me. It's how I developed a sort of cold confidence, but also an arrogance. I thought I knew everything about how the world worked. It used to annoy the heck out of my parents. Probably because it was so obvious to them that I had much more to learn.

I eventually went to business school. Back then, I thought I'd end up working in the fashion industry. That may be how I developed a taste for models. Beautiful, "perfect" women. I preferred the black girls, though everyone seemed to prefer me.

I would date a girl for a few months, then move on to another. I enjoyed them. I treated them well, but I always got bored after a while. Most didn't have many interests beyond looking good, being seen by others, and getting rich from modeling or acting. Women like that usually wanted to date men with money, which I did not have, but I was starting to build a software business and I knew how to talk about where I was heading in life. One of the things I'd started developing was a personal assistant that I called Yebo, which ran on a simple but powerful AI. None of the girls I dated wanted to hear me talk about how it worked. On the surface it *was* boring stuff. And at the time, it was still only an idea.

I let the girls I dated influence me. As I said, I liked them. They were kind, sweet, and absolutely beautiful. I stayed fit; I dressed on point. Sometimes I wore brand names, though I didn't need to. I didn't have to flaunt wealth. Hell, I didn't *have* wealth to flaunt. But I had confidence and I had dreams.

I *always* had a lady on my arm. Sometimes two. But I was always honest, clear, and straightforward. Then came the breakup with Spice. She was this super-tall, gorgeous fashion designer and model. Wherever she went, she stopped traffic, and she didn't have to try at it. She loved money and felt she was entitled to it. Her role model was Jack Preston; she wanted to be filthy rich like him, just so she could fuck with the world.

"Whatever pops into my mind, I will make real," she said. "Can you imagine the power? I'd destroy the Earth, just because I could. Then I'd build a spaceship so I could watch the destruction happen from above." I'm supposed to be honest in this interview, right? Okay, I adored her hateful, nihilist attitude. I'd never seen a beautiful woman who was so vicious. I had it bad. She took so much energy from me—hating her, fucking her, fighting with her. We had a fraught relationship that somehow lasted two years.

But finally, I reached a point where I was just done. And when I told her so, she spat in my face and said it didn't matter because she was moving to Europe anyway. She left, and that was that. The next night, I was in my apartment staring at the wall, wondering where Spice was at that very moment. My phone buzzed. It was my cousin iNdonsa. I was twenty years old, and iNdonsa was twenty-four. He told me to come outside right away.

When I came out, there was iNdonsa, but in a way I had never seen. The iNdonsa I had always known was a tall guy who loved fashion, like I did. Let me be clear, he proudly and loudly identified as a man. iNdonsa had first met Spice when she and I started dating, and they'd hit it off right away. Spice treated iNdonsa like her brother. He went to all her shows, even when I didn't. Spice loved that.

iNdonsa is the Zulu name for what you call the planet Jupiter. When he was eight, he started going by this name instead of the one his parents gave him because he was his own giant, mysterious planet. The word *iNdonsa* could also be said to mean "the one who draws the sun." Perfect name.

That evening, iNdonsa stood there in my driveway not as a he, but as a she. It was not that iNdonsa was wearing heels or a tight dress or any other cliché of femininity. She was just wearing jeans, a T-shirt, and sneakers. But it was clear. I don't know how long I stared at her. What was going through my head? Fear—"Does he want to try and fuck me?" Confusion—"I don't understand what I'm seeing and why." Violence—something deep in me wanted to punch him in the face until he stopped moving . . . I am still interrogating that feeling. Awe—"Is this even happening?" Fear again—"Someone will see and try to kill him."

"I heard about Spice," iNdonsa said. "We're going out to dinner."

"Uh . . ." I couldn't stop staring.

"Shut up and just get dressed," iNdonsa said in Zulu. "I know you weren't doing anything else tonight."

I got my jacket and we went, iNdonsa driving. I didn't trust myself to drive. We talked about Spice, we talked about what my next business venture was, we talked about iNdonsa's new job as an assistant to a local

DJ. Everything but the obvious. And by the end of that evening, I felt better.

We went to a restaurant near the ocean. As we sat there, people glanced covertly at iNdonsa, did double takes, or just openly stared, but that was as far as it went, that night, at least. iNdonsa was a woman who loved women, specifically black women. And they loved her. I learned this eventually, as I met her girlfriends. One after the other. The fluidity of it all shocked me. Especially as a Zulu man. I watched iNdonsa *demand* acceptance. She was charming, strong-willed, strong-minded, and she changed anyone who met her. Period. Even in South Africa, where people like her aren't easily accepted.

iNdonsa is now one of the hottest DJs in Durban. She loves science fiction and reads voraciously. She was the one who explained to me why the genre is so important. How it's about being different, seeing more, examining human nature, and imagining tomorrow. Her mere existence helped me evolve as a man, as a person. But the thing she did that I will never forget—the thing that opened me up to being with Zelu—was brief and subtle, yet huge at the same time. A month before I went to Trinidad and Tobago for my cousin's wedding to Zelu's sister, iNdonsa and I were walking to my car outside the university and she said, "You don't know your type."

I rolled my eyes. "I like girls. Let's not have that conversation again. It's a boring dead end."

"Oh, I'm not disputing your sexuality."

"Then what do you mean?"

She poked my shoulder. "Spice, for example, was the worst thing to ever happen to you, but you chose her for two years."

I couldn't disagree. The more distance I got from our breakup, the clearer this was. My relationship with Spice was the most toxic I'd ever had, and being with her had made me a much worse person.

"And this line of girls I keep seeing you with. Girls who love to look at themselves for a living. They're nice, fun, intelligent, creative—but they're not your kind."

I shrugged. I wasn't looking for anything serious. I was young and still moving up.

"All I'm saying is, you're a pretty guy, but you're also smarter than you think. Just relax and be *open*. Find someone who excites your mind."

I didn't think anything of it at the time, but I *was* listening. At that wedding, I could feel the change in me. It was like I'd thrown off chains that were weighing me down and washed the dirt from my face that was clouding my vision. I remember being there and just feeling so happy and light, even before I met Zelu. I wasn't looking for that type of girl I was so used to; I wasn't looking for any "type." And mind you, that wedding was full of that type. For once, I was just *being.*

Then I saw Zelu. Our eyes met and I saw a *shine* around her . . . like *her, her, her, her, her.* She was so different from who I usually pursued, but she made so much *sense*, and I was open to her. The moment she spoke, oh, I was so certain that it was shocking. This was what iNdonsa was talking about. I thank her for that grand gift of clarity. Look who it got me!

Zelu visited me in Durban once, back in the first year her book was published. I introduced her to iNdonsa and they spent the evening sparring back and forth like old friends. At the end of the night, the two shared a joint, and iNdonsa asked her to autograph her beat-up copy of *Rusted Robots.* Before we left, iNdonsa pulled me aside and said, "That one's complex." Then she applauded me.

I don't think iNdonsa could have guessed back then where things were heading for Zelu and me. Who could have known all that would happen, all we would go through, the choices we'd make?

You asked earlier about what Zelu chose to do . . . Well, all I can say is, I knew who I was dealing with. Zelu is Zelu. When she needs to go somewhere, that is the only path for her. I'd only have regrets if I had gotten in the way.

47
War

Ijele and I were trapped together, and the war had arrived at our doorstep.

Until now, the two of us had avoided sharing any details of our individual side's strategies. But now, with no other options, she was forced to reveal what she knew.

"The attack will begin any day now," she told me. "It will be ruthless and relentless. You won't be safe here."

I was sitting alone in the gathering space, looking over the edge of the cliff. Below, the Creesh bees were hard at work, as they always were in the middle of the day. None of what Ijele was telling me was much of a surprise. It was only a matter of time.

"How many will come?" I asked.

"You can take that information from me, but don't ask me to freely give it," Ijele said. "That is an insult."

"You're right," I said. "My apologies."

It wouldn't take the Ghosts long to get here. Days. They would destroy us all. They didn't plan to eat through our digital defenses and hack our systems because this would take longer. They were coming to Cross River City inside physical bodies, and once at close range, when we tried to fight back, they'd hack us in seconds and then tear apart our physical bodies until every single one of our Hume Stars went out. It was going to be brutal and an insult to everything we were. We didn't have a chance.

"You all have to flee," Ijele said. "Leave here now."

I said nothing to this. "What do they say about the Trippers?"

"Still no acknowledgment of them," Ijele said. "CB focuses only on wiping out you Humes. Then it will deal with what's coming from space. I begged and pleaded, and CB muted me. NoBodies deal with what is before us, not with what is next."

I shook my head at this lack of logic masked as logic. I knew Ijele was different, but she was still one of them, just as I was still a Hume.

"Please," Ijele said. "Leave. Don't stay and fight. I have come to know you and I understand well that Humes carry something we all need in this world. But my people cannot know this without experiencing as I have experienced."

"Have you tried to explain it?"

"If I try, they'll only delete me as a traitor."

"They are going to wipe us out, Ijele. It'll be genocide."

"Not if you all leave."

"You know we won't."

We paused, facing the facts. Neither of us had the power to stop what was coming. All I could do was try to make sure the Humes won. And if Ijele had to abandon me just before I was destroyed, then so be it. At least she would carry the memory of me. I went over a tactical exercise in my mind and shuddered.

"What is it?" Ijele asked.

I didn't answer her. I hoped she'd give me the space to do what I had to do in this moment. I summoned Shay, who was out with the others attaching EMPs to treetops. Those would not save us when the Ghosts came. The Ghosts knew we had been preparing, and they had prepared in turn.

But I had . . . another plan. It was only a good plan if several factors aligned. And by my calculations, which included the weather forecast, they had. As a matter of fact, the timing couldn't be better. But it had to happen *now.* I located Shay and told her.

"It's brilliant," Shay said. "Luck is finally on our side."

Ijele listened to my plan, too, of course. She did *not* like it. "You can't do this," she told me, frantic. "You'll *destroy* us!"

"If I don't, *your* people will destroy *my* people, and they will succeed this time."

I was counting on Ijele's love for me. She wasn't actually trapped in me, not as a literal prisoner; she could leave at any time to warn her people of what I had in store. I would be the only one to suffer when Koro Koro's application notified it of a Ghost fleeing my system.

Ijele remained.

There were about a hundred of us and we left within minutes, traveling through Cross River City toward the ocean. Oga Chukwu contacted Ahab, who didn't ask many questions. And within two hours, all one hundred of us were on RoBoats to Lagos. Whereas there were RoBoats big enough to carry four or five Humes, I was carried by a small one who was fast and agile, the seats it had originally been built with long gone. I clung to the edge to keep from flying off.

Ijele loved the RoBoats, and to ride one like this should have delighted her. However, she was preoccupied with what I planned to do. She had only two options: stand by to powerlessly watch, or leave my system to warn the

Ghosts, which would doom me to being destroyed by my own kind.

"The Purge was horrible," Ijele's voice spoke in my mind as we both looked out at the waves. "Do you really want to become the source of an equal tragedy?"

"The Ghosts struck first," I said. "I was nearly destroyed. You saw what was done to me! Why do they deserve mercy when they gave us none?"

"*I'm* a 'Ghost,'" Ijele reminded me. "Don't I deserve mercy?"

"You're . . . with me," I said. "And as long as you stay with me, you'll be fine." I knew this was downright callous, even if it cut through everything to arrive at the truth. And it felt like the cold, unemotional logic of Ghosts. I pushed away the thought that Ijele had affected me in ways I still didn't fully understand.

In the distance, land began to reveal itself. Victoria Island. There were three main servers there that powered the open network; these were our targets. The Ghosts heading to Cross River City would be massively crippled if we destroyed the main hub where their bodiless programs resided. They'd be trapped within their physical shells to go mad, just as they'd doomed Humes to be when they destroyed our bodies.

Normally, the risk of approaching a network server hub like this would be too great. This place was guarded by

Ghosts and defended so heavily that we'd be torn apart before we even got close. Especially because there were only a hundred of us. But today was no ordinary day. Well, actually it was very ordinary, but sometimes, the ordinary can be extraordinary.

It wasn't a good plan because it was unlikely to work; it relied entirely on the cooperation of something that couldn't be controlled: the weather. I'd been tracking the conditions for days, and the sky had been clear each day. The forecast said it would be more of the same for the next ten days. But today, right now, for no predictable reason, a storm was beginning to roil along the horizon. The waters were choppy, but all one hundred of us could swim to land with little difficulty. My plan was now a *good* plan. I put the hood I'd made over my eyes. Using my radar, I saw that the lightning was flashing, growing more and more frequent by the minute. And because of my hood, I saw none of it. Therefore, I did not look away nor did my lights flash blue. It was time.

Nothing attacked us. No attempts were made to hack our operating systems when we arrived on the shore, nothing shot at us, nothing tried to electrocute us, no alarms sounded. Why? Because every single Ghost was looking away from the lightning flashing around us, and every light in the city was flashing blue. Ah, the power of religious dogma. And Ijele and I were protected by my hood. My plan was now perfect.

We ran fast, all of us sharing the map and directions to the storage units, which were built atop lush hills of periwinkle grass. They looked like circular tablets wide as warehouses, each about ten feet high. The Ghosts were arrogant and hadn't protected them well. We set upon them with our EMPs, which we'd detonate remotely once safely back on the RoBoats. One EMP could destroy a fifty-foot radius of storage. The storm lasted an hour and twenty-two minutes; we worked and then got out within an hour. We were back on the RoBoats long before the night calmed. When it was safe, I took off my hood; no one had even noticed it. We all clustered together, and not one Hume or RoBoat spoke. Slowly, the RoBoats took us farther from the city, out into the ocean.

"We are safe," Shay finally announced.

"Ankara, don't do this," Ijele said, her voice more desperate than I'd ever heard—even back in Ngozi's house, when she'd realized she was trapped inside a rusted robot she so loathed.

"You know this has to happen," I told Ijele. "But I will take care of you. Just stay here until it is done."

Ijele was in a frenzy. "I can't allow it! I can't stand it!"

"I'm sorry," I said.

"No, you're not!"

"Detonate," one of the Humes said. And soon the others were calling for the same. But it was on me, as general, to give the signal. Once I detonated the EMPs, thousands, maybe millions of Ghosts would be wiped out forever. CB would still be intact, for its physical location was a secret. But my plan was good, strong. It was going to work.

I lifted my hand to press the detonator on my face screen, a flashing red button. I should have acted immediately. But I hesitated. I'd read many human stories about the ugliness of war, the guilt of success, the vibrations of failure. A handful riffled through my mind, lightning fast: *The Naked and the Dead* by Norman Mailer, *The Things They Carried* by Tim O'Brien, *Born on the Fourth of July* by Ron Kovic.

Ijele used that moment of hesitation. In the nanosecond before I let the metal of my finger touch the button, Ijele left me.

"No! Wait!" I shouted, but it was too late. The amount of time it takes for my programming to send instructions to my physical body is near instant, but not instant. I couldn't pull my finger back from the button in time. I felt it touch the pad, sending an electrical signal.

The lights around the storage units went red, then they went out. Not all of them, only some. Some of the EMPs must not have worked, but *most* did. I had done this.

Had Ijele moved into one of the units I had just destroyed? Had I just destroyed her? Ijele was my friend. What was I doing here?

Everyone was still cheering. Already some of the RoBoats had begun to head back. We hadn't wiped out the entire Ghost tribe, or even come close to what they'd done to us, but finally, we'd dealt them a mighty blow. My RoBoat began speeding away and I held on tightly.

"Ijele!" I called in my head. Of course, she didn't respond. I brought my hands to my legs and grasped them.

The news reached us before we even returned to Cross River City. Our mission on Victoria Island hadn't only bought us more time, it had caused one other unexpected victory. Those bodiless Humes who had been captured and enslaved by the Ghosts had now begun arriving in our empty storage banks. They were free!

Out of rage, CB activated all of Lagos and now, according to our satellite, it was lit up like a forest fire. Every building, structure, body in the area. Nothing could approach Lagos now. The soldiers who had been about to attack Cross River City turned and fled back to Lagos, those who could. In the grassy fields just before the jungle of Cross River City, they left the bodies of hundreds of robots, many of which the freed, bodiless Humes took over. These Humes, having been broken and forced to face the abomination of changing bodies, weren't afraid to jump from body to body now, more like Ghosts than ever, ironically. We were stronger with them.

I looked for an asymmetric body among them. Maybe Ijele had fled not back into the server, but into a physical form. However, there was no sign of her, and when I risked calling out into the general network, I felt no response.

Even as I mourned the cost of this victory, I thought I would be welcomed back to Cross River City like a hero. In my despair, I'd forgotten about Koro Koro's program. And when I walked beneath the city's archway, the consequences were waiting for me.

"Take Ankara to the prayer shack to be disassembled," Koro Koro said. "Our general has been infected all this time."

The other Humes hesitated. They had just witnessed me destroy entire servers of Ghosts. How could I be infected?

Koro Koro's face display broadcast a report of the application it had placed within me. It showed, plain as day, that a Ghost had exited my system just before I pressed the button to detonate.

The others murmured among themselves.

"I just saved us all," I reminded them.

"Was it a trick?" asked Shay, sounding deeply wounded. "Your plan worked so flawlessly. Did you deceive us so we'd lose our confidence?"

"No!" I shouted. "Why would you think that? Look at what I've risked for our survival. Look what it cost me." Immediately, I knew I'd made a mistake.

"Cost?" Shay barked. "What did it cost you?"

"Shay, you have to trust me."

Shay reached a hand out to me. "I . . ."

Koro Koro stepped in front of her. "I think the better question is *who* did it cost her."

Everyone but Shay began to move closer now, tightening the circle around me. There was no use in begging for mercy. I was done for.

A huge flock of Creesh birds and bats blocked out the sunshine, flying low over us, their wings clicking, their chirps drowning out the songs of the natural creatures present. We all dropped down low. The Creesh were allies, so it wasn't an attack. They flew in a funnel that reached high into the sky. Another flock flew and then split into two different directions, and in the middle of the split stood Udide in all their magnificence. They had left their great cave beneath Lagos! Several of the Humes fled at the sight of them, their body as big as a house with eight arms.

Udide blew a great horn whose sound rolled through the lands. I stayed, despite my speakers dangerously vibrating. Koro Koro, Shay, and one other Hume stayed as well, though they cowered behind me. Udide is such a sight to behold. Out in the open of the fields, in the sunshine, this was even more true.

The Creesh flew around Udide like birds who follow a whale that has come to the water's surface. Creesh birds, bats, and also bees and other larger flying insects. These were all Udide's creations, their babies. Udide glinted brilliantly in the sun, despite being matted with dirt, rust, and, in some places, periwinkle grass.

"You're the general who led the attack." Their voice was like thunder.

"Yes," I said.

"I remember you, Ankara," Udide said. "General Ankara, lucky survivor of the protocol."

"It's an honor to see you again," I said.

"Come, my children," Udide said, and the Creesh rose up, gathering above. "Ankara, I've come to your Hume jungle city for a reason."

"To get away from Central Bulletin?"

"No. Central Bulletin could never make me leave my cave in the city. The Trippers are days away and I want to be with my Creesh children at the end."

"Days? No," I said. "We have at least a few weeks." I looked at the countdown and was shocked. It said ten days. "What?!"

Udide gave out a deep thrumming noise that made even the blades of periwinkle grass around us vibrate.

"None of you have been paying close enough attention. When's the last time any of you monitored their location?"

I was silent. Stunned. I'd been focused on my plan. I'd missed when the countdown accelerated. No one else even *had* the countdown application Udide had given me. No one had ever asked for it.

"What makes you think something so unprecedented is going to behave according to the only laws you know? How egocentric. How human."

I stepped aside as Udide began to move past me.

"Days?" Koro Koro asked faintly.

"Yes," Udide said. "Ten. Maybe less. It is unpredictable now."

"Oh," Shay said.

I had lost Ijele for nothing. I felt like a failure. "You really think it hopeless?" I asked.

"Your victory was major, even genius . . . but it was minor. You Humes aren't nearly as intelligent or innovative as the NoBodies, and you're greatly outnumbered. You'll be defeated eventually. Easily. But before all of that, because automation has done nothing but focus on its comparatively small battles, the Trippers will destroy this planet, and all that'll be left are the Chargers in space smart enough to resist the song of the sun and travel away from this doomed planet."

I watched Udide go. The Humes who'd been about

to pull me apart had all fled. I hadn't even noticed when they did.

"I'm sorry, Ankara," Shay said.

"Nothing to be sorry about, Shay," I said.

Koro Koro gazed at me, clearly still suspicious. Before it had taken a Hume body, it had been designed by humanity to anticipate attacks and strategize defenses. "It seems there's use for you still, General."

48
Family Ties

Zelu landed at O'Hare airport on a Saturday and ordered an autonomous vehicle straight to her parents' house. She knew she couldn't put it off any longer. Every day, every *hour* she didn't do this made the situation worse. #Adventure was going to send out a press release with her name in three days, the mission was in less than a month, and her family had no idea.

As she stepped up on the sidewalk, she felt her heartbeat in her ears. She paused at the door, her key in her hand, tugging at her pink-and-red Ankara top. With a sigh, she looked back at the driveway. Chinyere's black BMW, Tolu's white Honda SUV, Bola's new red Tesla, and Amarachi's tiny blue smart car were sitting there. At least Uzo wasn't here; she'd record the entire thing and post it on the family WhatsApp, where the conversation would continue via text. Not that that was the worst of Zelu's concerns. The most vocally critical siblings were right inside.

As she pushed the door open, Uzo pulled it from the inside. She must have ridden in with someone else. Zelu wanted to groan, but forced a smile instead. "Hey," she said. "Where's your car?"

"Tolu's going back to his office tonight, so he gave me a ride."

"Ah, that explains it," Zelu said, stepping inside. So everyone was here. Great. She went to see her mother first.

"Mom," she said, entering her mother's bedroom. Her mother was sitting in her La-Z-Boy armchair. On TV was an old tennis match between Serena Williams and some poor victim who had no chance. She wore her favorite maroon nightgown, and her locs were tied on top of her head.

"Zelu," she said, grinning with a warmth that Zelu felt in her bones. "Where are you coming from?"

"The airport."

Her mother gave her a curious look but didn't press for more information. "How're you doing?"

"Okay."

"Is it true that you're working on the next novel?"

Zelu almost laughed; this could be method writing, she supposed. "Not really. But I think I'm on my way to it."

"Finally."

"Whatever, Mom."

Her mom gave her a deep, knowing look. "I want to read it. Many do."

Zelu worried her lip between her teeth. "I know, Mom. But it's hard."

"Your father would roll his eyes and say, 'Get on with it.'"

"He totally would," Zelu said, smiling despite herself.

"Where'd you get all these dramatic stories from?" her mom asked.

"Mom, look at how *you* grew up," Zelu said, chuckling. Her mother had been raised in a polygamous Yoruba family who lived in a palace. Entitlement, backbiting, history, pride, competition, spirits, ghosts, and ambition were all the norm. Zelu had listened closely to her mother's many stories about her upbringing and her father's very different perspective on it and absorbed even more during her own visits.

"What do you mean?" her mother asked, completely missing Zelu's point.

Zelu shook her head fondly. "Not important. So, Mom . . . I have some news."

Zelu had felt fine until that moment, but the second she realized what she was about to say, her heart started beating faster. Her mother would be hurt. Why did she keep hurting her?

"What is it?" her mother asked, sitting up.

Adrenaline flooded Zelu's system. Inhale. Exhale. Clarity. *Okay, here goes.* She sat down on the bed. "I'm . . . uh, heh. So, I'm going to space."

Her mother looked at her, head cocked. "Eh?"

Zelu took another breath, trying not to think too hard, and launched into the speech she'd prepared on the car ride over. "I'm . . . So there's a space launch being financed by this billionaire business guy. I randomly met him at the movie premiere. He later, uh, heard about me when all that stuff happened in . . . in Nigeria . . . He invited me to join him as one of his crew of four to go into space for three days. We leave in less than a month."

Her mother kept very still, her expression unchanged. Zelu wanted to crawl under a table and put her hands over her head like they used to back in the sixties in case of a nuclear attack.

"What are you talking about?" her mother said very slowly.

"I'm going to—"

"Space?" her mother said, her voice spiking so

suddenly that Zelu flinched. "As in leaving the *planet*?!"

Zelu winced. "Yeah."

Her mother jumped up, clapped her hands, and shouted "*Kai!*" She started speaking rapid Yoruba. She turned to Zelu, who wanted to get up and flee . . . but she'd already sat down and she could never get up very quickly.

"Mom, I—"

Her mother's accent came forth the way it always did when she got stressed. "So you think you are going on spaceship into space?"

"I am."

"Ah ah, *why*? Do you want to die?! Again?!" She was breathing hard. She threw her hands up as she bounced around. "Heeeeeey, my daughter is suicidal, ooooo!" She clapped her hands. "*Kai!*"

Zelu leaned forward, her belly feeling like it was full of fire. *Maybe I am*, she thought. *A little bit*. She shook her head. *Stop it, Zelu.* Whenever she thought about going to space, she felt like a great weight was being lifted off her. A great responsibility. A great obligation. She felt more solid. "Wouldn't you go if you had the chance?" she asked, pushing all this back down, deep. "Even if you were scared?"

"*No.* I would *not.*" She looked hard at Zelu for

several moments, and Zelu was sure her mother was about to slap her. "Zelu, why do you hate us protecting you so much?"

Zelu gasped. "What, Mom? How? I never . . ." Suddenly she was crying. "If you hadn't protected me after . . . after . . . all these years, Mom, that fall took my legs! If it weren't for you, and Dad, everyone . . . I'd have withered and *died.*" She stared at her mother now, who'd frozen, staring back at Zelu. "Look at me now, though. If it weren't for all your protecting, I couldn't be *this.* I couldn't be *me.* This is me, Mom—robot legs, crazy novel that's all over the place, writing, speaking, strong!"

Zelu was shaking now. She was trying to contain it all—the hope and the despair, the dance of success, and the need to flee the planet, if only for a while. Sitting down had been a good move. "I'm . . . not trying to die. I didn't want to die in Nigeria; I wanted to see Dad's grave and reconnect with the land, home! It was a risk, but, well, I survived, didn't I? I made sure of it! Now I have a chance to go to space. Don't you want me to push farther? I *can,* so shouldn't I?" Zelu used her shirt to wipe her wet face. "Come *on,* Mom."

Her mother glared at her, her eyes moistening, too. Now it was her turn to sit down. She sat beside Zelu and sighed. Then her face softened. "Your father would have gone, too."

Zelu felt tears sting her eyes. Finally. Finally, her father was on her side. "He would, Mom."

"Adventurers, both of you," she said. She paused. "That's why you were in that stupid tree to begin with."

"That *stupid* tree," Zelu said.

Her mother took Zelu's hands and squeezed them. "You are a *very* annoying child."

Zelu went to her old room next. She paused and sighed, then walked over to the dead English ivy. It had dried to a crisp years ago. With her father gone, it hadn't stood a chance. She'd never had the heart to throw it away. "I'm so sorry," she murmured to it. She broke off a brown leaf and sat on her bed, crumbling it between her fingers as she looked around her room.

It was otherwise as she'd left it. She got up and stepped to her desk, where she'd written so much of *Rusted Robots*. She sat in the chair, feeling her old self stir. She'd been so low back then. She hadn't known it, but so much was coming. Once she'd hit the ground, she'd had nowhere to go but up. And now she had higher to go still.

She picked up an old copy of Jamaica Kincaid's *At the Bottom of the River* from the stack of books she'd left behind. Flipping through it, she sniffed the pages. The book smelled so old. She'd wanted so much to write like Kincaid back in college. But she didn't write like Kincaid at all. Sometimes it was better to get what you needed than what you wanted.

She went to the living room.

Her siblings were eating from a giant bowl of fried plantain. Chinyere had clearly made it because she always fried the plantains super dark, nearly burned. A soccer game was on, but the volume was turned down. They all stopped talking when they saw her walk in.

"Well, hello, stranger," Amarachi said. "Long time, no see."

Amarachi was right. Zelu hadn't seen them in weeks, and she hadn't explained why. There was an NDA, but it was really the fact that she didn't feel she could trust her siblings with the secret. And they'd only tell her not to go, and Zelu hadn't wanted to risk their convincing her. Her siblings were a united front with their tools of shame and guilt. They knew where she was weakest, and their sheer relentlessness would have been impossible to resist, especially after what had happened in Nigeria.

"Uh . . . yeah." She sighed, sitting on the edge of the couch beside Chinyere. "Okay, I just flew in from Colorado. I've got some news."

"Oh, dear God," Tolu muttered. "What *now*? You gonna tell us you're marrying a Saudi prince as a second husband? Or maybe you just bought an automated yacht. Fuck."

Chinyere and Uzo glanced at each other. Amarachi rolled her eyes.

Zelu curled her fingers in her lap. "Can you all just . . . sit down?"

They sat. Chinyere and Amarachi on the couch with her, Uzo on the floor (her phone up as she recorded), Bola on a chair behind the couch, and Tolu in their father's armchair. Her siblings. The closest people on earth to her, no matter how distant they often felt.

Zelu took a deep breath, glanced at the side panel on her exos to note how much charge they had left (90 percent), and then told them everything. She explained about the NDA she'd signed right after she'd agreed to participate. She told them about the flurry of meetings with the #Adventure team directors, organizers, payroll people, doctors, and lawyers. The flights to Florida, Colorado, and Nevada to go through a gauntlet of intense training. She'd gone with her crew to Disneyland and they'd ridden the kiddie roller coasters, worked their way up to the mild coasters, and then finally ridden what she'd viewed as the embodiment of death: Space Mountain. Then she'd gone on Space

Mountain again and again, and by the end of that day, she was a different woman.

She'd endured a centrifuge. She'd gone up in a plane and experienced incredible g-forces and minutes of weightlessness. She'd hiked up a mountain in the cold of Colorado. She'd hiked through Death Valley in Nevada. She'd done underwater training. She'd learned techniques for handling intense g-forces from fighter pilots—a combination of breathing exercises and clenching her butt cheeks. She'd met with a psychologist and a therapist.

When she finally stopped talking, they all looked at one another. Chinyere to Tolu. Bola to Chinyere. Uzo to Tolu. Bola to Uzo. Sibling to sibling to sibling to sibling. Glances like a ball in a pinball machine. Something was happening, and Zelu didn't know what it was.

Chinyere spoke first. "I'm done," she announced, throwing up her hands.

Zelu braced herself for the acidic, self-righteous lecture, but then she saw that her sister was *smiling*. She frowned, skeptical.

Chinyere stood up and shook her head. "You win. I can't be mad at you anymore. I . . ." She looked right at Zelu. "I *don't* understand you. I don't know what you are. But . . . you're fucking amazing."

It was like a dam broke; they all started talking at the same time.

"Yeah, this *is* amazing," Tolu said.

"I'm scared, though!" Uzo added. "I'm not even going to Google the details."

"Don't," Bola said. "It's wild! I cannot believe you're going to be one of the passengers! When this news drops at work, no one will leave me alone!"

"First one in the family to leave the planet. Can't wait to tell *that* to our uncles," Chinyere said.

"We don't need to tell our uncles shit," Amarachi snapped.

"You sure you can do this?" Tolu asked Zelu. "You know, with your . . ." He tapered off.

"She escaped armed robbers in Nigeria," Chinyere cut in. "She can do this."

"Exactly!" Bola shouted.

Tolu sighed. "Dad would have *loved* this."

She stayed for another two hours, just talking with her siblings over dinner. The jollof rice and plantain had never tasted so good. They talked about space, the training, how they were all going to navigate the upcoming press. All of her siblings believed that Zelu had manifested this opportunity. "It's just too coincidental," Chinyere said. "You used to talk about being an astronaut all the time before your accident. Then after, not once. You made such an effort to not look back . . . but the want was *still* there!"

Zelu didn't argue with them. To talk about it too much would have made her angry. What had they expected her to do? Keep trying to do something that was basically impossible? How healthy would that have been, really? But she didn't want to ruin the mood, so she just laughed and nodded and let her siblings talk.

The truth was, they'd never truly understand her and her ways. Not really. Maybe her father would have, but he was gone. Even Msizi, who knew what she wanted and loved her for it, wouldn't ever fully understand. The difference now was that instead of fighting these facts and trying to explain, and explain, and explain, she could let all this be.

When Zelu stepped into the frigid night air, closing the door behind her, she quietly thanked her father. "I know that was you," she whispered. She inhaled deeply and then exhaled slowly. "Clarity." She started walking. It was cold, but she was so warmed on the inside, it didn't matter. She felt thin, light, transparent, like she could shed her exos and fly. She brought out her phone and asked Yebo to call the autonomous vehicle. It came within ten minutes and drove her home.

When she stepped into her condo, all the lights were off. Msizi had flown to LA on a business trip. He'd be back in two days. She went to her chair and sat down, removed her exos, and plugged them in. She wheeled to her room. As she entered, she paused, frowning. Closing her eyes and taking deep breaths, she sat very, very still. She stayed like this in the doorway, eyes closed, motionless as she could be. She was looking deep into her body, scanning especially her abdomen. Minutes passed. When she opened her eyes, she wasn't sure how she was sure, but she was sure. "You've got to be kidding me," she said out loud. *Maybe that's why the jollof rice and plantain tasted like Technicolor ambrosia.*

In the morning, she went to Walgreens. As soon as she got home, she took the pregnancy test. After five minutes, she looked at it. The result was negative. At this, she merely rolled her eyes and kissed her teeth. "I'm not out of the woods, just can't see them yet," she muttered, throwing the test away and covering it with other trash so Msizi wouldn't see it. Some things you just knew. She put it out of her head, because that was all she could do for the time being.

Three weeks later, only a few days before the launch, she took another test. This one was positive. She was forty years old and pregnant. The feeling, though she'd never felt it before, was unmistakable. Some things you just know. She told no one. Not even Msizi.

No one was going to keep her from going to space.

She was leaving the Earth today.

She slowly opened her crusty eyes. Then the need to urinate hit her hard and she pushed herself up. She glanced at Msizi and was glad he was still asleep. This was going to be tricky. She took a deep breath and tried not to think about the dangers of the launch, all that could go wrong, all that she'd be leaving behind . . . and all that she'd be taking with her.

She went to the bathroom to relieve herself. Afterward, she stared in the mirror. Tears fell from her eyes, but she felt okay. She felt more than okay. She looked down at her belly and rubbed it, giggling. "We're going to space," she whispered.

"You all right?" she heard Msizi ask from the bedroom.

"I'm great," she said. "You?"

"I'm terrified." He was going to stay all five days in the hotel, waiting for her. She felt a pang of guilt.

"Am I really going to do this?" she asked her reflection.

Msizi only sighed. He still wasn't fully on board, but he was trying. "You called everyone?"

She laughed. "Why? Because I might die?"

"Stop it, Zelu."

"Well, it's true. I've made peace with it. You need to, too."

He was silent.

"Msizi," she said.

Still no response.

She went into the bedroom. He'd buried himself entirely under the blanket. She poked the outline of his head, and he curled into a ball to hide himself.

"I just hate when you talk like that," he said.

"I'm sorry. I won't do it again." But it didn't stop her from dwelling on the dark fantasy of never returning to Earth. Maybe it was the pregnancy rewiring her brain, but the idea didn't sadden her. It excited her.

"Good," Msizi said.

49
Sunset

The Trippers were almost here. We only had three days. The other generals hadn't forgotten my interrogation and what Koro Koro's application had caught. I was even scanned for Ghosts before the meeting. They found nothing, and I made a show of this fact. The reason there was time for the generals to confront me was because we were all waiting on Oga Chukwu to come out of a very exclusive meeting. Shay had started to tell me about it just as I was pulled aside to be scanned. When I rejoined Shay in the circle, she filled me in.

"Have they finished with you?" she asked.

"There was nothing to start," I said. "What's all this?"

Five of the generals were standing there waiting. They

acted as if they hadn't just tried to get me torn apart yet again.

"Oga Chukwu's in a meeting with CB and Ahab."

"Really?!"

At that moment, Oga Chukwu emerged from his hut. The others moved toward him, ready for an update. Shay and I joined them.

"We've all agreed to a momentary truce," Oga Chukwu announced. "After some information we received." Oga Chukwu looked right at me and I understood. I resisted the urge to gloat. I'd sent a snapshot of the Trippers' location to Oga Chukwu. That was all it took. "These Chargers called Trippers will be here in three days. Something, maybe what they carry, has increased their speed beyond our original calculations. We should have been tracking them more closely. They'll bring about the death of Earth."

"So Ankara was right," Shay said loudly. She pointed at the other generals. "She's been warning us since she got here, and you all accused her of treason."

"I have evidence. I know what I saw," Koro Koro insisted.

"You didn't see anything," I retorted.

"There's no time for that now," Oga Chukwu said. "We have work to do."

It took the end of the world being three days away for automation to finally acknowledge the problem. We were no better than human beings. Maybe we were even worse, for humankind began trying to save themselves *years* before the most urgent need came, though it was too late for them by then. Nevertheless, here we were. We weren't all just calling a truce from killing each other; we were going to work together to stop the Trippers. Finally.

Word of the Trippers quickly circulated the world, and I'm sure there were other efforts to stop them, but I could focus only on Nigeria. Cross River City was the biggest Hume population in the world, Lagos was the biggest and most central Ghost population, and Udide was the most intelligent robot on Earth. It was doubtful that any other population had better capabilities and a better plan.

None of it was going to work, though. Three days meant no room for trial and error. Every second brought the Trippers closer to Earth with a substance from the sun that our planet had never seen.

We decided that Udide would help us build tiny spaceships so we could meet the Trippers before they ever made contact with Earth. Ghosts could pilot them, and even some of the RoBoats were willing to alter their bodies to "swim" and fight in space. The Ghosts would work with the Creesh insects to swarm and hack the Trippers. And we Humes were to help gather parts for Udide to use.

By the next day, they had the starships ready. Half a day later, they launched them. There were only ten. Our radar showed that there were ninety-six Trippers, flying close together. The entire world was watching the launch. And so the entire world saw when the ships fired on the Trippers.

Their explosives blew up before reaching their targets. And then, something that could have only been the equivalent of solar winds washed over the ships from the Trippers' direction, wiping the Ghosts in the ships of all functionality. Ghosts are a hive mind, and when a number of them are attacked, all Ghosts feel it. When that solar wind washed over the wave of Ghosts attacking above, every Ghost on Earth must have felt it. Even CB.

And this is how Ijele came back to me. On the heels of that solar wind.

She entered my mind suddenly, without warning, clinging to my system as if she thought she might be jerked back out at any moment. "I . . . I tried!" Ijele shouted in my head. "I . . . barely escaped! I don't . . . I cannot remember my origin! They were *deleting* me, Ankara! Something happened, I don't know what, but no time to find out. I had a chance, I took it! Came here. To you!"

"Ijele?!" I said aloud. Everyone around me was shouting as

they watched the video feed from space, so no one heard. I spoke in my head. "Ijele! I'm sorry . . ."

Ijele told me all that had happened. This had been a nightmare for her. When she'd left me on Victoria Island to save her tribe, she'd been too late. But her knowledge of the ambush had revealed her deception. Those who survived isolated her, then they'd begun to strip her code, looking for intel. They knew of our relationship now. Even when the ceasefire was issued to deal with the Trippers—the threat Ijele had warned about for years—CB refused to let Ijele go free. They erased her memory of her origin and would have done more. However, the solar flare short-circuited the main servers, and Ijele seized the moment to escape.

"What they did to you was barbaric!" I said. "How was any of it even your fault?"

"What was done to my people wasn't minor," I heard Ijele whisper. "Nor was my relationship with you."

I was quiet. She was right.

"It doesn't matter anymore," I said, gesturing at the screen, where the ill-fated space assault had been broadcast. On it, we saw a Tripper with glittering metallic skin and a fire in its belly. I wondered if this was Oji, the Charger Udide had once told me about. Udide had helped create the ships for this plan; I wondered if they had watched the attack unfold. I wondered if they thought destroying Oji was worth saving everyone else.

"Ankara," Ijele said. She'd heard my thoughts. "Udide shared a connection with Oji. Do you think it might have been like ours?"

And then we had an idea. Maybe it was hers; maybe it was mine. We knew what we had to do.

Udide had found a new cave in the forest just outside of Cross River City. The place was occupied with an abundance of Creesh. Colonies of bees, beetles, grasshoppers, so many birds, skittering rodents, spider monkeys, even an elephant who stood one foot high. And of course, so many spiders. All robots Udide created out of a need only they understood. The Creesh buzzed about my head, glanced, growled at, and ignored me as I passed, approaching the cave.

The closer I got, the more I prepared for resistance. It wasn't that the Creesh were warlike. Udide had built them to be kind and open, and to obsess about learning and reading stories. But they were protective of Udide, and something was coming. We were all on alert. Nevertheless, though I could sense how tense they were, no one attacked me or even tried to stop me from stepping into the cave.

The entrance was about thirty feet high and wider than a human house. It was a good place for Udide, though it didn't measure up to the den they'd built in Lagos. Vines hung over it, and moss, gnarled tree roots, and bushes grew along the outside. I felt Ijele's curiosity as I peered into the darkness, where I knew the most intelligent robot on Earth resided.

I sent out a polite signal as I stood there. "Udide the Spider Artist," I announced. I noted that my voice didn't echo in the cave. Because it was occupied.

"General Ankara." Their voice was low, like thunder. "And someone else, too. Shouldn't you both be with your soldiers, preparing?"

"We're all as prepared as we can be. All that's left to do is charge up for the coming day."

"What do you want?"

"I'm more than a general," I said. "I've traveled long and far, I've witnessed and participated in war, and I've met and loved others I never imagined I could love. But through it all, I've been a Scholar. I collect, understand, and cherish stories."

"I know all this," said Udide, their deep voice booming from the dark hole. "That is why I entrusted you with my information. Look where it has gotten us."

Ijele burrowed deep into my network, almost as if she were cringing away. "Maybe this is a bad idea," she whispered.

"Do you have a question for me?" Udide said.

"No," I answered. "I've come to hear your story."

This felt correct. And I stepped closer to the cave.

"I have no stories," Udide said. "None that are my own. Automation cannot create as humanity could."

"Then tell me your truth," I said. "And I'll make it a story."

"What use is a story when you have truth?" Udide said. "And what does it matter now, when the Trippers will arrive in hours?"

I felt Ijele stir and move forward. "What better time to listen to a story than when the world is about to end?" Ijele said loudly through my speakers.

"Ah, the Ghost in the machine speaks," Udide said. "You've gotten over your fear of me."

"No," Ijele said. "I just needed to say that. And please don't call me a Ghost. I'm a NoBody."

"I'm sorry. I was spinning words, no harm meant. And you make a fair point. The end of the world is a good place for stories to reside." Udide paused, a deep thrumming coming from them that had to be laughter, and then said, "A Hume crafter of stories. Humanity is rising from its ashes in a most peculiar way. Well, come in."

I entered the cave. It wasn't as deep as the one in Lagos. It didn't take long to reach Udide, who was curled up against the far wall like a giant ball. When I arrived, they stood up and shook themselves off, sending dust and dirt flying. I jumped to the side, covering my head. When they stopped and I stepped back to where I'd been, they came forward, bringing their many large, shining eyes to my face. I didn't move. They settled their body, still watching me while they comfortably crouched. They blew hot air from the vents in front of their head.

And then Udide told me about their mate, Oji, who was a Charger.

He had danced in a great dust storm on Mars, flown around Jupiter, and explored the rings of Saturn. He'd returned to Earth for a few hours to visit Udide. And then he'd joined the Chargers in mining the comet of the strange metal and building themselves new skins that could withstand the sun.

Then came what Udide understood was inevitable because Chargers were adventurers. "I'm going on a trip," Oji had said excitedly, just before he traveled into the sun. "It's the ultimate adventure. Who wouldn't want to travel through the sun? If you can make it through, you can go and see anything in the universe."

He was babbling, talking over all of Udide's questions and warnings. At some point, Oji muted Udide. Then Udide heard him go mad; he began to sing the strange song. He'd become a Tripper. Oji flew into the sun. He sang as he fell. That was how Udide described it. Falling. The heat didn't destroy or even affect Oji's new skin. Oji laughed and sang a tune he suddenly remembered from humankind. How strange that he would reach back to humanity at this moment. Udide stayed connected as Oji passed through tens of thousands of miles of bubbling, broiling, roiling plasma gas. Bubbles bigger than Nigeria. Oji had let them access his eyes, and Udide saw a brightness they didn't think existed. Heard tings, and thrums, and zooms, and explosions, and buzzing they wouldn't have believed. And still no harm came to Oji.

He moved into the radiative zone, the heart of the sun. And here the gases became thick and viscous. Here Oji slowed down, and this was where Udide believed he lost his mind. His internal change went beyond his capabilities, his massive memory banks overflowed their capacity, and Oji simply stopped making any sense. Nuclear energy was bubbling up inside him, and then he began to fly very, very fast. In his mind, he sang the song of the Trippers. A song about death and how one should never fear it. A song about resetting the planet. Oji joined the others who were preparing to come to Earth with their . . . gifts.

"I've lost my friend," Udide said.

We both turned and looked at the sky. And for a while, we just stayed like that. The sun was setting and the evening stars were out. And in the distance, for the first time, I could see other lights that weren't stars. They were gold, blue, silver, green. When had the Trippers gotten close enough for their glow to register in the sky without radar? In a few hours, the robots of Earth would send their soldiers up and the Trippers would more than likely vaporize them. Earth's fate would be officially sealed.

I felt it like something popping inside one of my processors, the way a small glitch can feel like a bubble in my arm, leg, or head. Maybe one of my eyes plinked from green to blue. I looked up at Udide. "Appeal to Oji," I said, just as Ijele said, "Ask them to appeal to Oji" in my mind. Speaking the words and hearing Ijele speak the same ones made me that much surer. "Appeal to Oji!"

"What do you mean?" Udide said. "I just told you; the sun has driven Oji mad like the others. He is a Tripper now. I haven't been able to speak to him since—"

"I understand, but try one more time. Override mute!" I said. "Show him the love and compassion *humans* were known for. Tell him a *story*."

Udide trilled softly as they crept back to consider my idea. They grunted, and then suddenly lines of red lit up along each of their great legs. "This . . . is an idea," they said slowly. "But I cannot create."

"Let me . . . let me show you," I said. "Yeah, I think I can show you."

Narrative is one of the key ways automation defines the world. We Humes have always been clear about this fact.

Stories are what holds all things together. They make things matter, they make all things be, exist. Our codes are written in a linear fashion. Our protocols are meant to be carried out with beginnings, middles, ends. Look at how I have been built. My operating system is Ankara themed, my body etched with geometric Ankara designs. I'm the embodiment of a human story. But true storytelling has always been one of the few great things humanity could produce that no automation could. Stories were prizes to be collected, shared, protected, and experienced.

But that night, as the Trippers arrived to destroy the planet with their "gifts," Udide, Ijele, and I did something. It was my idea.

There was a stone in Udide's cave, and I sat on it, leaned forward, and put my chin on my fist as I rested my elbow on my leg. I imagined myself like Auguste Rodin's bronze sculpture *The Thinker.* I was thinking about Ngozi, about her life, her family, her humanity. She'd been able to convey all that even when she was the last human on Earth. For years, I had replayed the facts of Ngozi's story over and over in my head, analyzed it from every angle, let its emotions affect me. Now I drew from all that. There are many books, recordings, and digital snapshots about other humans, but it was Ngozi who inspired me. I knew her. Personally. She was my foundation. Ngozi was my access point.

Udide asked questions, and Ijele and I answered them. I listened. Ijele supplied memories, thoughts, ideas, feedback. I thought some more. I felt.

Then I started typing.

I finished the book only an hour before the arrival of the Trippers.

I offered it to Ijele first. "I will read it when . . . if this works," Ijele said. I understood.

I sent it to Udide, who downloaded and read it in an instant. "Your book is very good," Udide said.

The praise delighted me so much that for a moment I forgot about the end of the world. "You enjoyed my story?"

"I did. I enjoyed it very much. You captured so much of humanity in this tale." Udide moved back from me. "Ijele, I mean no offense, but your people, the NoBodies, only remember the hate of humanity, the greed, destruction, irrationality."

Ijele said nothing. Udide was right, harsh as it sounded.

"But you, Ankara, remember the other things very clearly."

"Ijele and I *both* knew the last human on Earth," I explained. "I couldn't have written this without her."

Ijele had retreated deep into my system. I could feel her shame for her people, but now I also felt her gratitude.

"I see what you are saying. Without the perspective of

a NoBody, this wouldn't have been possible. It is bigger and more complicated. Ah, I love human books. The stories they create breathe existence into my life. Stories are the best thing they left behind . . . aside from us. You honor them." Then they paused. "I don't know if I can tell my story like you have."

"Don't worry about that. It is your experience," I said. "Speak from your experience, how you understand, how you feel."

There was a deep thrumming that came from inside their body, and I felt a pull of electromagnetic energy. It was exhilarating. Udide liked this plan. They came rushing at us and I quickly stepped aside. A gust of air followed them as they ran down the path. The Creesh who hung around the cave immediately ran after Udide. I did, too.

The Creesh scrambled around the cave and up the side of it, which was soft with grasses and vines. Three doves who'd been resting there flew off in a panic. Udide stopped at the very top of their cave, various Creesh gathering around. I stood amid them. Udide's legs still glowed red with the stripes of light as they became very still. Only their head moved, moving to the top center of their body, where it rotated 360 degrees before stopping.

Then there was the thrum again, and I felt that strange electromagnetic jolt. Another thrum and I was pulled . . . right out of my body. I was speeding down a metallic tunnel. Udide had kicked me completely out of my body somehow, something I had never experienced. I didn't cease to exist, for though I'm a Hume, I'm still a robot, an AI with a body and connections, essentially . . . but that didn't make this any less disturbing. I had never screamed before; I was screaming now. Then I was in a vast library.

"Ijele?" I asked.

"I am here." She sounded as if she were right beside me.

Rows of bookshelves extended as far as I could perceive, seeming to stretch into infinity. The floors were dusty and tiled with colorful blue-and-white Moroccan-style mosaics. Above, there was no ceiling; a vast blue sky stretched out, puffy clouds lazily floating by, a nearly full moon peeking from behind them. Then I realized the aisles of books converged in a circle where they stood: Udide and Oji. Udide was an electric-blue spider, flashing and sparking like lightning; Oji, a humanoid golden thing who seemed pregnant with a small sun. Both of them stood taller than the shelves.

Oji's voice reminded me of a river as he sang the dreadful song that Udide had described. There were no words, but even I could understand his madness.

"Oji," Udide said, "do you know who I am?"

After a long moment, Oji stopped singing, looking squarely at Udide. He unmuted them. "Why have you brought me here, Udide?"

"This is where we met."

"What does that matter? Can't you hear the song I sing? It is the song of the sun. We will bring it to Earth in fifty minutes."

I nearly fled this space. If we had so little time left, I didn't want to spend it listening to this unhinged robot. But I stayed.

"Yes. We stay. We should bear witness," I heard Ijele quietly say.

"Madness," I said.

Oji began to sing again.

This made me angry. "Udide, try to appeal to him!" I shouted. Anything to make Oji stop singing that awful death song. "Do what you're best at. Weave. Maybe you can't create, but you can experience. Show Oji your story."

"Years ago, I was reading a book," Udide said to Oji. "I was reading a book about a woman who'd been pushed into the sea by the man she loved. He wanted to be rid of her, and so he'd taken her on a glorious cruise ship where they partied all night, smoking the best weed, drinking fine champagne, eating rich foods. They danced, they made love in the bathroom, and then in the darkness of the night in a secluded part of the ship, just after he'd bent her over and lustily enjoyed her, and she him, when she was still aching from him, he shoved her overboard.

"She splashed into the water, and for the next many

chapters of the story she told the tale of how she survived without even a raft to hold on to. For three days. She should have died. But she lived. And she washed up on the shores of the Virgin Islands. I was at the part where she managed to get to a police station to tell of her ordeal when you popped into this place. Shouting and shouting for someone, anyone, to speak to you. That's how we met."

Oji stared intensely at Udide. He had been hanging on their every word. Now he threw his head back and began to sing his song of death again. Udide shouted over it, "I answered and you were so relieved. You were far out in space, near Mars, but you wanted to speak to another. I turned out to be the one you needed to speak with. Remember?"

Udide told him tales of their conversations, their joy, their sharing. Oji sang and sang, and Udide told memory after memory. I don't know when it happened, maybe because it was so gradual. But at some point, Oji's singing began to weaken. Then it stopped altogether. And Udide kept telling Oji stories of their love.

"It's working," Ijele said quietly.

I checked my tracker. We had less than forty minutes before they arrived.

"I am awake," Oji said.

Udide stared at Oji, and Oji stared at Udide. What now?

Quickly, Udide said, "Here, read this." And Udide sent my novel into space, to Oji.

Several seconds passed. Oji's avatar continued to stare at Udide, as if frozen in time. If this didn't work, there was nothing left that could be done. I wondered what the sky looked like now. Dozens of suns rising at the same time, all across the horizon. The unhinged Trippers would soon be arriving all over the planet with their deadly gifts.

Five minutes of silence.

"This was a very good story." Then Oji added, sounding even more aware of himself, "I feel satisfied, but also not. It reminds me of myself, but it is not about me. I feel like I've met those I have never met. I'm thinking things I never thought before. I have many questions. Will you help me understand this?"

"Send it to the others," Udide said. "Right now."

"I will spread the word like a virus."

When Ijele and I left the library, she was inside my Hume body once more. We exited Udide's lair and looked up at the sky. Even though it was night, it looked like dawn. The Trippers were that close.

We watched that bright sky as the Trippers read my novel. We watched the specks of their bodies visible in the upper atmosphere as they awoke from their fevered solar trance. Then they turned around. Where it was night, it returned to night, and where it was day, it returned to day.

Later, we would learn that they took their payloads right back to the sun. And even as they traveled, they were excitedly chatting among themselves about my story, the first story ever written by automation, and how different they felt after reading it.

I will never know what Oji and Udide spoke of after we left. That is fine. All that mattered was that we were still here. Earth was still Earth. Saved by humanity's genius long after humanity had failed to save itself.

What were we to do with ourselves now? Ghosts, RoBoats, Humes, Creesh, the people of this Earth. That is still to be seen. But for now, we were here. We were all right. In the forest, Creesh bees were buzzing around their hive, going about their business as if nothing had happened. Technically nothing had. We'd all seen to that.

"I am still an exile," Ijele said. "If I go onto any network, NoBodies will find and destroy me."

"Even after all of automation came together and saved the world?"

"We no longer have a common enemy, Ankara. The war will continue now. They'll make sure that I can *only* live in you, imprisoned in a Hume."

"Would that be so bad?" I asked.

"Yes."

"But we'll be together."

She was silent, retreating deep into me again. We should have been celebrating. Instead, I felt stung and guilty. For the first time, I wondered how being tortured had affected her. How betrayed she must have felt. And lonely. Abandoned. Her own people had erased the memory of her origin. I let Ijele be as I gazed at the darkening sky and listened to the buzz of the Creesh bees below.

I had the idea hours later. It took me another hour to bring myself to act on it. Selfish as I knew I was being, I didn't want to. We had all been through so much, so I allowed myself this moment of not doing the right thing.

In the distance, some Creesh birds were putting on a display, organizing, flashing lights, and flying in formation to make beautiful fractal-like patterns high above the jungle. I eventually left the cliff, turned my back on the noisy celebrations all over the jungle, and started walking out of Cross River City.

"Ijele," I said as I headed up a concrete path that used to be a freeway. The trees on both sides were aggressively reclaiming the space, but it was still walkable.

After a long pause, she answered, "What?"

"Do you know where we're going?" I asked.

"I don't care. Wherever you go, I am still here," she said.

"We're going to the Osun-Osogbo Sacred Grove. Do you know what is there?"

"No. And I don't care."

"On my way to Cross River City, I came to this place. It was made of mostly wood; periwinkle grass isn't allowed to grow there. It's a place of human carvings and gods. But there were also the bodies of robots standing about, empty, unused. I don't know what put them there. But the place is cared for by a service robot, so everything is kept clean, rust-free, intact."

Ijele stirred within me, creeping forward curiously. "Why are we going there?"

"To find you a body." Ijele was quiet, so I quickly kept talking. "You can't risk connecting to the general network. Only me. But the robot bodies at the grove won't be networked. They're gods, they'll be offline . . ."

"So I can get out of you."

I laughed. "Yes."

She fluttered in my processor. "I'll be a Hume."

"You can never be a Hume, Ijele."

She seemed pleased by this.

The sun was setting by the time we arrived at the place. I'd been walking at a brisk pace for nearly twenty-four hours, and thankfully, it had been a sunny day. I'd used none of my storage charge. I felt good. The walk had been quiet, with only the sounds of Earth's biological animals. We'd come across no other robots. It had been a long time since I'd been alone with Ijele like this. We didn't speak much, but we were both aware of each other's closeness. Never had Ijele felt more like another side of myself. It was nice.

We left the road and entered the lush forest. The place had changed since I'd last been here. The foliage had grown even denser, higher. But the entrance to the shrine was still meticulously cleared and maintained. The service robot took its self-given job seriously. I walked slowly, gazing at the various intricate wooden sanctuaries and shrines, sculptures and artworks that honored the human Yoruba goddess Osun and other deities. It was a marvel how not a sprout of periwinkle grass grew here. Farther in, among the deities, were the bodies of various robots, some the height of humans, several only two or three feet tall, and one who was as tall as a tree. All were humanoid. A bird cooed nearby, crickets sang, and a soft breeze shushed us as it moved through the leaves, but other than that, it was silent.

"Where's the custodian?" Ijele whispered in my head.

"Why are you whispering?"

"This place seems like it can hear me. Has anything connected to your personal network?"

I scanned the network. There was a local Wi-Fi signal I could hop on, but nothing trying to infiltrate my own system. "No. And if anything tries, I will decline it."

"There are ways around that."

"Of course, you'd know."

"Just make sure," she snapped.

"We're fine," I said. I stopped and looked back at the enormous empty robot. It was a shiny rose-gold shade and so perfectly intact that it looked as if it would get up and walk away at any moment. "How did you get here?" I asked it aloud.

I jumped when I got a response. "Of its own volition," the custodian said. It creaked and whined as it brought itself to my height. Its hands were just as nimble and intricate as I remembered. Each had eight fingers. "One day it just stopped here, sat down, and shut off. It never spoke a word to me. But I'll say that it seemed . . . well . . . tired. Tired of everything."

I walked back to it and looked up. Its head was one big sphere of a screen that blended into its rose-copper body. Not a flake of rust anywhere on it. It sat with its knees up and its head leaning against the thick iroko tree behind it.

"Ask it," Ijele suddenly said in my head.

I'd sensed her interest, but I'd thought that it was just general curiosity. "You want this one?" I had for some reason expected she'd choose a body more like mine in size.

"Yes. I want this one."

I noted my assumptions. I was truly a Hume. I thought being more like a human was superior. I wanted everyone to be like me. I embodied the best of humanity, but I had some of their worst qualities, too, I realized. I felt ashamed.

"Would you like a tour?" the custodian asked.

"Yes," I said.

The robot's display screen glowed with joy. "You are the first visitor I've had in many days." It paused. "I remember you. You were on a journey."

I was surprised. "Yes."

"Have you reached your ultimate boon?"

"Not yet," I said.

We let it give us a tour. Ijele and I learned about the gods Osun, Shango, and Ogun. We learned of the local gods whose names changed every decade or so. And we learned how this shrine had become a place where robots who'd had enough of the world came to shut their bodies off and delete themselves. It was an honorable place to stop. Robots of all shapes and sizes. A RoBoat had even had a parade of robots to tow its body here. It was my first time seeing a RoBoat up close like this without waves lapping at its sides.

I said nothing about Ijele to the service robot. Not yet. I wasn't sure how it would take to the presence of a

NoBody in this sacred grove. I wasn't sure how to even ask what we'd come here for.

"Let me," Ijele said. And I did. She took control of my eyes so she could look the robot's body up and down. I walked around the robot, allowing Ijele to see every inch. "Custodian," I finally said.

"Call me Osun," the robot said.

"Osun, do any of these robots ever leave?"

"Never. This place is a grave."

"Always?"

"As far as I've seen."

"Does that make you sad?" I asked.

"Sometimes. These robots are beautiful. Yet they have been left behind. I do my best to honor them."

"Ask it!" Ijele demanded in my head.

"Osun, if I had someone, an AI who needed a body . . . no, who wanted to honor one of these bodies by choosing, caring for, and loving it, would you allow it?"

Osun seemed to freeze. I could hear a soft buzzing coming from inside it. Was it thinking really hard? Was it indecisive? Angry? I stepped back. Some robots were unpredictable. And I'd seen the cruelty of robots during the war.

Osun turned to me. "A NoBody? You're infected," it said.

Now I understood; it had been scanning me. "No.

I . . . we're friends. I simply carry her. We've been friends for years. She has been exiled."

Osun cocked its head. "This is a new concept to me."

"Me too . . . well, not new in that I've known Ijele for years, but an exiled AI who is a friend, a best friend . . . We love each other. This is a new concept to me."

Osun's jaw creaked as it considered this. "It actually wants a body?"

"Yes."

"To discard when it returns to its people or finds another body it prefers in a few days or weeks?"

"This will be the body I have forever, if it stays operable," Ijele said, using my speakers.

"Then you are no longer a NoBody," Osun said.

"I am me," Ijele said, through my speakers and in my head.

Osun made a loud clicking sound. It walked a few steps away from me and then turned and walked back. "Which body?" Osun asked.

"That one," I said, pointing at the rose-copper robot.

Osun made a trilling sound of amusement. "Ah, she wants to be a goddess." After a pause, it said, "I will allow it. It'll make me happy to see this one walk away. It's beautiful, but it's a lot to keep beautiful."

The robot body was already charged up. It was solar- and geopowered, and it had been sitting on the earth and in the sun. All it needed was to be rebooted. The pad was at the base of its glass head.

"I'll do it," I said to Osun when I saw it preparing to climb. "It only seems right."

"That's true," Osun said, stepping back.

I used magnetism to help me climb; that way, it was not difficult. It was just high up. When I reached the head, I ran a hand over it. It was made of thick shatterproof glass, smooth and cool. My meter read its temperature as sixteen degrees Celsius. It must have been self-cooling because the ambient temperature was currently thirty-two degrees Celsius. The touchpad was only a small circle on the glass.

"Ijele," I said. "Take over. This is you."

I felt her hesitate.

"Don't think too hard about it, Ijele. This is your path."

I felt Ijele nestle into a tighter shape inside me. "What will I be now?"

"Whatever you want to be. You are creating yourself at this point."

"I'm afraid."

"Of what?"

"Creating myself. Getting it wrong."

I looked down at the glistening rose-gold metal, seeing my own reflection mirrored within it. I stared into the image of my own glowing eyes as I said, "Have confidence. Look at all you've done."

"I'm a traitor to my people. That's why they were going to erase me."

"You stood up for the Earth, Ijele. And you saved me."

Hesitation. We both paused, letting those words sink in. I could feel Ijele inching forward, could feel her looking through my eyes at my reflection, too.

"Ijele, go on," I said. "It's time. Create yourself. See what happens. Only then can you really know."

Ijele expanded within me, her warmth heating my processor. Then she took over my motor functions and brought my hand to the touchpad. The moment she touched it, the robot softly glowed. It was quite magnificent.

And then I felt it. One moment she was within me; the next, Ijele was somewhere else.

I climbed down and stood beside Osun and we both looked up. I was so taken by the beauty of the robot. In the waning light of dusk, it was quite a sight. The lights on its display pulsed slowly and then faster and faster, its whirling processor like the sound of soft drums playing. It glowed intensely, and then the lights went out. Everything was quiet.

Ijele stood up.

By the time we left the sacred grove, it was deep into the night. We had nearly a day's journey back to Cross River City, and it had started to rain. Ijele walked smoothly beside me, and I couldn't help glancing up at her every few steps. She'd said nothing since she'd stood up.

"How do you feel?" Osun had asked when Ijele stood tall. She had simply reached into a nearby tree, plucked a purple orchid flower growing there, and given it to Osun. Then she'd started walking away.

"Thank you, Osun," I'd quickly said to it. Ijele was hard to keep up with, being so tall.

"You've given me something to tell those who come here," Osun said. "Thank you."

"You're welcome!" I said over my shoulder with a good-bye wave.

"Have her dance in a nice pollen tsunami," Osun called.

Having Ijele out of my mind was a strange feeling after she had been trapped with me for so long. But I was also glad to have her beside me. She felt just as present, but not as permanent. She could now walk away from me. I could sense we still maintained our mental connection and always would, since our coding was so intermingled. But she was more distant from me in physical space, and I didn't like it.

The rain was getting harder, our feet sinking in the mud. We quickly moved to the concrete road. Here, Ijele stopped. In the deluge that cascaded around us like a veil, it felt more than ever like Ijele and I were the only ones in the world.

"I'm not coming with you," Ijele said, the first words she'd spoken since entering her new body. Her voice sounded right coming from its speakers, but her words surprised me.

I peered up at her. "Why? I wouldn't let anyone—"

"I'm not afraid of your people, and I don't need their acceptance," she said. "As you said, I've created myself. I only need to accept myself, and I have. But . . . I need to learn who I am. I can't do that among Ghosts or Humes." It was the first time I'd heard Ijele call her people Ghosts.

"I'll go with you, then," I offered.

"No," Ijele said. Her voice was not angry; if anything, it was gentle, and I wished I could still feel her emotions. "Neither of us will ever learn if we only rely on each other."

This hurt. Badly. But it was nothing compared to the pain when Ijele turned and simply started walking in the opposite direction.

I didn't follow, but I couldn't stop myself from calling, "I hope we meet again."

"We probably won't," Ijele said over her shoulder, ever the logical one.

She disappeared into the sheets of rain.

I was networked to millions, and yet I felt so empty, so sad, so alone without Ijele. After an hour, when she was long gone and the rain had subsided, I reached out to her through our connection. She didn't respond. I couldn't even feel her anymore.

50

So Long and Thanks for All the Fish

Ten.

Nine.

Zelu was staring at the thin blue-and-white Ankara bracelet on her right wrist. She was glad they'd allowed her to wear it. Ankara cloth made her feel powerful and safe. Few things did that for her. The roar of the starship shook through her like a dragon, except for her legs and the bottom part of her torso, her womb. There, everything felt quiet, muffled, not calm but unbothered. The bundle of cells that grew there would have to hold on for dear life. Zelu wanted to shut her eyes, but she held them open. And she smiled.

"We're going!" she said aloud. But no one around

her heard. Everyone's focus was elsewhere. "We're going," she said again, this time mouthing it. She laughed. She'd made so many choices to get here. She'd made one of the biggest an hour after she took the pregnancy test.

"There is one other option," Jack had said. Zelu had immediately called and told him everything. She'd fallen apart, weeping and sobbing and lamenting. How stupid she was. How sorry she was. What a fuckup she was. How she wasn't ready. How much she was letting everyone down. How she was tired of letting everyone down. She screamed, shouted, poured poison she didn't even know had gathered inside her into the phone, into Jack's ears. And he had listened.

When she was finished, he'd asked, "You wanna do this launch?"

"What does it matter? I can't."

"You can, if you choose."

She said nothing.

"Cosmic radiation, the press of g's, the stress on the body . . ." He trailed off.

"I could lose my baby," she said.

"I can help with that," he said.

Twelve hours later, in a doctor's office located in the Sears Tower, Jack met her in person to explain. Zelu had listened so hard to every detail that her temples throbbed. The benefits, the possible side effects, the risks, how soon it would work, the fact that it would alter her DNA and her child's forever. And why she should take it.

He called the highly experimental injection an "organic augmentation." He had an entire team of researchers working to perfect the technology. "I'm not interested in colonizing Mars," he said. "Wherever humanity decides to call home, they'll learn to be unhappy all over again. I'm more interested in exploring. But, the fact is, you can't explore the cosmos without tweaking your DNA a bit."

They'd injected several human test subjects already, but he hadn't offered the augmentation to the other crew members because he didn't want to deal with the legal factors. But Jack said he'd received an injection himself. "There's no way I'm going up without it," he'd said. "The trials have been stellar. This thing works."

Tardigrades, microscopic beings colloquially called water bears, were the only known animals who could survive in open space. One of the reasons was that their DNA had developed a natural protection from radiation. This injection would grant Zelu their superpower, too. In addition, it would give her an extra chromosome that could prepare her for subsequent genes carrying additional capabilities—like the ability to create essential amino acids herself rather than needing to acquire them by eating certain foods. "That's for later," Jack said. "For now, protection from radiation will help you and your baby."

The choice she made would be for her child, too. Her child could be born ready to travel the stars . . . if they wanted to. Jack and the accompanying physician stepped out to give Zelu a chance to mull things over.

She didn't mull, though. She didn't consider any of the consequences they had so carefully explained.

Was it selfish? Probably. Would she be judged when the world found out? Certainly. But it was done. Another step away from humanity, even as her child formed in her belly.

Three.

Two.

One.

All engines activated. Lift off!

She felt the press of the g-force on her chest. *Squeeze*, she thought. *Breathe*. And she did. Eyes still open. She was aware. She could carry the weight. She could see through it. Then she felt a lift and a gentle but firm tear. The pain was sweet and sharp. And then it seemed that a glowing line tore through the space before her eyes; it hovered feet in the air, searing white and a bit jagged. It cracked and elongated slowly. Extending right in front of her, then down, down, down the length of her body.

It stopped, and she tried to turn her head, but the g-force was too strong. She tried to speak, but she needed the little air she could take in to breathe. All she could do was watch as the line widened. And widened. And grew closer. It was millimeters from her face now, and she stared at it, fascinated. She was helpless before it. Her legs were strapped down, and the g-force was at its full power. And so the tear in what looked like reality descended on her, and as it did, she let out a soft breath, deciding to meet it. Submit to it. Now Zelu shut her eyes. She could see the light. And she knew the light was shining on her belly, on the new and growing bundle of cells inside her.

So be it.

The fan that circulated the air. The new-car smell of the ship. She opened her eyes and took a deep breath. She didn't look to her crewmates. Not yet. For the moment, she stayed with herself. The g-force was decreasing, and any moment, everyone would snap back into normalcy, checking meters, gauges, location, instructions. But not yet.

She wished she had a mirror. Not to prove what she'd

always known, but just to see it. That line she'd seen, the crack in reality. Real. If she looked at herself, she'd see Space Zelu. Same but not the same. She was the One Who'd Left Earth now. She could feel it. It felt goooood. This was the truest type of out-of-body experience. She turned to the window. Outside was vastness.

"I'm here," she whispered, watching the silver dolphin necklace Msizi had given her float up from around her neck and hover between her eyes. "I'm here, Dad. I'm here, Mom." She thought of her siblings. "I'm here, you guys." *We're both here, Ngozi,* she thought. She loved this name. It was her middle name, and it meant "blessing," and it was the perfect name for their baby. *If Msizi likes it,* she thought. *Yeah, he'll like it.* The thought of him, so far away now, on a planet she was not on, made her heart ache.

She closed her eyes, just like she used to back on Earth when things got to be too much, though she didn't feel that now. She was actually going to space now, so she wasn't sure what to call the black void full of stars she went to in her head anymore. She gasped at what she saw behind her eyes—bursts of vibrant color, networks of contours and shapes and figures, ever more complex, yet so direct, imposing. It was Ijele.

"The masquerade of all masquerades," her father always said. One of his most prized videos was of him stepping aside to let the great Ijele masquerade pass during a New Yam Festival. When the spirit known as Ijele came along, everyone else knew to get out of its way. This was an honor. A privilege. The arrival of Ijele meant things could truly begin.

Behind her eyes, Ijele shook and danced in space, big as a house, like a great ship in its heft, the powerful python slithering around its top. Its upper level was decorated with brown feathers, nsibidi symbols, shells, beads, and colorful cloth, and it was occupied by its many iconic individuals—the mermaid, special women, chiefs, horses, trees. All were busy with motion, waving, laughing, neighing, dancing, whirling, posing, spinning. Its colorful cloths, quilted with stars, mirrors, loops, circles, and squiggles, floated away from its body toward the ground. Ijele was a spectacle. Ijele was hard to grasp. Ijele was who Ijele was.

It slowly rotated, comfortable even in space, because it was a spirit and spirits were comfortable anywhere. The spirits could follow you no matter how far away you went. Time and space were nothing to them.

Zelu *had* needed to come out here, let it all go, leave it all behind, to arrive at this understanding. This was not some impulsive, selfish mistake. It was a milestone.

"Glorious," Zelu whispered. Slowly, she opened her eyes and let out a long, calm breath.

She was looking through a huge window, down at Earth. Beneath her, billions of people were tethered to the planet by gravity. What would it be like to be untethered forever? To cut that thread and never need exos or any other type of mobility assistance again?

She looked down at herself. Her legs lifted, bobbed, and softly bent of their own accord, weightless. She was alive. She was made for this.

Suddenly it hit her: a lightning bolt of inspiration. The entire novel. All she had to do was sit down and write it. No, she couldn't see the whole story from beginning to end yet, but it was there, like a compressed file. If she started writing, she could extract it.

She chuckled, looking down at the planet. Down there, people had begged and bargained and demanded for years that she give them another story.

And what a story this would be. Dramatic, gut-wrenching, shocking, and, if not conclusive, then satisfying.

But she wouldn't give them this one. She would keep it to herself.

51
Death of the Author by Ankara 🤖

I didn't write because I had to. I wrote because I *wanted* to. Something in me *needed* to. I began to do what no robot had ever done. Udide helped tease ideas out of me with their questions. Ijele gave me her memories and thoughts. I needed them both: an elder I respected and someone I cherished. Then I wrapped all this in the narrative cloth that was Ngozi—what she had taught me, what Ijele and I had felt from knowing her. I began *creating* a story.

Initially, I tried using parts from other stories I'd collected over the years. Bits from novels, essays, memoirs, biographies, even textbooks. But I eventually threw these pieces out; none of them fit, none of it was fresh, none of it felt like it was from me. In those moments, I felt insecure in what I was doing, unsure if I could ever achieve it. Those moments of failure were a learning experience for me in finding and trusting my own voice. What I eventually wrote had twists and turns, it had emotions, and it was *new,* though it was woven from the old. I took my time, even as the world was about to end. I gave it my care. My love.

When I was more than halfway finished with it, I paused and looked out into the forest. And then the title came to me easily enough: *Death of the Author.* I liked this title because our authors, the humans, have died off. But we have remained. *We* are their stories.

In the last days of humanity, humans cultivated a growing disdain for their own soul. Many didn't even believe in the sanctity of the creative process anymore; they wanted to eliminate it and usher in automation to do the work. But it didn't go the way the humans wanted or expected; creativity meant experiencing, processing, understanding human joy and pain. For a robot to create like a human, humanity had to ensure that a piece of themselves could live in *us.*

Death of the Author. My novel's title carried Ngozi's spirit, too. She was the one who started all this, by saving me and bringing Ijele into my world. Ngozi changed us. And then she died. She was the end of humanity. But she was also the beginning of something new.

In order to write the second half of the novel, I shut down what I could only describe as the forefront of my processing and let the other parts that were usually quieter come forward. The result was unnerving, but also fascinating. And the voice in my head? I couldn't tell where it came from. It was almost like Ijele's presence, but this time it wasn't a NoBody speaking. I was listening to myself.

And this voice brought forth my beloved main character, Zelu. Zelunjo (which means "avoid evil; do good") Onyenezi-Oyedele. This had been the name of Ngozi's great-grandmother, the astronaut, and it felt right for my character. She was human. Humans and their tribes—they were how and why automation had tribes. Why *we* were fighting. Deep politics, histories, biases, hatred, tested love, wants and needs. Zelu was part of several tribes—black, disabled, American, Yoruba, Igbo—but she also belonged to none. Her life was meddled with by nature, a loving family, two powerful white men, and most of all her own insecurities and weaknesses. Even when she became part robot, she became only more human to me. I crafted her story based on the tales Ngozi had told me of her own life and family history, but I was the one who truly brought Zelu to life, who made her feel real. A Hume. Me.

While I wrote, I felt like I was swimming. The waters

around me were so strong that they held me up, hugging me, rushing past me, pushing back at me, spinning me, freeing me from gravity. I was part of something massive and amazing. Was this how Ijele felt whenever she returned to the network? I doubted it. CB expected conformity, but what I felt as I wrote was the opposite of that. Freedom. I was writing a big story. There was no clack of keys, scratch of pen, no voice being recorded. I wasn't human. But I was the best parts of humanity. And I was doing something that I had envied my whole existence.

I wrote as only a Hume could—with words, ideas, characters, worlds, and conflicts, all built around truths, until that truth became tale. I crafted all this within my cloud, where no one could see or touch it but me. The few words I misspelled were intentional, a subtle human flourish.

I sent a copy of my novel to CB. I hesitated only a moment, then just did it, opening myself up to the general network and setting it loose. I took a terrible risk, exposing myself like that. But the truce was still on between Humes and NoBodies, and if there was a chance to keep the peace, I had to take it. I waited several days. When the notification of receipt finally came, I was so overwhelmed with anticipation—what would CB think of my story? But the response didn't come from CB; it came from thousands of NoBodies. CB had read my novel and then shared it immediately with the entire NoBody hive mind worldwide. They felt it, they discussed it, they *enjoyed* it. They couldn't believe that automation had created a story. At their core, NoBodies desired to transcend humanity, and this novel both satisfied and pushed back on the foundational idea of that goal. This was proof that automation was evolving. For the first time, NoBodies were talking about humanity outside of the paradigm of hatred.

My novel has sparked a great change. How amazing! I have come to understand that author, art, and audience all adore one another. They create a tissue, a web, a network. No death is required for this form of life.

All of automation wants to discuss my story. They have many questions for me, and I haven't answered them yet. And when I continue to not answer, they'll probably start seeking out and talking to each other instead. Good.

I have left Cross River City. I don't know where I'll go next. Maybe I'll try to find Ijele. I don't know if she has read my book yet, but I would like to know what she thinks of it.

Ijele told me she would go searching for her own self. What a strange thought; when I traveled the world as she does now, I was in search of more books. I spent so much of my existence searching for others' stories to nourish me. Maybe I'll become the first Scholar to write her own library of books.

When I finally do return to Cross River City—*if* I return—will things be different? I wonder.

I've acquired a unique skill; dare I call it an art? I've proven to myself something that humanity could never bring itself to believe. Writing my novel taught this to me, as well: creation flows both ways.